I0645627

ROCK
GOD IN
EXILE

ROCK GOD IN EXILE

Kella Campbell

TIED STAR BOOKS

Once I was a white belt, and now I am a black belt;
I did not make that journey alone.
My life has been changed by my taekwondo family.

An instructor who is also a writer and friend
helped me find the perseverance and commitment
to finish writing this book when it got hard.
This one's for you, ma'am.

chapter

I

ELL SAT ALONE AT THE BAR, READING A BOOK AND sipping a Frosty Peach. They were a little too easy to drink, as cocktails went, but the frozen slushy mixture with the peach candy on top felt like a treat, in a way that a nice glass of wine or a standard gin and tonic never quite did. Her Sunday nights belonged to books and a quiet seat at the bar, two drinks over two hours – never more – and a plate of sweet potato fries or cream cheese wontons to snack on.

The Frog and Ball tended to be quiet on Sundays, which suited her perfectly. A group of regulars ate nachos and watched baseball; a few couples were there for the Sunday dinner special. A pair of old guys at the other end of the bar worked their way steadily through a small fortune in pull tabs with their beer – Nell had seen them before. Over at the pool table, a man with wavy blond hair played against himself, shooting first for solids, then for stripes.

What a bastard of a week. The comforting buzz of the alcohol in her drink soothed Nell a little. She didn't believe in using booze to feel better – *it's a depressant, it dulls cognitive faculties, it's bad for self-discipline, and it costs too much* – but there was no denying that sometimes it could anesthetize the ache of a bad day. Or week. Or year.

The bartender never bothered Nell; after maybe a hundred or so Sunday nights at this point, he was used to her and her book. She tipped decently and didn't create trouble for him.

1

And if the occasional jerk tried to chat her up, or muttered a pointed "antisocial" when she refused to take her eyes off the page she was reading, she just ignored him. Sundays were Nell's Fridays, and after five straight days of dealing with mind-numbing ridiculousness, she needed her night off. Errands and socializing and necessary evils could wait for Monday or Tuesday – her "weekend" – but she didn't have any space or patience for fools or even friends on Sunday nights.

When the bartender placed a third Frosty Peach in front of Nell, he had a slight smirk on his face. She looked up at him, raising her eyebrows in a silent question. "Enjoy," he said.

"What's this about, Tim? You know I never have more than two," she told him.

"Courtesy of the gentleman at the pool table," said the bartender, with just the faintest inflection on the word gentleman.

Unable to help it, Nell glanced over. The pool player was nearly done with his game, stripes set for the definitive win, solids nowhere. He looked up at her, winked. And she realized that she wore a green striped shirt, and his muscle tank was a solid blue.

"I don't know," she said. The Frog and Ball wasn't the kind of place where men sent drinks over to her; it had never happened before, here. The book should have been armor enough.

The bartender shrugged. "He already paid for it. You might as well drink it."

The sports-watchers called for another round of beer and the bartender moved to pour it, leaving the unwanted drink in front of Nell. She sighed and picked the peach candy off the top of the frozen slush. *The best part. It would make more sense to just buy a bag of peach candies and eat them.* "I suppose a few sips more won't kill me," she said aloud, mostly for the bartender's benefit. And it meant she could put off going home for a little while longer.

But concentrating on her book had become difficult. *I will not look over at that man again,* she told herself. He might take it as an invitation.

He had blond hair, didn't he? Seemed tall enough. And the muscle shirt showed off toned arms with just the right amount of ink. *No.*

Nell pushed the slushy cocktail away and stuffed her book into her sling bag. "I'm done, Tim," she called to the bartender. "Thanks!"

As usual, she ducked into the bathroom on her way to the door. A twenty-minute walk home was no joke for someone holding it, and a couple of cocktails would have a predictable effect.

The lock was broken in the stall she'd chosen, but as Nell debated whether to shift herself to the other one, she heard the outer door to the bathroom swing open and decided she might as well stay put. As Nell awkwardly held the stall door closed with one hand while doing her business, she waited for footsteps to move into the adjacent stall. Nothing. Nor any sound of the sink being used. Perhaps it was just someone reapplying lipstick or getting something out of her teeth.

Nell opened the stall door and stepped out. Froze in surprise.

"Hey, baby."

The pool player lounged against the counter, arms crossed, pleased with himself.

"What the flipping hell?" Nell stared at the cocky length of him. "Did you follow me in here?"

"Sure – it's not like there's anyone else using it, and I thought you might appreciate a little company, gorgeous." His frank gaze fixed on her chest, blatantly admiring.

Nell shook her head. "Unbelievable. What I'd appreciate is a chance to wash my hands, if you could get your ass off the sink. *Please.*" Despite the sarcastic courtesy, her tone made it a command, not a request.

"Okay, sassy pants." Laughing, he slid to one side, just enough for her to reach the taps.

She assessed the situation, not pleased with her choices. Stepping up to the sink would put her too close to him for comfort; she'd otherwise have to leave with unwashed hands.

"Get out of my space." She stepped up to the sink as though he weren't even in the room. He moved away at her approach, and she thought at first her confidence had driven him back – until he looped around and came up behind her, trapping her against the counter with a hand on either side of her.

"What's your perfume? You smell good enough to eat," he murmured, his mouth flirtatiously close to her ear, her neck.

Whoa! Flipping crap. How had she let herself get into a position like this? She could feel the heat of his body and smell the alcohol on his breath mixed with his body wash or cologne or whatever it was. A shiver rippled through her.

"Haven't been able to take my eyes off you... sitting there, flirting with me over your book... and you've got such heavenly tits..." One of his hands left the counter and snaked around to caress Nell's waist.

"Get your hands off me," she snarled. When he didn't comply immediately, she lost it. "That's it. Fair warning was given. Flipping asshole." With everything she had in her, all the power from every training session, every self-defense drill, she raised an arm, torqued herself around and nailed him with a hammerfist in the side of the neck. *Pressure point. Brachial plexus origin.* As his arms slackened, she turned, gripped his shoulder for leverage and slammed a knee into his groin. He dropped, groaning and cursing. "Don't assume women are helpless. Some of us are black belts. Some of us will make you sorry you tried it." Kicking away a pawing hand with one foot, she stalked out of the bathroom.

Do I say anything to Tim? Or do I just leave?

Technically, she knew she should probably say something. But explanations would be complicated. And a martial artist's hands and feet can be considered weapons in a court of law.

The pool player could explain what had happened, if he wanted to – starting with why he'd been in the women's bathroom.

She left.

chapter 2

W EDNESDAY MORNING, THE FIRST DAY OF NELL'S workweek, came all too soon.

Her usual round of squats and pushups and crunches jump-started her body and put her into a better frame of mind than she'd woken up with, but didn't leave much time for anything except a quick shower and basic grooming. Not that anyone at the office would care if Nell Whelan did or did not wear eyeliner and mascara, as long as she followed the workplace dress code and looked like she was doing her job.

Pushing the vileness of business casual slacks and blouses into the back of her mind, she ate some cold leftover stir-fry for breakfast and made a protein shake to get herself through the rest of the morning.

I'll have a cup of tea when I get to the office, she told herself. She kept a stash of good tea in the bottom drawer of her desk, a small luxury that made her office existence a little bit more bearable.

She didn't get a seat on the bus, but that was normal, and at least her commute took only twenty minutes. The riders who got on early enough to have seats were coming in from the suburbs and had probably been on the bus for half an hour already. Tinny music from several sets of nearby earbuds buzzed softly around her, and she gazed out the bus window at the sunrise.

Work never changed. Nell was the first one to arrive, as usual, and she liked it that way. The elevators weren't yet as crowded as they would be later in the morning, but two early birds waiting by the elevator bank were enough for Nell to take the stairs. Six flights were nothing; she usually did the stairs both ways at lunch anyway without breaking a sweat, but an extra set in the morning would be good for her. She reached the sixth floor, unlocked the glass front doors of the office, and moved through the space turning on lights.

The office had its usual early morning smell of cleaning solution and electronics. No one was ever around this early. Nell liked to get a start on her day before the rest of the managers and assistants and booking agents turned up to fill the office.

She turned on her computer, made her tea, tidied the photocopier room and kitchenette – even though that wasn't technically her job. She couldn't bear to have the office's public and shared spaces in disarray, and Lila the receptionist never did it.

Basics attended to, she started on her email inbox.

I hate my job. I hate my job.

Nell was a supervisor for a vacation properties company. Wildforest Vacations Inc. owned assorted cottage resort parks – charming rustic cabins and cottages in picturesque rural areas, clustered around a restaurant and general store. Some were aimed at couples, some at families, some at singles and the party scene. Each property had a supervisor, and each supervisor was supposed to have an assistant in the office as well as an on-site manager at each property. But Nell's previous assistant had quit without notice the month before, and Wildforest hadn't yet hired her a new one. Two people's jobs to get done in one person's hours, on one salary. Not that Shannon had worked terribly hard. Lila had agreed to help Nell out until a new assistant could be found for her, but although the receptionist was friendly and had a great telephone voice, she wasn't much for organization skills or neatness or quick work.

Emails from the on-site managers were Nell's first priority each morning, in case something urgent needed to be dealt with right away. Brian at Winter Pine Cottages was practical and reliable, if a bit abrasive, and Nell tolerated working with him because he got things done, while Stuart at Secret Creek Lodge reminded her of a male version of Lila –

great voice, super friendly, not so organized and a bit short on common sense. Deep down, Nell thought both of them were lucky. They lived in jeans and plaid shirts – Wildforest's idea of what a "camp manager" ought to look like, but it was comfortable and much better than her stupid slacks and blouses.

"Why don't you apply to be a camp manager?" Nell's friend Amy had asked her one night, after listening to a frustrated outburst about office life. Amy lived for her acting career and didn't seem to mind sleeping on friends' couches or slinging coffee during the bad times; maybe she couldn't understand Nell's need for security, stability. Anyway, the camp manager life sounded idyllic in some ways, but not much of a challenge, and Nell couldn't imagine giving up her martial arts training as she'd have to if she moved out of the city.

Life is complicated. I can't have everything. Nell sighed.

At least, on this particular Wednesday morning, there were no urgent disasters for her to handle. One leaking pipe at Winter Pine, fixed by Brian, with a net result of two wet rugs that had been removed from the cottage in question for drying. The renters had been offered a move to another cottage but were fine where they were. Spare area rugs had been provided. Nell made a note to call Perks & Promos later, once everyone was in for the day, to see what they could do for those renters to make up for the burst pipe and boost goodwill. Apparently, nothing at all had happened at Secret Creek since Sunday afternoon – Stu's email basically said, "It's all good." She could picture him saying it, with a shrug and a laugh. As long as no one died, Stu would probably think things were *all good*.

Lila stuck her head in Nell's office doorway, saying, "Morning, sunshine!" with offensively cheerful enthusiasm. "I'm making coffee. Want some?"

Nell hadn't accepted a cup of coffee once in the four years she'd been with the company, but Lila still offered every morning. Sometimes Nell wished Lila would offer to make her a cup of tea, but really, she'd just decline anyway. Lila's idea of tea was probably a generic orange pekoe teabag with coffee creamer and two packets of sugar. A few times, Nell had offered to make tea for Lila, but the receptionist wrinkled her nose at the premium rooibos and whole-leaf green teas and said she thought regular tea was okay but liked coffee better. "No, thanks, Lila. I'll make myself a second cup of tea in a bit."

Lila giggled. "You and your tea. Are you drinking that vanilla spice rooibos you like so much?"

"Not this morning. Green tea tastes better with my protein shake."

"Eww," said Lila. "I hit the drive-thru and grabbed an Egg McMuffin on my way in." Lila had a smart little black Jetta, bought for her by her parents, and the Wildforest owners had somehow been prevailed on to grant her a parking stall in the underground lot as part of her employment contract.

"I like my protein shakes!" Nell shook her head. "And taking the bus is good for the environment. I don't mind not having a car." In her heart, Nell coveted a Tesla – all that sleek luxury and status in an environmentally friendly package.

Lila rolled her eyes. "I never *said* anything about you having a car, Nell. And I guess I'd be fit like you if I drank protein shakes and worked out all the time, but eww. I just want to enjoy my life and eat delicious things." Somehow, Lila was oblivious to the fact that she clearly weighed less than Nell – not that Nell wasn't all muscle, and nor did she care about dress sizes, but her solidity looked a bit chunky next to Lila's relatively ectomorphic frame. "I'm going to go make that coffee. Later!"

The kitchenette will have to be tidied again, Nell thought. Lila would leave the coffee canister out on the counter, the used filter and grounds in the machine, and a litter of spoons and stir sticks and sugar packets in the sink.

The front of the office looked spacious and calm – a prosperous and imposing reception desk, a sitting area for guests with a comfortable couch and two armchairs clustered around a coffee table. The nearby kitchenette meant that Lila could offer visitors coffee or tea without leaving the reception desk unsupervised. Behind this gracious front area lay a warren of small offices and passageways and cubicles. The photocopier and office supply room was right behind Nell's office, with a thin shared wall. She could hear every copy being made. She'd gotten to know the photocopier very well, in fact, and could fix most of its jams and troubles without having to call a technician. Not her job, but it made everyone's day go faster if they weren't held up waiting for a tech to come fix the machine, and a little mechanical aptitude came in handy.

She might as well make sure the paper drawers were full. It seemed a small thing, to fill up the various paper trays of the photocopier as needed so the next person wouldn't have to stop, job half done, and deal with refilling the paper. And that reminded Nell that she needed to order paper for both cabin sites – toilet paper, paper napkins, paper towels, paper for the site office printer, note pads for the guest cabins. *An assistant to take care of basic orders would be awesome.* But there was hardly a chance of them finding her someone anytime soon, so Nell would have to do the ordering and whatnot herself.

♥

Just before lunch, her boss swung into her tiny office without so much as a knock. "Nell. You're here. Good."

Suppressing a desire to ask where else she might likely be at 11:30 on a workday, particularly as they weren't supposed to go off-site without permission, she forced a smile and said, "Of course, Tommy. What can I do for you?"

"First of all, did you know? About Aidan?" He fixed her with a cold look.

"No, what about Aidan? I – we don't exactly *socialize* or anything. He's just a co-worker; I barely know him."

Tommy Baxter practically snarled with displeasure. "It's the height of our busy season, we're short-staffed as it is, and that turd went and quit without notice. Sent me a goddamn email and didn't come in today. Says he'll mail in his keys."

Nell struggled to control the expression on her face. "Wow. That's... so wrong of him." *And exactly what we all wish we could do.* Part of her wanted to applaud Aidan for getting out, but his defection would doubtless make life more difficult for the rest of them.

"His desk is already cleared out. He must have known on Sunday that he wasn't planning to come back. You're sure he didn't say anything to you?" Tommy's suspicious nature was legendary in the office.

"Literally the only thing Aidan said to me on Sunday was, 'Got any plans for your off days?' And I told him I was going to read the rest of *A Discovery of Witches* and bake bread. That's it."

Tommy huffed in a way that suggested he wasn't impressed by her weekend plans – but then, she hadn't mentioned to him or to Aidan that she also took an advanced combative self-defense course on Mondays and traditional taekwondo plus an MMA sparring session on Tuesdays, and taught classes both days as well. Aidan had abhorred violence of any sort, no matter how necessary and justified, and Tommy made it known on a regular basis that he admired women like Lila who "didn't need to work out to look good" and entertained themselves on weekends by going out to restaurants and clubs. He'd hate the thought that Nell might be stronger than he was, which would likely make him even more poisonous in her vicinity. Nell would much rather stay invisible around the office as a homebody bookworm and bread-baker, hiding her strength under the business casual clothes she hated, even if she'd overheard Tommy referring to her as Chunky Booty.

Quit the damn job, Amy had said to her once. *It sounds like a horrible place. You could get something else.* But she was trapped, as so many people got trapped, by a salary she'd worked up to within the company – from booking support to junior booking agent to senior booking agent, then she'd been promoted across departments to property assistant and then to property manager – and it was all just specific enough to be not very transferable in terms of skills and position. She'd have to start over completely, rent would become unaffordable without a roommate, and she'd have a hard time paying her martial arts training fees. *No.*

"–all going to need to pull together and cover Aidan's accounts until we can replace him, right?" Tommy was saying, and Nell nodded and tried to look appropriately concerned. "Good. Thank you." Tommy's satisfied tone puzzled Nell for a moment, then he plunked one of the folders he was holding onto her desk. *Oh, no. He can't possibly...* "I'm giving you Champagne Cascades for the moment, and Scott or Trina can take Applegarth Cabins. Unless you'd rather have Applegarth?"

"But... I already have two properties, and no assistant. Couldn't Scott and Trina take these ones?" Nell didn't believe in the word *can't*, but it was perilously close to forming in her mind at the thought of a third property to handle.

Tommy gave her a grimace of impatience. "I'm asking *you*, Nell. You're taking one of these. Which one?"

Nell swallowed her frustration. As usual with Tommy, she had to force a smile – he liked to see women smile, he'd said, and he had a way of making life difficult if you didn't accommodate him. "Champagne Cascades is fine." She knew nothing about either property, as Tommy would know if he thought about it for a flipping minute. "But I haven't got an assistant right now. I really will need some help managing three."

"You're on salary, Nell. That means you stay until your work is done, right? No running home at five. But I'll get you an assistant. In fact, I have an idea about that..." His words trailed off as he left her office.

"Okay, so where is Champagne Cascades?" Nell muttered to herself, picking up the folder and opening it. "Huh. Up near the Canadian border. Romantic cottages for two, no kids or singles. One of *those*." She read on. Rentals were at a higher price point, so this was obviously more luxurious than she was used to handling with Winter Pine and Secret Creek. Would it be interesting or just a hassle? The site manager's name was Jessalyn Roberts. *A woman?* Nell didn't know that Wildforest hired female site managers at all – she'd only ever dealt with men like Brian and Stu. What would this Jessalyn be like?

Soft chimes sounded over the office PA system, letting everyone know it was noon. They were allowed to leave the office for lunch as long as they were back before the chimes sounded again at one, as if they were at school, not adults working in an office. As soon as she heard the lunch chimes, Nell whisked her purse out of the desk drawer where she kept it and bolted for the stairs. Sure, it would be financially more responsible to bring a packed lunch, but then she'd have to eat at her desk and would have no escape all day from the Wildforest dungeon.

It was a matter of principle for her to get down the stairs in under three minutes, without running.

There was a little vegetarian café down the block from the office, barely a hole in the wall, it was so tiny – just a counter and a couple of tables, and some tall stools by the window. Nothing fancy, but Nell could eat in peace for half an hour. The tomato and avocado sandwich was her favorite, but she also liked the cucumber and cream cheese one, and egg salad some days for variety.

Refreshed, and a little more tolerant of the circus that was her workplace, Nell returned as usual just before the one o'clock chimes. On her desk was a yellow Post-It note from Tommy – *Assistant confirmed, will start ASAP.* No other details were provided, so she'd just have to wait. But at least help was coming.

She sent off an email to Jessalyn Roberts, introducing herself as the new property supervisor and inquiring about paper supplies at Champagne Cascades since the folder had no recent inventory report. And then Lila transferred a call to her desk with the warning, "Incoming hot top, Nell." A hot top was the interoffice term for an actively angry guest.

Nell spent the next forty-five minutes listening to an enraged woman who claimed that Brian at Winter Pine had been rude and disrespectful, and ended up offering her a voucher for a night at Secret Creek to make amends. Forty-five minutes she'd never get back. And while it was quite possibly true – Brian was, in general, a rude and disrespectful sort of person, though she believed he mostly held his attitude in check around the guests to keep his job – Nell also had the feeling that the woman was milking a probably mild incident to get freebies in compensation, so it galled her a bit to play into that game. And now she'd have to call Brian and find out what happened from his point of view.

♥

About twenty-four hours later, Nell returned from lunch to find another of Tommy's yellow Post-It notes on her desk: *My office – 1:30 pm.* Everyone else at Wildforest seemed able to use the interoffice calendar and messaging app to arrange meetings, but Tommy liked his Post-Its, or maybe he just liked that one couldn't decline or reschedule them.

Feeling all the relaxation of her lunch break boiling away, Nell bent down to grab her favorite vanilla spice rooibos from the tin box where she stashed her tea in a bottom drawer. She usually waited until later in the afternoon, but today she'd need it to handle Tommy's meeting calmly. He'd probably tell her that it would be weeks until a new assistant could be hired, or that she'd have to share Trina's assistant – putting a strain on both of their files and probably their relationship. Then she became aware of some thumping noises and swearing from the photocopier room behind her. Plainly, someone was having trouble with the copier and not handling it particularly well.

Stifling a wry snicker, Nell decided to see if she could help, like some kind of photocopier superhero. All she needed was a cape. She whipped around the corner and into the copier room.

A man in beat-up jeans and a Queen t-shirt bent over the copier, prodding its innards unsuccessfully, and giving the base of the machine a desultory kick when it continued to beep and flash error messages. *Tall enough. Toned arms with just the right amount of ink. Blond wavy hair. Oh, hell no.*

The man stood up.

Their eyes met.

It was definitely, without a doubt, the pool player from the Frog and Ball – the man she'd left writhing on the floor of the women's bathroom. And there was no question that he recognized her.

"What are *you* doing here?" Nell asked, before he could say anything.

He looked down at his hands, which were streaked with copier toner. "Tommy Baxter is my uncle. It seems I'm going to be working here for a bit. I'm, ah, not used to being in an office – do you know anything about these beasts?"

"Right," said Nell. "Let me have a look at it." She gave him a cold look and a jerk of her chin to let him know that he needed to move out of her space before she'd approach. Somewhat warily, he backed away to lean against the office supply cupboards. Stepping up to the copier, she turned the handle that would open the inner section of the machine, then rotated the wheel to move the jammed paper forward.

As she eased the crumpled and smudged paper out of the copier, the blond man moved closer, leaned down next to her ear and asked quietly, "What the hell was up with you putting me on the ground at the pub like that?" His unexpected nearness startled her, and she jumped back, only narrowly controlling her impulse to take down the threat. "Whoa!" he said, seeing her half-fisted hands and ready stance.

"You were in the women's can, where you had no business being. You wouldn't listen when I told you to back off. So yeah, I put you on the ground. And I'll do it again if I have to."

The man laughed, a sexy, throaty laugh. Flirty. "I would never have hurt you, gorgeous."

Nell rolled her eyes. "You *couldn't* hurt me even if you wanted to, and I don't care about your intentions. Stay out of the women's bathroom here at work, and stay away from me at the Frog and Ball on Sundays."

"All right." The man's chuckle told her he wasn't taking her seriously.

She finished putting the photocopier back together. "There. The copier is fixed. Try not to break it again."

"Thanks. What's your name, ninja woman?"

"Nell." She didn't want to tell him, but he'd find out from Tommy soon enough. No point in creating a war over something minor.

"That's pretty. I'm Eamonn."

Nell shrugged. *Damned if I'll show him I like anything about him.* She didn't want to find even his name appealing. "Right. Well, I'd better get back to my desk."

Not waiting for a response, she swirled out of the room and ducked back into her office, grabbing her tin of tea and her mug. A soothing cup of vanilla spice rooibos would be just the thing to settle her agitation over finding *him* here, in her office.

♥

At the dot of half past one, Nell knocked on Tommy's office door. He didn't like late, or early. But instead of his usual barked "Come in," she heard footsteps, and he opened the door for her himself. "Nell, you're here," he said, in an unusually affable tone. "Come and sit down. There's someone I want you to meet."

Oh, crap. Eamonn the photocopy room guy, the pool player from the Frog and Ball, was sprawled in one of Tommy's guest chairs. "Hi, Nell. Uncle Tommy, we've met – she helped me with a paper jam in the copy machine."

"Well, good. Nell, Eamonn's going to be your assistant for a while. No experience, but he can learn on the job. Changing careers isn't easy, so I trust you'll help him out and not be too hard on him?" The inflection made it a question and asked for her agreement, but the wording didn't give her a choice.

"Of course. I'm... sure we'll work things out."

Eamonn looked across at her and gave her a slow wink, making the words *work things out* seem somehow dirty, like a double entendre she hadn't intended. "It'll be a pleasure to work things out with you, baby."

Tommy or no Tommy, that couldn't stand. "Do *not* call me baby," Nell gritted out.

"Calm down, Nell. Eamonn isn't used to an office environment; it'll take him some time to learn all the niceties."

"Right. Eamonn, if we're going to work harmoniously together, you'll have to call me Nell – or Miss Whelan." No one used last names at Wildforest, not even the most senior management or the board of directors. But Nell was accustomed to being Miss Whelan in a martial arts setting, and she could use a little of that respect from Eamonn.

That only got a laugh from him. "*Miss* Whelan, is it?" And she realized that the title didn't have quite the same meaning as it did in martial arts circles; his emphasis made it something dainty, maybe even a bit southern belle, rather than the earned title of a black belt. *Damn.* Well, in ten years she'd qualify as Master Whelan, and then... That wouldn't show him anything. She wouldn't even know him a decade on. But her goal of attaining mastership had sustained her through a lot of things. She held onto it now and straightened her spine.

"The Wildforest board prefers that we use first names here," Tommy explained to Eamonn. "Friendly corporate culture and all that. Run along now and Nell will show you your office – Shannon's is still empty, right, Nell?"

"Yes. Thank you, Tommy. Let's go, Eamonn." She turned to leave Tommy's office and nearly ran smack into Lila, who was carrying two cups of coffee.

"Whoops! Didn't know you were in here, Nell. I was just bringing some coffee for Tommy and Easy – it's okay if I call you Easy, right? I'll never remember to say Eamonn." Lila held out the coffee to the men, practically purring and batting her eyelashes. "Let me know if there's anything else I can get you."

"Thanks, sugar." Eamonn took the coffee, seeming to accept the nickname and Lila's fawning behavior as normal and his due. *Weird.*

Tommy accepted his coffee with a shrug and a muttered, "Typical."

"Let's go," Nell repeated, nearly taking Eamonn's arm to drag him away from Lila's fluttering attention. But she jerked her hand back just in time; he might take the contact the wrong way. Who knew what went through that man's mind?

As they filed down the narrow corridors to Nell's office and the empty one beside it, now Eamonn's, she wondered about Lila nicknaming him "Easy" – and how readily he'd accepted it. That seemed pretty brazen of Lila, in retrospect, although it did somehow suit him. Maybe the receptionist had heard Tommy call him that, or perhaps he'd leaned over the reception desk and suggested it. Without thinking it through, she turned back to him and asked, "Hey, why did Lila call you Easy? Is it a nickname? Something you prefer?"

He looked at her in stunned incredulity, coming to a stop in the hallway. "You don't know?"

"Should I know something about you? Other than your habit of entering women's bathrooms uninvited?" And she didn't even know that was a habit, but it didn't strike her as a one-time effort.

Eamonn still looked stunned. "You don't, ah, recognize me?" She blinked at him, still drawing a blank. "Rock band? Bass player?" he prompted. "Stage names?"

Crap. "Smidge," she said, as the puzzle pieces fell into place in her mind. She wasn't a huge rock fan, preferring classical music and jazz, but she didn't live in a convent. She'd seen them on television, on bus shelter posters, heard their songs on friends' playlists. She hadn't expected one of them to be *here*. "You're Easy from Smidge." And then, "So what the ever-loving hell are you doing in an office, working for Wildforest?"

His face closed up, grew hard, stony. "If you have to ask, do you think we could talk about it somewhere more private?" The icy tone to his voice told her something had gone very wrong and he was raw about it right to his core.

"It's none of my business," Nell said at once. "I'm sorry I asked."

Eamonn shrugged. "Whatever. Show me my office so I can get settled in, okay?" A faint hint of a flush around his neck and jaw told her he wasn't as blasé about it as he seemed. *A complicated man. A rock god. An office assistant?*

"Would you rather I call you Eamonn, or Easy?" she asked.

"Either. I'll answer to both."

She shrugged, letting him have his privacy. "Here's your office. Mine's next door. Have you been given a username and password for the office computer system yet?"

For answer, he fished a crumpled Post-It note out of his pocket and held it up.

"Okay, then, go ahead and get logged in and configure your email and chat profile and stuff. I've got a couple of things I want to get done, then I'll come back and walk you through the basics of managing a Wildforest property. All right?"

"Cool," Eamonn said, sliding into the desk chair with a smoothly graceful movement that shouldn't have made Nell shiver.

She needed more tea. Hell, she needed a Frosty Peach and some sweet potato fries.

How is it only Thursday? Sunday night seemed an eternity away.

Did it bother him that she didn't recognize him at first glance? The question had troubled her a few times in the night. Presumably, he'd earned his place in the music world every bit as much as she'd earned hers in martial arts; she was familiar with the infuriating feeling of having one's skill disregarded – she hated it when people assumed she was helpless just because she was female. If being recognized was inherent to being a rock star, then to go unrecognized...

Still, Nell refused to vary her routine for a new assistant, especially one who was so presumptuous with women and so sure of himself and his fame and sex appeal. She felt particularly glad that she hadn't done something silly – like buy a new blouse or put on makeup – when Lila floated in, early for a miraculous first time ever, in a ruffled peach chiffon dress and smoky, sparkly eye makeup. "Hot date after work, Lila?" Nell asked, although she was pretty sure she knew the cause of Lila's extra efforts.

Lila giggled. "Not unless Easy asks me out. Is he here yet?"

"No. Haven't seen him."

"Do me a favor and let me know when he comes in, 'kay? I want to be the one who brings him coffee."

Nell snorted. "Sure, but you've got feathers for brains if you think that's going to get you anywhere. The man probably has a dozen girlfriends."

Eamonn didn't turn up until after ten o'clock, eating a doughnut and drinking coffee from a Top Pot to-go cup. He propped himself against the open door of her office and said, "Morning, baby."

Suppressing an eye-roll, Nell said mildly, "You have to stop calling me baby. Also, the office opens at nine."

"Mm. I'm not good with mornings," he said. "But I'll try. Brought you a doughnut."

He tossed a paper bag onto her desk and vanished into his office without another word. Through the thin walls, she could hear the squeak of his desk chair and the burbling start-up noises of his computer.

A doughnut. Nell hadn't eaten one in – she couldn't remember how long – it must have been years.

The paper bag was slightly warm and smelled amazing: a doughy, sugary smell that reminded her of fairgrounds and bakeries. She ripped the paper open, exposing the fried goodness within. A jelly doughnut, no less. Round, plump, covered in powdered sugar, with a tiny bit of raspberry filling dripping from a hole in the side.

I shouldn't. But why would it be so wrong to eat the doughnut? It didn't mean she'd owe Eamonn anything. It had been freely offered, without conditions; he hadn't given her a chance to refuse it.

She lifted it to her mouth and bit into it, closing her eyes to better savor the combination of flavors. *Damn, that's good.* She nearly moaned with the pleasure of tart raspberry jelly and sweet sugar on her tongue.

A soft chuckle made her open her eyes. Eamonn was leaning in her doorway again, grinning at her. He'd been watching her eat the doughnut. "You like it," he said.

"Yeah." Couldn't very well deny it. "Thanks."

"You've got jelly on your lip."

"Oh." She stuck out her tongue and licked the jelly up.

The way he looked at her mouth made her feel like she'd just stripped for him. "I want to be that doughnut, gorgeous," he muttered.

"Get out of my office, pervert," she told him, but without much fire. "And follow up with Champagne about their paper order. I need to put the order in by five." *Stick with business. Don't even acknowledge that look.* They'd have to work together for an unspecified amount of time, and anything less than total professionalism would be awkward as hell.

♥

Nell felt angry and discombobulated all afternoon. *It's ridiculous. I'm an adult, a woman, a feminist, a martial artist. He's a pervert – he hit on me at the pub in the women's bathroom – and he uses the most inappropriate language.* Accepting a doughnut from him felt like a low point in her personal account book.

Part of her wanted to put him on the ground and teach him some manners, some respect and appreciation for women. An angry, frustrated side of her flared up. Ordinarily, self-control and a disciplined outlook on life were things she took pride in: the ability to tap an opponent's headgear with a precise kick that showcased her aim, the measured speed and strength she brought to self-defense drills – enough to be realistic as a defender and provide some resistance and force as an attacker without either partner actually getting injured. But now and then the anger flared up, particularly when a cocky teenage boy started showing off with her at training, trying to score points on a senior black belt, out to win rather than train and improve. This was especially true if she caught a sense that he thought he could beat her because she was female, that he didn't think girls could hit hard or take hard hits. On a couple of occasions, and she was not proud of them, she'd lost her temper during training and tried to nail a sparring partner hard or put him into the mat during self-defense. She'd done it, too, swearing under her breath and jangling with adrenaline, earning herself some surprised looks for the loss of control.

She could feel the anger burning in the same way here, the urge to fight and win, to take him down and teach him his place in her world. *That's ridiculous. He doesn't even do martial arts.*

But it wasn't about sports or sparring. She was just angry.

Angry at herself?

The twinges of attraction, the dirty way he looked at her, it all added up to something that shouldn't *be*. How could she want to like him, let alone be attracted to him? Everything about him was reprehensible to her and stood against her values and the way she tried to live her life, with integrity and respect for life and individual autonomy. And it wasn't as though she had some kind of subconscious fetish for disrespect; she'd been catcalled and propositioned plenty of times, and there'd been no turn-on in it, no flutter of appeal, just a sort of scornful distaste. But she kept thinking about how he'd looked at her mouth as she'd eaten the doughnut. How he'd flushed and closed himself off when asked why he was working in an office. How he'd never once presumed on his fame to ingratiate himself with her. Hell, he'd introduced himself as Eamonn, not Easy.

Easy. He sure acted like he'd be easy to get into bed. *Flirt.*

That ought to gross her out, repel her. Why didn't it? *Ugh.*

So when Eamonn popped into her office, she snapped, "Even if it's open, you can still knock on the frame before walking in, you know."

"Right," he said, with a *what got your panties in a knot* expression on his face. "So I got a hold of that chick Jessalyn at Champagne Cascades."

"Did she say why she didn't bother to return my call or email yesterday?" Nell didn't even bother to correct his use of *chick*, though she did raise a disapproving eyebrow.

"She wasn't feeling good yesterday. She didn't say exactly but I'm thinking it's woman stuff, you know? She says she was at work but had a hard time getting much done."

"She really unbuttoned for you, didn't she?" The moment she said it, Nell knew her choice of words was a mistake. But it burned her that the unknown Jessalyn had taken his call when she'd been ignored the day before.

Eamonn laughed. "I wouldn't say *unbuttoned*, gorgeous – that's what I want *you* to do for me. I can't help it that women like to talk to me. Anyway, if it works... I got the paper inventory figures from her and forwarded them to you. Good?"

"Thanks. Could you stop calling me that, though?"

"Why? You *are* gorgeous. You've got heavenly tits and–"

Nell growled, actually growled, in frustration. "We're in an *office*. I'm technically your supervisor. Your uncle is my boss and I don't need him walking by and hearing that – I really, really, absolutely don't need him to be thinking about my personal attributes in any way. Okay?"

Eamonn shook his head. "Uncle Tommy's married, he'd never... well, okay, yeah, that'd be weird."

An awkward silence settled between them. *You think I have nice breasts?* The question burned on Nell's tongue, tempting her, but there was no way she'd ask such a ridiculous thing.

He watched her, considering, a half-smile on his lips. "Yes," he said.

"I was *not* thinking about–"

"Of course you were, and you do. But I won't refer to your tits in the office again. Nell." The way he said her name made her think that maybe he was getting it, that he could see the difference between an office and backstage, and that he understood the differences, the things you could say there and not here.

"Thanks," she said, and she didn't know if she was thanking him for using her name, or for the compliment he'd given her. *Easy from Smidge. Bass player, rock star, sex god.* Given all the females he must have known, the array of chests available for him to sample, his commendation meant a lot to her. Not that she'd let herself care. Her body was strong and muscular and solid, perfect for a fighter, a competitor. "Thanks for getting me those numbers from Champagne. I need to get the order in before the paper supplier closes."

"I'm off, then. See you tomorrow." And he was gone.

I should make him stay until the clock hits five, Nell thought. But he was Tommy's nephew, so she suspected the usual Wildforest regulations didn't apply to him.

chapter

3

HE FIRST SIGN OF ANYTHING WRONG CAME WITH A phone call. Someone from booking and customer service pinged Nell on the intercom line. "Got a hot top on line four calling from Champagne Cascades. Goes beyond what we can handle in booking. Will you take it?"

"Saying no isn't a choice, is it? Sure." Nell sighed, looking at the button for line four, flashing red, on hold. Coping with an angry guest was never fun, but it was part of dealing with resort properties and their temporary residents – people paid for pleasant vacations, after all, and tended to get bent out of shape when little things didn't go their way. She took a sip of tea and hit the button to take the call. "Hi there, this is Nell Whelan, property supervisor for Champagne Cascades. I understand there's a problem?"

"Well, yeah. Been standing here forty minutes waiting to get our keys, but your office is closed up tight and there's no sign of when someone will be coming or anything."

"You're saying that you're at Champagne Cascades *now*, and there's no one in the office there to book you in and give you keys?"

"Yes. We've been waiting forty minutes. Ridiculous! There's not even a sign on the door saying when they'll be back."

Nell brought up the booking system on her computer. "Could I get your name, ma'am? I just want to check and make sure we were expecting you." She spoke slowly, pitching her voice quietly, aiming for a calm and respectful tone that would help the infuriated woman settle down.

"Annie and Michael Prince. We got a confirmation email yesterday."

"Right. I see Veuve Cliquot is reserved for you." The booking was there in the system, as it should be – apparently, all the cottages were named after famous champagne brands. At three in the afternoon, there was absolutely no reason the site office at Champagne should be closed. And the policy at all sites was, if you had to close up the office during business hours for any amount of time, even five minutes, you had to place a notice on the door saying why the office was closed and for how long. "Well, the office should not be closed at this hour. If I may put you on hold, Mrs. Prince, I'll see what I can do from here."

Mrs. Prince made a frustrated noise into the phone, a sort of huffing sigh of annoyance. "I guess, okay. I'll hold."

As soon as Nell placed Mrs. Prince on hold, she tried the office line, but as expected got no answer. She then tried the mobile number in the company records for Jessalyn Roberts and got no answer there either. Now what? She decided to try the restaurant – there should be two full-time staff there, though she couldn't remember their names off-hand from her glance through the information binder: a cook and a waitress.

A man with a thick Québécois accent answered. "Allo, Pink Champagne Dining Room. François speaking."

"François, this is Nell Whelan. I'm the new property supervisor for Champagne Cascades. Have you seen Jessalyn today?"

"*Non.* She hasn't been here today. Mary and I didn't know what to do. Guests at breakfast ask us when they can check out, but we don't know. We had Aidan's cell number but he says he doesn't work for the company anymore."

And you didn't think to call the main office? But recriminations wouldn't help anything now. "Either you or Mary is going to need to go and open the office. I'll have to walk you through the check-in and check-out process over the phone."

"Better be Mary," said François. "She's better with computers and things. I'm just a cook."

"Don't knock yourself. It's a gift to be good with food. Okay. Send Mary up to the office and have her call me when she gets there. Oh, and warn her there's a hot top waiting to be checked in."

"Hot top?" the cook asked, sounding puzzled.

"Angry guest," Nell clarified, surprised to find that they didn't use the office code words on-site. She gave François her phone number to give Mary, in case Jessalyn hadn't updated the site office's speed dial and emergency call list, and then hung up. Taking a deep breath, she picked up line four. "Mrs. Prince, thanks for waiting. We don't know what's happened to our site manager at this time, but Mary from the dining room is on her way to the office and I'll help her check you in. You should be all right for this evening, and someone from Wildforest Vacations will be up there tomorrow morning to take charge."

"Will *you* come?" Mrs. Prince asked. "You seem like a sensible person."

"I'll ask my boss," Nell said, knowing that she would indeed likely be the person sent up, but thinking it wouldn't hurt to have Mrs. Prince believe she'd asked to come.

"Good."

"I'll hang up with you now, but I'll be here waiting to take Mary's call once she gets into the office." Hopefully, Mary would prove competent to follow instructions over the phone, just to get them by overnight. What had happened to Jessalyn Roberts? Why had she not turned up for work that morning?

♥

Nell knocked on Tommy's door. "Come in!" he barked. Not a happy afternoon, then.

"Tommy, you're not going to like this, but one of our site managers seems to have disappeared."

"You're kidding me, right? Tell me you're kidding me."

"Unfortunately, no. Jessalyn Roberts from Champagne Cascades didn't turn up for work this morning – no note, no message, nothing. I've got the waitress from the restaurant doing office duty for tonight, but she's not trained and has to be talked through everything over the phone."

"Smart thinking, Nell. You and Eamonn will have to get up there tomorrow to take over, of course. Sign out a company vehicle; here's the authorization slip. I'll get HR working on finding a new site manager right away."

The thought of the unknown Jessalyn losing her job made Nell wince, no matter what difficulties she was causing. "Give me twenty-four hours to look into it up there, Tommy? If she's just down with a violent flu or something, it may not be worth the expense of finding a new site manager."

"Twenty-four hours, then," Tommy said, looking displeased. *Torn between wanting to fire her and wanting to save the cost of hiring and training someone new, probably.* "And only if she has a damn good reason."

Then something else he'd said struck Nell. "I can make the trip alone," she said quickly. "I've never taken an assistant along on site visits before."

"You've never had to cover for and investigate a missing site manager before, either," Tommy snapped back. "Plus, I want him to get some on-site experience, and it's safer for you to have a man along on trips like this."

Seriously? She was plenty safe on her own. But that wasn't a conversation Nell wanted to have with Tommy. "Fine."

"It had better be fine with you, Nell. You're taking Eamonn with you, and that's an order. Now, send him down to see me. And get Lila to bring us coffee."

I hate my job. I hate my job. Nell nodded, not trusting her voice to come out evenly over the fury inside her. At least she'd get to go on-site for two or three days. If nothing else, it would get her away from the office. But it wouldn't get her away from Eamonn.

♥

Lila came floating into Nell's office. "You lucky bitch."

"What, now?" Nell gave Lila a hard look.

"I hear you're going on a road trip with Easy Yarrow, and I'm green with envy over it. And the sad thing is, you probably won't even get laid while you have the chance."

"What in the ever-loving hell are you talking about, Lila? Just because his stage name is Easy, it doesn't mean he'll roll over for any woman he happens to be around, right? Otherwise, you'd have had him in the janitor's closet by now, I expect."

Lila gaped at her. "Don't be catty, Nell. I'm just saying you're lucky, that's all. And that if I were in your shoes, I'd be packing condoms with the rest of my shit tonight." Giggling, Lila turned to leave.

"Wait. Easy Yarrow? I assumed it was Baxter. Tommy's his uncle."

"Dunno. His HR file says Yarrow."

Nell tried not to let her surprise show on her face. *Lila went snooping in Eamonn's HR file?* She hadn't figured Lila would have the computer skills to get into a restricted part of the database. "What else did you learn?"

Lila giggled again. "Oh, his birthday, his age, where he lives, how much he's being paid."

"Pretty sure I can find out that stuff by asking him, Lila."

"Enjoy your trip. Aidan told me one time that Champagne Cascades is a pretty freaking romantic place."

"Do you *want* me to sleep with Eamonn?" Nell asked, puzzled. "I thought *you* were crushing on him."

"Oh, I am, who wouldn't be? But you need to get laid, sunshine. And I think he could do the job just fine. Besides, I've got a boyfriend."

"Well, all that's pretty... ah... enlightening," said Eamonn from the doorway, where he'd obviously caught at least the last little bit of their exchange.

Lila turned bright red, muttered, "We were just joking around," and scuttled out of Nell's office.

Eamonn stepped into the office and closed the door. "Uncle Tommy tells me we're going on a road trip."

"Door open, please," Nell ordered, using her no-nonsense instructor voice. It was way too intimate with the door closed. And she didn't get involved with co-workers.

"Why?" he asked. "I'm not going to do anything to you. Like you said, we're at the office. We're just talking."

"I just... it just feels weirdly private." Nell shrugged, not wanting to make too big a deal of it. "Whatever."

With a thoughtful look, Eamonn turned and cracked the door so it stood open a few inches. "Better?" The look on his face said he was humoring her. *Bastard.*

"Oh, sure, an inch or two makes so much difference."

Eamonn burst out laughing. "I'm told my extra inches make a pretty nice difference." Nell fixed him with a murderous gaze, and he raised his hands to ward off her anger. "Hey, hey, I'm just winding you up. Tell me about this road trip."

Nell sighed. "I don't know. I've never been to Champagne Cascades before – I only got assigned the property the day before you started. And I've always done site visits alone and left my assistant in the office. But Tommy wants me to take you with me."

"He says it's a long drive, through mountains and shit."

"And he thinks I'm a little lady who can't take care of myself without a man's protection. Screw that!" Nell couldn't keep the scowl off her face. Tommy's antiquated attitude toward women always enraged her.

"Simmer down. I know you can take care of yourself. Black belt, I think you said? I was on the ground and in pain at the time, so... you made your point."

Nell, who never blushed, felt her cheeks getting hot. "So maybe I overreacted. I thought you were planning on stepping up from harassment to assault, though, and – adrenaline took over. Muscle memory and training. I didn't think, I just... acted."

"Dude. I never thought – I was just flirting – I'd never *rape* anyone!"

"You think an unwanted grope is just *flirting*?"

"No. Fuck me, I – all the time I was playing with Smidge, girls were practically lining up to have a go with me in the bathrooms. Like, where else can you do it at a bar? And they wanted to say they'd screwed a rock star. I just lived up to my name." *Easy.*

Nell shook her head. "So you assumed I'd be into it too. Yeah, no."

"Sorry," Eamonn muttered.

"Forgiven. Just remember that any time you get that close to a woman who's not actively saying yes, there's a strong chance she's wondering if you're planning to rape her. Let's move on."

He looked a bit stunned. "I, ah, never thought of it like that." When she gave him a prompting look, he nodded. "Sure, moving on. You were saying you haven't been to Champagne Cascades before?"

"That's right. From Google Maps, it looks pretty remote, up toward the Canadian border on the other side of Wenatchee National Park. The nearest town is called Winthrop. It'll be upwards of a four-hour drive, so we'll have to leave really early." She pulled the map up on her computer and angled the screen so he could see it. The blue line of the recommended route followed a scooping curve, taking I-90 across the narrowest part of the mountains and then US-97 up through Wenatchee on the other side, until they'd get to smaller local roads after Brewster.

"Just how early are you talking about?"

Four hours. Need to be there for checkout at ten. "You're not a fan of mornings, are you? We're going to have to be on the road by six."

"Oh, that's ugly. I don't function before ten. How come we don't head out now and sleep there tonight?" Eamonn asked.

Nell blinked. She hadn't even thought of it. "I haven't packed. And even if we left in less than an hour, we'd be driving 'til at least nine, later if we stop anywhere."

He shrugged. "Just an idea. Your call."

"I'm not a fan of night driving, especially in the mountains," she admitted. She never liked to have her weaknesses brought to light, but she'd been a city dweller all her life and her experience was more tied to public transit than rural highways.

Eamonn reached out, as if to rub her shoulder in reassurance, then jerked his hand back as if reminded that his touch might not be welcome. "Hey, it's okay. I love to drive, especially highways at night. Could we take my truck? Four-wheel drive, good tires, and I promise it's a comfortable ride."

Nell smiled at his wheedling tone. "I'd imagine a truck owned by a rock god would be pretty comfortable. We're supposed to take a company vehicle, but I bet you could persuade Tommy to waive that rule."

"Yeah. I'll go ask him. I've got my bike here today, so I'll have to whip home and get the truck. You want to take transit to your place to pack, or are you willing to ride with me? I've got a spare helmet."

She grinned. "I've been on bikes before. I'd appreciate a lift home."

"Sounds good. I'll go talk to Uncle Tommy. Meet you at the elevators in ten minutes?"

Elevators? Let's see what the man is made of. "Afraid to take the stairs?"

He stared at her. "Six floors?"

"It only takes a couple of minutes. Good cardio. But you can meet me at the bottom if you'd rather."

"All right." He shrugged. "I guess I can take the stairs with you."

Eamonn was a bit out of breath when they reached the parking level, but not as much as Nell had expected. "You're not in bad shape," she said. *Especially given that he's carrying his helmet.*

"Mm. Playing rock concerts can be pretty intense and I work out when I'm able. Keeps me fit enough." His voice sounded casual, almost deliberately casual, and she wondered if he was taking their relative fitness as a competition. So many men, in and out of martial arts, took it as a personal challenge when they met a woman who was physically strong. *Maybe I should have taken the elevator.*

She didn't have to ask where he was parked. There was just the one motorcycle in the parking garage. She'd assumed a guy whose stage name was Easy would have a sleek crotch rocket in a flashy cherry red or something equally attention-screaming, but the bike they walked toward was a big, comfortable touring Harley in silver and black. "Nice ride," she said, and he grinned.

Reaching the bike, he unlocked the trunk on the back and lifted out a spare helmet. "Full helmet," he said, handing it to her. "I like my passengers to be safe. You said you'd ridden on the back of someone's bike before?"

"A few times, yeah. Some of the guys I train with have bikes and I get a ride home now and then."

"Good. Here, give me your bag and I'll lock it in the top box so you don't need to worry about it." Then he swung his leg over the bike and adjusted his weight. "Let me just pull out and turn before you hop on." Nell stepped back against a concrete pillar while Eamonn rolled his bike out of the parking spot and got it positioned toward the parking lot exit. He waved her over. "Okay, climb on up. You know you've gotta hold tight, right? Can't be shy on a bike."

"I'm not shy." *I just don't know that it's a good idea to get so close to you.* But her only other choice was to refuse to get on the bike, and then she'd have to waste time on the bus when they could be getting on the road. She hadn't been on a touring motorcycle before. It was bigger than she was used to, with a high back behind the passenger seat. "Looks like an armchair, all that leather padding." Feeling fortunate that her training had given her so much flexibility, she grabbed the back of the seat, got a leg up, and slid into position. The padded seat gave her no choice – her legs were pretty much snug around his hips, and unless she leaned back awkwardly, her chest was right up against his back, like a sitting piggyback ride.

He didn't seem to mind. "I like road trips. I like being comfortable. We could ride to Champagne like this without too much trouble, but I think the truck will be better, especially if you want to nap while I drive."

Nell snorted. "I don't nap."

"We'll see. My truck is comfortable too. Anyway, you know the drill, right? Keep your feet up even at stops, keep your arms around my waist, and keep your shoulders in line with mine. Tap my shoulder if there's a problem and I'll pull over. Good?"

"Don't you need my address?"

"Got it from Uncle Tommy on my way out. Let's go." He revved the motor, a smooth rumble that vibrated right through her like a cat's purr, and pushed off.

No goddamn privacy in that place.

She couldn't feel much of his body through his leather jacket, just a sense of lean hardness and warmth. It was still too close for comfort. *He doesn't respect women,* she reminded herself. He may not have intended to harass her in the Frog and Ball, and he may have meant 'gorgeous' as a compliment, but it still didn't make him acceptable. But in her mind, she kept hearing Lila saying *you need to get laid.* "I do not," she said out loud, knowing that the wind would eat her words without him hearing them. *I'm quite capable of taking care of my own needs in between lovers, thank you.* She wasn't so desperate that she'd need to take someone called Easy into her bed. *Think about packing,* she told herself. *Think about planning. Don't think about him.*

She wrapped her arms tighter around him and closed her eyes against the afternoon sun. It seemed like no time at all before he pulled up in front of her apartment building.

"How long do you need to pack?" he asked, as he turned and offered her a hand to steady her as she dismounted. Then he got up too and opened the top box to get her bag.

"Not long," she said without thinking. *I am totally unprepared for this.* She'd planned on doing laundry in the evening, packing methodically, leaving in the morning after a good sleep. "How long will it take you to get your truck and get back here? And you have to pack too."

"I'm a guy," he said. "Packing takes me a few minutes, tops. I can be back here in forty, if that works for you?"

"You bet." She'd be on the front step waiting when he arrived if it killed her. *Do I even have clean pajamas?* "I'll be ready."

His truck was gorgeous. Nicer than the bike, even. She hadn't been expecting cherry red, especially after the bike had surprised her by being such a subtle silver and black. It was a fully tricked-out Chevy Silverado 1500 High Country, and as he opened the door, she could see leather seats.

Getting up from the front steps of her building where she'd been sitting, Nell hoisted her travel bag onto her shoulder and walked slowly down to the curb. By the time she reached the truck, Eamonn had gotten out and was waiting for her next to the passenger door. "Bet this thing eats a lot of gas," she blurted out. It was rude, and not at all what she'd meant to say, but she was feeling discombobulated from having packed in a hurry, and slightly angry with herself for liking his toys so much.

"It's not too bad," he said mildly, and she wondered if he'd ever had to worry about gas prices. *Rock star.* But then he gave her a half-smile and added, "It's not a full hybrid, but it has e-assist, so that helps a fair bit."

"It's a lovely color," she said, wishing she'd just said that to begin with.

"Thanks, babe." He took her bag and tossed it onto the second row of seats – the truck was a big crew cab style with four doors and seats enough to fit all of Smidge plus a girlfriend or two – then offered her a steadying hand for the step up into the passenger seat. "Let's get on the road."

Nell ignored his hand and hauled herself up into the high seat on her own. *Don't call me babe,* she thought grumpily. But she bit her tongue on the thought – no sense starting an argument when they'd be stuck in the vehicle for the next four or more hours. As she settled into her seat and buckled up, he closed the door and went around to the driver's side.

The Silverado's cab could sit three across, but the middle seat was folded down to provide a console with cupholders. *Good, a bulwark between us.* The motorcycle ride had been more than enough coziness between them, and Nell didn't want any more of it. Once Eamonn was in the truck and buckled, he leaned over and pointed to something on the dash. "Here's the AC, feel free to adjust it to whatever's comfortable for you. If the night gets cold later, there's a heated seat switch there. It's a long way, so let me know if there's anything you need, like a pit stop or food, right?" He started up the truck and pulled out smoothly onto the road. "I'm going to go through the Starbucks drive-thru on our way out of here – coffee goes with highway driving for me. Want anything?"

"I can get my own."

"Just let me get you a coffee, all right? It doesn't mean anything."

"Yeah, no, because I don't drink coffee."

Eamonn laughed, a full-throated genuine laugh. "Figures. Green tea latte? Chai? I'm guessing you're a green tea kind of girl."

Because she liked both, and because she just plain didn't want him to be right about her, she said, "Chai. Half sweet, with coconut milk. And I'm a woman, not a girl."

He laughed even more. "Oh, you're all woman, that's for sure." *Damn, I walked into that one.* But she hated being called a girl. "Okay, complicated-drink woman, I'll get your half-sweet coconut milk chai. Now, what about music?"

♥

They stopped for dinner at a pub in Wenatchee around half past seven, just over two hours after they'd set out. They were making good time and Nell suspected Eamonn wasn't sticking to the speed limit, but she refused to give him the satisfaction of seeing her peering at the speedometer so she deliberately kept her eyes averted. He was a smooth driver, in any case, and the big truck ate up the miles like they were nothing. "I'm good to keep going," he'd said when they reached the outskirts of Wenatchee, but Nell reminded him they didn't know what they'd find in the smaller towns ahead and pointed out that the kitchen at Champagne wouldn't still be doing dinner after nine, even if he wanted to wait another two hours or more to eat. "All right," he'd agreed, "but let's get a proper meal if we're stopping. Not shitty road food."

Nell wasn't sure if they'd agree on what constituted a proper meal, but he pulled into a parking lot next to a pub and turned to her with raised eyebrows as if to ask, *will this do?*

"We only get ten dollars a day in travel allowance," she reminded him.

He shrugged. "Yeah, they expect us to eat Mickey D's. I'm okay with covering the extra."

"I can afford my own dinner. I'm not broke. It's just... natural caution, I suppose."

"You always color inside the lines?"

I draw my own lines, she wanted to say. *My life isn't a coloring book.* But he was right. She recognized in herself a tendency to follow rules, to stay where things were clearly black and white, no mess or blurring of what was expected. The structure and hierarchy of martial arts never left room for doubt, and she'd been living within it for most of her life. Even her own rules for herself... She smiled ruefully. "Pub night is Sunday. It's not Sunday today."

"Well, let's pretend." He jumped down from the truck and came around to open her door.

"Dude, you don't have to open doors for me. I can do it."

He shook his head. "Mom would skin me alive if I let a lady open her own door. But you can jump down without touching my hand, if you'd rather."

Feeling as though she'd been ungracious, Nell rested her hand lightly on his as she stepped down to the sidewalk. "Thanks," she muttered. Although she broke the contact immediately, she could still feel the imprint where her palm had touched his fingers. Rubbing the offending palm against the thigh of her jeans, she strode ahead to the door of the pub, opening it before he could get there. Her first glance around showed her warm wooden tables and brick walls, bell-shaped glass lights and rustic open rafters overhead, a long bar counter. "This place looks all right," she said, reaching back to hold the door open for him.

"Thank you, gorgeous." He winked at her.

"Don't–" Then she realized he was winding her up on purpose.

"We're not in the office." He took a burning good look at her below the neck before meeting her eyes again. "Yup, still as nice as before."

"You're unbelievable." She felt a reluctant smile twitching at the corners of her mouth.

The hostess showed them to a cozy table for two up against one of the brick walls, put some menus on the table, and told them their server would be with them in a moment. Nell barely had a chance to look around before the server showed up. "Hi, my name is Aris. I'll be taking care of you this evening. Can I get you started with some drinks?"

Nell asked for water.

"Dead Guy Ale sounds interesting," said Eamonn. "I'll have a pint of that. And a glass of the Stemilt Creek merlot for my dinner companion, but you can put it on my check."

"But..." Nell opened, then closed her mouth. Not wanting to argue in front of the server, she fixed him with a disapproving look, holding her tongue until Aris walked away. Then she said, "But this is a work trip. And you're driving."

"Oh, Nella-bella, I'm perfectly safe to drive on one beer." The jaded look he gave her suggested that he'd driven on much more alcohol and much worse substances than that. "And a little bit of wine won't hurt you. Come on, I know you drink, I've seen you enjoying those peachy things at the Frog and Ball."

"Did you just call me Nella-bella?"

He grinned. "Bella means beautiful."

Just then, Aris returned, flipping a couple of coasters onto the table with one hand as she balanced her tray on the other. "The Stemilt Creek Caring Passion Merlot for you, ma'am, and a pint of Dead Guy Ale for you, sir. Have you had a chance to look at the menu?"

"We'll get right on that," said Eamonn.

Nell stared down at the menu in front of her. *He ordered me a wine called Caring Passion?* Every time she turned around, Eamonn "Easy"

Yarrow had her more and more confused. *The menu. Concentrate on the menu.*

The food choices were extensive, for a pub. Lots of substitution options – veggie patties and gluten-free buns in the burger section, a gluten-free pizza crust choice, a quinoa pasta option, lots of extras and sides. She ended up choosing a salad entrée that sounded both substantial and healthy, with tomato and avocado, grated carrot and parmesan and jicama, pistachio nuts and cucumber slices. He ordered a burger with bacon and cheese.

"Vegetarian?" he asked. "Or dieting?"

She wasn't sure if she wished she could answer yes. "Conflicted," she said, after a moment. "I'm about seventy percent vegetarian. I like a lot of vegan recipes and could *almost* do it, but then there's that other thirty percent where I'm a hardcore carnivore and I just want a burger or steak, damn it. Today isn't one of those days, though. And I don't diet. I really do like salads."

"Sure." He took a long sip of his beer, a tiny bit of suds catching on his upper lip. "This is good beer. I hope you're happy with eating dinner here?"

"The wine is all right." She nodded, glad now that he'd insisted she have it. One glass wouldn't hurt. She could relax a little. Maybe she'd even sleep away some of the highway left to go. When the food came, it was as good as the menu had promised, and she ate with a hearty appetite.

By the time they walked back out to the truck forty minutes later, the wind had picked up a bit, whipping awnings and signs around. Nell looked up at the sky. "My weather app didn't say anything about rain, but those clouds over there..."

"I've got good tires on my truck," Eamonn said, "and four-wheel drive. Even if it rained hard, we'd be fine. Probably just a summer shower coming, though."

"I wasn't worried," she told him.

This time, when he popped the passenger door open for her, she just gave him a nod and got in. *I won't thank him. I didn't ask him to open it for me. But I won't complain.*

She settled herself into the seat and buckled up.

"I'm going to stop and get another coffee for the drive," he told her. "Want anything?"

"Not me. I'm pretty full, and caffeine keeps me up at night."

"That's kind of the idea." Once they'd been through the Starbucks drive-thru and were back on Highway 97, he plugged his phone into the truck's sound system – but instead of loading up the classic rock playlist he'd been running earlier, he chose jazz.

"*You* like jazz music?" she asked. It was just so unexpected, so incongruous with his rock-and-roll persona and the country-boy truck he drove.

"Don't look so surprised," he said, with a wry twist to his mouth. "If you don't like it, we can go back to rock, or I've got a classical playlist or some country. Your choice."

Oops. "No, jazz is nice. I just didn't expect..."

"No one does. I'm just Easy, Smidge's bastard ex-bassist. Why would I listen to jazz?"

Crap. "I didn't mean–"

"Sure you did. Just look out the window and go to sleep, babe. We've got a long drive ahead and I don't want to debate public personas and musical taste with you."

"Rude, much?" she muttered, but turned her head to stare at the passing countryside. *Great, what a way to start off the next few days being stuck together at Champagne.* The clouds had completely filled the sky now and the dry gravel and scrubby bushes on the side of the highway were being blown about by the wind. When the first few drops of rain splattered on the windshield, Nell resigned herself to a miserable and frustrating site visit. Even with rain and Eamonn being a bear, it was better than being stuck in the office.

The buttery smooth jazz music soothed her. Just the right thing for a road trip and rain. Eamonn's big truck was comfortable and well-insulated, keeping out the engine and traffic noise. As the windshield wipers began to swish away the rain, she found herself nodding off. She'd had no intention of falling asleep, especially after he'd suggested twice that she might, but the glass of wine with dinner had taken the edge off her resolve and the jazz music and rain were doing the rest.

I'm just Easy, Smidge's bastard ex-bassist. His voice echoed in her half-asleep mind. *Ex-bassist?* She wondered, remembering that she'd asked him about what he was doing at Wildforest. *If you have to ask, do you think we could talk about it somewhere more private?* He'd sounded bitter, troubled, and she hadn't pried. Had he quit, or been kicked out? The temptation to search the internet for answers warred with a conviction that she ought to grant him the respect of privacy. And she slept.

He woke her on the outskirts of Winthrop. "Sorry to wake you, Nell. Where now?"

"Agh. What time is it?" She rubbed her eyes and looked out the window. Dusk had fallen, and through the rain, she could see that they were in a parking lot in front of something called Pardner's Mini Market that had gas pumps and looked like a general store.

"Just after ten."

"Right." Sleepily, she dug out the sheet of printed directions from her pocket – she always took printed travel directions with her in case cell service was a problem – and unfolded it. He switched on the truck's cabin light for her. "North on Chewuch River Road," she read. "Should be less than ten minutes away, I think. I wrote down seven miles? Then we should turn onto a private road called Bereche Avenue, and we're there."

"Might be a little more than ten minutes. Road conditions aren't great."

"Yeah."

Eamonn reached up to switch off the cabin light, then put the big truck into gear and pulled out of the parking lot. Visibility wasn't great, even with high beam headlights on, and it was closer to fifteen minutes before they saw the turn sign for Bereche Avenue and a billboard showing the delights of Champagne Cascades – Romantic Cottages at the Prettiest Falls In The Northwest. A smaller sign said *Private Road:*

Guests Only and an ornate metal gate stood open but could clearly be used to close the road. *Lucky that's not closed.*

Eamonn didn't turn into the lot marked *Guest Parking*, but continued along the grand circular driveway to pull right up under the portico of the building with the carved wooden sign reading *Site Office*. Being in the Pacific Northwest, presumably it rained a fair bit of the time even at the Prettiest Falls Ever, so a drive-up portico had been a clever and necessary part of the building's design. "Come on," said Nell. "Let's go in and see what we can find."

The office was locked, naturally, but she'd brought keys with her. Inside, it was tidy and looked normal – a few papers in the in and out trays, the computer in sleep mode, a pink fluffy sweater over the back of the desk chair, and a half-full mug of stone-cold coffee with pink lipstick on the rim sitting on the desk. Concern prickled in her mind more strongly than before. Whatever had happened to Jessalyn, she hadn't meant to abandon the office. She'd started a cup of coffee and had expected to drink the rest of it.

Nell noticed an insulated lunch bag tucked under the counter, and when she peeked inside, she saw a sandwich and muffin. "Well, I think we can say for sure that Jessalyn didn't just bail on the job because she got another one she liked better. It looks like she was here at some point relatively recently – maybe early this morning?"

"Are there guests who might have seen her? Seen what happened to her?" Eamonn asked.

"Maybe. Let me look at the guest register – and we can also pick where we're going to stay."

"I assumed there'd be staff sleeping accommodations," Eamonn said.

"There's a bunk room for staff behind the store, and the site manager has an apartment upstairs in this building. But we're management; we're supposed to act like bosses. We get cottage accommodation if they're not fully booked, and meals in the dining room."

"The lap of luxury," he said, his tone dry, and she thought about the five-star hotels he'd undoubtedly stayed in and how much of a come-down even the nicest of Wildforest's properties must seem to him.

"You know, we should probably go up and have a look at the apartment, in case..." She didn't want to voice the horrible thought she'd had, that Jessalyn might be up there, injured and trapped somehow, in a coma or dead.

But he knew what she meant without her having to spell it out. "You want me to go up and look around? You can get on with the computer stuff here."

"Thanks. That would be helpful. Here's the key, the one with the purple cap." She held out her key ring, which had all the keys identified with stretchy silicone caps in different colors.

As he headed down the staff-only passage to find the way upstairs, she woke the computer and logged on with her administrator password. By the time he got back, she'd checked Jessalyn's email and browser history for any information about where the woman might have gone, with no luck, and called up the booking program. "Anything?" she asked.

"Nothing. There's milk in the fridge, a few dirty dishes in the sink, and laundry in the hamper. It doesn't look like she expected to be away."

"Hmm. Well, maybe one of the guests will have seen or heard something. We've got three occupied cottages: Annie and Michael Prince are in Veuve Clicquot, Pauline Morton and Jason Butcher are in Krug, Jude Leith and Finn Halliday are in Dom Perignon. Pol Roger is closed for plumbing issues, Bollinger and Gallimard haven't been cleaned–" She scrolled down the screen– "Oh, and nor has Taittinger, or Pommery... or Moet & Chandon. Why is the cleaning so far behind? Half the cottages shouldn't be sitting dirty..." *Crap.* The cleaning service ought to have been brought in as soon as each cottage was vacated; why hadn't that happened? She'd need to call them first thing in the morning. "It, uh, looks like only Cristal is available."

"We can make it work." Eamonn shrugged. "I can sleep anywhere – bonus if it's soft and there's a pillow, but I've slept on floors and in the backs of vans."

"And in top hotels with actual champagne flowing like water," Nell pointed out.

"True."

"If I'm reading this right, Cristal should have a daybed as well as a king. I know you said you're fine sleeping anywhere, but I'm betting you'd rather not sleep on the floor if there's a choice, and I'm not sharing a bed with you."

"True."

"If I'm reading this right, Cristal should have a daybed as well as a king. I know you said you're fine sleeping anywhere, but I'm betting you'd rather not sleep on the floor if there's a choice, and I'm not sharing a bed with you."

THE COTTAGES AT CHAMPAGNE CASCADES WERE SPREAD out in the woods along the river for as much romantic privacy as possible, with neat gravel paths winding through the trees and ferns and salal bushes leading to each one. Although none of the cabins were far from the main area where the office building and the main dining room and laundry were located, the artful illusion of distance and privacy seemed very real in the rainy night, even with the strings of white fairy lights along the paths.

After a quick search, Nell found a couple of heavy-duty flashlights in a box in the office and handed one to Eamonn. "These will help. There are supposed to be umbrellas, too, but I have no idea where, so we'll just have to get wet. Let's go."

"Which one is ours?" he asked, looking at the pouring rain and the faintly twinkling strands of lights leading off between the trees.

She locked the office behind her and turned. "Far end," she told him, pointing to the right. "I've got a copy of the site map in my bag, just in case, but I'm pretty sure it's the last cabin to the north."

"Can we drive closer?" He unlocked his truck and reached to open the passenger door for her.

"No such luck," she said. "Guest parking is on the south side, and the staff spots are behind the office. Just leave your truck under the portico for the night and we'll move it in the morning."

"All right." He opened the door to the crew cab's second row instead, handed Nell her bag, then grabbed his backpack. "We're going to get soaked. Want to run?"

"On gravel paths, in the rain, in the dark. Great idea." Nell laughed. "But sure. Why not?" She waited for him to lock his truck, then took off, her bag bouncing on her shoulder, getting wetter in the rain with every step she took. She didn't think he'd meant it as a race, but his footsteps close behind her triggered a competitive burst of speed and she pulled ahead for a moment before he caught on and upped his pace. With his longer legs, he caught up with her quickly, though she thought – hoped? – he had to put more effort into it than he might have expected. She pushed herself for more speed and he matched her, their flashlight beams swinging wildly. Then one of her feet skidded on a slick patch of gravel and she instinctively braced herself to roll and break her fall safely.

"Hey," he said, and he grabbed her just in time, saving her from a nasty tumble. "You okay?" He steadied her back onto her feet, his hands still curled protectively around her upper arms. She could feel the heat of his palms through her wet shirt.

"Thanks." He stood there, ignoring the rain, looking down with admiring eyes at the front of her shirt, which had become rather transparent. When he didn't move, didn't let go, she snapped, "Okay, I'm not falling anymore. Hands off."

He dropped his hands and marched away from her down the path, reaching the end of it before he remembered that she had the key and he couldn't get in without her. A carved wooden sign over the door read *Cristal.* "Are you coming?"

Slowly, almost grudgingly, she caught up with him. They were both soaked through at this point and speed didn't seem to matter anymore. *Sharing a cottage is a bad idea if he's going to look at me like that.* Separate beds were beside the point. But they couldn't stand outside in the rain all night, so she got the key out of her pocket and closed the distance between them.

A light by the door came on automatically as they stepped inside, and Nell smiled for the clever idea – a motion sensor light would always make sure that guests were greeted with a friendly glow, no matter what time it was. No fumbling around for a light switch in an unknown position or trying to find a lamp. The door light was enough to show her where the main light switches were, and she flipped on the overhead lights in the open living space and kitchenette area. Everything was decorated in shades of champagne and gold. Any wood she could see – the legs of the high stools at the breakfast bar, the coffee table, some bookshelves, a piano – was pale, maybe birch or maple, polished to a high gloss. The kitchenette's granite countertop sparkled white.

She shuffled forward to make room as Eamonn came through the door behind her, but she didn't want to leave the tiled door well and drip all over the hardwood floor and area rugs. She kicked off her shoes. "I'm going to find the bathroom and get dry," she said. "Unless you want to go first?"

"You go ahead, baby."

"Don't call me baby," she muttered as she jogged to the door that presumably led to the bedroom and its en suite bathroom. "Wow!"

The bed was enormous, a king-size four-poster in pale birchwood, with pale gold satin sheets and pillows and a darker gold comforter, plus a patchwork quilt in shades of cream and champagne folded over the end of the bed. It looked spectacular, warm and inviting. And massive. More than enough room for two, and whatever acrobatic activity they wanted to engage in. *Nope. Not going to happen.* She took a quick look around for the daybed the office description had mentioned and was ridiculously glad to see it under the window – more of a chaise longue, but there'd be enough room to stretch out. She'd take the quilt from the bed and leave Eamonn the comforter. She noticed with pleasure that the gas fireplace was a two-sided one so they could enjoy its warmth in the bedroom as well as the living area. Sad to need a fireplace in summer, but it would be nice with this rain. *Oh, Pacific Northwest, how I love you.* This last thought was accompanied by a bit of sarcasm, but in truth, she didn't mind the rain. It kept things green and fresh.

The bathroom was every bit as luxurious as the rest of the cottage. As she skinned out of her wet things, she eyed the deep whirlpool bathtub and separate glass-walled shower stall that filled one side of the room. On the opposite side, the toilet was tucked behind a half-wall for semi-privacy, and it had what looked like a bidet attachment. Nell wasn't about to mess with that, at least until she had more of a chance to inspect the operating instructions, but she appreciated the heated seat. She put on her sleepwear, a girly set she hated – a gag gift from Amy, frilly pale pink with little hearts for a woman who wouldn't be caught dead in something like that, just so Amy could see the expression on her face when she opened it – but they'd been the only clean set in the drawer when she'd had to pack so quickly. She covered herself with one of the fluffy cream-colored bathrobes hanging on the bathroom door and hung her wet clothes over the glass wall of the shower to dry.

With a sigh, she headed back out through the bedroom to the living area. "Your turn," she said to Eamonn, then stifled a gasp.

He stood in the kitchenette area, next to the electric kettle, poking through a basket of what Nell guessed to be packets of tea, hot chocolate mix, and instant coffee. "Want some tea or something?" he asked. Just as if he weren't standing there shirtless and barefoot, nothing keeping him decent except for a pair of very snug wet jeans. When he'd been fully dressed, she hadn't noticed his jeans. They were jeans, unobtrusively blending with his hoodie and boots, the rock-and-roll man on a road trip. Now, she could see how the sodden denim molded itself to him, outlining every muscle and... everything.

"I hope you're wearing underwear under those," she blurted out before she could censor herself.

He stared at her in amused disbelief. "You're asking me if I'm going commando?"

She could feel herself blushing. *Ugh.* How did he do that to her? She didn't blurt things out without thinking. She didn't blush. And yet, when she was around him, these things kept happening. "Yeah, no. I don't want to know. That was a rhetorical statement, not a question,

Eamonn Yarrow. Based on the fact that you're half-naked, and I'm your co-worker and supervisor."

"Don't be prickly," he said mildly. "My hoodie and t-shirt were soaked, so I took them off. You've seen a man shirtless before, yeah? So it's not a big deal. Cup of tea? There are a bunch of flavors here – white vanilla grapefruit, pomegranate oolong, mint verbena, English Breakfast, something called Paris, rooibos chai..." He poked through the basket again. "I think that's it. Or hot chocolate."

Thoughtful. She hadn't expected that of him. Because rock stars aren't supposed to be thoughtful. Still a sexist pig, though. "I'll have mint verbena, please. Paris is my favorite, but I don't need the caffeine right now," she said, then after a moment, she added, "Thank you."

She crossed the room to turn on the fireplace. Pleasant flames leapt up behind the glass, and soon a glow of warmth began to fill the room. Two overstuffed cream-colored loveseats faced each other across a coffee table by the fire. She sank into the corner of one of them, tucking her feet up and snugging the ends of the bathrobe around herself.

"Milk and sugar?" Eamonn asked, and Nell shook her head.

"Just black, please." When he brought the mug to her, she looked up at him and gave him a rueful grimace as she accepted it. "I don't mean to be prickly, you know? I've just never worked with someone like you. I know how to shut down flirty guys in bars and I know how to train and compete with all kinds of people, but work? It's weird."

"That's okay, ninja woman. I'm not really an office kind of guy."

"I can't imagine you would be, all things considered. Can I ask what it was like? I mean, what was a workday like for you, being in a band and all?"

He shrugged and propped himself against the arm of her loveseat as he took a sip from his mug. She could smell that it was hot chocolate and saw that it made a little milk mustache on his upper lip. *Yum.* "A lot of travel," he said. "And not the nice kind on your own with a truck or a bike. All schedules and sleeping on tour buses, then as Smidge got bigger it was schedules and flights and hotels. A lot of drinking and drugs, if I'm being honest. A lot of getting laid."

"Not much like the office," Nell said. "Except schedules. We have those." The hot mint tea soothed her, put her in a better frame of mind. Wildforest's premium tier of vacation properties all stocked a nice selection of good quality Harney and Sons teas. It crossed her mind to be glad this emergency site visit wasn't at Winter Pine, since the economy tier of properties got whatever basic black tea could be had cheapest from their supplier, plus one caffeine-free option – usually something with chamomile, which made her gag. A quiet moment settled over them. She sipped her tea and watched the gas flames flickering in the fireplace.

"We should go to bed," Eamonn said with a lazy stretch, spreading his arms over the back of the loveseat. When had he moved from the arm of it onto the seat next to her? Too much of his bare skin was disturbingly close to her – she didn't let anyone into her personal space like this, especially not a half-naked and flirty near-stranger with a hot body and a dirty reputation.

"True." She got up and crossed the room into the kitchenette area to put her mug in the sink. "I'll take the quilt and some of the pillows and sleep on the daybed. You can have the big bed and keep the comforter."

Sitting there, his long legs stretched out and crossed at the ankles, he was a picture of laid-back unconcern, but his eyes were bright with interest and appraisal. "You don't want to sleep on that little cot, do you? King size is plenty of room for us to share."

"Don't start with that. We are *not* sharing a bed tonight, and that's final." Why had she added *tonight* to that? She should have told him they were not sharing a bed ever.

His slow smile challenged her words. "Why not, gorgeous? We're both single grownups and we've got chemistry in spades. So what if we have a little cuddle? Who'd even know?"

"I'd know." Nell crossed her arms and planted her feet, falling into her pissed-off martial arts instructor stance. He was like a bratty student, not paying attention, wanting to get to the fun stuff without doing the work. "Easy, you're not sharing my bed because you haven't earned it. And I'm not sharing your bed because I don't know yet if I want to be there. When I make love with someone, it's mutual, consensual, and respectful. And I'm not seeing that from you right now."

He winced at her use of his stage name, apparently recognizing that she'd meant it as a reprimand. "Fuck me," he muttered, sounding grumpy and put out. "Okay, whatever." Then, with grudging resignation, "D'you want the big bed? A lady should sleep in comfort. I can take the daybed."

"Pretty sure you'd be uncomfortable, given your height, and I'll fit nicely. Thanks for the offer, though."

"Enjoy your little bed, then."

"I'm using the bathroom first," she told him.

"Fine."

After she was done in the bathroom, she snagged the quilt and two of the four pillows from the big bed and made up the daybed for herself. But she waited until Eamonn was taking his turn in the bathroom before skinning out of the bathrobe and diving under the quilt. She had no intention of letting him see the silly sleep set Amy had given her. She wasn't that kind of woman, and she didn't want him getting any more ideas than he already had. She set the alarm on her phone to wake her and propped it where she could see it before burrowing in.

He grinned when he saw her under the quilt on the day bed, tucked in right up to her nose. "You're sure you're comfy all alone there?"

"I'm perfect," she said. "Get into your bed and go to sleep, already." His striped pajama pants were adorable.

He turned down the fireplace and put out the lights. "All right, then. Sweet dreams, Nell Whelan. Dream of me, will you?"

"Ugh. You wish. Goodnight, Eamonn." She heard the rustle of sheets and the sigh of the mattress as he got into the king-sized bed a few feet away. Then a bit more rustling and shifting, getting-comfortable noises, or... "You'd better not be masturbating."

He laughed out loud in the dark. "Oh, babe, I love how you say what's on your mind like that. Do you really think I'm such a pervert, that I'd lie here jerking myself off and thinking about you while you're right over there listening to it? I don't think I could be that quiet."

"No, I suppose not. I don't know why I..."

Eamonn laughed again. "I'd like to, though. Yeah, I'd enjoy the hell out of that. If I thought you'd be even halfway okay with it, I'd be reaching into my pajama pants right now and stroking myself until I came, pretending it was your hand instead of my own, knowing you were lying there in the dark hearing me gasp and groan as I got myself off. I'm so hard right now, I don't know how I'll be able to fall asleep."

"That's intense," Nell muttered. Her skin felt like it had been touched by fire all over.

"You've got a banging body, Nell, but what really turns me on is your sassy no-nonsense talk and your sharp mind. You don't suffer fools, and I don't want to be a fool around you. So my hands are outside the blanket, even though it damn well hurts, because I want you to still be talking to me in the morning." He sighed, and she heard more rustling and a mattress noise – had he rolled onto his side to settle for sleep? "How come you're not smacking me down for being inappropriate, I wonder?" he asked, and his voice sounded amused.

"I don't know." Honesty seemed to come naturally in the dark.

"Go to sleep now, Nella-bella," he said. "Unless you're going to come over here and get in with me. This flirting is torture, and I can't stand much more of it."

She wouldn't dignify that with an answer. "Goodnight," she told him firmly.

"Night."

After a while, his breathing settled into sleep, and then she let herself drift off.

♥

Her phone alarm woke her. For a moment she was disoriented, seeing the room around her that wasn't her apartment bedroom – groggy with sleep, she'd forgotten for half a moment that she was on a site visit. She sat up, silenced her phone, and looked around at the daybed where she slept and the cream-and-gold décor. Champagne

Cascades. The rainy drive up the night before. Eamonn sleeping in the big bed. *Right.*

He appeared to be fast asleep, undisturbed by the alarm from her phone. Thankful for this small mercy, Nell slid out of bed and padded quietly to the bathroom. She always felt more human after brushing her teeth. She did a quick round of squats but decided the bathroom floor was no place for pushups or crunches. She promised herself she'd find somewhere to do them later in the morning. Somewhere Eamonn wouldn't see her. The glass-walled shower stall looked inviting, but her clothes and toiletries were in her bag at the foot of the daybed in the bedroom. And she hadn't brought the bathrobe in with her either. *I'll just get my things. He's sleeping.*

Only he wasn't. "Cute," he commented from where he lay in the bed with arms folded behind his head, admiring her in the ruffled sleep shorts and babydoll top she found so absurd.

Damn. "I don't do cute. I don't do pink or ruffles or hearts. This was a gift and I feel ridiculous, but I didn't have time to do laundry." She hoped her flat tone and don't-go-there face would be warning enough for him to drop the subject – with most people, it was sufficient.

But no, of course it wasn't. "Aww, come on. You look adorable. Pink suits you."

That's it. She could feel the burn of anger rising inside her. Needed to work it off. Needed to show off a little, to show him there wasn't an ounce of *adorable* in her. With a quick glance around to make sure she had enough space, she dropped into pushup position. "Don't mind me – I've got a morning workout to take care of." Smooth pushups, perfect form, straight back, right down until her nose nearly touched the floor. She could feel him watching her. *Ten... twenty... thirty...* She'd usually stop there, but today she kept going. At thirty-five, he got off the bed and walked over to her. At forty, he got down on the floor and did the last ten with her. *Fifty.* She flipped over onto her back, shooting him a quizzical look as she did so. He raised his eyebrows and continued with his pushups, just another ten, but presumably that was enough to satisfy his macho competitive instinct.

When she started her crunches, he followed suit. She normally did fifty, but in this moment she pushed onward to sixty, purely because she could hear him beginning to breathe hard and slow down. *Good.* Nell sat up and stretched, mostly to show him how flexible she was. *Am I still adorable when I can do this?* Legs so wide they were almost in the splits, hands on her ankles, nose to the floor. She heard him mutter, "Fuck me." He was still sprawled on the floor after his crunches, a light sheen of sweat on his bare chest and shoulders. *Maybe you lift, but you don't do enough core.*

Planting one hand and one foot, she kicked out with the other foot and bounced to a standing position. "Much better. I'm off to shower. I imagine you'll want to as well, so I won't use all the hot water." In a substantially improved mood, feeling that she'd paid him nicely for his comments, she grabbed her bag and practically floated into the bathroom. *He's lucky I didn't make him do a round of squats.*

♥

One of Nell's favorite things about site visits was that she could, out of sight of the office and Tommy's critical eye, dress to suit herself. She vastly preferred stretchy, comfortable athletic pants – usually yoga or running pants that gave her the flexibility to move. Slacks and even jeans always made her wonder if she'd be able to fight and defend herself, if needed, or if they'd impede her movements with their tightness and resistant fabrics. Because of the rain and the cool air it had brought with it, she pulled a baggy hoodie with a picture of a martial artist breaking a board and the words *Personal Victory* over her tank top. She wished she'd brought boots and a rain jacket, but there hadn't been so much as a cloud in the sky when they'd set out, and given that it was June, she hadn't thought of it. Living in the Pacific Northwest, she should have known better, but it couldn't be helped. She emerged from the bathroom and slipped past Eamonn who was waiting to go in. "Enjoy your shower," she said to him. "Should I wait for you or go along to breakfast?"

"I'll just be five minutes," he said, and she nodded.

While he showered, she looked in the various cupboards and closets in the cottage and found what she was looking for – a pair of large umbrellas. Every Wildforest vacation cottage, even on the economy sites, came equipped with umbrellas for exactly this sort of unexpected weather. These were clear plastic, printed with a pattern of ivory and pale gold bubbles and the Champagne Cascades logo. As soon as Eamonn opened the bathroom door and came out, still toweling his hair dry, she held one out to him and said, "I'm hungry. Let's go eat."

If anything, the rain was heavier than it had been the night before, and the wind seemed angrier. Eamonn and Nell hurried along the path to the center of the resort and made a beeline for the portico of the office building, where they took shelter for a moment as they looked for a sign to lead them to the dining room. The office building also had signs for laundry, a games room, and a library. To one side of it, another building appeared to be a sort of boutique general store, and on the far side of that, they could see a signboard that read *Pink Champagne Dining Room*. They splashed along the driveway that curved around in front of the three buildings, making their way to the far side and taking shelter under the restaurant's porch roof before collapsing their umbrellas. Fortunately, the dining room had lights on and seemed to be open.

Even though Nell arrived at the French doors to the restaurant in front of Eamonn, he managed to reach past her and pull the door open for her. She suppressed a sigh, remembering that he'd said his mother taught him to open doors for women. A guy who remembered what his mother taught him couldn't be all bad. The dining room was empty, but a little bunch of bells chimed with the door's movement and a moment later a woman with a mess of blonde curls popped out from the pass-through to the kitchen.

"Good morning," she said, then, "You're not guests – oh, are you... Nell, and...?"

Nell stuck her umbrella in the brass holder by the door and strode over to the woman with a smile, holding out a hand to shake. "Yes. I'm

Nell, and you must be Mary. We talked on the phone. This is Eamonn, my assistant."

Mary looked at Eamonn as though she'd like to pour caramel sauce all over him and eat him up. "Hi, Eamonn!" Then she grabbed a couple of menus from the hostess desk and waved for them to choose a table. The room was a pleasant one. Ten tables were spaced just right for intimate dining, with cream linen tablecloths and white roses in crystal bud vases. A cheerful gas fireplace gave the room a warm and inviting coziness, much needed on such a rainy morning. "Come and sit, you two. I'll go tell François you've arrived. Have a look at the menu – he'll make you anything you like. We're so glad you're here! Are you going to find out what happened to Jessalyn? I've been so worried!"

"Of course," said Nell, as though there couldn't be any doubt. *Act with confidence, be decisive, don't show weakness.* Wanting to look authoritative in front of Mary, she marched over to a table by the window and sat down, assuming Eamonn would join her. She scanned the menu. By the time he'd seated himself across from her, she'd decided on the mushroom hollandaise omelet with fruit salad.

Mary popped back out of the kitchen with her order notebook and asked if they knew what they wanted or if she could start them with some drinks. "François says if you don't see anything that appeals to you on the menu, he'll make you whatever you like. Just ask. Now, tea or coffee? Or hot chocolate? And will you have orange or grapefruit juice as well? We usually do a hot beverage and a juice – the breakfast comes with both. But you don't have to."

"I'll have grapefruit juice and Paris tea, please."

"Just coffee with cream and sugar for me, sweetheart," said Eamonn. Mary turned pink and fluttered her eyelashes at him before whirling away to get the drinks, her blonde curls bobbing like fancy ribbons on a gift.

Nell shook her head. "You oughtn't call women by pet names like that. You'll either make her feel like you don't respect her or you'll give her the wrong idea and have her all over you." She couldn't put her finger on why she felt so irritated with him. It wasn't as though she wanted his attention – why shouldn't he flirt with Mary the waitress and even potentially roll around with her in the staff bunk room? He'd said he was turned on by her mind, but maybe that was just a line and he was equally up for sex with a bubbly dumb-as-rocks Barbie doll.

"Come on, Nell," he said, "I get that *you* don't like being called baby and sweetheart and stuff, but not everyone's offended by it. Mary seemed pretty content just now. And maybe having her all over me isn't such a bad – hey!" Without meaning to, Nell had shoved her chair back and stood up, popping with adrenaline, ready to – she didn't know what she was ready to do, only that all her fight-or-flight instincts had kicked in. "Sit down," Eamonn was saying. "Please? Don't go off mad. I shouldn't have joked about that."

She flopped back down in her chair, feeling like a puppet whose strings had been cut. "Whatever. Why shouldn't you go have a cuddle with Mary, then? Why the ever-loving hell should I care?" She forced a neutral expression onto her face as Mary came over to the table with their drinks.

"Here's your Paris tea, Nell." Mary placed a small brown teapot on the table in front of Nell and set an empty mug next to it. "Do you want any milk or honey or lemon? Just black, is it? And coffee for you, Eamonn. Here's the cream and sugar you asked for." It was proper cream in a little pitcher, and a bowl of sugar cubes. No plastic cups of synthetic creamer or paper sugar packets in the Pink Champagne Dining Room. "I'll be right back with that grapefruit juice."

As soon as Mary had vanished back into the kitchen, Eamonn leaned across the table and looked into Nell's eyes, his blue eyes intense and darkening with desire. "Because I'm flirting with *you*, lovely. Because I'm trying to get into *your* pants. Because there's no denying I've done some pretty dirty things in my life, but just talking to you in the dark last night was sexy as fuck, and there's no way I'd go hump some random chick when I might have even half a chance of getting somewhere with you."

"Okay, then," said Nell, nonplussed, crossing her arms across her chest and feeling defensive. "Not sure quite where to go with that, but okay."

He relaxed, laughing softly at her discomfiture. "If you tell me it's never going to happen, I'll leave you alone. Promise. Otherwise... I'll keep trying."

Nell gave him a narrow look. *I ought to be able to tell him it's never going to happen, but...* She couldn't do it, couldn't shut him down and close the door on that tantalizing possibility she could barely even admit to being curious about. "We're co-workers. I'm your supervisor. It's against the rules, and it could get awkward."

"I'm not going to be at Wildforest forever," he said. "Uncle Tommy thought it'd be good for me to have something to do with my days, and I was bored enough to go along with it, but I don't have to stay. So I'll make you a deal – if things get awkward, I'll leave. I won't mess up your job."

"I'm not agreeing to anything," said Nell, "I just... I don't know."

He grinned, his face lighting up. "You don't have to know anything. Oh, Nell, if you give me a chance, I'll blow your mind."

"You're not cocky at all, are you?" She rolled her eyes but couldn't stop herself from grinning back at him.

Mary brought Nell's grapefruit juice in a glass with a sugar-frosted rim. "Ready to order?" she asked. Eamonn, looking as though he'd forgotten they were in a restaurant, grabbed one of the menus. "Or do you need more time?"

"It's okay. I'll be ready by the time Nell has ordered hers."

"Sure thing. Nell?" Mary turned to her with a peppy smile.

"The mushroom omelet, please."

"With breakfast potatoes or fruit salad?"

"Fruit salad would be great, thanks."

Mary looked over at Eamonn with an inquiring expression, and he nodded. "I'm going with a Benny and potatoes." At Nell's sharp look, he added, "Please. And a dash more coffee when you have a minute, sweetheart?"

Mary glowed. "Of course. I'll be right over with it; just let me get your food order in to François." *She does seem to like being called sweetheart,* Nell thought uncomfortably. But weren't pet names for women diminishing and disrespectful?

More hot water for Nell's tea arrived along with Eamonn's fresh coffee.

The French doors swung open, letting in a gust of wind. A middle-aged couple dripped their way in and deposited their wet umbrellas into the brass umbrella stand. They settled themselves at a table near the fireplace, and as Mary went to greet them and take their beverage order, the door opened again and a young couple in *Bride* and *Groom* t-shirts drifted in, holding hands and not seeming to mind how windy and wet it was. The honeymooners, as they obviously were, called a greeting to Mary and the older couple, then settled themselves at what was presumably their regular table.

Nell leaned closer to Eamonn to talk quietly. "I'm guessing the older woman is the one I talked to on the phone: Mrs. Prince, here with her husband, arrived yesterday. So the bride and groom are probably Pauline Morton and Jason Butcher, because Krug is one of the two 'bridal suite' cottages – you know, heart-shaped bathtubs, that kind of stuff. They've been here since Sunday, so they will have been checked in by Jessalyn, and I'm hoping they can give us some clue what happened to her."

Mary brought their breakfasts. The eggs were cooked to perfection – her omelet fluffy and fork-tender, his Benny poached just right. The hollandaise sauce was a taste of heaven; the unseen François clearly knew his way around a kitchen. Nell licked some sugar from the rim of her juice glass and felt a happy glow of contentment.

The door banged open again, and a tall, thin man in a long leather coat stepped in, carrying a suitcase. "Mary?" he called, and she popped out from the kitchen with a wave and smile.

"Hi, Mr. Leith. Where's Mr. Halliday? Isn't he having breakfast this morning?"

"He's getting the car. We've decided to head home a day early, my dear. He doesn't like to admit it, but his lungs aren't strong, and all this rain isn't helping."

Mary tsked regretfully, her usual smile dissolving into a moue of disappointment. "Aww, that's a shame. Tell him to come in and have breakfast before you go, or at least a coffee."

"We want to get an early start. We were thinking of stopping to eat somewhere on the road," Mr. Leith said. "I was hoping you could open the office and do our checkout."

"I can't leave the dining room right now, Mr. Leith." Mary fluttered her hands apologetically. "Maybe if you and Mr. Halliday have your coffee here, Nell from head office will be able to do your checkout after she's finished her breakfast." Mary gestured toward Nell and Eamonn's table.

Nell waved acknowledgment and called out, "I won't be long, nearly done here, then I'll be happy to take you over to the office to do your checkout."

"Don't hurry on my account," the man said graciously. "Perhaps I may have a cup of coffee after all, Mary, and one of François's delectable chocolate croissants, if he's made any this morning. After all, there's no sense getting on the road with an empty stomach." He fished a phone out of one of his coat pockets and tapped away with both thumbs, paused, and tapped some more. "Finn will be joining me in a minute or two," he told Mary as he settled himself at one of the tables, "if you could bring him a coffee as well, and an avocado toast."

Once Mr. Leith had made himself comfortable, Nell realized there was no hurry in finishing her breakfast. His partner Finn arrived and tucked into avocado toast, and they started a conversation about horse racing, of all things, with the newlyweds. They'd be content for a while. Nell enjoyed every last bite of her mushroom hollandaise omelet and every sip of her grapefruit juice and tea.

After she was done, and Eamonn had cleared every bit of food from his plate too, she suggested they go over and open the office, ready to do the Leith-Halliday checkout and tend to any further business for the day. He agreed.

As they passed the men's table on their way out, Nell stopped and greeted them with a professional smile. "I'm sorry you've decided to head out a day early, but I quite understand why, with all this rain – it's a bit over the top for June. My co-worker and I are just going over to open up the office. Please take your time with your coffee, and we'll be ready to do your check-out whenever it's convenient for you."

"Thank you, dear. We won't be long," said the second man, Finn.

Nell could feel Eamonn's astonished eyes on her. As soon as they got outside, he turned to her and asked, "Why didn't you object to him calling you *dear?*"

Uh, because I didn't even notice? She'd been thinking of several things at once, planning ahead, doing the courtesy thing with one part of her brain. In the moment, it just hadn't mattered what a polite and well-mannered stranger called her, because he didn't mean it with ill intent, and it just wasn't important. "Because he didn't say it like I was *lesser.* He probably calls everyone dear, male or female. Like people saying ma'am in martial arts – lots of women are put off by being called ma'am in regular life, like it makes them feel old or helpless or something, but when we're in uniform, we just say sir and ma'am to everyone, regardless of age or belt level. Context, right?"

He snickered. "And you've never accidentally called someone sir or ma'am when you're not in uniform? You've *never* said it automatically, respectfully, and had someone think you were patronizing them or calling them old?"

Nell pulled up the hood of her oversized hoodie, jerking it forward so it would hide her face a bit. She busied herself putting up her umbrella, kept her eyes moving between the slick pavement of the driveway and the office they headed toward – anything to avoid looking at Eamonn. *Of course I have.* She could think of dozens of incidents where the familiar, respectful *ma'am* had come automatically from her lips, especially when she was under pressure, and been met with sneers, an offended rise of eyebrows or chins, and even the occasional snappy "I'm not a ma'am!" or "Do I look that old to you?" *Crap.*

"I hate having wet shoes," she muttered, as she splashed through a particularly deep puddle. *Wet shoes, wet socks, and wet pants up to the ankles. Also a blatant change of subject, but whatever.* She wasn't sure if Eamonn had even heard her.

They reached the office building. A sleek silver Lexus RC350 was now parked behind Eamonn's truck, not leaving room for any more vehicles under the portico. "I'd better move my truck," he said. "We're obviously stuck here for a few days and it's taking up prime space."

"Site map says there's staff parking behind this building," she told him, glad to move on to less a less uncomfortable subject. "I think you need to loop around the restaurant to get there, but at least you don't have to put it in the guest lot and walk back. I'll go through inside and see if there's a back door I can open for you."

"Thanks."

Nell got the office keys out of her hoodie pocket and unlocked the front door. Behind her, she heard the truck door open and close. She didn't look back or wave to him, though she wanted to. *That's silly. He'll be back here in five minutes.* She collapsed her umbrella and stepped inside, sticking it in the umbrella holder by the door. Her feet squelched on the tile floor, wet shoes oozing puddle water. *Ugh.* After turning on the office lights, she slipped through the "staff only" passageway to the back of the building, where she found a bathroom, a small break room with a microwave and television, and a back door that opened onto the staff parking lot – all four stalls of it. Two were occupied, presumably by cars belonging to Mary and François. Nell guessed that the turquoise Kia Soul with a tiny disco ball hanging from its rearview mirror belonged to Mary, so that made François the driver of the old grey Jeep.

As she stood there, she heard the smooth purr of Eamonn's big truck's engine, and he pulled into view through the rain, turning smoothly into one of the remaining spaces. Something about the way he handled the big vehicle made *her* feel like purring – but then, she'd always been turned on by competence, and he handled his vehicles, both the truck and the bike, with smooth and unfaltering skill.

She waved and held the door open as he ran for it, shoulders hunched and eyes squinted against the rain. "What'd you do with your umbrella?" she asked, and he shrugged.

"I think I left it by the front of the office. It's not in my truck."

He came in, dripping, and began to peel off his hoodie. She turned away to lead him down the passageway to the front office, trying to shut out of her mind the glimpse of taut stomach she'd had when his t-shirt clung to his hoodie and was pulled upward. Not to mention the memory of his bare torso during their sit-ups that morning and while he was making tea the night before. *The man has a good body, I'll grant him that much.*

The two men from the dining room were sitting on one of the sofas in the front office, waiting to check out. "I hope you weren't waiting long," Nell said, putting as much upbeat energy into her tone and expression as she could. *You get back what you put out – positive staff attitudes lead to happy guests.* She'd told new Wildforest staff that too many times to count, and she'd learned it first-hand in her martial arts training: if the instructor is having a good day, the class will too, and a grumpy instructor's mood spreads like the plague. "Now, I understand that you're leaving a day early because of the weather. Is that right?"

"Regretfully, yes," said the thin man.

"It's my health," said his partner, looking rueful. "Jude wants to get me home. It's nothing against the resort, we've had a lovely time here."

"I'm sorry to hear you're not well, s–" Nell began, then caught herself; she'd been about to use *sir* outside of training. Men tended to object to that less than women minded *ma'am*, but still. She glanced down at the computer screen. Mary had called the thin man Mr. Leith, so... "Mr. Halliday. I expect you'll feel better once you're in your own home. And since you're leaving for health reasons, I can waive the early departure fee for you."

Mr. Halliday smiled. "That's very kind. And please, call me Finn. He's Jude. We aren't formal."

She printed out the summary of their stay and charges and tax, tucked it into a cream-colored cardstock folder, and turned to where Eamonn lounged against the wall. "Could you take this over to the gentlemen so they don't need to get up?" He took it with an agreeable nod and carried it over to them, while she looked around for the credit and debit card terminal that had to be around somewhere but wasn't in evidence on the desk. *Must be a wireless model,* she thought, and sure enough, she spotted a base for it. *Locked up overnight, maybe?* One of the keys on her ring was for the desk's two lockable drawers, and she found the unit in the second one, along with the petty cash box. "Are you paying with a card? I can bring the terminal to you if you are."

"Please," said Jude. He produced a leather wallet from his coat pocket and drew out a platinum Visa. Nell took a seat on the other sofa as she punched in the necessary information, then handed the device to him.

She felt the sofa compress as Eamonn sat down beside her. "I'll be honest with you," he said to the men. "We're trying to find out what happened to the person who usually works in the office here. She seems to have disappeared."

"That nice young woman? Oh, dear," said Finn. "I hope you find her. We haven't seen her since Tuesday afternoon, when she replenished the tea and coffee in our cottage. That would have been around four."

Jude looked thoughtful. "You might try the hospital. I thought I heard a siren yesterday morning but we're isolated enough here that I figured I must have been dreaming. It was early."

"Nine o'clock is early for you, dear," Finn teased, but he nodded. "I thought I heard a siren too, around seven thirty – and I was definitely awake, but no one else said anything so I assumed I must have imagined it."

Site managers were expected to be awake and in the office at seven. At seven thirty in the morning, on an ordinary day, Jessalyn would have been at her desk right there in the office, preparing check-in and check-out packages for the day, dealing with her email, drinking her coffee, and resolving any problems that had come up the night before;

that is, anything she hadn't had to get up in the night for. As a site manager, she'd signed up to live on the premises for the summer and be on call twenty-four hours a day, hadn't she?

"A siren," said Eamonn. "That's interesting. Not a fire, presumably, so… ambulance, or police?"

And wouldn't that be a disaster, Nell thought, *if the site manager had been arrested.* Wildforest management had a tendency to hold the site supervisor – her – responsible for anything that happened, no matter how surprising or out of her control it might be. "Let's assume it was an ambulance, for now," she said firmly. "There'll be information here somewhere on emergency services and the closest hospital. That gives us somewhere to start. Thank you both so much."

Jude held out a business card. "If you wouldn't mind emailing to let us know when you find her, we'd appreciate it." Finn nodded agreement, and coughed. They got up and shook hands with Nell and Eamonn. Nell held out the receipt from the card terminal, which she realized she'd been holding all that time, and Jude tucked it into the folder that held their summary of charges and stay information. "We'll come again," he said.

"I hope you do," Nell told him. "Finn, I hope you feel better soon."

He smiled, the sort of smile that people with chronic conditions give to those statements, and shrugged a little. "I'm lucky I have Jude to take care of me."

"Have a safe drive home," Eamonn said, and then Finn and Jude were out the door, and shortly the silver Lexus roared off down the rainy drive.

Nell got up from the sofa and went behind the desk to look for the site's information binder. Every site had to have one so that the site manager could answer guests' questions about the area and find relevant contact information for any situation. She found it in one of the drawers and opened it, hoping it was comprehensive. Fortunately, there was a tab marked *Emergencies,* and along with state-licensed wildlife control operators, listings for a couple of dentists and an optometrist, she found a listing for a health clinic in Winthrop and one for Three Rivers Hospital in Brewster, as well as information for the area's ambulance service provider. "Okay, then," she said to herself. "She's probably at Three Rivers if it was so much of an emergency that she couldn't leave a note."

She heard the door open and looked up to see Eamonn leaving. *That's odd.* She wondered where he was going, since there was a bathroom in the staff area at the back. But she told herself he couldn't be going far, and she didn't have time to think about what he was up to. She thought of calling Three Rivers but hadn't a clue what department to ask for, and a large hospital might not give out information without a lot of circling around. She called the ambulance service.

"Hello, this is Nell Whelan calling from Champagne Cascades. We're trying to track down a missing employee and I was told there might have been an ambulance out this way yesterday?"

"Champagne Cascades," said the female voice on the other end of the phone. "That's the resort at the falls up past Winthrop?"

"That's right," Nell said. "Can you tell me if you had a call here?"

"Yes. We took a young woman to Three Rivers Hospital. Is she your missing employee?"

"Jessalyn Roberts," said Nell. "I know there might be privacy issues, but would you be able to tell me what department of the hospital I should be calling to check on her?"

There was a brief pause on the phone, as though the woman was surprised. "Labor and Delivery, of course," she said.

"She's... pregnant?" Nell asked, her voice rather weak and showing her astonishment.

"Visibly so, according to our team," the woman said. "I don't think she could have kept it a secret. I wouldn't have said anything..."

"Understood. I'm from the company's head office and just took over the property from a different supervisor, so I've never met Jessalyn in person. They sent me up to find out what happened to her. I'm just glad she's alive."

"I need to take another call now," the woman said. "You have a great day."

Just as Nell hung up the phone, the door opened and Eamonn returned, carrying two steaming mugs. He put one down in front of her. "Paris tea," he said. "Thought you could use it, baby." The pet name was added deliberately, ironically, with an arched eyebrow. *Not going to rise to it,* she told herself.

"*Baby* is apparently the operative word," she said. "I've found Jessalyn, and she's in the labor and delivery section of the nearest hospital."

"Huh." He looked as stunned as she felt. Being a site manager for a vacation property was a job you *lived* in the summer season, not just one you went to for your allotted hours each day. Quieter in the fall and winter, sure, but still no place to have a baby. Jessalyn hadn't given any indication that she was pregnant, nor had she told them she'd be quitting or taking maternity leave or anything. "Well. What do we do?"

"I'm thinking I won't get anywhere on the phone with them. Big hospital, privacy concerns, and all that. Maybe the best thing to do is go visit her. Brewster is a little over an hour away, according to Google Maps. But you're the one with the vehicle, so it's your call."

He grinned. "I'd be happy to go for a drive with you. Bet I can get us there in under an hour."

"Don't be a fool. We're in no hurry; keep to the speed limit."

He just laughed. "Do we need to do anything else first, or are we going now?"

Oh, the attitude of him. She gave him a quelling look, the one that warned students on the training floor they'd better settle down because Miss Whelan was done with their goofing around. "Since you were so kind as to bring me this nice mug of tea, I'm going to drink it. Without rushing. I also need to see if we have any check-ins coming this afternoon that we'd have to be back for. Then we can go." She turned to the computer and called up the booking program again.

"Right." He dropped onto one of the sofas, leaning back and hooking one ankle over the other in a nonchalant fashion as he sipped his coffee. "Anything I can do?" He didn't look like he was aiming to do much of anything, sitting there like that. He got his phone out of a pocket and began playing with it.

"Just drink your coffee."

Rock God in Exile

do much of anything, sitting there like that. He got his phone out of a pocket and began playing with it.

"Just drink your coffee."

67

chapter

5

THE RAIN WAS COMING DOWN HARD ENOUGH THAT EVEN Eamonn couldn't rocket along the freeway as he pleased. It took them an hour and a half to get to the hospital in Brewster, and gusts of hard wind rocked the sturdy truck. He drove with both hands on the wheel.

"We were supposed to have one check-in this afternoon and two tomorrow, and all three of them have canceled because of the weather," Nell told him. "Looking on the bright side, we don't have to hurry back for anything, but that's about it. June's part of our peak season and Wildforest expects all properties to be full or nearly full, especially coming into the weekend."

He blew a raspberry at that. "And they think you can control the weather?"

"They don't look at that. They look at the sales figures for the month and how they compare to other properties and previous years." Once again, all the reasons she hated her job pressed in on her. She particularly hated the pressure to magically produce ever-better sales figures and glowing reviews from happy guests.

"We're a team now. Uncle Tommy won't give us any grief." He didn't take his eyes off the road, but she could see him smile.

Don't you see how that's worse? That I'm being protected because he's your uncle? She took a deep breath. He couldn't help benefiting from nepotism, and why should she fight it? After all, she had to swallow the casual misogyny that made her job harder, so maybe it was only fair that she benefit from his protection, even if it was unjust and infuriating and not even meant for her.

They drove for a while without talking, listening to a mix of classic rock.

"You don't listen to current stuff much," she said after a while. "Don't you like to discover new music?"

He didn't answer for a moment, then replied, "I don't want to hear any Smidge songs." Something about the way his mouth was set, and his white knuckles as he gripped the steering wheel harder, told her he didn't want to discuss it.

"Fair enough." She liked classic rock as much as newer music, anyway; she'd only asked out of idle curiosity. Signs for Brewster began to show up on the freeway and the GPS prompted them to take the next exit. "Let's stop somewhere and get flowers," she said. "We'll get in to see Jessalyn more easily and with less questions if we look like visitors."

He nodded. "Clever." A quick online search found a florist nearby, and he pulled up to wait while she ran in to choose something.

At the hospital, they followed the directions for the labor and delivery department, then simply asked for Jessalyn Roberts at the nursing station. The nurse sitting there smiled, seeing the pretty bunch of white freesias and baby's breath that Nell carried. "Aren't those flowers lovely? I'm so glad she has some visitors, the poor girl — all alone, with her husband deployed. She had quite a scare, but with proper care, she should be all right now."

"We were worried," Nell said.

"And how do you know her?" the nurse asked. Clearly, they didn't just let any random people walk in without questions.

"Work," said Eamonn, with a charming smile that caused the nurse to take a second look as she wondered why he looked so familiar.

"I'm her supervisor," Nell added.

The nurse nodded, apparently satisfied. "Aren't you kind, to visit a co-worker. She's in 4B, just down there on your left. And you'll find a vase under the sink in the bathroom."

When they walked into Jessalyn's room, the first thing they noticed was how young she was – young, very thin, and all round belly under the blanket on the bed. She looked fragile, with an IV in one arm and a vital signs monitor hooked up to the other. She gazed at them in surprise and a blend of pleasure at having visitors and puzzlement as to why they'd come.

"Hi there, Jessalyn," said Eamonn, again with that charming rock star smile.

The young woman's eyes widened in astonishment. "Oh my goodness! You're..." Her mouth opened in wordless surprise, then she squealed, "You really are! You're Easy from Smidge!"

"And you must be Jessalyn from Champagne Cascades," he replied. Nell jabbed him with her elbow and handed him the flowers. *Might as well let him do the whole rock god act. She can tell her friends Easy brought her flowers in the hospital.* He winked at Nell, closed the distance to the bed, and held the bouquet out to Jessalyn with a flourish.

Nell ducked into the bathroom to find the vase that the nurse had mentioned. When she emerged with it, Jessalyn was clutching her flowers and gazing up at Eamonn – Easy, because he was wearing his rocker persona and doing the suave charm thing – with a gooey fan-girl expression on her face. *Meet-and-greet man.* Nell wanted to stomp her feet and kick things out of rage, have a full-on toddler tantrum. *Can't you see this is fake? He's putting on an act for you! There's no such person as Easy! And you lick it up like cream for a cat, Jessalyn. Have some dignity.* She was just wondering how to break into the conversation and bring it around to the subject of work and what had happened, when he turned to her with a smile and drew her forward to the bedside, saying, "Jessalyn, this is my friend Nell. She works for Wildforest, and she's here because we got a phone call saying you were missing."

"Missing!" Jessalyn's eyes got really round. "Oh my goodness, I guess no one told Mary or François. My husband is down as my next of kin but he's on deployment – he's in the Navy – and I never thought…" She looked worried. "Oooh, that's really bad. Am I fired?"

"No one gets fired for a medical emergency," Eamonn assured her, in a tone of voice that suggested it wasn't even a possibility. *Oh, you've never been poor, or a woman, my friend,* Nell thought wryly. *We get fired for medical emergencies all the time, especially baby ones. They just come up with something that sounds plausible.* But he could probably pull strings with his uncle to make sure Jessalyn kept her job, if he wanted to.

"We just need to put something in our report to explain your absence," Nell said soothingly, taking the flowers from Jessalyn and placing them into the vase, which she set on the bedside table.

"Oh. I was at work, you know, having my coffee and doing all the things, and I know I should have eaten something, but I woke up late and… you know how it is sometimes. The thing is, last week I failed my glucose test and my doctor started me on insulin right away because it was so bad. I've been really good for a whole week about not eating sugar – or anything nice…" And Jessalyn burst into tears.

"Fuck me," Eamonn muttered, looking at Nell with a what-do-we-do expression on his face.

Nell pushed him out of the way, gently, and perched on the bed next to Jessalyn, patting her shoulder. She snagged the tissue box from the bedside table and put it into the younger woman's hands. "Giving up sugar sucks ass at first," she agreed. "But it's not so bad once you get used to it."

Jessalyn sniffled. "So I went hypoglycemic. Got confused and dizzy and might have had a seizure, apparently. They say I passed out and gave myself a concussion, falling. I came around on the office floor and somehow managed to call 911. I didn't know what had happened at that point. I should have just eaten a cookie or something." She sobbed again, probably thinking about the cookies she wasn't supposed to eat.

Blow your nose already, Nell wanted to snap. "Okay. So you're pregnant and have gestational diabetes. Are you okay to keep working 'til your due date?"

"I have to! I need the money and benefits. It scares me to be totally dependent on Mike's salary, especially when he's out of the country and in harm's way for months at a time."

Nell nodded. "Fair enough. But you have to take care of yourself. With your permission, we should tell Mary so she can keep an eye on you in case you have another hypoglycemic episode, okay?"

"Sure. Mary's nice."

Is she implying that I'm not nice? But Nell decided that Jessalyn just meant she didn't mind having Mary keeping tabs on her health and safety. "I understand why you didn't want to tell Aidan about your pregnancy, but if you'd like, I can help you sort out things like maternity leave coverage and a childcare plan if you're coming back to work afterward. Don't worry about that now, though. We'll talk when you're back at Champagne."

"Okay. I'm supposed to meet with a dietician tomorrow. Maybe they'll release me after that?"

With a concussion and poorly-controlled blood sugar, Nell thought that was unlikely. "There's no pressure. You're on sick days right now, so it's all good, even if they keep you 'til Saturday. Eam– Easy and I will take care of everything at Champagne." She corrected herself before using his name. He was wearing his stage persona for Jessalyn, and maybe he didn't like to mix that with his private self. She made a mental note to ask him.

Jessalyn shot an admiring glance at Eamonn. "How come he's here with you? You're so lucky! Are you guys dating?"

Nell shook her head, just as he said, "Not yet, but I live in hope." And he winked at her.

That made Jessalyn giggle, apparently delighted by what she saw as a romance unfolding.

Then a nurse came in to check Jessalyn's blood sugar, and she shooed the visitors away. As they were leaving, Nell overheard the nurse saying to Jessalyn, "Your visitor, honey, he looked a heck of a lot like that bass player who was part of Smidge and–"

"Not just looked like, it really was him!" Jessalyn replied. "Easy. He's my new work supervisor's friend..." Nell rolled her eyes as they headed down the hall to the elevators, with Eamonn being Easy and flashing his star-quality winks and smiles for all the nurses.

♥

As they got into the truck, Eamonn swiped at the rain soaking into his hoodie, then looked something up on his phone. "I don't know that I can do another two days of this rain without a jacket, and there's a Walmart in Chelan. Want to go shopping?"

Nell looked down at her wet shoes. The idea of having a rain shell and gumboots was awfully appealing. "The weather's getting worse, though. Shouldn't we get back to Champagne and off the road?"

"It's only half an hour down the freeway," he said. "My truck has good tires. It'll be fine. Come on, you don't want to spend the next forty-eight hours getting soaked every time we have to run from the office to the dining room, do you?"

"Not really, but..."

"I mean, that's altogether the wrong kind of wet, isn't it? I'd much rather you were wet for me." He shot her a flirty look, then laughed as she processed what he'd said.

"Ugh, pervert." She smacked him on the upper arm, not hard, but deliberately hitting a pressure point.

"Ow. Peace! I was just kidding."

The wind and rain were truly nasty. Nell looked at the sodden parking lot and how everything that could move was shaking and banging in the wind. *Not nice to drive in.* But Eamonn was a confident driver and he seemed to think they'd be fine. And she hadn't planned to be on-site longer than overnight, or in bad weather – she definitely needed a few things. "All right," she told him. "Let's go shopping."

They didn't talk much on the road, and this time he didn't put music on.

"I'm definitely buying rain boots," Nell said, after a while. "Having wet shoes is the worst." She made a mental list – a pack of cotton panties, because she hadn't brought enough for more than the night or two she'd expected to be there, and a pack of athletic socks so she wouldn't have to suffer damp or bare feet while she waited for the two pairs she'd brought to dry. Something to read. A rain shell. *Could I splurge for less-embarrassing pajamas?*

"My work boots are all right in the rain," he replied. "But I need a jacket."

In the Walmart, they took baskets and split up to find what they needed. She didn't want him watching her choose underwear and presumed he didn't need her looking over his shoulder while he picked out whatever necessities he had on his list.

Socks and undies were inexpensive and she just wanted basic white; the same ones she usually bought to wear with her taekwondo uniform. No issue there. But there were no black rain boots in her size – only bubblegum pink, a pastel floral pattern, electric orange, and dark purple with silver stars. She opted for the purple with a resigned sigh, wondering why footwear manufacturers seemed to think grown women would want colors and patterns that looked like they belonged on Barbie dolls. At least the price was acceptable.

She made her way to the women's outerwear section, hoping she could find something marginally tolerable. At least in terms of cheaper rain shells, the color selection was painfully pastel and not at all her style. *It just has to keep the rain off.* She shuddered at the thought of voluntarily walking around in a lilac or rose jacket, even for the bargain price of $19.95. But some of the nicer jackets came in sensible colors. She stroked her fingers over the sleeve of a hip-length hooded jacket in olive green. Waterproof, lightweight but warm enough for a summer storm. Fleece-lined and machine washable. It cost a bit more than she'd wanted to spend, but if she put up with the pink sleep set she had and didn't buy new pajamas, she could make it work. She ought to skip getting a book as well, but she wanted to have something new to read in bed at night, as long as they were stuck at Champagne.

"Hey." Eamonn appeared behind her. "Found something you like?"

She shrugged. "I was just trying to decide..."

"Nice color for you. What makes you hesitate?" When her involuntary glance toward the price tag betrayed her, he nodded and flipped it over to see the price. "I'll buy it for you, no problem. You'll look cute in it."

Nell grabbed the jacket and stuffed it in her basket. "No. You can't buy me something like this. I've got it." She stomped away, turning back to add, "I just need to look at books, then I'm good to go. And I'm not damn well cute."

The amused look on his face told her he'd been deliberately winding her up. *He's impossible!* As she strode away, she indulged in a little fantasy of meeting up with him at an MMA sparring session and taking him down. But she wasn't imagining him bruised and bleeding, she realized – she didn't actually want to see him damaged. She was thinking about having him pinned down under her, tapping out, admitting that she'd won.

♥

They heard the first roll of thunder just as they got back to Champagne Cascades. "Looks like we've upgraded ourselves from heavy rain to all-out storm," Eamonn said.

"I like thunderstorms," Nell said, "all that power."

He laughed. "You might regret saying that. Let's go get some lunch."

They got their umbrellas and splashed over to the dining room. It made a pleasant change to step inside with feet still dry inside her rain boots, and peel off her wet jacket to hang on the coat rack by the door.

The Princes and the newlyweds were sitting together, consuming soup and sandwiches. Mary seemed glad to see Nell and Eamonn, and waved them over to where she stood at the pass-through to the kitchen. "Come in with me, if you don't mind," she said. "François and I want to talk to you. Not in front of the guests."

"Sure," said Nell. They followed Mary into the kitchen. "What's up?"

François looked up from the broad worktable in the middle of the room, where he was doing something with pastry. "Allo! How are you liking the food?"

"It's great," Eamonn said.

"Delicious," Nell chimed in. "We're lucky to have you here. Mary said you two wanted to talk to us?"

The cook nodded. "We've been hearing the weather reports on the radio. Storm warnings and now a flood watch."

Flood watch. For a resort on a river, floods were naturally a concern, though not usually in the summer. "That's not good." Nell pulled out her phone to check the weather app. "Do we get flooded out often?"

"Eh, no, it's not a worry for our safety here," François assured them. "We're on high ground; the cascades take the water downhill and well away from the resort. But if the river floods further down, it can wash out the freeway. Sometimes the State Patrol closes the roads if there's a high risk of flash flooding."

Nell thought for a minute. It wouldn't fall under site safety if the site was on high ground. Travel safety risk, then? "Okay. We need to inform the guests."

The Wildforest emergency procedure for impending or threatened travel safety risks was to let guests know that traveling to and from the resort may become unsafe or impossible, so they'd have the option to leave while it was still possible, with no early departure charges, plus a voucher for a free night's future stay at any Wildforest vacation property. The manual didn't say what to do if any guests decided to stay on – but who would? Being trapped at a resort with no road access wouldn't be anyone's idea of a fun adventure.

François and Mary nodded their agreement, having been at their jobs long enough that they'd experienced the situation before. They seemed relieved that she was taking the textbook course of action. "We've never had a supervisor on-site during a flood warning before," Mary said. "Harry, the site manager before Jessalyn, he used to like to tell the guests himself when we had a weather or safety issue."

"Right. Well, no sense in wasting time, and they're all here in the dining room. I'll go talk to them." *All four of them.* At least it wasn't a full house. That made it less of a disaster, somehow.

"Want me to do it for you?" Eamonn offered.

"That's a good idea," said François. "A man's confidence is reassuring to the guests in these situations."

Nell gave him, and all of them for good measure, a deadly look. "I'm good. My confidence is quite up to the task, even though I don't have a penis. But you can come along to back me up, if you like."

She heard a snort of suppressed laughter from Eamonn as she turned on her heel and moved off. "Did you just say 'even though I don't have a penis' to François?" he asked under his breath.

"A penis isn't required for confidence, or competence."

She thought she heard him mutter an infuriatingly sarcastic "Yes, ma'am" to that, which made her ponder the exact moves it would take to have him on the floor with a knee on his back and his arm in a lock that would let him know exactly how much confidence and competence she had. *Such a pity that it wouldn't be appropriate.*

"You're only coming with me in case any of our guests are as doubtful of my abilities as François and Mary apparently are. In case you need to *mansplain* things for me," she snapped. Then she took a calming breath. It wasn't Eamonn's fault. She'd expected him to act like a jerk, to laugh with François – but he didn't. "I'm going to call it right now: the honeymooners will jump at the chance to go home early and christen their bed as a married couple, and the Princes will be difficult until we give them an extra voucher or a bottle of champagne to take home... both, probably."

Eamonn laughed, a deep chuckle that made Nell want to purr. "I never bet on a sure outcome, babe. Let's go so you can do your thing."

♥

She was right. Of course she was.

Mrs. Prince crossed her arms, with a dissatisfied twist to her mouth and an ever-so-slightly calculating glint in her eyes. "A voucher for *just one night* isn't much compensation for having to leave early. I mean, we're not likely to drive all this way another time just to stay the single night, are we? Is that the idea behind the policy – to hope we either leave the voucher unused or pay for more nights to go with it?"

Probably, yes. Nell fought the urge to say the words aloud.

Eamonn stood slightly behind her, so she couldn't see his face, but she heard him snicker. "Very likely," he muttered, just loud enough for the Princes to hear. *Craptastic.*

"My assistant Eamonn has been with the company less than a week and is just being a smartass." He'd wisely shifted out of reach, so she couldn't jab him with her elbow.

But Mrs. Prince's eyes had fixed on Eamonn's all-too-recognizable face. "Say, do I recognize you from somewhere...? Are you...?" Her voice trailed off.

Nell waited for him to switch on his Easy persona, to flash that charming smile and take over the conversation. *Why yes, and aren't you sweet to recognize me, darling...*

But he didn't. "People often say that," he mumbled. As Nell turned to look at him, he waved a dismissive hand, and a red flush crept up his neck. "I guess I look like some pop star."

Embarrassed? Oh. She'd introduced him as her assistant with the company – and no plausible way to backpedal on that. He wouldn't want to be recognized here, like this, with the inevitable questions that would come and the gossip that would follow. Nell took pity on him. "Fortunately, I have the discretion to offer a second voucher. Would two nights' stay make the drive worthwhile, Mrs. Prince?"

The woman pursed her lips, considering. "I don't know..."

Considering whether she can wring anything more out of us by pretending to hesitate. Nell gave Mrs. Prince an artificially benign smile. *That's enough.* "Of course, you're not obliged to leave at all. If the flood warning for the freeway doesn't worry you, you're more than welcome to stay for the full visit you booked – and there'd be no need for a return visit. Or vouchers."

She heard a snort from Eamonn, just as Mrs. Prince huffed and said, "Well. I don't want to be *stuck* here. Two nights' vouchers will do.

And our package included a bottle of champagne with each night's stay. Do we get tomorrow's bottle to take with us?"

The smug look on Mrs. Prince's face as she got into her car, clutching her bottle of champagne, galled Nell a little. But being right about her sort of made up for it. And giving the honeymooners a totally unexpected and appreciated bottle of champagne too – in the interest of fairness – felt good.

♥

The rain and wind had picked up to an alarming degree by midafternoon. "Time to go," Nell said to François and Mary. "You both live off-site, right? Do you have far to drive?"

"I live in Omak – it's about an hour away," Mary said. "He has a place in Twisp."

The cook shrugged. "Fifteen minutes, more or less. Where are you going? Back to Seattle now?"

"Eamonn can do as he pleases, but I'm staying. Company policy, unless the site itself is in actual danger, and it's not." Nell braced herself for their worries and protests. A woman alone, and all that.

But François had his mind on the food in his kitchen. "You'll have plenty to eat – too much, eh? Mary, you must take some meals with you. Nell, if the power goes out, you must get the generator going right away or everything in the freezer will be lost." His efficient hands were packaging and labeling portions of food as he talked. Some he loaded into bags for himself and Mary, and the rest went into the fridge. "Beef stew, maple salmon, chicken pot pie, pulled pork... these will all go bad if they're not eaten. I've put heating and preparation instructions on the containers for you. Are you sure you don't need me to stay?"

"We'll take good care of your kitchen, François," Eamonn said. "You just get home while the roads are still good."

As Mary and François headed to their cars, Mary turned back with a quizzical expression on her face. "Eamonn, I feel like I know you from somewhere..."

"Well, maybe you do, sugar. Let me know if you remember, all right?" Eamonn waved her off with a laugh, which Nell thought sounded a little forced. A gust of wind slammed the back door of the kitchen as soon as François let go of it, leaving Eamonn and Nell alone.

"You should go too," Nell said at once. "You've got a solid truck and you're a good driver. Get home to Seattle and come back for me when the rain stops."

"And leave you here by yourself? You've got to be kidding me."

She gave him a dirty look. "I'm not helpless." She turned her back on him, stalking to the bucket by the door where she'd left her umbrella.

"I *know*. You're the furthest thing from helpless I've ever met. But fuck me, you're frustrating – here we are, totally alone in a place made for lovers, and you won't tell me I've got no hope, but you want me to leave?"

"Don't assume we'll have sex if you stay," she warned him, feeling surly and stubborn, then she glanced back for a moment and caught the expression on his face.

Undone, confused, humbled, and desiring.

"I can hope, can't I?" he muttered.

For a moment, all of Nell's defenses fell away as a ripple of something powerful and urgent washed over her, sensitizing her skin and liquifying her core. *Maybe this isn't just a game for him.* His unconcealed lust made her feel... sexy – not something she was accustomed to feeling. *Too strong, too much in control. Chunky Booty.* That one was Tommy's voice in her mind. *Scary woman. Robotic, cold.* She got admiration in plenty, but it was usually for being able to fight hard and break things, or for being competent and efficient, and the lewd variety was so often of the any-hole-will-do sort. Eamonn couldn't take his eyes off her. And she felt wanted, warm, and glorious.

"Yes, you can. And I'm allowed to be frustrating." She could feel a twisted smile spreading across her face, almost against her will. "Stay, then."

His answering smile was equal parts hungry, dirty, and grateful. "We'll have fun, lovely." And he lowered his gaze to her chest for a moment, blatantly admiring. "There's a hot tub, and I've got a bottle of tequila in my truck – pretty sure we could find what we need to make margaritas or something."

She laughed. "Are you suggesting your intention is to get me drunk?"

He blew a raspberry at her, his eyes teasing. "I think you know exactly how much you can drink without losing control, and I bet you never let yourself go there, so... no."

"Fair guess." Nell shrugged, as though it didn't mean a thing. *Why does that sting a little?* Staying alert and in control was a good choice, a smart choice.

"But you'll have a margarita or two with me, won't you? Relax, soak in the hot tub, forget about the rain?"

"I don't have a bathing suit."

"Your sports bra and boyshorts probably cover more than most bikinis – hey, no, I didn't peek!" He raised his hands as if to ward off any violence she might do. "Are you going to tell me you're *not* a sports-bra-and-boyshorts kind of woman?"

He had a point. "You probably prefer your women in lace and butt-floss."

That just made him laugh. "Oh, babe, the gift wrap doesn't matter – it's what's underneath that counts."

"Awkward," she said. "Don't push me, but we'll see." He winked at her, and she raised her chin. "I should go over to the office and call Tommy now in case we lose phone service later."

"All right. How about I gather up some supper and snacks, and we can take the food back to our cabin? The dining room is a bit big and lonely when it's just the two of us."

"Sure. Good plan."

♥

Alone in the office, Nell felt unaccountably anxious as she picked up the phone and dialed. "Hi, Lila, it's Nell. Could you put me through to Tommy?"

"Nell!" Lila's voice bubbled with giggles over the phone. "How's the romantic cascades? Get laid yet?"

"No. Lila, someone will hear you. Please just put me through to Tommy."

The hold music played for a moment and then Tommy picked it up. "Nell. Good. Did you find that manager?"

"Yes. She's in the hospital, but she'll be back to work as soon as she's released, probably in a day or two, and–"

"Did you say hospital?" he snapped. "What's wrong with her? Anything that will make her unreliable or cause problems for us? If we need to get rid of her, I want to start the hiring process right away."

If I say anything about the baby, Jessalyn will lose her job. "From what I understand, she fell and hit her head, gave herself a concussion." Which wasn't a lie. Jessalyn *did* have a concussion from falling, if one left out the part about gestational diabetes and a hypoglycemic seizure. But even lies of omission didn't sit well with Nell's integrity. *It's the lesser evil,* she told herself.

"All right. But you'd better conduct a performance review as soon as she's back on the job, and don't renew her contract at the end of the season without talking to me first. We can't have clumsy site managers falling everywhere."

"Yes, Tommy," said Nell. In her heart, she knew that Jessalyn wouldn't last at Wildforest once a single word was said about maternity leave, never mind childcare. She sighed, not wanting to be the one to burst that bubble.

"Is that all you called about?" Tommy asked. She could hear him tapping his coffee mug against the desk.

"Unfortunately, no. We also have a flood warning for the highway below the property, so we've had to voucher the guests out, and I've sent the staff home. Eamonn and I will stay onsite until we're back to operation."

Tommy swore, ostensibly under his breath, but she felt the words were directed at her. "How can you have a flood warning in June?"

he demanded, as though she had some kind of responsibility for the weather. "This is ridiculous. I need to see better things from that property, Nell."

"I'm working on it, Tommy."

"Good. Call me when you're on your way back." And before she could ask him to put her through to booking so she could let them know about the flood warning, he'd hung up.

Not wanting to talk to Lila again, Nell looked up the direct number for booking instead of dialing the main line she knew by heart.

♥

"How's it going, babe?"

Startled, Nell spun around in her desk chair to face the threat before she managed to process that it was just Eamonn. "Oh. Hi. I'm just about done here."

"Good. I hope you're hungry. I wasn't sure if you were, ah, feeling vegetarian today, so I heated up a bunch of different stuff. Probably too much, even." He had a plastic milk crate full of stacked covered dishes, and a tote bag over his shoulder with what looked like a blender sticking out of the top. A delicious smell wafted over to her and her stomach growled in response.

"Apparently, I'm hungry enough not to care what it is. Let me just finish this–" She brought her attention back to the screen, where the out-of-office autoresponder sequence waited for activation. *There.* She shut down the computer, punched in the code on the phone to redirect calls to head office. "And we're done until the storm passes and the roads are open." She pulled the large, high-powered flashlight from the desk drawer where she'd found it and stood up. "I know there are flashlights in the cottages, but I want this big one if we lose power. Let's go. Can I carry something?"

"I'm good, if you get the doors and light switches?"

Nell shot him a grin. "Oh, you're letting *me* get doors for *you* now?" She almost bounced ahead of him to the office door, feeling full of freedom and holiday – it was raining and horrible out and they were caught in a storm, but until the flood watch was lifted, they were on a private, almost secret vacation. Alone together.

As she flipped off the lights, she realized how dark the day had become under the heavy cloud cover and gusting rain. It was flying all but sideways, and they were going to get soaked. Eamonn must have seen the thought written on her face, because he said, "I don't think I can run with all this and my umbrella, but you go ahead if you want to. I'll follow as quick as I can."

"We're getting wet anyway. We'll stick together."

As they strode out into the rain, Eamonn laughed. "I wanted to see you wet, babe, but not like this."

And for no reason that Nell could think of, she smiled sweetly at him and said, "Add in the hot tub, and we can try for three kinds of wet tonight..." It was worth it, just to see the incredulous anticipation light up his face. She moved ahead of him and added a bit of extra sway to her hips as she walked, guessing that his eyes would be fixed on her rear view and feeling oddly fine with that.

By the time they reached the cottage, Nell's yoga pants were drenched from the bottom of her jacket to the tops of her boots, and rain had run up the sleeves of her coat to saturate the cuffs of her hoodie. As she peeled off her coat and stepped out of her boots on the doormat, she saw that Eamonn's jeans were soaked across the thighs too, and the rain had blown in under his umbrella to dampen strands of his hair and scatter droplets across his face. *Flipping hell, he has no right to be so handsome.* It was as though the weather itself had somehow made him more approachable, more touchable – or was that the privacy of being alone, where no one would know or judge what they did?

Damn. Maybe Lila was right that she needed to get laid. She hadn't wanted to feel this attraction, but there it was, a ridiculous urge to run her fingers through his wet hair and lick the raindrops from his face. *Simmer down, Miss Whelan, we're not rushing into anything.* Skipping dinner wouldn't do anyone any good, no matter what the blatant desire in Eamonn's eyes promised.

"You want to go get out of those wet things?" he asked, setting down the things he'd been carrying to shrug out of his jacket. "Dinner could be clothing-optional..."

A rush of heat flowed over her, and she wasn't sure if it was embarrassment or just plain arousal. "Slow down. I need a little foreplay – and maybe a drink – before we get to the clothing-optional part."

"Babe, you really do speak your mind. I've never met anyone quite like you. And foreplay can definitely be arranged." He took a step toward her, and she could see the kiss coming, see the moment where he'd take her in his arms and press his mouth to hers.

She shuffled backward. "Dinner first." *I can't be nervous about this, can I?* She'd always taken a practical approach to sex, never shy about her body or safety or making sure she got her needs met.

"Sure thing." He shrugged, maybe a little bit frustrated or confused, then picked up the milk crate and bag, carried them over to the kitchenette area, and started to unpack. "Go get some dry pants on, then. Or a bathrobe."

"What about you?" she asked.

"Me?" He stopped shuffling dishes around and turned to face her.

"You can't be comfortable like that–" She'd only meant his wet jeans, but the moment she said it, she thought of his obvious arousal tenting those jeans, and her eyes flickered there without her meaning to look.

He smirked, and boldly reached down to adjust himself. "I can wait, Nell. And you're right; if we got started now, even a little, I'm thinking I might forget about eating anything but you. Go strip down to your underwear – for the hot tub, don't panic – then cover up with your bathrobe and come have some supper before we get into that foreplay you mentioned."

She couldn't think of a single thing to say to that. Finally, she muttered, "You're so sure of yourself," and stomped away to the bedroom. It infuriated her that she couldn't even tell him it wasn't going to happen, because it so obviously *was* happening. Nell Whelan disliked not having the upper hand, or at least a controlling position, and she was slightly afraid she'd bitten off more than she could chew with this man.

Well, I'm not sitting at the table in nothing but a bathrobe and my undies, waiting for him to seduce me, she thought, pulling on her last dry pair of pants. She'd only brought the one hoodie, but her t-shirt was dry, and it was warm enough inside the cottage not to be an issue. She tied back her hair as though she were heading to the training floor rather than dinner with a potential lover, then looked in the mirror and pulled the elastic free with a snort of disgust.

And even though she was about to eat dinner, she brushed her teeth.

chapter

6

AN ASSORTMENT OF DISHES COVERED THE SMALL TABLE in the kitchenette, steaming and redolent with heavenly smells, and Eamonn stood at the counter, pouring tequila into a blender. He must have been listening for Nell because he turned the moment she stepped out of the bedroom.

"Fix yourself a plate, babe." He gestured toward the food on the table. "I'll join you in a minute; I'm working on that drink you said you needed."

Her first impulse was to snap that she did not *need* a drink, but she took a deep breath and reminded herself that maybe a little liquid relaxation wouldn't hurt. "Where did you get the Cointreau?" she asked instead, seeing it on the counter.

"Oh, I had it in my truck too," he said with a shrug.

"Seriously? You got a full liquor cabinet in there?"

He grinned. "I have far too much alcohol in my truck. Comes in handy sometimes. And François had frozen limeade concentrate and strawberries, so we're all set. Now, eat." He held out a plate.

"Thanks." She took the plate. Then he hit the ice crush button and the blender's noise made conversation impossible, so she turned to the table and looked at the offerings laid out there. He'd picked out things that could be eaten easily, with fingers or at least minimal mess – quesadillas that François must have frozen for easy reheating, crusty rolls stuffed with pulled pork and coleslaw, bruschetta. Delicious.

The blender noise stopped, and Eamonn turned to snag a triangle of quesadilla, dipping it in the sauce. As he bit into the wedge, a dollop of sauce slid off and dripped down his hand. "Oops!" He licked the sauce off his fingers, winking at Nell. "Mmm, that's good stuff. Try it." As she narrowed her eyes at him, he nodded toward the dish of sauce. "I'm not even going to tease you about licking it off me. You can get your own."

"All right." She took a quesadilla and dipped it in the sauce. Started eating it as slowly and sensually as she could, licking her lips and fingers as she went, getting an unreasonable amount of satisfaction from his look of astonishment. *Flirting? Well, I suppose I am.*

"You trying to speed things up here?"

"No. No, I–" Flustered, she dropped the last bit of quesadilla – it slipped out of her fingers, landing with a splat on the floor. "Crap."

Before she could move, he grabbed a paper towel from the kitchenette counter and knelt to wipe up the small mess. *Kneeling at my feet.* Then he looked up at her.

"We need those margaritas," he said, his voice husky. He stood. Got two tumblers out of the small cabinet and poured pink slush from the blender into them. Handed her one. "Cheers. Sorry there's no salt."

As he clunked his glass against hers, a glob of frozen margarita slopped over the edge of her glass onto her hand. She looked around for the paper towels.

Eamonn put a hand on her wrist, stopping her. "Let me get that," he said, and drew her hand up to his mouth, closing his lips over the sweet-tart slush and sweeping his tongue along the sensitive skin between her thumb and forefinger.

"Did you just *lick* me?" Nell's voice came out breathy, sounding as stunned as she felt.

"Yup." He grinned. "Are you going to put me on the ground for it, ninja woman?"

She took a big slurp of her margarita, debating how to answer that. Too late to play a careful game, wasn't it? Silly to take things slow, when the path ahead was burningly clear. "Only if you want me on top."

"Fuck me." Eamonn put his drink down, then gently took hers and placed it on the table next to his. Stepped into her space and rested a hand on her hip, pulling her in. His eyes were dark with desire. "Can I assume I've got consent here, babe?"

"Are you making fun of me?" She tensed, ready to push him away.

He laughed softly. "No – I just want to be sure. Don't want to ruin the moment. Are we good?"

The room felt suddenly short of oxygen, and Nell gathered her scattered brain cells to mutter a breathless "Yes."

"Good." He snaked one hand behind her head, gently cupping the base of her skull. With his other arm, he settled her more firmly against him. She tensed for a moment – his hands on her head and hip gave up too much leverage, too much control, and she found the vulnerability of her position unnerving – then his hand slid further down to rest intimately on her ass. She could feel his arousal, evident right through his jeans, and the awareness of it blotted everything else from her mind.

She could feel the warmth of his breath, his lips inches from hers. Time froze. And then he closed the distance, bending his head to bring his mouth down to hers.

His lips were firm and slightly cool from the margarita, and he tasted of strawberry and lime and tequila. "I've wanted to do this since we met," he murmured against her mouth. He probed at her lips with his tongue and she opened for him, welcoming the deepening of the kiss.

Eventually, he drew back and smiled down at her. "All right?" he asked, but as the haze of desire faded, the specific position of his hands on her triggered an automatic muscle memory, embedded deep in her mind after years of self-defense training. Without thinking, she gripped his upper arm with one hand and slid the other into a choke position against his throat, preparatory to shoving him away. "Whoa! Maybe you *do* need to be on top..." He leaned away from the pressure of her hand on his throat and loosened his arms so that she could put space between them if she so chose. "I thought you wanted a kiss, babe."

He sounded puzzled, and a bit concerned. "Did I do something to freak you out?"

A wave of embarrassment washed over Nell. "I – no. It's habit. I don't like being in a position where I can be pinned down or controlled. Anyone having a grip of my head and hip like that... it's too much like what we train to avoid in self-defense. I just..." She stepped away from him, shaking her head. "I feel like kind of a fool now."

As she turned to go, not sure where but away from him and the ruin of what had promised to be an enjoyable evening, he put a gentle hand on her arm and said, "Hey, it's okay."

She gave him a deadly look over her shoulder, designed to make him back off. *I don't need your tolerance and sympathy for my weirdness.* "Right."

"Come on." He picked up her margarita and held it out to her, waiting, until she turned back to him and accepted it. Then he watched her with one eyebrow cocked until she took a drink. "Let's go try out that hot tub, all right? You go on out to the porch with the drinks and I'll get us some towels."

♥

The covered and screened porch kept the rain out and was somewhat protected from the wind, but the air felt damp. Although the temperature wasn't exactly cold, getting undressed in it didn't have much appeal. Still, the view was beautiful, even in poor weather; the porch overlooked the river, churning away toward the cascades.

To one side of the door, a pair of deck chairs were positioned on either side of a small coffee table. On the other side, a tubular metal handrail and a beige vinyl cover were all that showed of the hot tub sunken into the deck; a slatted wooden bench set against the wall was probably intended to hold towels and discarded clothes. Several thick pillar candles in glass chimneys were lined up against the wall.

Nell set the drinks on the bench, then crouched down and pulled up one corner of the hot tub cover – heat and steam wafted out with a clean and inviting whiff of properly sanitized water. *Good maintenance,* the professional part of her mind noted. She dipped her fingers into the water and sighed with pleasure at the warmth. Maybe testing out the hot tub was a good idea after all.

She knew better than to trust the water's look and smell, though. Looking around, she spotted the wall-mounted box that she knew had to be present, containing the maintenance record for the hot tub and a bottle of test strips. She knelt down and lifted the corner of the hot tub cover again so she could dip the little strip into the water.

Behind her, she heard the sliding door open and close, and Eamonn said, "Let's get that cover off and hop in. It's chilly out here."

"Ten seconds. I just want to make sure the chlorine and bromate levels are where they should be..." She turned. He stood there, his arms full of towels, wearing the skimpiest pair of black swim trunks printed with nebulas and galaxies. *Well, damn, he has a fine body.* He was all lean muscle with a golden dusting of hair, and the ink on his arms was matched by more art on his abs and thighs. "You're wearing a bathing suit." As she spoke, she could hear the accusatory tone in her voice.

"Well, yeah." He shrugged. "I've stayed in far too many hotels – with the band, you know? I learned a long time ago never to go anywhere without swim shorts."

"And I learned from *this* job never to get into a hot tub 'til I've tested the water." She looked at the strip in her hand, compared it to the chart on the bottle. "It's good."

He dropped the towels onto the bench, then reached down and flipped the cover open without waiting for her help. Before she could even sort out the words to say *slow down* or *I'm not ready for this,* he was in the water, sliding over to the jet controls to send them purring into life. "Come on in."

"I should light the candles," Nell said. "It's getting dark."

Eamonn touched a button, and the hot tub's underwater mood lighting came on in a shifting display of LED colors. "There we go. That should be enough light."

With one tense look at him in the water, she began to place the big pillar candles around the hot tub, one at a time. Found the waterproof box of matches and lit every candle, methodically lowering the glass chimneys back into place.

He watched her. Oh, how he watched her. She could feel his gaze on her like a caress. "Don't be shy," he murmured at last, his voice thick with desire. "Get your gear off and come play."

"I don't do shy," Nell snapped. And it wasn't a lie. She'd been sparring and grappling with mostly men since she'd been a preteen, she thought nothing of getting changed in mixed company when the need arose, and she refused to harbor any notion of body modesty or bashfulness. But Eamonn had her on edge, discombobulated.

"Then prove it, gorgeous. Strip for me."

"You wish." But she heard her words come out in a way that sounded more like *challenge accepted* than *go stroke yourself*. Or maybe she meant both.

He laughed, a low and sexy sound. "I do wish."

And that lit something up in her, something that said *game on*. Holding his gaze, she hooked her thumbs into the waistband of her yoga pants and slowly inched them down. The cool damp air brought up gooseflesh on her bared hips, but a furnace was overheating inside her. When she got to mid-thigh, she turned to give him a good back view as she bent over to push the stretchy fabric the rest of the way down. Her grey athletic boyshorts covered more than most bikinis, but a choking groan from his direction assured her that he was getting a satisfactory eyeful. Could he tell that the crotch of her underwear was already wet, just from this stripping business and the way he looked at her?

She straightened and turned back to face him. Crossed her arms and raised the hem of her t-shirt to show her belly button, then a little more, until she had it bunched just under her breasts.

"Come on, show me those heavenly tits," he muttered. "You're killing me here."

So she paused a moment more, hugging herself and doing a little twist wiggle. "Why? You got a rocket ship ready for blast-off under those galaxy shorts?"

"Bigger and harder than the Saturn V – you're absolute rocket fuel, Nell."

Hot damn. "Modest, much?"

"I've got what it takes to send you into space, and you know it. Do you want me to beg?"

Maybe I do. But she'd never been inclined to play bedroom games. Blowing out a shaky breath, she whipped her t-shirt off and slid into the hot tub, sinking up to her neck in the steaming water. Pulsating jets of water massaged her. "Ooh, that's nice."

"Now, how is that fair?" Eamonn asked, with a teasing grin. "I barely got to see anything." Between all the ripples and bubbles, and the candlelight reflecting off the water, and the shifting colored lights underwater, a clear view couldn't be had. "And our margaritas are way over there on the bench. Someone's going to have to get out and fetch them."

Crap. Now what?

He gazed at her across the hot tub, a wicked look in his eyes. "If you go get the drinks, I'll take any dare you give me. Or I'll get the drinks and you take the dare. Your choice."

The thought nearly took her breath away. What might he dare her to do if she stayed in the water and told him to get the drinks? What would she ask him to do if she had the choice? "Dares? Are we in middle school or something?" she asked.

"Aren't you even a little bit intrigued about where this could go?" he asked, with a smirk that implied he knew exactly how much the idea was affecting her.

Maybe he would think the heat in her face was from the hot tub. "I just... dares are about giving up control, and backing out after agreeing to one would be giving up integrity." That didn't mean she didn't *want* to go there.

"Oh, babe, dares are about having an excuse to do something you know you want to do anyway. But how about we make it truth or dare instead? You like honest talk, don't you? And if I'm lucky, it'll get a little dirty..." He paused, cocking an eyebrow. "Now, you want me to get up and get those margaritas for us?"

I can deal with that. Her mind flashed back to them lying in their separate beds the previous night, and how his words about touching himself had electrified her. "Sure," she said, meeting his eyes so he'd know she was agreeing to his game.

He stood up. As the water streamed off his beautiful inked body, she licked her lips. Those soaking wet cosmic swim shorts clung to his hips and – he hadn't been lying about the rocket ship in there. He saw the direction of her eyes and laughed. "Oh, hell yes."

It took him only moments to get their drinks and splash back into the hot tub, thigh-deep in the steaming water and close enough to touch. As he handed her glass to her – at least, she assumed it was hers, but they'd already swapped spit so it hardly mattered – she blurted out, "Truth." Before he could ask. No way was she entertaining a dare.

"*Sláinte.*" He clinked his glass against hers before sinking down onto the seat opposite her, grinning. "So, how about you tell me what dares you were thinking about when I first mentioned it? What you thought I'd ask you to do. What you considered asking of me."

The hot tub suddenly seemed ten degrees warmer as thoughts raced through Nell's mind. She took a sip of her margarita, then another. The slushy sweet-tart liquid didn't make any of this more sensible, but she gathered her nerve and decided to just blurt it all out. "Okay. Honest answer. I thought you'd try to get me to take off my bra. Make me sit on your lap, or maybe... maybe touch myself for you..." The last bit came out as sort of a gasping whisper, but Eamonn heard it.

"Good girl." He sounded thoroughly turned on and approving. "I like the way you think. So, would any of that have been so bad?"

"No, actually. I like being in charge of my choices, but... we'll see. A little more truth and a little more tequila, maybe we'll get to that dare stuff after all."

He crossed his arms behind his head and stretched, looking much too relaxed and satisfied. "Your turn now. And I'll make it easy on you and take truth. For the moment."

Too cocky. He wants me to ask him something dirty. About fantasies or kink. She wouldn't give him that satisfaction. "You said *sláinte* before we drank. Are you Irish?"

He reached for his drink and took a big gulp, half shrugging but looking a bit wary. "Could be. A few of the guys who might have contributed to my DNA were Irish."

"A few...?"

"Oh, come on. Even *you've* heard of my mother, right? Amanda Joy Yarrow – of *course* I don't know who the fuck my father is." And when Nell still looked puzzled, Eamonn gave her a disbelieving lift of his eyebrows. "Candy Bar Mandy? Sweet Almond Joy? She was a groupie, Nell. The only thing I'll ever know for sure is I've got rock music in my blood."

"That... wasn't meant to be an awkward question," Nell muttered, waving her hand as if she could wave away the words or rewind time. The words *Candy Bar Mandy* and *Almond Joy* did trigger a vague memory of clickbait articles about groupies of decades past and glamorous pictures of girls with long legs and big hair clinging to rock stars.

Eamonn snorted. "It's not awkward. I love my mom. I'm not ashamed of who she was, or who I am. But some people make it into this big weird thing."

"Right. Let's move along, then. It's your turn to ask me something."

His eyes widened slightly, as if he were unprepared for how easily she let the subject go. Then he narrowed his gaze and leaned forward with a devilish grin. "All right, then. Do you do anal?"

Well. Was that a serious question, or was he just being dirty to get a reaction from her? "Is it a deal-breaker if I don't? I'm not morally opposed to it or anything, but that kind of trust and vulnerability..." She looked down at her drink and sloshed it around. "You want the truth? Any time I've felt remotely close to the level of respect and safety I'd need to try something like that, I didn't have the sense that the guy would know how to do it right, so... no."

"Not a deal-breaker. But for the record, I *do* know how to do it right – slow, fingers first, tons of lube. In case you're curious."

She shook her head. "Nope. My turn. Do you give oral?"

He laughed. "Hey, hey. I didn't say *truth* yet. I'd love to go down on you, babe – do you want a demonstration? Because I'm choosing *dare* this time..." He waggled his tongue at her.

"Whoa, that's..." She couldn't find words. The hot tub water swirled around her like a caress and her skin tingled. He was teasing, but she could tell by the intensity in his eyes that he meant it; all she'd have to do is say *yes please* or *I dare you* and he'd have her up on the tiled edge of the tub, underwear off, thighs spread...

"You're thinking about it, aren't you?"

Nell couldn't honestly deny it. "Who could listen to a suggestion like that and not think about it?"

"And... are you considering it?"

"I don't move quite that quick. I need a bit of kissing and making out before I let you into my pants, okay?" And even putting that statement out there felt like too much, too fast, but playing games had never been her style. She waited. Would he close the gap between them now?

He grinned. "Babe, you aren't wearing pants. And there's a dare on the table right now – what're you going to ask me to do?"

Dare. Right. Her mind spun with possibilities. But she'd just asked for slow, so she could hardly suggest anything too extreme. "The tattoo covering your left side... is it an angel?" She couldn't see much of it now in the rolling water of the hot tub, but she'd noticed it earlier. Black-inked wings and flowing robes stretched from his belly button around to his back, from his ribs down past his waistband. Dramatic and gorgeous. *How far down does it go?* She took a breath. "Will you show me all of it?"

He wasn't expecting that. And from the look on his face, she'd just asked to see most of what his swim trunks covered, if not everything.

He glanced down toward his abdomen, under the water. "My guardian angel? She's crying over all the bad shit I've done." Standing up, he moved into the middle of the hot tub, close enough for Nell to reach out and touch him, if she wanted to. Candlelight and underwater rainbows lit up his wet skin. "You want to see the whole thing?"

"Yeah." Nell's mouth felt dry.

"Okay, then." He tugged his swim trunks down a bit, showing more of the angel's sleeve. "I feel like a stripper." Another inch. He turned his body so she'd get a better view of his side and hip. There were music notes and a black broken heart blended into the trailing robes, and as he pushed the fabric right down to fully expose one exquisitely formed buttock, she could see the crown and lettering that unmistakably formed the logo for Smidge – the band he was no longer part of. "You like?"

She licked her lips, overcome with an urge to touch and taste him. She'd seen handsome men before, but there was something about Eamonn Yarrow that undid her. "You're freaking glorious," she muttered.

Pulling his swim trunks back into place, he sank down into the water, but instead of retreating to the far side of the hot tub, he slid onto the bench next to her, his leg touching hers. And he waited.

"Dare," she said at last.

He looked at her, his eyes so loaded with sexual intent that she shivered. "Touch me," he commanded.

"Where?"

"Anywhere you like." His voice, husky with need, lit her up like phosphorus to a safety match. She started with his chest, laid a hand over his heart underwater and then stroked down across his abs, across the angel tattoo. She brushed his waistband with her fingertips, and paused. "You know you want to," he said.

"Do *you* want me to?"

An involuntary upward thrust of his hips answered that question. "Do you need to ask?" He chuckled, slightly breathless.

So shaken by the electricity between them that she could barely move, she slid her hand down inside his shorts, prompting another thrust and a gasp from him as the touch became intimate. "Whoa, you weren't kidding about the size of this rocket." Her guts clenched and went gooey at the thought of having all that inside her.

"All the better to please you with," he said with a shaky grin, his voice ragged. And then he cursed under his breath and laid a hand on her wrist to stop her, gently drawing her hand out of his shorts. "Your touch is heaven. But the first time I come for you, Nella-bella, I want to be with you, in you." He leaned forward and kissed her, fierce and hungry, his tongue stroking into her mouth with urgent need. Then he pulled away, breathing hard. "I need a moment. You're wrecking my self-control here – why do I fall apart when you touch me?"

It shocked her a little, that he'd admit to so much vulnerability. But it was also a gift and a huge turn-on to know how intensely she affected him. "Don't know. But yeah, I want to ride that explosion when it happens."

He found his margarita on the edge of the hot tub and took a drink. The way he bit his lower lip told her that her words hadn't helped him cool down. *Ride that explosion.* The air between the two of them was charged with sensuality.

She took a drink too, waiting for his next move. *I need a moment,* he'd said. She could see his chest rising and falling as he breathed hard, as though he couldn't get enough air.

"Talk to me," he said. "Tell me something, ask me something, doesn't matter what."

"Okay." Nell tried to think of something that could serve for conversation. "I think your crying angel tattoo is beautiful. You want to tell me more about it? How come it has a broken heart at the bottom?"

He looked away from her, the lust in his eyes shifting into something more complex and bittersweet. "And the Smidge logo that you're too polite to mention? You want to know what happened, don't you?"

Crap. That was the wrong question to ask, wasn't it? "You don't have to tell me. I'm just making conversation. I really do think your ink is gorgeous."

Eamonn sighed. "Thanks." He knocked back the rest of his drink and gazed out into the dark, toward the rain and the river.

"You *can* tell me, if you want to," Nell said softly. "I'll listen." She wanted to touch him, to close the distance between them and erase the trouble from his mind, but some small doubt held her back.

He was silent for a while, then said, "You know I wasn't their first bassist, right? Angel and Blade were best friends in school, and Dice was their neighbor down the street. They performed at school dances and did gigs in local bars before they were even legal to drink, I guess, and one of their friends played bass okay, but maybe not up to a pro standard, or maybe he wasn't hot enough, didn't fit the look. I don't know. So, the label persuaded them to drop him, and pushed me on them instead – their hired eye candy."

"More than that, surely."

"Oh, I'm a competent musician, no doubt about that, but Angel and Blade never really let me in. Even when we were at our worst, high all the time and barely able to keep everything together, they watched out for each other and tried to protect Dice from the worst of it and I was on my own."

"But you didn't leave them?"

"No." Something stark and lonely was etched across his face for a moment and then was gone.

"So, they dumped you? Kicked you out? Why?"

He forced a laugh. "Forget it. Let's just go to bed. A truly epic fuck will help me forget." He slid toward her, swirls of displaced water eddying around him. She wanted to reach for him, knew it would be epic, needed that release maybe as much as he did. Instead, she slid away, keeping a bit of space between them.

"Tell me," she said, aching with regret. "I think I need to know."

"Fuck me. You're not going to let this go, are you, ninja woman?"

She wished that she could. But she needed to know. "I can't."

"I wanted to feel like I belonged, okay? But as Angel got clean and Blade was working on it, we didn't even party together anymore. Smiles for the media, efficient rehearsals and performances, that was it. Trying to fill that void with sex worked for a while." He shrugged. "It felt less like being abandoned after a show if I was busy screwing my brains out. And there were always groupies up for it. That's their calling, right? Didn't feel so bad if I was making some girl's night."

He trailed his fingers through the water around him as though bemused by the colored lights and jet bubbles.

She reached over and shut off the lights and jets. "Just tell me," she said.

"Well, I found Blade alone. He was mucking around with his guitar, maybe writing a song, I don't know. And I wanted to get my bass and jam with him, craft the song together. But he stopped playing when I walked in, put his guitar in its case like he couldn't bear for me to be a part of that. So I offered the only thing we'd ever really done together – said let's go out and get trashed. Just booze, he said, because he was supposed to be getting clean. But I'd only ever felt part of Smidge when we were all high."

Nell felt sick. "You knew he was a recovering addict and you encouraged him to relapse?"

Eamonn was silent for a moment, then he nodded. "It didn't seem so terrible at the time," he muttered.

"Ugh." She hoisted herself out of the hot tub, shivering a little in the cool air, and grabbed a towel from the bench. "Honestly, *Easy*," and she spat his band name out like an insult, "I can't even – how *could* you? Don't come into the bedroom. Sleep on the couch or go find another cabin. I'm done."

She wanted to stomp away and slam the door, make a dramatic exit to show how disgusted she was. But she'd lit the candles, and they needed to be extinguished. Her responsibility. In silence, she circled the hot tub, blowing out each one.

"Nell?" Eamonn said, his voice rising to make it a question. She shot him a *this is not a good moment to talk* look, one she'd perfected over years of martial arts classes and hundreds of students. His shoulders slumped and all hope faded from his face. Then the last candle was out, and she strode inside, spine straight and chin high, refusing to look back.

Nell woke to music, haunting piano sounds that morphed from classical lament to grieving fatalistic jazz, accompanied by the rhythm of heavy rain. At first, it felt like part of her disturbed dreams, but gradually she concluded that she was actually hearing the melody coming from somewhere. It didn't strike her as Eamonn's kind of thing, but she remembered him saying on the drive up that he had a classical playlist if she'd prefer it. Although what she was hearing didn't sound like any of the jazz she'd listened to in his truck, she knew she'd slept for some of the drive. Perhaps he'd found a sound system in the cottage and plugged his phone in, or maybe he had a portable speaker. Either way, it made her angry.

He had a lot of nerve to play music while she was sleeping. At full volume, no less.

And how dare he listen to – and like – something so beautiful? *He's scum for enabling an addict like that. Cocky, self-entitled scum.*

She had not slept well.

Unfortunately, she was not the kind of person who could roll over and snooze or go back to sleep, no matter how much or little sleep she'd had. Once awake, Nell was switched on for the day and felt an overwhelming urge to get up. Mornings lounging about in bed weren't in her nature.

She launched into her morning workout, doing twice the usual reps at a furious pace, and it failed to soothe her. Usually, the burn of well-worked muscles would induce a pleasant glow of satisfaction, but today she just felt sore and drained. A scalding hot shower didn't help, either.

The music cut through everything, and it sounded like grief and loss and an apology. *I'm sorry, I did wrong. I'm ashamed, forgive me. I miss them.*

Nell seethed inside. The man was just listening to music; it didn't mean a thing. *I refuse to feel sympathy or find excuses for what he did,* she told herself. *Why should I care, anyway? He's nothing but a co-worker at a job I hate.* Still, she couldn't shake the memory of his sexy gasps and shaky self-control as she'd touched him. And she didn't want to face him.

Putting this off is cowardly. At least her hoodie had dried overnight – though it didn't provide much armor, she thought grimly that it did a better job than the previous night's wet underwear. Summoning a neutral expression to her face, she crossed the bedroom and opened the door, strode into the sitting room like a competitor into a ring.

The music wasn't from a playlist, wasn't recorded at all.

Eamonn sat at the piano, his whole body moving with the music that flowed from his fingertips. He wore nothing but a pair of jeans. In daylight, the crying angel tattoo wrapped around his left side looked even more tragic than it had in the romantic glow of the night before. *Oh, ever-loving hell, he's spectacular,* Nell thought helplessly. *How can I stay angry at that?*

Then he became aware of her presence, and his hands froze over the keyboard as he turned his head to look at her in apprehension.

"But you're a bass player," she said, breaking the silence in the stupidest way possible.

That prompted a bark of bitter laughter from him. "I started with piano," he explained. "Played since before I can remember. Then guitar and bass once I could hold them properly, I guess. I'm not a good drummer, but I can fill the role if needed. Flute and saxophone too, and weirdly enough, harp – one of Mom's groupie friends taught me that one, hanging out on someone's tour bus on the road."

She blinked at him. *All that?* "Why?" she asked, then frowned at him. "Also, could you put a shirt on?"

"Sorry. You were pretty clear that you didn't want me in the bedroom last night, and all my stuff was in there. It's lucky I hung these jeans over a chair out here to dry." He pushed the piano bench back and stood up, glancing over to where his damp swim trunks now graced the back of one of the kitchenette chairs.

If he'd had nothing else to put on... *He's definitely going commando under those jeans, then.* Nell shook her head at that irrelevant conclusion. She did *not* need to be thinking about the equipment he was packing behind his button fly, or how thick and firm he'd felt in her hand the night before. "I should have thought to toss your bag out here. I was..." *Angry. Disappointed. Frustrated.* But she refused to apologize.

"Yeah. I'll get my shirt." He headed for the bedroom but stopped in the doorway and looked back at her, with a wry half-smile and a resigned look in his eyes. "I know this has sunk any chance I had with you, and I won't push it." He nodded as if to emphasize that he meant it before disappearing through the door. She heard rummaging-in-bag noises and then the sound of the bathroom door closing.

No more of his flirting, no more being coaxed to spend a night with him, no more hearing him call her Nella-bella – or any of his other words for her. No more of his eyes on her, hungry and admiring.

He's a lost cause, she told herself. But now that he was walking away, she didn't want to give him up.

"I have some rules," Nell said, as Eamonn came back into the main area of the cottage, slicking back hair damp from the shower. She saw that he'd put on his other jeans – and presumably underwear – and his hoodie as well as a shirt.

"You have what, now?" he asked, cocking his head at her.

"Rules. For if you..." She paused, steeling herself with a deep breath. It wasn't easy to back down, or to expose her own complicated feelings on the matter. "If you wanted to salvage that shipwrecked chance, you know?" *Well, that got his attention.* He froze, his eyes widening, and she could feel the heat rising in her face as he stared at her. She forced herself to shrug like it didn't mean much.

"Fuck me. Nell, are you saying–"

"I don't know what I'm saying," she admitted. "Just... maybe sometimes things aren't as clear-cut and binary as I'd like them to be. Good and bad, right and wrong... I don't believe in excuses, but I want to think there's a way forward from this, if you're serious about making amends for what you did."

He sighed. "You have no idea."

She crossed her arms and fixed him with a hard look. "You're going to have to apologize, you know."

"A hundred times, yes. Babe, I am more sorry than you can–"

"No. To him, your addict friend. He's the one you hurt."

Eamonn scrubbed a hand through his damp hair. "I can't. Angel kicked me out, right? Told me not to call or write, told me I wouldn't be welcome again. I wasn't even given a chance to say goodbye to anyone, especially not Blade. So, no, I don't think I'll be apologizing."

Nell shook her head at the hard look on his face. *Putting up walls. Time to change the subject, for now.* "Look, we need to eat something," she said. "Let's find some food, and you can tell me how you ended up playing, what, seven instruments?"

That made him smile. "We've got all we need right here. Will strawberry crêpes do? There was a stack of crêpes in François's fridge. They just need microwaving. And strawberries in syrup – I got two containers out of the freezer but only used one for the margaritas last night – and a can of whipped cream."

She didn't usually like sweet things for breakfast, but he seemed so pleased that she nodded. "All right."

When she moved toward the fridge in the kitchenette area, he waved her away. "Go sit by the fire," he said. "I've got this."

"I can get my own breakfast," she told him, tensing. *I'm not helpless. I can feed myself.*

He nodded. "I know. But I *want* to do this for you, since I wrecked everything last night."

You didn't wreck everything, she wanted to say. But deep conversation wasn't what they needed right now. "Okay, then, get my breakfast for me. That would be nice."

"Yes, ma'am," he said with a grin, a bit of his confidence resurfacing.

"Hold on." She stopped him as he turned toward the kitchen. "Bow properly, please. Feet together, hands at your sides." As though he were one of her students, being corrected for proper protocol on the training floor.

He stopped and stared at her for a moment, slightly shocked but with a flash of something unexpected in his eyes. Arousal? *What the hell?* She'd been kidding, but he slowly made a deep bow. "Yes, ma'am.

Like this?" She could see his throat move as he swallowed, then his chest rose and fell as he took a deep breath. *Weird.*

"Like that. Yeah."

He moved into the kitchen, started setting out plates and microwaving the crêpes. "You asked why I play so many instruments," he said casually, as though nothing intense had just happened.

"Right. Seven, is it?"

"Eight if you count harmonica, more if you count percussion stuff – tambourines and shit. I basically grew up on the road with whatever bands Mom was following, right? Other groupies were my aunties, roadies were my babysitters. Piano was Mom's thing, so she taught me that, probably as soon as I could sit upright at the keyboard, I don't really remember. Then I picked up whatever anyone wanted to teach me, did any job I was given, played whatever they threw at me. I was fourteen the first time I got shoved in front of a crowd, hat and sunglasses to hide my age, to fill in for a support band guitarist who was too drunk to go onstage."

"Didn't you go to school?"

"Oh, sure, two dozen different schools. Mom would stop and rent an apartment somewhere and teach piano, I'd go to school for a term, then she'd fall head over heels for another band and we'd move on."

Nell suppressed a shudder. "I don't think I could handle living like that."

"It was all right," Eamonn said, bringing her a plate of warm crêpes rolled up around strawberry filling, syrupy red sweetness oozing from the ends. He had a can of whipped cream in his other hand. "You want cream?"

"I don't know." She looked at the confection in front of her, shaking her head. "Protein shakes are usually more my speed."

He held out the can with a tempting lift of one eyebrow. When she hesitated, he gave the cream a shake, holding the tip down toward her plate. "You're on vacation. Splurge a little." He glanced down at the can in his hand and then toward her chest, his voice deepening as he added, "If I don't get to lick this off you, at least let me watch you eat it."

Damn. Her breath left her in a rush. "You, uh..." She couldn't articulate the thought, held tight to the plate on her lap so it wouldn't slide to the floor. He knelt in front of her.

"If you had your shirt off, babe, I'd lay you down and put this–" he squeezed a ruffled line of whipped cream across her crêpes "–right across there." He reached out and drew a line in the air, his eyes dark with desire, and she felt it as though he'd actually stroked his finger across her chest. "Then I'd lick up every bit of it."

Unable to hold his gaze, she looked at her plate, feeling conflicted. "I'm... I'm not ready to not be mad at you yet."

"That's okay," he said. "As long as I still have a chance, I'm a happy man. Eat."

He'd forgotten to give her a knife and fork, so she scooped up a bit of cream with one finger and licked it off, watching as a sexy smile spread across his face. "This'll be a bit messy if I have to eat it all with my fingers."

That made him laugh and broke the tension. "Let me get you a knife and fork." He jumped up and strode over to the kitchenette. When he came back, he had silverware in one hand and a mug of tea for her in the other. "I thought you'd want tea with your breakfast, yeah?"

And though her first impulse was to tell him he should ask rather than assuming what she wanted, she swallowed the words and said, "Thank you. That's perfect." Because it was.

After they'd eaten, Nell decided to do a load of laundry, since the rain and wind seemed heavier and she thought the power might go out. Who knew how long they'd be stuck at Champagne Cascades? The generator would run the emergency lighting and keep the kitchen fridge and freezer on, but it wouldn't be enough for extras like laundry.

She'd planned to read while she waited for the dryer to finish, but Eamonn came and lounged against the doorway to the laundry room, saying, "Hey, I found a fun-looking board game in that games room across there. D'you like fantasy games? This one's called *Crowns &* *Exiles*." He held out a small plastic crown, evidently a game piece. "You want to check it out with me?"

As he was setting up the pieces and she was reading the instructions, the faint but unmistakable sound of a siren made them look at each other in puzzlement, and then concern as it grew louder.

"That sounds like it's on its way here," he said.

Nell nodded. "I'd better go outside. Coming?"

As they reached the driveway in front of the office, a truck marked *Sheriff* pulled up, and a man in uniform jumped out. "Is it just the two of you still onsite?" he asked.

"Yes. I'm Nell Whelan, property supervisor, and this is my assistant Eamonn Yarrow. What can we do for you?"

"Leave with me now," the sheriff said. "There's flash flooding coming down the river and we need to evacuate the area immediately."

chapter

7

ORTUNATELY, THE DEPUTY AGREED THAT EAMONN could drive his own truck, following the official vehicle until they were out of the flood zone. It seemed that a dam farther up the river was in danger of giving way after some seismic activity, and even though the resort was on high ground, flash flooding was unpredictable. The Sheriff's Department rules superseded any Wildforest Vacations dictums about the supervisor or manager staying on-site.

They stopped briefly in Twisp so Nell could call the office while she was able to get a phone signal. She left a message for Tommy, updating him on the situation and their planned return, and then she and Eamonn stopped at a bakery for his coffee and her tea – and some heavenly cinnamon twists – before they hit the road.

He cranked up his classic rock playlist, and she stared out the window at the rain.

"Are you hungry?" he asked when they passed through Wenatchee.

"Not really," she said.

It wasn't that she wasn't hungry, more that she couldn't bear the thought of stopping for a cozy pub dinner as they'd done before. Then, she'd been fending off his teasing and flirting, a sort of game that both of them had been well equipped to play. Now, she had a *vacation's ended* feeling hanging over her, and the teasing and flirting had blown up into full-on sexual tension she didn't know how they'd resolve now that their fairytale vacation was coming to an end.

They weren't going to date, were they? Rock star Easy Yarrow wasn't going to take her to the movies and out for dinner back in Seattle. But the idea of just being a casual booty call for him didn't sit well with her either. *Why not, though? Nothing wrong with getting our mutual needs met.* Still, she didn't know how she'd be able to deal with him in the office even now – she kept thinking of the hot tub, and the feel of that giant rocket in her hand and how she'd almost wrecked his self-control, the explosive kiss they'd shared and the way he'd needed a moment to just breathe. If she let him into her bed…

All too soon, his big truck was parked in front of her apartment building. He clicked open his seatbelt but made no move to get out. *I suppose he's not opening doors for me anymore,* she thought, knowing that it ought to make her feel strong and equal, but somehow feeling that she'd lost something. She unbuckled herself and reached toward her door.

"Hey," Eamonn said. When she turned to look at him, he gave her a hesitant half-smile and slid an arm around her shoulders, slowly, as though giving her the chance to pull away if she wanted to. They hadn't kissed or even really touched since she'd gotten out of the hot tub. "Come here, lovely," he murmured, easing her toward him. It wasn't quite a question, but it sounded like one, or at least a request for permission.

"You and your nicknames," she said softly, but she could feel herself starting to smile. And without meaning to, she let herself be drawn in, saw all the hunger and need and aching in his eyes in that split moment before she lifted her face to his and he leaned down and his lips touched hers.

Maybe he'd only meant a brief kiss goodnight, or goodbye, but the moment his mouth covered hers, it blew up into shattering need, his tongue pushing between her lips like he was making love to her. She felt his free hand cup her breast and she moaned and pressed into his touch. Their kisses almost absorbed his gasp of delight, the urgency with which he sucked on her lower lip, biting gently. Everything in the world vanished but his touch, his strength, his mouth, and the dizzying sweetness between them.

"Nella-bella," he murmured between kisses, "I'm feeling pretty damn desperate, enough to start stripping us down right here in my truck where anyone can see." A hand trailed down to play with the waistband of her yoga pants, dipping toward tempting heaven. "You want to invite me upstairs?"

In some fuzzy part of her brain, Nell knew they'd already complicated things beyond belief. But taking him upstairs? She wrenched herself upright, and said, "No. Eamonn, I... I don't want to stop either, but I don't know what we're doing here, and..."

He stopped. Let her go with a groan, popped open his door, and jumped down. For a moment, she saw him lean against the side of the truck and press his face into his arm, then he came around and opened her door for her, holding out a hand to help her descend.

She took it. Stepped down onto the sidewalk. "Thank you."

"Is this just not tonight, or not ever?" he asked slowly, his face tense.

"This is – we have to see each other at work tomorrow. We're not strangers, we're not dating. You shake me up, Eamonn. I don't know what we are or where this is going, but right at this moment I can't handle being a bed buddy tonight and a co-worker tomorrow."

He sighed. "Yeah. Well, let me know." He opened the rear door and grabbed her bag, handed it to her. "Walking you up to the door is too damned much temptation. I'll watch you from here, to see you get inside safely."

"I can take care of myself," she reminded him, but the words came out sounding more resigned than fierce.

"I know, ninja woman. I'm still going to watch you until you're in."

"Fine, then maybe you should call me when you get home, so I know *you're* safe."

"Fishing for my phone number?" he asked with a muted laugh, but he got out his phone and handed it to her, open to the New Contact screen. "Give me yours, and I'll call you when I'm in bed."

"Right." She handed his phone back to him, settled the strap of her bag on her shoulder, and nodded. "I'm off."

He leaned down and kissed her forehead, lightly, but it made her scalp tingle. "I'll talk to you in a bit," he said.

"Yeah." She turned and sprinted for the front door of her building, though running made no sense and her bag bumped awkwardly against her hip.

♥

Home. It felt good to be back in her space – small and nothing fancy, but all hers. She took a two-minute shower and pulled on an old district championships t-shirt in place of pajamas. She'd got the t-shirt the first time she'd competed at the district level as a teenager, before she'd ever gone to nationals. It was a tighter fit now than it had been back then and the graphics were faded from washing, but the old shirt still brought up happy memories and a security blanket feeling. *It's just a clean t-shirt,* she told herself. *Nothing to do with wanting comfort.*

But she couldn't avoid the thought that she'd chosen to be alone, that Eamonn could have been there with her if she hadn't stopped him. Yes, it would have been complicated afterward. But damn, the fireworks might have been worth it.

She didn't really think he'd call to say he'd made it home safely, but just after she'd gotten into bed with her book, her phone rang, an unknown number on the call display. "Hello?"

"Hey, ninja woman. I'm safe at home," Eamonn's voice came over the line, low and intimate. "Where are you? In bed yet?"

She'd never been a liar. "Yes."

"Wish I were there with you."

And what could she say to that? "Regret is a waste of time."

She heard him chuckle softly. "You regret sending me home, do you?"

"Tomorrow's going to be weird anyway, isn't it? And if you were here…" She couldn't finish that sentence. *You'd be inside me right now? We'd be falling apart together?*

"I know, babe," he said, his voice deepening, with that thick quality she now knew meant he was aroused. She heard a rustling of sheets and a muffled squeak: the sound a mattress makes when someone shifts position.

"Are you in bed too?" she asked. There was something oddly intimate about that, both of them in bed, talking. Not together, but together.

"Yeah." He was quiet for a moment, then said, "Just talking to you like this has got me so hard, it's ridiculous."

His words sent a rush of heat over Nell and she snuggled deeper into her blankets, wondering if he slept naked, if... "Are you getting yourself off?" she blurted, before she could censor the words.

"No, but I will before I sleep." That admission came out in a low, sexy voice that made the air in the room seem somehow thin. "As soon as we hang up. And I'll be thinking of you."

And that was it, fuse lit. Didn't matter that she'd done the smart thing and sent him home earlier, she'd gone off the deep end now, thrown herself into the fire. She couldn't deny it, might as well embrace it. "Why hang up?"

"You want me to..." He didn't finish the sentence, and she heard a gasping breath as he wrapped his mind around what she'd just said.

"I want to listen as you come," she told him. "Be loud for me. Let me hear it."

"Fuck me," he muttered, then a deep groan told her he'd settled himself to it, and a rush of answering wetness soaked her underpants. "Just thinking about you is wrecking me, lovely." His voice sounded ragged, barely coherent.

"Hearing you like this..." She pictured his beautiful inked body, his big hands and the massive cock she'd wrapped her hand around in the hot tub – she imagined him stroking himself now, and a little moan of frustration and hunger escaped her as she listened to him work.

A gasping laugh answered her. "You're turned on too, huh? Join me?"

She'd never considered taking care of herself with someone listening, knowing, but in this moment she was so achy and frustrated – and the sounds he made were so deliciously sexy – that she murmured, "Okay," and rubbed a hand across her aching nipples before sliding downward into her underpants to ease the tension there. "I can't believe I'm doing this." And then in surprise, "Whoa, I am *never* this wet!" She imagined his fingers instead of her own.

"Oh, Nell, baby... stroke that juicy peach for me... I'm so hard right now, I think I'd split you in two..." His gritty murmur told her he was almost there.

"I'm tough enough to take you," she choked out. Sensation swirled and crashed over her, with frantic fingers and imagination and hearing his gasps and groans over the phone, until she just barely managed to whisper, "Coming..." in the split second before her climax rocked through her. And his wordless growl in response was the sweetest sound she'd ever heard.

They lay there in silence for a minute, in their separate beds but somehow feeling close, listening over the phone to each other's breathing as it gradually slowed back to normal.

"That pretty much blew my mind, Nella-bella," Eamonn said at last, his voice hoarse.

"It was something," Nell agreed sleepily. "I'll see you tomorrow, Eamonn. Sleep well."

♥

It was Wednesday again – Nell's equivalent to Monday. Even though she'd worked through her "weekend" up at Champagne Cascades, she was expected to be in the office. She'd have to go through the HR department to arrange days in lieu; she couldn't just take them.

She did her workout and made her protein shake, as always. Refused to put on makeup or fuss with her hair, but she chose the least terrible of her hated business casual outfits, a black cap-sleeved wrap blouse and black slacks that at least had pockets and a bit of stretch. She'd never told anyone that she imagined herself as a ninja in that particular combination.

And she spent the whole bus ride to work thinking about Eamonn. Like iron pulled toward a magnet, she wanted to see him, but she also dreaded it a little. *How will we handle this? Will he keep things professional at work?* It seemed a lot to hope for. She didn't want to be the subject of gossip and titillation.

She felt her familiar sense of satisfaction at being the first to arrive at work, the one to unlock the glass doors. As usual, it soothed her to get herself established before anyone else arrived. Especially Eamonn.

In Nell's absence, Lila had allowed the reception area and kitchenette to devolve into mild chaos – the glossy vacation magazines were haphazardly stacked on the end tables, with sticky coffee rings showing that the tables hadn't been wiped down at all, and the kitchen sink was full of dirty mugs and a coffee filter full of grounds that hadn't been disposed of. Nell allowed herself the private luxury of a headshake and sigh before she set to work sorting out the situation. Squaring everything away eased her tension a bit and made her feel more in control, as always. She filled up the photocopier with paper, since five of the six trays were nearly empty, made herself a cup of tea, and headed for her office to get started on her own day's work.

Before long, Lila rapped on the doorframe and popped her head in. "Morning, Nell, how was the site visit? I'm making coffee, if you want some."

"I'm good with my tea, thanks." Nell nodded toward her steaming cup, sitting right in Lila's line of sight on the desk. *Brilliant observation skills, there.* "The site manager was taken to the hospital for concussion, and then we had to voucher the guests out on a flood warning, and then we got evacuated."

Lila made dramatic big eyes at that, then leaned closer and asked in what was probably meant to be a hushed tone, "And what about Easy? You had him all to yourself for two whole nights! Did anything happen? Is he as good as they say?"

"Really, Lila? Eamonn Yarrow is my assistant, our co-worker, not some kind of man candy that I could just have for the taking," Nell said firmly, schooling her face to show nothing.

"Come on – he's a rocker and apparently a sex god – I bet he'd have been up for it if you'd shown the least sign of interest." Lila shook her head and rolled her eyes at the same time, her move to convey peak frustration. "I'm trying to be your friend and help you out here. You'd have so much more fun in life if you took that stick out of your butt and enjoyed your opportunities a little."

"Nell doesn't have a stick up her butt, princess." Eamonn's amused voice broke into their conversation, and Nell looked over in horror to see him lounging against the wall in the hallway. Who knew how long he'd been listening?

Lila spun around with a gasp and giggle. "Oooh, hi, Easy! I was just kidding, right? Do you want coffee? I was just making coffee…" She fluttered away without waiting for an answer.

Eamonn watched her disappear with a cynical look on his face. "She'll no doubt be back with a cup of weak coffee, too much cream and not enough sugar." Then he crossed the hall into Nell's office and shut the door behind him. "Thanks for telling Lila that I'm not just man candy, but for the record, *you* absolutely can have me for the taking, anytime, anywhere. You have a beautiful ass, you know, and I'd love to put something up–" She remembered him saying *slow, fingers first, tons of lube*, and flushed.

"Eamonn! We're at work, and what did I tell you about keeping the door open?" She pushed her desk chair back and stood, feeling a strange tingle of adrenaline, like she was about to step into a sparring ring with an unfamiliar opponent.

He raised his eyebrows. "I know, but which is the worse evil here: a closed door, or having someone listen to us talk about last night?"

"We're not talking about that *here*."

"Where else am I going to talk to you, babe?"

She shrugged, seeing the sense of that, but all too conscious of the closed door. Every minute it stayed closed increased the chance that someone would notice. "All right. What, then?"

"You said you couldn't do bed buddies at night and co-workers during the day." He ran a hand through his hair, looking a bit uncertain. "So, do you want to, well, date?"

That made her blink. "You're asking me out?"

He grinned. "Whatever it takes. I mean, it's a little awkward, the whole fame thing. I tend to stick to low-profile places like the Frog and Ball, my hair is shorter these days and I dress down and wear shades a lot. Don't want to be recognized. So, we won't be fancy. But if you don't mind..."

"I'm not fancy," Nell said. Surely he could tell that, just from looking? But maybe rock stars were used to women expecting red carpet affairs. "I don't want anything like that. I told you before, though – I've got rules."

Eamonn raised his eyebrows. "I thought going out *was* your rule."

"Nope. Going out just means we're not ashamed of each other. I've got no issue with one-night stands or casual sex; it's the idea of us coming to work and pretending to be just colleagues afterward that I couldn't deal with. I don't want to be anybody's under-the-table affair." She pressed her lips together, feeling that she'd said too much.

He cocked his head to one side, looking oddly sympathetic. "Did someone try to do that to you?"

"Not here. I know better than to get involved at work. Or, I used to know better. But I'll never be a Barbie doll, and I learned the hard way that some guys think I'm good enough for a cuddle but too–" *Too strong, too rigid, too opinionated, too blunt.* She won trophies, but she'd never be one.

"Well, shit," he said. "Anyone who thinks like that about you is a tool." And he came around her desk and put a hand on her shoulder like he wanted to comfort her, but his hand felt really nice, and she couldn't help turning a little toward him and then she was in his arms, being hugged and sort of rocked against him. It felt too damn safe and nice. "So, what are your rules, babe?" he asked.

"I've just got three." She pulled away from his all-too-comfortable embrace and perched on the edge of her desk. "First of all, if you're polyamorous or something, tell me now, all right? I'm not knocking non-monogamy; I just need to know what our deal is."

He looked a little taken aback at that. "Okay, I won't deny that I've done some pretty kinky shit here and there, and some of it involved more than two people. But do I *need* that? No. You've got my full attention."

"Good. I don't want to be worrying about where else you've been or if you're clean. So as long as you're in my bed, you're not in anyone else's. Is that acceptable?"

"Sure. I'd actually kind of assumed that was part of going out. What's rule number two?"

"My martial arts training is really important to me. I need you to understand that. I'm not going to skip training or put social stuff first. You can come watch me train, you can train with me if you want to, or you can do your own thing while I'm training. That's up to you. But it's my thing. My life."

"Okay, I get that. I can respect it."

"Thank you." *You'd be surprised how many guys don't get it.*

"What's the third thing?"

"You have to live with integrity. I can't be with someone who doesn't."

He laughed, and it sounded a little defensive. "What does that even mean? I already said I wouldn't cheat on you."

"Integrity. It means doing the right thing even when no one's looking." She crossed her arms and gave him her instructor face. "No lies. No illegal drug crap. And you're going to have to apologize to your guitarist, you know – make things right."

At her words, he froze, his expression hard. "I, ah, think I already told you that's not going to happen. That bridge is so fucking burned." His flat tone didn't quite mask the layers of hurt and shame underneath.

"He may not be willing to hear it, but you should at least try." She could tell that he didn't want to discuss Smidge or what had happened – that she might even push him away – but she still felt compelled to speak up. The idea that he hadn't even tried to repair his damage ate at her.

"Not really your business, is it?"

"No." *Crap.* Her heart sank as he turned to leave. An apology stuck in her mouth, and she couldn't say it. *He's right – it isn't my business. But I'm not going to say sorry for caring.*

He turned back, hand on the doorknob. "Am I going to regret telling you what happened?"

"I told you, regret is a waste of time." Nell sighed. "Okay, no lies, no drugs, and we'll leave this sore spot alone. As you say, it's not really my business."

She could see the relief in his posture as he opened the door. "What're you doing tonight?" he asked, his voice and expression casual, neutral, like they hadn't nearly argued. Like he wasn't asking her about potentially... what was it? An official *date*? Or just an invitation to get horizontal?

It would be so easy to say, *I'm busy, tomorrow is better.* But... "I've got a sparring class after work. You can come watch if you like." He might as well see all of her. *Violent, unfeminine, too much muscle.* And if it put him off, at least she'd know.

♥

She could have changed at home, because he'd picked her up at her apartment in his truck, which made a nice change from public transit. But she stuck to her usual routine of putting her uniform on in the changing room at the dojang.

It held a kind of magic for her, the ritual of changing, stepping out of the work world and into her space, seeking the focused mindset she needed – the clean, crisp feeling of heavy white cotton, creases down the arms and legs ironed sharp. The black of her instructor collar and the vivid colors of her patches stood out boldly against the white. And when she tied on her black belt, she felt complete.

She pulled back her hair, secured it with an elastic, and closed her locker. *I'm ready.*

♥

"Evening, ma'am."

"Hi, Miss Whelan."

"Hey, Nell!"

Various people greeted her as she entered – students, classmates, and teachers – each according to their history with her, some formal and some familiar. This was a black belt sparring class, and she'd been training with a few of them for over a decade. *My place, my world.* She glanced over at Eamonn, sitting alone on the row of chairs set up for spectators.

"Who's the dude, Miss Whelan?" asked a fifth-degree instructor she'd been training and teaching with for what felt like forever. He smiled encouragingly at her, and she realized that she'd *never* brought a guy, a date, to a training session like this.

It doesn't mean anything. Her first impulse was to tell him it was none of his business, but doing so would betray that she even cared. And Riley Kahn had a wicked sense of humor underneath his perfectionist exterior – Nell didn't want to face the endless teasing she'd get if she gave him an opening. Nor did she want to lie. "Co-worker. But he asked me out, so I figured this would be a good test. If he sees me spar and runs screaming, it wasn't meant to be. And if he's cool with this, I'll take him to an MMA session sometime."

Mr. Kahn laughed. "Practical as always. You should bring him to a self-defense class. See how he likes getting put on the ground."

"Oh, I've already done *that*." She allowed herself to show a bit of satisfaction at the open-mouthed surprise on his face. But bringing Eamonn to a self-defense class did have some appeal.

The chief instructor called them to bow in, which put an end to the chit-chat. As always, they warmed up with kickboxing combinations on targets, partnered by height, which usually meant that Nell was matched with a teenage boy or one of the few other women present. Today, her warm-up partner was a young man preparing for his second-degree rank test – he showed off a bit by doing the drill at warp speed, sacrificing accuracy and technique in favor of finishing ahead of other pairs around them. "Great power, sir, but you should take care not to hook your punches like that or you'll end up with a broken finger," she warned him, her instructor instinct coming to the surface despite the fact that she was a student in this class.

"Thank you, ma'am," the kid mumbled, looking a bit sheepish.

When the chief instructor called out for them to switch holders, Nell bounced on the balls of her feet, thinking *light*, thinking *hard*. She enjoyed these warm-up drills, and launched into the kicking and punching combination with full power. Her partner staggered backward a bit, apparently unprepared for her to have that kind of force. "Do you want me to hold the targets for Miss Whelan, Mr. Tibbett?" called out Mr. Kahn, seeing what was happening.

"No, sir, I've got this," the kid said.

"Take a stronger front stance and breathe out as her kicks are coming at you, then. She's got a lot of power." Mr. Kahn moved on, circulating through the room, but Nell was aware that another instructor moved into their area – keeping an eye on the young Mr. Tibbett. She eased back her power just a notch, not wanting to embarrass the teenager in front of so many senior belts, but also not wanting to give him an easy ride. *You thought a woman couldn't kick so hard, Mr. Tibbett?* It was a common mistake.

When they were released to get a drink from their water bottles after the warm-up, Nell glanced over at Eamonn, wondering if he'd be looking bored or playing with his phone. He watched her, smiling slightly, so she toasted him with her water bottle, mouthing, "Cheers." He winked at her, definitely flirting.

She felt a tiny, unwelcome flutter of hope. He didn't seem put off by this world she loved so much. *No. It's just going to be sex, maybe a few drinks somewhere or a movie or two. Casual dating.* If feelings got involved, they'd leave a mess.

When they paired up and bowed to their opponents, she bit down on her mouthguard and put everything out of her mind but her partner and the contact she could make, the points she could score. Set. Bow, rotate to a new partner, and repeat. After a few rounds, they'd stop and listen to one of the instructors talk about technique, or something to work on. Breathe, drink water. Then pair off and spar again.

For her last round of the night, she lucked out and got matched up with Mr. Kahn. He was fast, strong, had long legs, could take hard contact, outranked her, and didn't underestimate her – a challenge. She didn't have to hold back or worry about accidentally hurting him if she did land a solid kick. As they bowed and shook hands, he winked at her. "Showing off for the dude a bit?"

"Fighting to win, sir, as always," she told him. Not that there was really winning in class, but she liked to train as though it were a competition or a test. Always doing her best, eye on the prize. *Someday I'll be a Master.* Step back, sparring stance. *Sijak.* She dodged away from his twist kick, faked a kick, tested his guard with a couple of punches and danced back, circling. Butterfly kick. He landed one on her chest pad, but she got him back with an inner crescent kick to the head. *Two points for me.* By the time the round was over, she was sweating and had worked hard, but felt she'd held her own. "Thank you, sir."

He gave her a fighter's hug instead of shaking hands. "Great round, Miss Whelan."

Praise from a senior belt, especially one she admired, made her glow.

And it didn't look like Eamonn had been put off at all.

She didn't want to put her street clothes on, sweaty as she was, so she decided to just gather up her gear and wear her whites home in his truck. She'd shower at home, and if Eamonn came up to her place, he could watch TV for five minutes while she did so.

But he walked her up to her front door, gave her a crooked grin, and said, "Goodnight, Nell. I'll see you tomorrow."

She blinked. "Uh, what?"

"Oh, lovely, of course I want to come upstairs with you." He chuckled softly. "Never doubt that."

"I didn't say–" She knew as she tried to speak that it was thin bluster and he'd see right through it, but she still wanted to save face. She'd basically admitted that she was assuming he'd come upstairs.

"Listen. We have to work tomorrow. I could blow it off and not care, call in sick or just tell Uncle Tommy that I'm taking the day off, but I don't think you would; am I right?"

Nell nodded. She couldn't risk her job, no matter what the temptation.

"And I want more than a quick wham-bam from you. I want to have the whole night, at least the first time, and I want you to walk like you've been well fucked the next day. You want to go into the office like that – sleepless, worn out, and walking funny?"

"It'd take a lot to change my walk," she said, chin in the air.

"I'm up for that challenge," he shot back.

They stared at each other.

Then she shrugged. "I see your point. Another night."

"Sunday." He grinned. "I'll take you to the Frog and Ball. Buy your peachy drinks for you. Take you home to bed after."

She nodded. "That's *my* time, but just this once, you can come along."

"Good. Now, am I going to get slapped if I kiss you?"

She crossed her arms and gave him a dirty look. "I don't slap people. I'll hit your pressure points and put you in a joint lock or choke to defend myself, if I have to, but I don't *slap*."

He looked down at her, shaking his head and chuckling. "Ninja woman, I just want a kiss goodnight."

"Okay." But Nell hadn't made a habit of goodnight kisses – it seemed impractical if it wasn't going to lead to bed – so she wasn't sure where to start, and stood waiting.

Glancing around, Eamonn grabbed her hand and pulled her around the corner of the building, into the shadow of a large shrub. She let him, feeling giddy, and just as glad that he preferred not to give the neighbors a show. *Privacy is good.* He gathered her into his arms and backed her up until her shoulders touched the wall of the building. *Back against the wall.* She stiffened, suddenly tense. *No.* "What is it?" he asked, relaxing his hold, maybe a bit wary of her reflexes.

"It puts me on edge to have my back against a wall," she muttered. "Not a good self-defense situation, and all that. Force of habit. But you're not going to hurt me."

"No, I'm not. I *promise* I'm not going to hurt you. Let's do this nice and slow." He moved in close, hands on her shoulders, pressing her against the wall as he fitted his hips against hers. "Feel me against you.

How's this? Are we good?" His voice dropped into the low sexy register she knew meant he was turned on – borne out by the hard evidence jutting against her belly. "You're going to have to trust me a little, give up some of that control. The wall at your back's going to hold you up when your knees give out."

That's what I'm afraid of. It wasn't him, or the wall. He had no training to make him dangerous and they weren't in an MMA cage. But *letting* him put her up against a wall carried a submissive undertone that unnerved her as much as it tempted.

He slid his hands from her shoulders down to her breasts, cupping them in his big hands, his thumbs just underneath the sensitive tips. She squirmed against his hands, and he gave her a wicked half-smile and stroked just a little. And then he bent his head and covered her lips with his, firm and knowing. She expected him to ravage her, but instead, he gave her the sweetest kiss she'd ever had. The world spun, and Nell leaned into the wall at her back, surprised at how grateful she was for its presence and how oddly seductive it was to just trust him and enjoy the consuming tenderness of his mouth on hers. She parted her lips and darted the tip of her tongue out to see if he'd open for her, because she wanted to taste him again the way she had in the hot tub.

"Oh, you're testing my self-control, Nella-bella," he murmured against her neck. Then he wrenched himself away from her, with a twisted grin for the effort it took. "I'll see you at work tomorrow."

Sometime in the night, the flood warnings for Okanogan County were relaxed and the highway below Champagne Cascades was listed as open. Nell hit the workday running.

By some small miracle, Jessalyn had been released from the hospital the day before. She answered Nell's phone call with a gush of gratitude for her supervisor's kindness and promised to go straight up to the site to report on any damage and how quickly it could be opened for bookings.

"Uh, you're not at – where *are* you now?"

"I'm at my mom's place in Chelan. She didn't want me to be living on my own with this gestational diabetic thing in case I have another seizure. But I can drive up right away."

Nell wanted to throw something. Would it be wrong to chuck an eraser at the wall? "Jessalyn, are you... sure this job is still a good fit for you right now?" Site managers needed to have initiative for things like going up to the site as soon as the roads were opened, without waiting for specific instructions. But she couldn't snap at Jessalyn for not thinking, not when the poor woman was just coming off a concussion.

Jessalyn gasped. "Oh, please, I need my job! Especially right now. No one would hire me, pregnant like this, and I need the benefits."

"I know." Nell pitched her voice to be reassuring. "It *is* a live-in position, though. You need to be onsite. Call me when you get there?" *This isn't going to end well.*

She let out a long sigh after she ended the call. Shook her head. Picked up the eraser she'd been eyeing before and rocketed it at her corkboard, knocking a couple of Tommy's Post-It notes to the ground.

A familiar masculine laugh drew her eyes to the doorway, and there was Eamonn, chuckling to himself. He'd apparently seen her throw the eraser and was enjoying her little loss of temper. "What?! Also, did you just get here? It's after eleven."

"Uncle Tommy doesn't care," said Eamonn, with a shrug. "Hey, I brought you this." He plunked a Starbucks cup down on her desk, gave her a look like he wanted to say something more, then strolled out the door. Moments later, she could hear him moving around in his office next door – the shoddy thin walls let every sound through. She sniffed the drink, then looked at the cardboard sleeve around the cup. *Yes.* A half-sweet coconut milk chai latte, the same thing she'd asked for as they were heading out on their road trip. *He remembered.*

And just like that, her day brightened.

When Nell got back from her lunch break the next day, she found one of Tommy's yellow Post-It notes on her desk: *My office – 2:30 pm.*

She stuck her head into Eamonn's office, announcing her presence with a quick rap on the doorframe. "Tommy wants to see me this afternoon. You don't happen to know what he wants, do you?"

"No, sorry. He stopped by to give me some of Aunt Betty's lasagna, that's it." Eamonn gestured toward a Tupperware container on the corner of his desk, which held a half-eaten slab of lasagna with a fork stuck in it. "He probably just wants you to reassure him that the bubbles will continue to be profitable."

"The bubbles? Oh, you mean Champagne Cascades."

Fortunately, the resort had been spared the worst of the flooding, due mostly to its placement on higher ground but also some sheer luck. Jessalyn had called in the landscaping service and cleaners, François was back in charge of his kitchen, and the existing bookings for the weekend did *not* have to be canceled.

Maybe she could salvage her figures for the month. *It's only the thirteenth, still lots of time,* she told herself. But she had a bad feeling about Tommy's summons, and even though she tried to believe that you could make your own luck with perseverance and positive energy, the sinking feeling in the pit of her stomach persisted.

Instead of making tea and returning a call from Stu about the laundry service at Secret Creek as she'd planned, she printed out the Champagne Cascades bookings for the month and whipped up a quick analysis of what the closure had cost in lost revenue, vouchers, and person-hours, along with bookings and revenue for the same time period over the past three years. There hadn't been a similar flood incident at Champagne Cascades in June previously, but there was a much longer closure recorded at the end of May two years before, so she printed out a report on that, and statistics on flooding across all Wildforest properties going back ten years. It was a regular occurrence at the riverside and lakeside properties, and the numbers bore that out, no matter how badly Tommy would like to lay blame.

Armed with a folder full of data, as prepared as she could be, Nell headed for Tommy's office. *Project confidence.* But he'd make it personal; he'd find a way to criticize her. *I hate my job.*

"You wanted to see me, Tommy?"

"Nell." He looked up at her in the doorway, then glanced at his watch, almost ostentatiously, pretending he'd lost track of time. "Right, it's almost two thirty. You're... three minutes early."

She gave him a neutral smile to mask her frustration with his little power games. If she'd been right on time, he would have made a joke about it. "Do you need me to come back in three minutes?"

"No, you can come in. Oh – close the door, please. And have a seat."

Close the door? Doors were never closed at Wildforest.

As she stepped into the office, she realized there was another person in the room. In the corner, out of the door's line of sight, sat a woman in a grey suit, with a clipboard. "I'm Melody," the woman said, "from Human Resources." She did not get up or offer to shake Nell's hand.

Nell perched on the edge of the chair Tommy indicated.

"Tell me," he said, in the manner of a prosecutor, "when did you first find out that Jessalyn Roberts was pregnant?"

chapter 8

OMMY HAD HANDED NELL A CARDBOARD BOX ALONG with the letter of termination. No quiet chance to be escorted in after hours for the collection of her personal items – instead, he'd orchestrated the ultimate walk of shame. As she strode down the hall, chin up and game face on, she could feel herself jangling with fight-or-flight adrenaline and knew that she had hardly any time before she'd lose the fine motor control in her hands and maybe her grip on the box. Melody from Human Resources followed her. "We won't need to call Security, will we?" the woman had asked with a faux-sympathetic smile. The building's security staff – mostly retirees who'd taken a five-day basic security training course and passed an exam – were available to provide this kind of escort, for a fee. *None of those guys would stand a chance against me.*

She couldn't focus on anything except her desire not to drop the cardboard box she carried, not to show pain or let anyone see her fear and despair. Would she lose her apartment? How would she pay for her training? They'd given her a month's severance on the condition that she signed waivers and disclaimers – no right to talk about it, no right to sue, no recourse. And she'd signed where they told her to, of course; she'd had no choice. At least the severance would buy her a little time.

She shivered. *Why am I so cold?*

They reached her office – no longer her office, now – and she stared at the desk. She couldn't think.

"That mug is yours, isn't it? Let's put it in the box," the HR woman prompted her after a minute. Nell picked it up, looked at the quarter-inch of cold tea in the bottom of it, and drank it because she didn't know what else to do. Her stomach churned. She held onto the mug with both hands and couldn't remember what was supposed to come next.

A knock on the doorframe startled her into dropping the mug. It tumbled into the box, dribbling the last drops of tea onto the termination letter, as Eamonn leaned into the room, swinging himself off the doorjamb. "Hey, Nell, do you have–" He froze, his eyes on the cardboard box as she turned toward the sound of his voice. "Oh, shit."

"They took my *phone*," she said. "It was a company phone, but on an unlimited plan, and Tommy encouraged me to use it for everything so I'd have it with me all the time; he didn't *want* me to have another. I never thought..." Appalled at how her voice shook, she fell silent.

Eamonn shook his head. "This has to be a mistake. They'd be fools to fire you. I'll go talk to Uncle Tommy–"

"Please don't." She could barely say the words. "He... he found out that I knew Jessalyn was pregnant and I didn't tell him."

"What the fuck does that have to do with anything?" he asked.

"Don't be obtuse. They'll fire her now so Wildforest doesn't have to cover her medical care or deal with maternity leave."

Melody from Human Resources pursed her lips. "I have to advise against that sort of speculation. Wildforest would only terminate Ms. Roberts's employment if she were unable to fulfill the requirements of her position. Nothing more, nothing less."

Nell laughed, a hard and bitter sound. "It's the flipping Dark Ages around here, if you hadn't noticed. I gather you're the token HR female they send to supervise females being fired so no one can claim anything inappropriate happened."

A tinge of pink darkened Melody's cheeks, telling Nell that her assumption had been accurate. "I hardly think my colleagues' gender is relevant here, and I'm not a token anything."

"No? Open your eyes; what they'll do to others, they'll eventually do to you. I knew this place was dodgy and I shouldn't have stayed. I shouldn't be surprised to find myself canned like this, but... I am." The wobble in Nell's voice surprised her, but for once she wasn't capable of controlling her tone or projecting an assured face.

"Oh, babe..." Eamonn said, crossing the room to put his arms around her. Nell flinched and stiffened, and he looked at her in dismay, his arms dropping to his sides.

"You can't hug me right now," she muttered. "I refuse to cry in this hellhole, and a kind touch right now would break me. Just let me tough it out 'til I get out the door, all right?"

He raised his hands in a helpless gesture, then nodded and turned to Melody. "You can leave. I'll escort Nell out, and you can tell Uncle Tommy that I'm not coming back, either."

"I can't. I have to see her off the premises," Melody said, having the grace to look slightly embarrassed.

"Then be helpful, would you? What would she have that she'd need to take?" Eamonn gave Melody the sort of look that a rock star would give an incompetent roadie.

"A purse? Do you have a purse, honey?" The woman's voice was almost kind.

"I'm not your honey," Nell snapped, but she opened the desk drawer where she'd kept her purse since she'd moved to this office. Then she remembered her tea and dug it out of the bottom drawer. "That's it, I think." *Think. I can't think.* Everything felt numb, surreal.

"I'll carry your box," Eamonn said, taking it. "Hold my hand? I want to show them all how lucky I am to be with you, even just to walk out for the last time."

She remembered telling him that she didn't want to be anyone's under-the-table affair. It was rather adorable of him to get up and wave that flag at a time like this; it made the walk of shame hurt a little bit less. "Okay. Let's do this." She let him take her hand, his touch unexpectedly warm – or maybe her hands were just cold. She felt cold, inasmuch as she was feeling anything at all.

One foot in front of the other, chin high. Eamonn's hand around hers gave her strength. Word had spread; curious and dismayed faces peered out of offices, and people passing in the hall stopped and turned to look, sympathy warring with an apparent fear of contamination. There were a few people Nell might have wanted to say goodbye to, but she couldn't go looking for them, and she couldn't think of what she'd say anyway.

They walked through the reception area, where Lila looked troubled as she waved goodbye. "I'll miss you, Nell," the receptionist offered with a weak smile.

"No, you won't," Nell said, feeling tired. "But that's okay." At Lila's nonplussed look, she shrugged. *Why pretend?* Eamonn pushed open one side of the heavy glass double doors, and Nell passed through the Wildforest Vacations office entryway for the last time. Then she turned back and called to Lila, "I'm taking your advice, though. Just so you know."

Lila's eyes shot to Eamonn and she giggled, cheerfulness restored to her face. "Have fun, then. Take care, Nell. Bye, Easy!"

In the elevator, he held her. Just held her, as he pushed the P button to take them to the parking level. "I have my bike here today. Are you okay to ride with me? You'll hold on?"

"You don't have to take me home. I'll be fine," she told him, pushing herself away from the comfort of his arms as the elevator doors opened.

"Fine or not, I'm not just going to put you on the bus."

Nell blinked at him in the dim light of the parking garage. "Don't you have to go back up there?" She tried to remember what he'd said to them as he was walking her out, but it all seemed to blur in her memory and she only had the haziest sense of how the previous half-hour had unfolded.

He chuckled. "I think you might have missed one small fact about me, babe. I don't *need* that job. Uncle Tommy thought it would be good for me to do something with my days while I figured my next steps out, and I agreed because Mom wanted me to and I honestly wasn't doing anything much else." They reached his bike and he took the two helmets out of the top box, holding the spare out to her. "Ride with me?"

She didn't have it in her to push him away. Why not get a lift home? A little bit of speed and thrill on the back of a bike might blow the cobwebs out of her mind. "Fine." She took the helmet and put it on while he transferred her things into the top box and kicked the empty cardboard box into a corner. And when she settled herself behind him on the big motorcycle and wrapped her arms around his waist, the world felt a little less dark.

The last time she'd been on his bike, she'd been focused on not getting close to him. This time, she snuggled into his back and let herself savor the feeling of having his hips wedged between her thighs atop the smooth purr of the motor. In all the mess – the humiliation of walking out with her cardboard box and everyone staring, the sudden financial vulnerability, the sick fear of losing her apartment and being unable to pay for training if she didn't find work soon, and the anger that she hadn't been able to protect Jessalyn and had lost her own position for it anyway – it couldn't be wrong to take comfort in holding close to Eamonn's fine body for a short while, could it? Just for the ride home. And maybe the night, if he'd stay? Her guts cramped in visceral, achy need. *No more waiting.*

Unexpectedly, Eamonn turned down a side street and pulled over. They were nowhere Nell recognized as being part of her route home. Still astride the bike, he pulled his helmet off and gestured for her to do the same. "I was thinking," he said, turning his head to look at her over his shoulder. "If I take you back to your place, you'll just worry, right?" Then his voice deepened, and his eyes met hers with unmistakable desire. "So, you wanna come home with me instead?"

"You're asking me to stay the night with you?" she clarified, as the urgency inside her turned into a swarm of fiery butterflies.

"Yeah. Let me be your distraction."

She nodded slowly. *I want to have the whole night,* he'd said, *at least the first time, and I want you to walk like you've been well fucked the next day.*

And the way he was looking at her now told her he meant to give that his best shot. "Okay."

"Good. Helmet on and hold tight. I'm going to go fast."

She locked her arms around him, letting the adrenaline wash through her as he pushed off and picked up speed. The big bike hugged the road and screamed around corners, faster than Nell had ever experienced on the back of a motorcycle. Did he mean to give her a thrill, or was he just eager to get to their destination? Either way, it made her heart pound as the air whipped around them and she felt the muted thunder of the engine and Eamonn's masterful control of all that speed and power.

On a tree-lined street with modern brick townhouses and gated driveways, they slowed. One of the gates opened, the wrought-iron halves sliding apart on tracks in the pavement, and Eamonn turned the bike into the driveway, coming to a stop in front of the garage door that was slowly rising. "If you want to hop off, I'll just roll in here and park, then I can take you inside properly through the front door. Makes a better first impression than the laundry room, you know?"

She looked around as he put his motorbike away – it was a nice street. Capitol Hill wasn't an overly fancy neighborhood, but these townhouses were maybe a dozen years old and beautifully maintained, definitely in the three-million-dollar range. She wasn't sure what she'd expected his home to be like – perhaps a Playboy mansion or some sort of rock-and-roll frat house – but it wasn't this quietly elegant place.

"There. Come on," he said, and took her hand, leading her up a few steps at the side of the driveway to reach the gleaming black front door with its small brass knocker and keyless entry deadbolt. He punched in the code and turned the knob, snickering. She looked at him with a curious lift of her eyebrows. "The code is sixty-nine sixty-nine," he explained. "Easy to remember."

"Oh, grow up." But she laughed. *So typical.*

As he pushed the door open, revealing an expanse of hardwood floor, a thought seemed to strike him. "Humor me?" he asked, sounding amused. Nell nodded her assent, waiting to see what he wanted. "I'm going to lift you." And that split second of warning was enough to keep her from going fully into self-defense mode as he scooped her up in his arms to carry her over the threshold.

"Put me down," she told him. "I don't like being picked up." She'd instinctively taken a solid grip on the back of his jacket collar as an anchor point, and actively considered moving into a choke hold instead if he didn't put her down right away.

"I'm not going to drop you," he said, laughing.

"I don't care." And then she *did* slide her hand around to grab the front of his collar so she could put some pressure on the side of his neck with her forearm.

"Ow." He set her on her feet, only a few paces inside the house, with the front door still open. "That was supposed to be fun."

She gave him a hard look. "Yes. If I thought you were actually trying to hurt me, you'd be incapacitated at this point. But I asked you to put me down."

"Yes, ma'am." And he snapped to attention and bowed, just as she'd taught him. Kidding around, but also with a hint of an actual apology behind it, and definite admiration. "Fuck me, your ninja skills are sexy, woman," he muttered, turning to close the door. "Anyway, welcome to my home. You want a glass of wine? Beer? Or tea, or I've got Perrier or lemonade."

Nell reached instinctively for her pocket, for the phone she no longer had. *Can't even check the time.* "It's probably not four o'clock yet."

"So? If you want a glass of wine now, you've had a hell of a day and more than earned it. Merlot?"

She sighed. "Yes, please."

He waved toward the furniture around the fireplace in the front room – a pair of green suede loveseats faced each other across a glass coffee table, masculine and solid. "Make yourself comfortable."

"Thanks." She chose one of the loveseats and sat down, cross-legged with her feet tucked up, as though she were on a mat rather than a couch.

He cocked his head at her, eyeing the way she sat, all knees and elbows and nothing to snuggle up to. "You've still got your prickles out. I'm sorry." He crossed to a dark wooden cabinet against the far wall and opened it to reveal a fully stocked bar and wine rack.

"Well, what were you thinking?" she asked. "Did you really expect picking me up would end well?"

That made him smile. "I don't know. I just thought of carrying you inside and right upstairs to bed, all romantic, like *Gone with the Wind* or something."

"Apart from the whole movie being problematic, you do realize that when Rhett carries Scarlett up the stairs in *Gone with the Wind*, he's explicitly intending to force himself on her, right?"

Eamonn handed Nell a glass of wine, looking nonplussed. "Fuck me, no, I thought it was supposed to be all passionate and stuff. I've only ever seen a clip. So – totally *not* romantic. Got it." He stood there, holding his glass of wine. He looked at it, then at her. "Well, cheers."

She held up her glass and clinked it against his. "Cheers." When he sat down on the other loveseat, facing her, she grimaced. "Mood-killer, that's me."

"Oh, babe, not at all." He stretched out his legs and took a sip of his wine, a small smile threatening to break out into full sunshine as he looked at her.

"You're *amused*?" she asked, stunned. "Do you *like* it when I go into self-defense mode on you, or something?"

He nodded slowly, his eyes intense, and she knew before he spoke that his voice would be thick and deep with arousal. "I find it incredibly sexy that you can make me behave if I get out of line. I wouldn't try to trigger you on purpose, I swear, but it doesn't turn me off at all."

An uncomfortable thought struck her. "I have to ask – is it a kink thing? Do you like being hurt, or something?"

He shook his head, not even remotely offended by the question. "I don't enjoy pain. I can tolerate it, like getting a tattoo or playing a concert injured, but... definitely not my thing. You?"

"I don't think I could voluntarily let someone hurt me. I've got a pretty strong instinct to defend myself."

That made him chuckle. "I'd noticed. Ninja woman, I've found it far too easy to have my way with anyone I wanted, and I hope like hell they were all as willing as they seemed at the time. You make me think; you make me listen. You demand respect, and I don't know why that's hot, but it is."

Eamonn's words washed over Nell, soothing balm to her heart after the humiliation of being fired. She sipped her wine and let some of the tension go. "I didn't want to like you, but I kind of do," she told him, remembering what she'd thought of him when they first met, surprised at how much her opinion of him had changed.

"Enough to go to bed with me?" he asked idly, his voice so deadpan casual that she took a sharper look at him and realized he wasn't relaxed at all. He seemed on edge, his lounging pose not consistent with the taut muscles she now noticed.

"Are you... nervous?"

Instead of denying it, he blew out a long breath and then raised his hands in a *what can I say* gesture. "I don't want to ruin this," he admitted.

"It's just sex. You make sure I come, I make sure you come, it'll be all right." Nell couldn't suppress a bubble of laughter at the surprise on Eamonn's face. "What? I'm practical about these things." She stood up, looked at the rest of the wine in her glass and chugged it down, then carefully set the empty glass on the coffee table before walking around it to stand in front of him. "You want to show me your bedroom?"

He gazed up at her, and the world went still for a moment. She saw his throat move as he swallowed. "Now?"

"Yes, now."

He reached up and caught one of her hands in both of his. She thought maybe he'd pull her down onto his lap or something, but he only stroked her palm with his thumb for a moment, a subtle caress that sent tiny shivers of chemistry tingling all over her.

Then he stood up, and since she'd been nearly leaning over him on the couch, that put him inside the boundaries of her comfort zone, close enough that if she leaned forward even a tiny bit, she'd be pressed up against him. But she stood, straight-backed, leaving that tiny inch of space between them, waiting. Her pulse raced.

"I promised you the whole night," he murmured. "Are you ready for that?"

"Bring it on. If you can make me forget this crappy day, I'll be impressed."

"Challenge accepted." He grinned. "I'm going to blow your mind, Nella-bella." Then he settled his free hand on the small of her back and pulled her gently against him, closed that last tiny gap between them, and bent his head to kiss her.

He tasted of wine. This was no hesitant lip to lip kiss – there was nothing gradual or coy about it. No pretense that they were going anywhere except to bed, and soon. Her mouth was open to taste him before he'd even got there, and his tongue plunged deep in a sensual caress that she met with glorious urgency. His hand slid down to get an unrestrained feel of her butt, as he broke the kiss just enough to murmur, "Upstairs?"

Part of Nell wouldn't have cared at that point if he'd just bent her over the sofa, right there in the front room with the drapes open, but with some remaining shred of dignity, she managed to say, "Okay. Upstairs."

With a last squeeze and a murmur of pleasure, Eamonn took his hand off her backside and put a little space between them, but his other hand had never let go of hers, and he didn't release her fingers now. He tugged her toward the stairs. "After you."

"This 'ladies first' stuff isn't–"

He shook his head, a wicked grin spreading across his face. "Honestly, I want to look at your ass while you go up the stairs. All right?" He was right behind as she climbed the steps, close enough to still be holding her hand. She could feel his eyes fixed on her, so she put a bit of a wiggle in her hips and laughed out loud when she heard an admiring muttered "Fuck me" in response. It felt good, to have him looking at her like that.

She reached the top of the stairs and stopped, looking around at the small hallway, wondering which of the four closed doors led to the bedroom. With a gentle tug on her hand, Eamonn twirled her around to face him and then they were kissing again, even as he moved them to one of the doors and pushed it open.

His bedroom made her think of sunshine, with yellow walls and creamy curtains, and a sunburst patchwork quilt on a vast king-sized bed with an old-fashioned metal frame. "Are you still feeling cold?" he asked, releasing her and crossing to the gas fireplace opposite the foot of the bed. "I can turn this on."

"You're warming me up all right," she told him. "But I've never had sex in front of a fireplace. Might be nice."

He flipped the switch and an instant fire sprang to life behind the glass. "Come on, then." He leaned against the mantelpiece, waiting for her, one eyebrow cocked.

Suddenly, the expanse of bedroom carpet between them seemed miles wide. *It's just a bit of fun,* Nell reminded herself. *Two consenting adults scratching a mutual itch, no big deal.* But the tense anticipation running through her as she closed the distance between them was unusual, unlike anything she'd felt before. *Maybe it's the day I've had. Strange circumstances, and all that.*

She stepped into his personal space, hyperaware that she was putting herself within his reach. This wasn't a sparring ring, and yet, she had a clear sense of stepping inside his guard. He reached out and squeezed her shoulder before running his hand down her arm until he could take her hand in his. His grip was warm and comforting, with fingers callused from the strings of his instrument. "So, how d'you want it, then?" His voice sounded casual, but his gaze held a delicious intensity, pupils so dilated with desire that his eyes seemed dark rather than blue. "I know we've joked about you needing to be on top, but... is that something you need tonight? Or would you rather just lie back and let me take charge, or what?"

"I..." Nell drew in a deep breath, a little overwhelmed. *Sex is just sex, isn't it? We get naked and do the thing?* But she didn't like to be pinned down; she usually *did* find herself on top. And the thought of letting go of that, of having Eamonn's big body covering hers–it was too much: overwhelmingly sexy, and the mental image of it made her bite her lip to hold in a wanton sound, but... too much. "Yeah, I think I need to feel in control of things right now. On top would be good. If you don't mind."

That earned a soft chuckle from him, a husky, intimate laugh. "Either way is good for me, Nella-bella. I'll do whatever you need."

Her knees felt unaccountably weak at the offer. Wanting to deny it, to maintain the upper hand, she perched on the end of the bed and said, "Strip for me, rock god."

"Fuck me, you don't mess around, do you?" he muttered. "All right. Game on."

He took his phone from his pocket and fiddled with it for a minute before setting it down on the mantelpiece, a dirty grin on his face. Moments later, she realized what he was up to, as the opening to "Pour Some Sugar on Me" filled the room. He met her raised eyebrows with a wink and swaggered across the room to take up a spot in front of her, close enough to reach out and touch, just as the lyrics kicked in. He started to move, completely unselfconscious as he danced, taking evident pleasure in the sensuality of it. She tried not to stare at the thrust and grind of his hips, and then his hands went to the hem of his t-shirt and he began to work it upward.

She could feel her face getting hot. "I didn't really think you'd–"

"You asked, babe. Just enjoy it." Inch by inch, to the rhythm of the music, he uncovered the inked skin of his abdomen, taut and lean, with a fine trail of dark gold hair running down into his jeans. He kept going until the t-shirt was up around his shoulders, giving her a good look at the tattooed angel and how extremely good he was at rhythmic movement. Then, as his face disappeared under the fabric for a moment, he put a little extra bump and grind into his hips, drawing her attention to the evident arousal there, straining the denim.

The t-shirt hit the floor, and he was grinning at her, all too clearly enjoying his performance. He clasped his hands behind his head and did a smooth body roll, showing off his control and muscles. It was unabashedly sexual – a promise, a demonstration. *He's owning this. Reveling in it, even.* And he really did have a spectacular body to show off.

He kicked off his boots, then brought his hands to his belt, playing with the buckle before slowly unbuckling it and sliding the leather free, stripper-dancing with it like he'd been on the wrong kind of stage all his life.

The belt dropped to the floor and Eamonn thumbed the button at the waistband of his jeans as if to ask, *are you ready for this?* Nell felt her mouth go dry. She nodded.

He slowly unbuttoned his fly and shimmied the denim down his thighs, revealing black boxer briefs that left little to the imagination. *Very nice.* He gave his hips a little pump to the music, pushed the jeans down farther – stopped with everything bunched around his knees. Their eyes met. *There's no graceful way to remove tight jeans while standing up,* Nell thought, unable to suppress a bubble of laughter at his predicament. So sexy and slick, but those jeans weren't coming off easily.

"A stripper wouldn't wear jeans like this," Eamonn muttered as the song came to an end. He came and sat beside her on the end of the bed, skinning out of his pants and socks and kicking them away. "Now you're overdressed," he said, putting a hand on her thigh. His palm felt hot against her leg. She felt as though, with the slightest slip of her self-control, she could burn up like a parched forest in fire season.

"I despise work clothes. Business flipping casual," she said, starting to unbutton her blouse.

"Want me to do that?" he offered.

"I've got it." Her voice sounded a touch firmer than she'd intended. *I'm in charge of how this will unfold; I refuse to get swept away.* And his fingers fiddling with buttons down her front, near but not quite touching her breasts, felt like handing control of the situation back to him. Trying for a lighter tone, she said, "You looked like you were enjoying that. Dancing."

"I like dancing," he agreed. His hand stroked her thigh, and she almost squirmed.

"And the stripper moves?"

"Choreography for music videos. You didn't see the one for 'Human Lollipop'?" He stood up and did another body roll, close enough that she could pretty much count it as a lap dance. Cupped himself and gave his erection a stroke through his underwear, his eyes steady on her with overwhelming desire. "Dancing for *you*, lovely..." He shook his head. "You've got me so hard, I can't think about anything else. It's taking everything I've got not to throw you down on my bed and fuck you senseless."

"You couldn't throw me anywhere," Nell reminded him, refusing to acknowledge the thrill his words gave her.

"I know. I'm just telling you I want you." He was already standing between her thighs, and he cocked an eyebrow in question before he rested his hands lightly on her shoulders and bent his head, giving her plenty of time and room to evade his kiss if she wished. But she lifted her mouth to his, instantly delighting in the pressure of his lips against hers, opening to his tongue and licking into his mouth in turn.

A rush of heat washed over her, stripping away all the hesitation as his mouth moved to her ear, her neck. *Now. I need this, him, now.* She fumbled open the last couple of buttons to get rid of her blouse and he helped her push it off her shoulders – then he murmured something inaudible as he ran a finger around the scooped front of her athletic bra. "I don't do lacy lingerie," she said, thinking he might be less than thrilled by the plain black spandex.

"You don't need to." He cupped her breasts and stroked his thumbs across her nipples through the stretchy fabric, causing her to arch her back and lean into his touch like a cat being petted. And then he was watching her disentangle herself from her bra, and the look on his face reminded her that this was the first time he'd seen her bare. "Fuck me, you have the prettiest tits I've ever seen," he told her, lowering himself to his knees in front of her so he could use his mouth, licking and sucking and gently nipping until she was squirming and moaning in a haze of pleasure. She barely heard him when he said, "Stand up for a second, babe. I want to take your pants off, all right?" But she felt his hands at her waist, undoing the annoying hook-and-bar fastener of her pants and lowering the zipper, and then his hands on her hips, encouraging her to stand.

It was only when she stepped out of the pants that she realized he'd slid her underwear down too, and he was still kneeling in front of her, staring at the triangle of hair between her legs as though she had some kind of heavenly dessert there for him to eat.

In a strained voice, he said, "I'm dying to taste you – may I?" And his hands were guiding her to sit again, to spread her legs wide for him.

But that was altogether too intimate.

"I don't need foreplay; I just want you inside me," she said, pulling away from the terrifying temptation, scooting herself backwards toward the middle of the bed where she got onto her knees, a stronger position. And he still knelt on the floor at the foot of the bed, gazing up at her in such blatant admiration that she arched her back and stuck out her chest proudly because for once she felt gorgeously sexy and desirable and fabulous. *The prettiest tits I've ever seen,* he'd said. "Come and lie down so I can ride you, all right?"

He groaned and chuckled at the same time, and complied, getting up and stretching out on the bed beside her, still wearing his boxer briefs. He hitched his thumbs into the waistband, preparing to remove them, then paused. "Aww, gorgeous, I'm afraid I won't last long enough for you – just *looking* at you has me almost to the edge."

"What happened to your big talk about going all night?"

"Oh, I'm good for that, never doubt it, but I might have to explode and reload."

"Fair enough. Condom?" Nell took refuge in practicality. Prophylactics had never embarrassed her, and it was easier to think about safety than to let her mind dwell on the beautiful tattooed body and shredding self-control of the man stretched out in front of her.

"Ah, right." He twisted to reach the bedside table drawer, giving her a full view of the angelic wingspan wrapped around his ribs. He snagged a foil packet and tossed it through the air to her, then lifted his hips and removed his underwear.

"Dude," said Nell. "You're freaking huge."

Eamonn grinned. "I think you can handle it, ninja woman." But he sounded breathless, and when she placed a hand at the base of his cock, about to put the condom on, his whole body trembled slightly.

"Put your hands on the headboard," she told him.

"Wha–?" But he obeyed, reaching up to grip the metal spindles above his head.

She looked deep into his eyes and said, "Self-control."

"It's... not usually a problem for me." His words came slowly, his cocky façade slipping so that she could see how shaken he was by his reaction to her. "You're like a lightning strike, babe. So electric..."

I feel it too. "Chemistry's a good thing," she said lightly. *Maybe sometimes too much of a good thing.* It wasn't comfortable to feel so overwhelmed. "Now, breathe." His hips jerked as she rolled the condom on, and she placed a steadying hand on his taut abdomen, suppressing a wild desire to lick him all over – they were both too far gone for that. "Keep your hands on that headboard. Here we go." She swung a leg over and straddled him, reached down to adjust the angle of entry, and eased down onto him.

Instinct took over. Her whole world shrank down to nothing but the feel of him inside her. *So big. So full. So freaking amazing.* Her inner muscles clenched, and he groaned, thrusting up to meet her as she rode him, beyond conscious thought.

She hadn't expected any magic to happen – figured she'd get hers on the next round – but the blissful friction spiraled into fireworks out of nowhere, flowing over her, blinding and dazzling her. She was barely aware of Eamonn's shout of delight, only that his arms came up to wrap around her as she collapsed onto him, that his face was buried against her neck with small nips and kisses in the aftermath.

She rolled off him, sprawling, limp. Beside her, she could feel his small movements as he dealt with the condom. "Bathroom's just there, if you want to..." he said, his voice slow and sleepy.

"I will, in a minute... just... so comfortable..."

His big body was warm and firm against her back, and the sheets were silky and soft and clean. In a minute, she would go freshen up, she told herself. There would be more pleasure, a whole night of fun. Thoroughly relaxed in a way she hadn't felt for a long time, if ever, she let her eyes drift closed. *In a minute...*

♥

She stood in her apartment, holding a cardboard box full of bills and alarm clocks, watching as Tommy and Lila and her landlord carried her possessions away. Jessalyn panhandled in the street outside, an infant car seat beside her, covered with a blanket. Then, in a flash, Nell was banging on the locked door of her dojang, and all the students and instructors inside ignored her because she had no money to pay for tournaments and training.

Then she woke, shaking and sobbing, to a moment of total disorientation at not being in her own bed – and not alone.

"Hey, now, it's all right," murmured a sleepy male voice in the dark. "Bad dream?"

Eamonn. His house, his bed.

She felt the mattress shift as he reached for the bedside lamp, and then it clicked on, with warm golden light that felt momentarily too bright after the darkness. *I'm fine,* she wanted to say, but the words wouldn't come.

"You want to tell me about it?" he asked.

"No." She curled over on her side, away from him. And she wasn't going to say anything more, but she found herself muttering, "They've taken everything away from me."

"Have they?"

He didn't ask who *they* were. His question was infuriating. "You wouldn't understand," she snarled, and was horrified to hear that her voice sounded close to tears.

"Wouldn't I?" His quiet words were so laced with bitterness and hurt that she uncurled herself, flopping onto her back to look at him in surprise. He lay on his side, propped up on one elbow, looking down at her as though she hadn't a clue. "You lost a job you hated."

"Hate's a waste of energy," Nell said, even as she vividly remembered reciting *I hate my job* in her head and biting her lip to not react to yet another inane rule or requirement.

"Whatever you want to call it, then. You were fired by my ass of an uncle from a job you won't miss, and you can find something better in a heartbeat." He paused, as if deciding whether to keep talking. When he did continue, his voice was so low that she almost couldn't hear the words. "I was kicked out of something I loved, my whole world, and it's irreplaceable."

How do I even respond to that? She took a breath. "But you–"

"Yes, I could find another band needing a bassist – or guitarist or keyboards – or start my own. Yes, I could easily get work as a session musician. But it wouldn't be *them*; it wouldn't be Smidge." He clearly hadn't meant to say so much, and fell silent.

She didn't think he'd accept a hug, and she wasn't the hugging kind anyway, but she laid a hand on his shoulder to offer some kind of comfort, suppressing a surge of sensual awareness at the skin-to-skin reminder that they were both naked under the covers. *We have all night.* "I bet they miss your talent. You couldn't be easy to replace."

He grimaced. "Depends. Maybe they wanted something new. Bass drives the whole sound of the band, deep down, so if you want to make a change..."

"Well, you're right about one thing; I'm out of a crap job with unethical people. And I didn't mean to compare that to... I'm just afraid of losing my apartment before I can find something new, and... I don't know how I'll pay for my training. But those are small things."

"You teach martial arts, don't you? Surely they pay you?"

She snorted. "Most of what I make from that goes to my own training fees and gear and tournaments. It's not a cheap sport." Even as she spoke, she realized that what she spent on her classes and competitions each month might seem like pocket change to him. *Different worlds.* And all at once, she'd had enough of this awkward conversation, half small talk and half deep feelings. She slid out of the bed, deliberately not looking for anything to cover herself. *I'm no Barbie doll, but I earned these muscles. And he's seen all I've got, anyway.* "Be right back." She could feel his eyes on her as she crossed the room.

Just as she was closing the door to the bathroom, she heard him say, "Spare toothbrushes are in the bottom right drawer. Help yourself. And there are clean towels in the cabinet."

Well. She pulled open the bottom right drawer and found a handful of brightly-colored toothbrushes sealed in plastic sleeves, each one saying HAPPY SMILES WITH DR. BETRAN and a phone number, which gave her an inward chuckle of approval. *He acts like such a rock star, but he trots off to the dentist for his checkup on the regular.* It felt good to be able to clean her teeth properly – much better than rubbing toothpaste on with a fingertip. And because he'd mentioned clean towels, she decided to take a two-minute shower, even though it was the middle of the night.

She'd barely stepped into the hot spray when she heard a knock, and Eamonn called through the door, "You want company in that shower, babe? 'Cause I could use a wash too."

"Shower sex is always a disaster," Nell called back, but her body was already responding, eager for his company, sensitized for more than shower water.

"Not if you do it right," he said, his voice loaded with promise.

"Oh, come in, then."

chapter 9

ELL WOKE TO AN UNFAMILIAR RINGTONE, THEN Eamonn's voice answering his phone.

He lay behind her, big spoon to her little spoon, his warmth and scent enveloping her, one arm snuggled around her waist with his hand resting just under her breasts. *And morning wood. Oh, very much so.* She blinked, impressed despite herself. If she was counting right, he'd managed three more rounds after the first one, and she'd seen stars at least five times – maybe six, if the last time counted as two rather than one extended bout of ecstasy, peaking and ebbing and peaking again. *Surely he's not ready for more...*

"I'm fine," he was saying on the phone. "No, I'm at home." He paused, listening – she could hear the faint sound of a voice talking on the other end of the line. "Yes, I *did* have to, Mom! ... No, I couldn't. I know you love Uncle Tommy, but he was being a tool."

Nell smiled to herself, trying to imagine the other side of the conversation. Eamonn sounded affectionate, even if slightly exasperated. Evidently, his mother had heard something about the events of the previous day from her brother. *Tommy.* A complex jumble of feelings bubbled up inside Nell at the reminder of her lost job and the string of decisions and events that had led to it.

"Yeah, she's here," Eamonn said. *Me?* That got Nell's full attention. "Oh, you don't need to do that– ... No, really, Mom, don't come over." She flipped over to stare at him in horror, hoping he was kidding or something. "Mom! She doesn't even drink coffee!" he said into the phone, but she could see the laughter dancing in his eyes and knew he'd already lost the argument. "Sure, but see if they have coconut milk. I don't know if she can't drink dairy or just likes coconut milk better, but–" His mother evidently interrupted him, saying something that made him smile and redden a bit. "Whatever," he muttered, and then, "I love you too, Mom."

He ended the call and put his phone down, grinning rather ruefully at Nell.

His mother was coming over, apparently. *This shouldn't be happening,* she wanted to tell him. *I agreed to a night of amazing sex, and I got it, but I have no desire to meet your mother.* It was bad enough that she knew his uncle. *Couldn't you have just told her no?* Still, there was something sweet about the way he'd spoken on the phone, something about his face as he told his mom he loved her – she couldn't be angry at him for that. "Coconut milk tastes better in tea," she said, because she couldn't find words for anything else, torn between an impulse to escape before his mother arrived and a ridiculously sentimental pleasure that he kept her minor preferences in mind.

He nodded, as though he'd heard what she hadn't said. "My mother doesn't hear *no* very well. It's a groupie thing. The serious ones do whatever it takes to get where they want to be."

"Okay, well, I don't think I need to meet her." Nell whipped out of the bed and gathered up her clothes, bolting into the bathroom to get dressed. Only after she'd locked the door and stepped into her underpants did she realize that she hadn't managed to pick up her bra with the rest of her things. *Crap.* She cracked the door open. "Eamonn? Could you possibly pass me–"

"This?" Standing in the middle of the bedroom, still completely and beautifully bare, he held up her black sports bra, twitching it lazily back and forth. "You don't need it. Go without."

Her hand slipped off the doorknob, letting the door swing open. "You've got to be kidding. Please? I need to get dressed and get out of here."

"Just put your shirt on." He gave her a panty-melting smile, one that said last night wasn't enough and he'd like to have her up against the wall right this minute. "Go braless."

Nell shook her head, refusing to be swayed. "All I have is my work blouse – thin flipping rayon. I am *not* walking around with my headlights on to give you a thrill."

Eamonn laughed. "I could lend you a t-shirt?"

She took a step toward him. "Don't make me come and get my bra."

"That could be fun–" he began, then broke off at the dirty look she gave him. "Whoa, okay. It's all yours." He tossed it to her, and she caught it without breaking eye contact.

"You should have to do pushups for giving me that kind of sass," she muttered. "And put some underwear on, already."

He cocked one eyebrow at her, but took a clean pair of boxer briefs from a drawer and put them on. "I'll do pushups for you," he said with a grin. "Or we could do them together. Morning workout?"

So tempting, but... "No time. I need to be gone already." She finished buttoning her blouse and looked around for her socks.

"Running away?" he asked, his back to her as he rummaged through a dresser drawer, choosing a t-shirt.

She froze. "No." *Yes.*

"Stay for breakfast. Mom's bringing doughnuts." His voice was slightly muffled as he pulled the t-shirt over his head.

"Seriously?" *Doughnuts aren't breakfast. I don't want to meet your mother. It's not about running away.*

"I never joke about doughnuts." He turned to face her; she read the words emblazoned across his chest and burst out laughing.

"Eye candy?"

"What can I say? This shirt is awesome." He smoothed it over his torso, giving a flirty and deliberate impression of self-pleasure.

But she wouldn't be distracted. "I don't like being railroaded into having breakfast with anyone, especially..." *Your mother, when I've just had spectacular sex with you all night. Who's also Tommy Baxter's sister, when he fired me yesterday, and I'm still all kinds of bitter about it.*

Eamonn nodded. "I can see that. This... wasn't planned. I guess Uncle Tommy got in Mom's ear about something, and now she wants to meet you. I'll call you a car if you want to be gone when she gets here, but – Nella-bella, I'm not ready for you to leave." He picked up his phone from the bedside table and looked at her, eyebrows raised, waiting.

She couldn't tell him to make the call. Somehow, by giving her the choice instead of resisting and insisting, he'd made it impossible for her to go. "I don't run away," she said – it had nothing to do with him wanting more of her company or the warm feeling his admission had given her.

"Speaking of mothers," he said, "I should have asked before: is there anyone you want to call? Family, I mean? You can use my phone."

Nell shook her head. "My mother lives in Australia with my stepfather now. It won't even be dawn there yet, and I don't know her current number by heart anyway."

"You got a father?"

She thought of her dad, smiling in his crisp uniform, on his way off to save the world again. *Chin up, Nells. You can take whatever the world throws at you. I'll see you in a while.* "He's an Air Force flight surgeon. I'll email him when I get home and we'll video chat when he's able."

The doorbell chimed several times in succession, and was quickly followed by the sound of the front door opening and a woman's voice calling out, "Hope you're decent, darlings!"

"Be right down, Mom – don't come up!" Eamonn bellowed back, then turned to Nell with a hesitant half-grin. "She knows the key code. For when I'm away on tour, and such." He held out a hand for her to take. "Come and meet her. She's... oh, probably not much like any mom you've ever met."

Maybe his words should have prepared her as they descended the stairs and turned toward the kitchen; still, she wasn't expecting the thigh-high white leather boots or the floaty silk chiffon tunic that probably *was* vintage Zandra Rhodes but put a lot of well-maintained skin on display. A vivid turquoise manicure, giant sunglasses, and feathered blonde 80s hair completed the astounding first impression Nell had of Amanda Joy Yarrow. *This woman does not look old enough to have a son Eamonn's age,* she thought wildly.

A gurgle of amused laughter greeted her. "Oh, I was only seventeen when I had him, honey – don't judge!" the older woman said, as though Nell had spoken aloud.

Honey? "My name is Nell, Ms. Yarrow."

"Of course, honey – I'm so pleased to meet you! Call me Mandy. Here's your tea; I got you a London Fog with coconut milk, so it's a tea latte, really. I hope that suits you." And Nell found a warm to-go cup pressed into her hands, steaming and deliciously fragrant with the sharp bergamot of Earl Grey and the sweetness of vanilla.

"I see where you get the pet-names habit from," Nell muttered to Eamonn.

He just shrugged and grinned at her. "*Honey* means Mom likes you; *darling* is being generic or sociable; *sugar* is a storm front warning."

Overhearing the last bit, Mandy Yarrow chuckled, seeming good-humored and not at all offended. "That's right, and if I have to resort to *sweet thing,* I'm probably contemplating murder. You want to sit out on the patio?" She gestured toward the French doors at the back of the townhouse.

"You and Nell go on out with the doughnuts, Mom. I'll bring some plates and napkins."

"That's my Easy." Mandy snagged the box of pastries from the kitchen counter and headed outside, somehow managing to juggle it and her coffee and still open the doors before Nell could even offer to help. She followed.

At the back of the townhouse, a tiny but very private patio was surrounded by tall fences, further screened by vines and bamboo. A few strategically placed ornamental trees and pots of colorful flowers completed the illusion of a postage-stamp oasis. Mandy placed the doughnuts on the coffee table and settled herself on the lounger, leaving the loveseat for Nell and Eamonn.

"You... even *you* call him Easy?" Nell asked, sitting down. It didn't seem like a nickname a mother would use.

"Oh, heavens, yes. My foolish boy likes to let people think it's just a band name brought on by his reputation with women, but *we* called him Easy long before he met Smidge or any of that. Before he'd ever been with a woman, far 's I know." Mandy propped her sunglasses up on top of her voluminous teased bangs and leaned forward, contemplating the dozen doughnuts in the box before selecting a Boston cream. "Have one," she said, before biting into hers.

Awkward. Nell took a sip of her tea. Her mind balked at picturing a teenage Eamonn Yarrow, and failed utterly at imagining him a virgin. Surely he was born confident and cocky? Or maybe life on an endless rock tour had given him that. "Why's he called Easy, then?" she asked.

"Oh, Mom, you're not going to tell her that old story, are you?" Eamonn said, coming out to the patio with a stack of melamine plates and a roll of paper towels.

His mother gave him a smile that was a mirror of his own – anyone could see he'd got his well-formed mouth and wide smile from her, along with his coloring. "I know you've got an image to maintain, love, but you don't mind Nell hearing where you got your name, do you?"

"Guess not." He handed his mother a plate for her partially eaten doughnut and passed one to Nell before plunking the paper towel roll down on the table next to the box. "You going to have a doughnut, babe?" The way he looked at the pastries told Nell that he was hungry, and it occurred to her that he might be waiting for her to have her choice before he took one.

"I..." *Doughnuts aren't breakfast. I'm an athlete,* she thought, *I shouldn't be eating any of this.* But they did look and smell delicious. The bigger problem was that she didn't want to inadvertently take his favorite one.

"Next time you sleep over, I promise I'll have something healthy for your breakfast," he said softly, as he sat down beside her.

Next time? "It's not that. I don't want to take whichever one your mom got for you."

Mandy shook her head, clearly amused. "Don't worry, honey, he likes all the jelly-filled ones. Take your pick." There were four jelly doughnuts in the box, along with some crullers and dipped and glazed ones.

I can't even choose.

Eamonn put a reassuring hand on her thigh. "You liked the raspberry one I brought you the other morning, yeah?" When she nodded, he picked one from the box and put it on her plate, then took another for himself, both of them oozing dark raspberry jelly. "I knew Mom would get two, just in case. I do like all the jelly ones, but raspberry's the best." He bit into his pastry with such pure sensual pleasure that Nell had to look away.

She turned to Mandy. "You were about to tell me where Eamonn got his nickname?" *Any distraction is good, even if it's not a story he wants to brag about.*

"Oh, yes. Well, you know he's been working as a musician since his early teens, right?" The way Mandy said this implied that it was something everyone knew, and indeed, when Nell had eventually searched online for information about him, it was plainly public knowledge that he'd started his music career before he could drive or vote. "Wasn't in a garage or bar band, though. His first time on a real stage was with Mad Gilbert when they were opening for the Bad Luck Opals' *Dark Jewelry* tour – the guitarist they had at the time was a tool who couldn't hold his booze, and the dumbfuck was passed out cold at showtime. Gil knew Eamonn had been learning their songs and he just took the boy on stage with them like it was no big thing. You're maybe too young to remember, but it was a big-ass arena tour with all the usual pyrotechnics and shit. So, the Opals' guitar tech was watching with a few of us from the side of the stage, and after the first song, he turned to look at me and said, 'Damn, that takes balls, and he's making it look easy. Your boy has a gift, Mandy. *Easy!*' And the crew started calling him Easy after that, and eventually we all did."

"True story," said Eamonn, seeming faintly embarrassed. "At least, I didn't hear Ritchie say it, but I went onstage with Mad Gilbert and played the set without rehearsal, and that was the day they started calling me Easy." He laughed self-consciously and took a big bite of his doughnut.

Nell watched him out of the corner of her eye. She didn't want to embarrass him, but was unexpectedly blown away by what she'd just heard. She'd been in eighth grade when *Dark Jewelry* had come out and all the cool girls had posters of the Bad Luck Opals in their lockers, but she'd thought Mad Gilbert was cooler. And Eamonn had played with them. *I was fourteen the first time I got shoved in front of a crowd,* she remembered him saying. He hadn't mentioned it was in an arena, though – hardly the bar scene she'd pictured. "That's a great story," she said. "Why'd you let people think you got the name from..."

"Being a manwhore?" Eamonn finished when her words trailed off. "It fits. I just give people what they expect, what they want."

There was a hint of frost in Mandy's voice and expression as she asked, "And is there anything wrong with enjoying sex, as long as everyone involved is willing and clear about their expectations?"

It wasn't immediately obvious whether she was addressing Nell or Eamonn with that. *Oops! Sensitive point for an ex-groupie, maybe.* And then Nell couldn't help but wonder whether the older woman had fully retired from that pursuit. "Of course not," she hurried to say. "I didn't–"

"Sorry, Mom," Eamonn cut in. "Good times were had. No regrets." Nell wondered if he was repeating something his mother had told him in the past. A philosophy of life, a lesson learned? She picked up her untouched doughnut and bit into it.

The sweet deliciousness filled her mouth, and she suppressed a moan of pleasure. *So good.* She could feel Eamonn watching her eat, taking pleasure in her enjoyment of it. If his mother hadn't been there...

"Easy, love, do you think you could get me a glass of water?" Mandy asked.

"Sure thing." He got to his feet at once.

As soon as he'd vanished inside, she fixed her eyes on Nell, with an air of getting down to business at last. "You seem to like my son. You know Tommy Baxter is his uncle, right?"

"I no longer work for your brother, and he has nothing to do with how I feel about Eamonn," Nell said firmly.

Mandy's eyebrows rose. "Well, you're a confident one, aren't you? Tommy has it in his mind that you're planning to make a fuss about wrongful dismissal."

"I signed his waiver and took the severance. I'm sure he told you that."

"He's more concerned about a media circus."

That gave Nell cause to raise her own eyebrows. *A media circus?* "Even if I hadn't signed a non-disparagement thing, who would listen to me? I've got no platform."

"I think you've missed a key point about my son, honey." Mandy spoke with laughter in her voice now, and her eyes were kind, making Nell feel like she'd inadvertently given the right answer in an exam she hadn't prepared for. "He could give you a platform, and Tommy knows it."

"And apparently doesn't know a thing about *me*, for all the years I worked there. I'm a martial artist; integrity is my life. When I sign something, I honor the spirit as well as the letter of it – no matter how crappy the terms were. I'm not going to use Eamonn to work some kind of end-around on that."

"An end-around on what?" His voice startled her; he'd come back out to the patio on quiet feet, and she wasn't sure what he'd heard or how long he'd been standing behind her.

But Mandy looked satisfied. "I can tell Tommy you're not going down that road, then?"

And in some way, Nell understood. The older woman was defending her family, protecting her brother and making sure her son wasn't being used for his fame. That was fair. "Yes. But you might also ask him why he fired me, while you're at it." Understanding didn't mean sympathy. People needed to look at what they chose to defend. Perhaps Tommy would like to explain to his sister who'd had a baby at seventeen that women who got pregnant and women who tried to protect them weren't welcome under his management. Nell got to her feet. "I need to go. Nice to meet you, Mandy."

"What? No," Eamonn said. He was in the act of handing the glass he carried to his mother, and his hand jerked so that water slopped over the edge. "Nell, you can't–"

She raised her eyebrows at him. "You're going to try to stop me?" she asked drily.

"But–"

"I've got to shower, sort out my resume and get some job hunting started, and I'm teaching two classes tonight. I really do have to go," she told him.

He rubbed his hands against his thighs to get rid of the water droplets that had splashed him. "But I can't even call you," he said.

She smiled at that, and wondered if he'd always been the one to do the leaving. "Tomorrow's Sunday. I'll be at the Frog and Ball around five thirty. You can buy me a drink, all right?"

♥

Chin up, Nells. You can handle anything life throws at you. Her dad had taught her well, and her martial arts training reinforced it.

Once she'd recovered from the first shock of losing her job, she made a plan and set herself to coping with the situation. A quick workout, a hot shower, a protein shake, and a multivitamin tablet put her back on track within her body. She researched and prepared a dozen job applications – none of the opportunities were terribly exciting, but any of them would help pay her rent, and if she could only pick up one or two more teaching hours a week, she'd be able to make ends meet and keep training. But without a phone number, she was at a disadvantage. Who would hire someone with no phone?

Without a job, she figured she wouldn't be able to get an expensive new phone on an installment plan or as part of a contract – it would doubtless require payment up front. Every article on cheap phones and budget options pushed a different opinion, and Nell couldn't decide how far she dared dip into her savings or what features were truly necessary. Maybe a temporary option would do: there were virtual phone number apps that claimed she'd be able to make phone calls from her tablet for only a few dollars a month.

No one was going to be looking at job applications before Monday morning. *If I haven't made a decision about a phone by then, I'll sign up for a burner number to use 'til I get a job.*

She read and re-read her dad's email. *Those nuthatches couldn't find their ethics or their brains with two flashlights and a GPS tracker. I'll be home in a month and I'll take you out to dinner, and if you haven't found a job by then, I'll see what I can do. There's always the Service, you know.* "I'm not joining the Air Force, Dad," she muttered to herself. It would interfere with her training, and they'd want her to do things their way rather than her own. He knew that. But he'd always held it out as an option if she got desperate, and the mention of it was as familiar as him calling her *Nells* or calling people who'd displeased him *nuthatches* – a substitute curse-word for use in front of his daughter, something he'd never once slipped up on.

Her mother's email was predictable in a different way, offering airfare to Australia for a visit, as if running away would solve the problem. Of course, a change of scenery and sunshine and cocktail parties *had* solved Nell's mother's problems – she'd met Anthony – and she no doubt thought that if Nell would just come and meet some nice young Australian men, the same fix would occur. *Call me when you get your new phone,* she wrote.

Amy was up in Vancouver filming, but made a shocked face and sympathetic noises via video chat and promised to come over with a huge bottle of gin and a box of Cheese Nips as soon as she was back home. "You'll be okay, bestie! I've been unemployed or underemployed a million times, and it always works out."

Nell arrived at the Frog and Ball just after five o'clock – nearly half an hour before she'd told Eamonn she'd be there. To her profound dismay, he'd arrived ahead of her.

Crap. Not what I'd planned. She'd intended to sit at the bar, as usual, counting on the bartender's presence to keep the conversation on a not too personal track. Instead, he'd settled into one of the booths behind the pool table – as private as one could get in a drinking establishment. Before she could wrap her mind around a decision, a plan of action, he spotted her and stood up, his face brightening as he waved her over.

A couple of the sports-watching regulars looked up from their nachos as she made her way between the tables, and she nodded in brief acknowledgment as she passed. *Will they realize I'm here on a date?*

"Hey," said Eamonn, when she reached him. His arms were open, inviting a hug, and – without thinking about it – she stepped into his space and let him wrap himself around her. He murmured in her ear, "You came. I wasn't sure you would."

"I said I'd be here," she reminded him, tensing a little at the suggestion that she might not have kept her word. He must have felt her body stiffen because he immediately loosened his hug to let her pull away if she so chose. And for a split second, she wanted to stay in the lovely warmth of his arms, smelling his skin and soap. Then she pulled herself together and stepped back. "So, I'm here."

"Yeah, well, after Mom pushed her way in on us the other morning, I wouldn't have blamed you for bailing. She's kind of a force of nature." He gestured to the booth. "Let's sit."

She slid into the booth on the opposite side from where he'd been, saying, "I'll sit across from you," to squash any potential awkwardness of the *across or beside* conundrum. Eye contact meant more than snuggling – or did it? She wondered if he'd try to hold her hands across the table or touch her feet with his underneath it.

In all of that, Eamonn must have caught the server's attention somehow, because even as he sat down, she scurried up to the table and placed a Frosty Peach in front of Nell. "Tim says that's your usual, right?"

"Yes, but how–?"

The server laughed. "Your date here said to ask the bartender to make your usual drink as soon as you came in. So, there you go." She unloaded a couple of appetizers from her tray as well. "Cream cheese wontons and coconut shrimp. And are you ready for another Dark 'n Stormy, there?" she asked, turning to Eamonn, whose glass was three-quarters empty.

"Sure, but no hurry."

"Dark and stormy?" Nell asked. The liquid in his glass was amber in color, and a lime wedge lay among the ice cubes.

"It's Black Seal rum with ginger beer. Want a taste?"

"Sure." She eyed the straw in his drink, unsure of the protocol. Use the straw from her own drink? Sip from the edge of his glass? Share his straw?

He chuckled. "You can use my straw, Nella-bella. You're my girl."

She cut him a sharp look at that. "I'm not a *girl*."

"Okay, you're my woman... No? How about my sweetheart?"

"Ugh." She took his glass and sipped from the straw. "Oh, that's seriously good. You want to try mine?"

He chuckled. "Sure, if you'll take a sip and kiss me with it..."

"I don't kiss in public places," Nell said firmly, though the idea itself was tempting. She picked the peach candy off the top of her drink and ate it.

Then Eamonn leaned in a little and said, "I brought you something."

She raised her eyebrows at him, not sure how she felt about gifts so early in their getting to know each other. It seemed a bit much.

"So, you might have already got one since I saw you last, but if not – I want you to have a phone, okay? I want to be able to call you." He reached into his back pocket and pulled out an oblong object, plunked it on the table in front of her.

A smartphone. Not new, evidently, as the screen had a small chip in one corner and the finish was a bit worn in places where a case wouldn't have protected it. "Uh... I can't–"

"It's just an old one of mine, and you do need a phone, right?"

She sighed. "I was *planning* to get a burner number for my tablet, 'til I'm working again."

"This one's been lying around in a drawer since I upgraded. I got it set up for now on a pay as you go plan so you can use it right away, but it's unlocked, so you can switch it to anywhere you like."

"I can't." Reluctantly, regretfully, Nell pushed the phone back toward Eamonn. "It's too much."

"But you need a phone, and it's just an old one. Take it. Please?"

She shook her head. "Can't." Sipped her drink, and bit her lip. *Why am I resisting so hard?* A used phone, older model – it couldn't even be worth much. *I could let him give it to me.*

He drained his glass, looking stubborn and thoughtful. Then he smirked. "D'you play pool?"

"I do. Why?"

He nodded at the pool table. "If I win, you keep the phone."

Persistent, much? Nell suppressed an urge to roll her eyes. "Strange kind of stake. Shouldn't you *get* something if you win?"

"Oh, but I do. I get to talk to you... and on nights when we can't be together," his voice dropped into the thick, husky range that told her he was turned on, "if I'm lucky, maybe you'll call me from your bed..." And just like that, she was filled with vivid memories of the night he'd called her to say he'd got home safe, both of them in their beds and aching for each other.

Nope. She refused to think about that here. "And what happens if *I* win?"

"Name your prize, babe – anything you want."

Her mind went blank. *This is worse than truth or dare.* "Fine. If we're going to do ridiculous wagers, when I win, you can get down and do twenty pushups for me right here in the Frog and Ball."

Eamonn raised one eyebrow. "You know you could ask me for a trip to Paris, or a car, right?"

"Yeah, no. If you ever take me to Paris, it'll be because you want to take me there, not because I've won it. I mean, not that you'd ever–"

"Point taken." He stood up and gestured toward the pool table. "Pushups if I lose. Let's play?" He didn't sound like he thought he'd lose.

Whatever happens, I'll make you work for it. Nell took a sip of her drink, then stood too. "Sure."

Eamonn racked the balls efficiently, reminding her of how he'd played against himself the day she first saw him – with confidence and ease, never doubting his game. "You can break," he said, offering her the chalk.

"We flip a coin for the break," she countered, feeling her stubbornness rise in the face of his expertise. "Otherwise, it's like… breaking a rebreakable board that isn't fully snapped together. Our dojang uses them instead of real wood; they're just as hard, with plastic teeth that click together, and if the two pieces aren't fully engaged when you go to break… I don't know, there's less satisfaction. The achievement is weakened, even if the technique is perfect."

She thought he'd brush her explanation off or laugh, but he nodded thoughtfully. "Like using Auto-Tune, I guess. Doesn't mean you *can't* stay on key, but you're not fully proving that you *can*, either. Okay. I flip, you call it." He fished a coin out of his pocket and flicked it into the air in a fancy behind-the-back move.

"Heads," she said, just as he caught it.

He brought his hand around in a swooping motion to slap the coin down on the edge of the pool table, then lifted his fingers away. "Tails." He winked at her. "But I'm a gentleman, so I won't sink them all on my first turn."

"As if you could," she muttered, choosing a cue.

At first, he flirted – brushing her hand as he passed her the chalk, bumping her with his hip as he leaned over the pool table. But as the balls left on the table grew fewer and fewer, he focused harder on the game. *Competitive,* she thought with respect.

"Corner pocket," he said, and neatly sank the eight ball to win.

Nell grimaced. "Nicely played."

Eamonn didn't gloat, just handed her the phone. "Honestly, I'll feel better knowing you have a phone. Not that you can't take care of yourself. I just – I really want to be able to call you."

"I'll borrow it," she said. "Only until I can buy the one I want. Thanks."

And before the moment could get awkward, he put a hand right on her butt, which made her tense up momentarily until she saw that he was laughing at her. *He's my... boyfriend, I suppose? Stupid word. But this is... okay.* The feel of his strong hand there made her tingle and want to squirm, and for once in her life, she had no urge to pull away, even when their server came over with Eamonn's drink and asked Nell if she was ready for another. "Sure." She wondered if the server noticed the flirty, intimate touch.

After the server had moved away, Eamonn gave Nell's butt a little squeeze and said, "Now, how about a rematch? Different stakes."

She grinned. "Fine. If I win this time, you come to my MMA sparring session on Tuesday. Just watch if you want to, get in the ring and dance with me if you're willing."

"Dance, you call it?" That made him chuckle. "Sure, and if I win, we'll put a song on that jukebox and you'll slow-dance with me right here. Deal?"

"Exhibitionist, that's what you are," she muttered. It wasn't the sort of pub where people danced – everyone would stare.

"Rockstar territory, babe. What can I say?" He shrugged and turned to rack the balls. "It's your break."

No way am I making a fool of myself like that. This game's mine. Determined, Nell switched her pool cue to her left hand, something she'd pulled before – a strategy intended to rattle her opponent. Something about the ability to shoot on either side of her body tended to be profoundly intimidating and distracting to those who couldn't do it, but she'd been training to use both hands equally since preschool. And it was enough. He didn't scratch or do anything overtly foolish, but she managed to put away her last two balls and then the eight ball while he still had four of his solids on the table. "Tuesday?" she confirmed with a lift of her eyebrows.

He accepted with an easygoing nod, not seeming troubled by having lost. "Stripes are lucky for you."

I like a man who can lose graciously. It was one of the qualities she'd look for in a forever partner, if she believed in forever partners. "We can have a third game, if you want," she said.

Before he could answer, the server brought Nell's drink over, and she paid for it right away, not giving Eamonn a chance to get in ahead of her or have it put on his tab.

"I was going to take care of everything tonight," he said, as soon as the server was out of earshot.

"Yeah, well, no." Nell crossed her arms, feeling defensive. "I ordered a second drink and I paid for it. Sometimes life is like that."

"All right, but I'll get your next one."

"Two's my limit."

"Two is barely even buzzed. Don't you ever want to just let go, without worrying about being in control and protecting yourself and doing right?"

She thought at first that he was mocking her, but he didn't sound mocking, only curious. "Of course I do," she said. "But this is who I am. I don't know how to *not* be me, if that makes sense." She took a sip of her drink, filling her mouth so she wouldn't say anything more.

"Ninja woman, did someone... hurt you, to make you so on guard?"

"Nothing terrible. I've never been raped, if that's what you're asking." She sighed. How could he even understand? *Chunky Booty. Can't you just smile?* Unwanted touches and pinches. "But the small things add up. And if I weren't who I am? I had to threaten to break my prom date's arm." A decade ago, and she'd never forget the fear and fury, her date's yelp of pain, or the effort it had taken to let him go despite her visceral urge to damage him.

"Wow. That blows," Eamonn said, looking rather stunned. It probably wasn't a reality he'd had to think much about, after all.

"I don't need sympathy," Nell reminded him. "Just leave it." But concern still hovered in his brow and an uncertain twist to his mouth. "Look, I train with a lot of guys; it's a male-dominated sport. I'm tough and I hold my ground so they'll take me seriously. And that's not something I can turn on and off – I've lived in my armor so long, it's become part of me."

That seemed to reassure him. "Okay. I understand wearing armor." He waved toward the pool table. "What about that third game, then? Got an idea of what to play for? Because I do."

"Oh?"

The grin he gave her was half dirty, half sweet. "There's something I wanted to do with you in bed the other night, Nella-bella..."

She felt herself tensing. "I do *not* know you well enough for butt stuff. If ever."

"That's not it – though if you ever want to, I'd love to show you how good that can be – and fuck me, you're sexy when you blush." He stroked a finger along the curve of her cheek, and his eyes on her were intent and blatantly aroused.

"What, then?" she managed to say.

"I want to taste you." His voice was thick, raspy. "I want you to come on my tongue. I want your peach juice all over my face."

Well, flipping hell. "You can't really want to... I mean..."

"Oh, believe me, I do."

"But it's awkward, and too vulnerable." Her voice came out small and choked.

Gently, he put his arms around her, pulling her into a hug, brushing softly urgent kisses against her forehead and temples. "Nell. You can trust me. And the thought of going down on you turns me on so hard it makes me dizzy. I won't push you, but if you'll let me, that's what I'd most want to win in this pool game."

She pushed away from him and took a big gulp of her drink, then another, and the icy slush gave her brain-freeze. "Crap, I can't drink this as fast as I want to right now," she grumbled to herself, pinching the bridge of her nose.

"Hey," he said, "we don't have to do anything you don't want to do."

"I know." She gave him a long look, steeling herself. "And I'll agree to let you have your prize if you win. I just... I don't do vulnerable well."

"Oh, Nella-bella..." For a moment, he looked pole-axed, beyond conscious thought, awash in desire. "And if you win? What will you ask of me?"

Focus. What do I want from him? "Well, I'm not fragile, right? I won't break if you play a little rough."

His eyebrows shot up at that. She'd surprised him, then.

"I could do that for you," he said slowly. He picked up her cue and held it out to her, and then the chalk.

They were both clumsy this time. Missing easy angles, scratching repeatedly. Nell's fingers felt numb and shaky so that she could barely hold the pool cue steady. Losing fine motor control. Adrenaline would do that. She wasn't sure if Eamonn was riding the adrenaline rollercoaster too, or if his mind was just in his pants rather than on the game, but he wasn't playing with nearly the skill he'd shown before. *I can win,* she thought, but then he bit his lip as he lined up his cue, and she started thinking about his mouth all over again. She took her shot to sink the eight ball for the win, scratched, and the game was his.

chapter

10.

EAMONN TOOK THE CUE FROM NELL'S SUDDENLY nerveless fingers and set it down on the pool table. "I think you'll find we've both won," he said, with an arm around her shoulders as he guided her back to their booth.

She made herself smile, reminding herself that losing graciously was part of being a good martial artist, whatever the circumstances. "You're good at pool."

"Thanks. Not sure either of us had our minds on the game in that last one, though."

That made her laugh. "You think?"

She sat. Instead of resuming his place across from her, he slid into the booth on her side, close, his thigh brushing against hers. Denim against yoga pants. "So, what now?" he asked. "Dinner? Another drink? Get out of here?"

"Well, I'm not all that hungry..."

He gave her a considering look, and she found herself struggling to stay cool, trying not to think too hard about anything ahead between them. "You like doing shots? We could knock a couple back before we head out."

Not a good idea. I don't need to drink to relax, and doing shots only leads to trouble. But she heard herself saying, "Just one. And we go to my place, not yours." His hand on her thigh felt so very warm.

"Sure. For that shot – how d'you feel about lychee as a flavor?"

"It's been years since I've eaten any." She thought of the round translucent fruits in their tough red husks, and the remembered pleasure of peeling them and biting into the pearly sweet flesh. "Funny, I haven't even thought about lychees in ages. I like them, though."

"So you're up for trying lychee liqueur? It mixes beautifully with tequila."

That sounds dangerous. But Nell nodded.

Their server was chatting with the bartender, so Eamonn got up and went over to them. He spoke briefly and held out a credit card, presumably settling their tab. Then he was striding back toward Nell, sliding in beside her, his hand returning at once to her upper thigh, easy and affectionate.

He makes life look easy; he really does. And in that moment, Nell could see how his nickname suited him.

The shots arrived, tinted palest pink and harmless looking. He clinked his glass against hers and drank, and she followed suit.

♥

He wanted to call his car service, but she insisted on walking. "I always walk home from the Frog and Ball," she said. "It's only twenty minutes."

"Would it matter if you got a ride this one time?"

"Would it kill you to walk with me? And I thought you were trying not to draw attention to yourself. Having some limousine roll up would be like waving a flag. Right now, no one's paying attention – or is *that* the problem? You *want* to be recognized?"

Eamonn scrubbed his hands through his hair, fingering the ends. *My hair is shorter these days,* he'd said. "Fuck me, you're so direct, Nell. And yeah, maybe I miss it a bit. But we'll walk."

♥

Nell's apartment was orderly and spotless, as always. "It's not much, but at least I don't have to share," she told Eamonn as she unlocked the door. *Small and plain,* she thought, *but it's all I need.* The sheets on her bed were clean, the apartment smelled of fresh laundry and citrus-bergamot candles, and her framed black belt certificate hung on the wall. *Good enough.*

"It's nice," he said. "I like the cactus."

She glanced at her spiky little plant on the windowsill above the kitchen sink. "Yeah, well, it suits me – prickly, low-maintenance, and it rarely flowers. You want some tea? I don't have any coffee."

As she turned toward the electric kettle on the counter, he stepped up behind her and traced one finger down her spine. "We can have tea later." His strong hands began to massage her shoulders.

It was ridiculous how much she wanted to lean into his hands. His thumbs digging into her trapezius and rhomboid muscles felt like heaven, soothing her, releasing tension. But she couldn't relax. "I'm... uh, got to go freshen up," she managed to say, and shot through her bedroom into the bathroom before he could respond.

When she came out, he was sitting on her bed, propped up against the headboard with his legs stretched out and crossed at the ankles like it was all no big thing. "Nella-bella, we don't have to do anything you don't want to do," he said, his voice both raspy and gentle. "Just come and cuddle a bit. Let me hold you."

She crawled onto the bed but sat cross-legged, like a student in class with her hands on her knees.

So he leaned forward and snagged one of her ankles, giving it a gentle tug to get her foot into his lap. She tensed for a moment, then relaxed. *Chill,* she told herself. *He's not a threat.*

His strong, clever hands massaged her foot, kneading and stroking into the arch, and the pure pleasure of it made her sigh with contentment. "Other foot?" he asked after a while, and she shifted position to unfold her other leg, then flopped onto her back to better enjoy the massage. He was only touching her feet, but there was something sensual about it, his touch running from the nerve endings in her soles right up her legs and into her core. And it went on and on, like he had all the time in the world and was happy just to rub her feet.

It didn't seem fair, and she reluctantly raised a hand to let him know he could stop. "You don't have to–"

"But I *like* touching you. Anywhere and in any way I can. And your face when you feel good is so fucking beautiful it blows my mind..."

"Whatever," she said, but the sincerity and desire on his face were so vivid she had to close her eyes. "You want sex, already?"

"I want to taste you, if you'll let me." The husky, thick sound to his voice couldn't be faked.

Heat washed over her. And she wanted it. But... "It just takes a lot of... trust, is all. Sex doesn't have to be intimate, but this..."

"Nella-bella, you're the most practical goddess I've ever met. But what we're doing? It's kind of *supposed* to be intimate. Let me inside your guard, lovely."

"Ugh." *I'm so uncomfortable.* Why would this man want any kind of real intimacy with her, when it was so much easier to bounce around on the bed and keep everything light and fun?

Holding her gaze, he licked his lip – not overtly, just a tiny subtle lizard-flick of the tip of his tongue – and it broke her.

Because a martial artist does need to have trust. Trust for instructors, trust for training partners, and maybe trust for lovers too. *Something I've always struggled with. Is it time to push past that?* "Fine," she said, and skinned out of her pants and underwear all in one tangled lot, leaving her lower half bare.

He grinned. "Arms up," he said, and whisked her t-shirt over her head and off, adding, "I'll let you get the sports bra off yourself. Extra hands don't make some jobs any easier."

That made her laugh as she wriggled out of it, remembering various instances of dudes attempting to help. But he was still fully dressed. "What about you?"

"I'm good for now. Lie back and open your legs for me." He spoke with such command and assurance, and somehow also such admiration, that she found herself gasping and complying – spreading herself open for him, with both her body and her mind. *Trust.* And the erotic contrast between her bareness and his clothes intensified it.

He laid a firm hand on her abdomen, and it scorched her.

"Flipping hell," Nell muttered, part of her wanting to curl away from the devastating intimacy as he settled himself between her thighs, but the part of her that had any control over actual movement and choices was transfixed by electric excitement at the warmth of his breath and the subtle stroking of his other hand at the top of her thigh.

"All right?" he asked.

"Awkward, but yeah," she choked out. *I can trust this man.*

His eyes were full of laughter and arousal as he looked up at her. "The idea is for you to enjoy it." He stuck his tongue out at her, waggled it until she laughed. And then – it was then, when she was undone by unexpected mirth, that he began a delicate exploration with his lips and tongue.

At first, she was tense, but the sheer pleasure of it and his evident enjoyment overcame her, and gradually everything around her coalesced into the slippery, talented stroking of his tongue. Slowly her universe turned inside out and she fractured into pure bliss.

♥

She woke sated – and alone. Suppressed a twinge of disappointment. *He's gone, then?* But when she sat up, she saw the note that must have slid off the pillow and into the sheets. *Getting coffee. Back soon,* it said, signed with an untidy, scrawled E and a scribble that looked suspiciously like a heart. *No way. Just a scribble.*

Well. A movie heroine would stay in bed, naked under the sheets, lounging sensually as she waited for her lover to return. But after about three minutes, Nell grew twitchy and couldn't lie still – lazy inactivity had never been a good fit for her. She kicked the sheets off and rolled out of bed, landing on her feet with more of a bounce than she'd felt in a while. Once she'd made the bed and snagged a pair of workout shorts and a top, she put a playlist of power-up songs on her tablet and blew through her morning workout like it was nothing – doing squat kicks instead of plain squats, just for fun, and opting for Spiderman pushups because she was feeling strong and fine.

"I could do more," she said aloud, to herself or no one in particular since she was alone, but decided on a quick shower instead.

When she got out, an unfamiliar electronic guitar riff called her attention, and she tracked it down to her new phone on the bedside table. There was a message from Eamonn: *I'm downstairs, forgot the front door would lock me out.*

Press #32 on the intercom and I'll buzz you in, she texted back, and by the time he was knocking at her apartment door, she'd figured out how to change the alert sound on the phone.

"I'm guessing you found the Coffee Witch?" she asked as he came in with a paper bag balanced atop a drinks tray. The Coffee Witch Café was the nearest source of caffeine, two blocks away, and she couldn't imagine he'd walk farther.

"Nice place. They, ah, had more than one kind of chai, so… I picked the marzipan chai for you. That okay?" He lowered everything onto the kitchen table, set the paper bag aside, extracted one to-go cup from the tray and handed it to her.

My favorite. "Perfect, thanks."

And then he held out another cup, clear plastic and full of something that looked like a sunrise, red at the bottom swirling up to orange at the top. "Yesterday, I promised you a better breakfast than doughnuts. The Coffee Witch barista said these smoothies are popular and have protein and antioxidants and stuff, so…"

Nell couldn't stop a wide smile from spreading across her face. "How did you read my mind? I love these!" A marzipan chai latte in one hand and a tropical dawn smoothie in the other was essentially her definition of a perfect morning. *Maybe this relationship thing is okay.*

"There are scones in the bag too, if you want one." He laughed, with a self-deprecating twist to his mouth. "The smoothie is… surprisingly good, and the coffee is fantastic, but I just can't get through the morning without something solid."

"Maybe later. I've got all I need for now – thank you!" And before she'd thought it through or even made a conscious decision, she closed the gap between them and planted an appreciative kiss on his cheek. It wasn't a sexy kiss, though the chemistry between them seemed to be always simmering and ready to flare up; no, the tender brush of her lips against his skin and the soft prickle of hair on his jaw felt unexpectedly, purely, and almost unbearably romantic.

A pleased flush spread over his face, and his eyes seemed brighter and more intensely blue than ever as he looked down at her with a bemused smile. "I like making you happy, Nella bella."

What happened to the cocky pool player from the Frog and Ball? It was as though she'd peeled an onion and discovered a mango inside – pleasant, but disconcerting. "People catch feelings from oral sex," she blurted out, turning away from him to go sit on the couch. "It doesn't mean anything."

"I already caught feelings for you a while back, so don't worry, nothing's changed." As he flopped down next to her, his wry grin told her that he didn't much like that she'd said *it doesn't mean anything.* "Or were you talking about yourself?"

I don't know. Nell shook her head. "I've got too much on my mind right now. I've got to send out resumes, find a job. I've got to talk to Master Simran about picking up more teaching hours, and I should call the MMA gym to see if I can put my membership there on hold until I'm working again. I–"

He stopped her with a gentle finger touching her lower lip. "It's okay. I'll head out and let you get stuff done. What're you doing tonight?"

"I've got a self-defense class at five, then I'm teaching until eight."

"I'll pick you up after." He stood up. "Same place as your sparring class, right?"

She nodded, and when he leaned down to kiss her, she tilted her head up for him, parting her lips for his tongue as the heat between them flared up immediately. *So good.* She found herself standing, swept up into his arms, both of them trying to get more of each other.

"If you didn't have stuff to do, babe, I'd take you back to bed and keep you there all day," he said, his lips next to her ear as he licked and kissed her neck and earlobe. "But I know you'll feel better once you've checked some things off your list, so I can wait." And with a final nip at her lower lip and then one last kiss on her forehead, like a blessing, he released her and walked to the door. "I'd really like to stay. But I'll see you tonight." And he was gone.

She sat back down, biting her lip. *Well.*

Long minutes later, she could still feel the phantom imprint of his kiss on her forehead. His self-control and the consideration he showed for her needs and day were definitely a turn-on, to the point of distraction.

She worked her way through the dozen job applications she'd started, adding her new phone number and submitting them. Then she found another three possibilities and applied for them too, even though one was a long shot and one wanted qualifications that she didn't quite meet. *Can't hurt to try.* But she kept thinking about Eamonn.

Every time she looked at the time display on her tablet or phone, more time had passed than she'd expected.

In the end, Nell was nearly late for her self-defense class at the dojang. She had to rush through getting changed – nearly everyone was already out on the mats, stretching – and was still in the process of tying her hair back as she left the changing room, just as they were called to line up.

"Where've you been, Whelan?" someone whispered from the row behind her. "You're usually the first one here." Fortunately, good discipline didn't allow for talking during bow-in, so Nell could justifiably ignore the question.

The class was not a particularly successful one for her. Because she hadn't stretched, she felt tight and unprepared, and while doing shoulder rolls at one of the warm-up stations she pulled something in her lower back – nothing major, but it was enough to give her stabbing twinges of discomfort as she kept on with the class. She took an accidental elbow to the jaw as they practiced countering chokes, hard enough that it would probably develop into a pretty bruise. *Just what I need for job interviews.* But some training sessions went that way; there would always be low points to go with the high points.

"Where's Master Simran, sir?" she asked Mr. Kahn during the short break between self-defense and the next class. Usually, the dojang owner was around, in and out of the office, even if he wasn't teaching.

"He and Mr. Price have gone to an instructors conference in Hawai'i, remember?" Mr. Kahn said. "So I'm in charge 'til they get back next week – Acting Chief Instructor, that's me!"

Crap. Once he'd mentioned it, she remembered some discussion of the conference in their instructors' meeting at the beginning of the month. She hadn't paid attention to the dates since it didn't directly affect her. "Right. Well, I'm available if you need any classes covered. I was going to ask Master Simran about picking up some extra hours."

"I think we're good, but I'll keep that in mind." Mr. Kahn finger-combed his hair into place and gave his belt a tug to tighten the knot. "We'd better get this class started. Could you line them up, Miss Whalen?"

"Yes, sir."

As Mr. Kahn led the warm-up, Nell glanced at the class planner, noticing that she'd been given the intermediate color belt group in the children's class and then the junior color belts in the teen class. *It's just as well I wasn't given any senior belts tonight,* she told herself. Her back ached, and it wouldn't have been fun to demonstrate hook kicks or jump round kicks like that. But powering through discomfort was a point of pride with her.

During the break between classes, she snuck an extra-strength ibuprofen caplet from the little first aid kit in her bag, making sure none of the other instructors saw. She'd been late, she hadn't stretched, and a pulled muscle was a natural consequence, but being teased for it by Riley Kahn or any of the others would *not* make her day any better, and concern or advice would be much worse.

The next class was often not an easy one, with teens who could bring a lot of energy to the dojang and didn't always channel it in productive ways. It was best to keep them busy.

Halfway through the class, she glanced over at the door, and there was Eamonn – a bit early to pick her up. *Early is good.* Did he want to watch her teaching, then, or was he just impatient to see her? Either of those things could be positive if she let herself feel optimistic. She saw Mr. Kahn notice and nod a greeting in Eamonn's direction, or maybe it was a nod of approval.

She could feel a smile spreading across her face, and quickly turned it on her students. "You've been working super hard this cycle, and I see most of you have got all three stripes on your belts, so we're going to break some boards today!"

The immediate "yes, ma'am" response, disciplined and enthusiastic, was gratifying. Today she could show Eamonn the admirable, socially acceptable side of martial arts – working with young people, inspiring them to find their confidence and personal victories. Board breaks were an excellent way to do that.

After she'd checked their technique on a target to make sure they were doing their front kicks correctly and safely, she explained the rotation – bow to the instructor and ask permission, break the board, then take a turn holding it with her for the next student. She could have asked for a couple of students from the senior belt group to come over and hold the board, but it was good training for the juniors to learn how to hold as well as break. The intermediate group was sparring, and some of her students' eyes were focused there instead of on her and the boards, so she called them to attention and reminded them that it didn't matter what the other groups were up to; even a white belt should be demonstrating black belt focus and self-control. She herself would *not* look over to see what the sparring group was up to, even if they did sound rambunctious and the thumps of hard contact suggested they were a bit out of control. *Not my group. Not my place to interfere.*

She took a solid stance and coached the young woman holding the board with her on how to get into position and lock up. She prompted the first breaker, who'd forgotten what to say when requesting permission to break. The impact of the unsuccessful kick against the board made her back protest, but she kept her encouraging-instructor expression at full glow. "Don't worry, we'll just reset the board – say 'second attempt, ma'am' – and you'll have it this time if you use your hips." This time he was successful, so he came to hold the board with her for the next student.

As they locked up for the next student's kick, there was a shout from the sparring group behind her, more hard contact thumps and heavy feet. A rush of air at her back was her only warning, and she half-turned her head, but she had no chance to disengage with the board or the kid holding it as a pair of big boys crashed into them, limbs swinging, and an elbow connected with her head.

♥

Nell! That had been Eamonn's voice she'd heard, hadn't it? But she was lying on her back looking at the ceiling of the dojang, and Mr. Kahn was kneeling over her, telling her to focus on his finger as he moved it back and forth. At the edge of her peripheral vision, two figures in sparring gear hovered, offering anxious apologies and concern.

"I'm fine. Let me get up." She tried to sit, but Mr. Kahn stopped her with a gentle hand on her shoulder.

"Nell, you were hit pretty hard. Just lie still a moment. You could have a concussion."

He called me Nell, even though we're in uniform. That seemed wrong. They could call each other Riley and Nell outside of class, in street clothes, but of all the instructors and masters she knew, he adhered most to the formality of titles within the dojang and in uniform. *He's worried.*

Her head throbbed. "I'm good, sir," she said. "I'm not concussed. I've been hit harder in the ring. Just let me get a drink of water and I'll go back to my students."

Mr. Kahn snorted with grudging amusement but helped her get to her feet and ushered her toward a chair that one of the leadership students brought over. "I know how you feel, Miss Whalen, but you're sitting out for a week, and–"

"I can't! I *need* the hours, sir." Her voice wobbled with horror and frustration.

He shook his head slowly, his eyes sympathetic but the set of his mouth unyielding. "Sorry. If Master Simran were here, I might look the other way and let you make the call for yourself, but... I'm responsible for the dojang right now. I'm responsible for *you*. Don't fight me on this, all right?"

Years of ingrained respect for senior belts and the martial arts hierarchy, years of discipline and self-control, forced her to choke out "yes, sir" when she wanted to scream and rage and even beg. *This isn't how it's supposed to go...*

"I think your dude wants to come see that you're okay." Mr. Kahn tilted his head toward the guest seating area where Eamonn stood with his arms crossed, tapping a foot in a twitchy rhythm – not hovering, exactly, but definitely on alert while still trying to appear cool. "Will you let him take you to Urgent Care? Or at least keep an eye on you overnight?"

Nell huffed out a disbelieving breath. "I don't need to be taken care of, sir."

"All right." His raised eyebrows said he doubted that, but she couldn't very well argue with eyebrows. "Go take care of yourself, then. I'll see you next week."

"Yes, sir." That came out sounding more defeated than she'd have liked, and she automatically raised her chin and straightened her shoulders, triggering various twinges of discomfort. He gave her an encouraging pat on the shoulder before walking away – back to students, back to training, back to everything she'd be missing. At least he had the sense not to go talking to Eamonn about her care or anything.

She got up from the chair and dragged it over to the audience seating area, placing it back on the end of the row it had been taken from. Only then did she acknowledge Eamonn, turning to him with a sigh, saying, "Well, that wasn't me at my best tonight."

"You are absolutely the toughest woman I've ever met," he said, shaking his head. "And I've spent my whole life around groupies and roadies and rockers, so that's saying a lot."

"Thanks," she muttered. *That doesn't scare you off?* She put on her shoes and picked up her gear bag. "I can change at home. Let's go."

"Can I carry your bag?" he offered.

"No."

"Of course not," he said. But he held the door for her as they left, and when they reached his truck, he tossed her bag into the back for her, and opened the passenger door for her too, giving her an arm to lean on as she climbed in.

"I'm fine," she said firmly, even as she appreciated his steady arm and the comfortable ride home. "I don't have a freaking concussion. I don't need to be babied."

He stood at the open door of his truck, leaning on the frame, regarding her with a bit of concern. "Ninja woman, it was a hard hit. I believe you when you say you don't have a concussion – I figure you'd know, right? – but it's still okay to be hurting, to need a little care." He gave her thigh an encouraging pat, his big hand lingering just enough that she knew it could easily become a caress if she encouraged him at all.

"Yeah. Well, I don't want to go get my head looked at, but you can stay the night with me if you like."

"You want to come to my place instead? I've got ice packs, and a really comfy bed, and a clean t-shirt you can sleep in."

It is *a really comfy bed.* The thought of his silky high-thread-count sheets and fluffy pillows called to her. *Nicer than mine.* "Sure."

He closed her door and strode around to the driver's side. Straight back, confident, not even scared off by seeing her take a hard hit.

Everything I've ever wanted. As he got in and put the truck into gear, she watched him out of the corner of her eye. After a bit, she said, "I... uh, might not be much use to you tonight. Not that I – I'm just so *tired*..."

His eyes were on the road, one hand on the wheel, and his other hand reached out, open, inviting her to take it. So she did. His fingers closed around hers, giving them a comforting squeeze. "Nella-bella, it'll be a pleasure to just cuddle with you," he said, and she heard something unexpected in his voice. *Warmth. Affection?*

She knew she ought to say something, to respond in some way, but her head throbbed and her back ached, and the truck's leather seat cradled her so well, and the warmth of Eamonn's hand and his thumb circling her palm in a light massage lulled her into the neutrality of silence as they drove.

❤

"You want me to carry you inside?"

Nell blinked. *Must have dozed off.* She unbuckled herself and eased her way out of the truck, grimacing. Every muscle in her body seemed to have stiffened up and was protesting. "My legs work just fine. And you've got to stop trying to carry me across thresholds, already." She wanted to call back the words as soon as she'd spoken them – being carried *across a threshold* had echoes of wedding bells around it, and there was absolutely no way she'd entertain that sort of nonsense, even in theory and far in the future.

The truck was parked inside the garage, and Eamonn led the way through a small laundry area into a room with soundproofing tiles on the walls and ceiling – a music room, clearly, since a grand piano sat in the center of it, half a dozen guitars and bass guitars hung from hooks on the walls, and a Celtic-style lap harp and gleaming brass saxophone were displayed on stands in the corners. Nell thought she ought to say something admiring about the impressive setup, but he didn't seem to expect it, waving dismissively at the instruments and saying, "This is my workspace, as you can probably tell. Have to go through it to get to and from the garage. The stairs are over here. Hungry?"

She was.

He made them grilled cheese sandwiches and cream of tomato soup.

I ought to be content, she told herself, sitting at his kitchen table, dipping a corner of her sandwich into her mug of soup. She wasn't damaged, only a little sore. A week off wouldn't kill her. But the blue feelings welled up inside her anyway, and she was having trouble suppressing an unfamiliar urge to cry.

"Hey, now," he said, apparently seeing something of that in her face. "Everything will be all right." He pushed his chair back as though he might get up and come around the table to hug her.

"Don't. I can't do comfort."

"Okay, let's do something fun instead. So you're on vacation for a week. There's nowhere I have to be. Wanna go to Paris?"

"Not helpful." But she felt her lips curving into a reluctant smile.

He chuckled, not seeming put out. Apparently, he hadn't expected her to roll with that suggestion. "Well, is there *anything* you want to do that you haven't been able to do because of your training?"

"Get a tattoo." The words popped out of her mouth before she could even think about the question. "I've wanted one for years, but I roll around on the mat so much…"

"This is your lucky week, then."

"How? I don't have an appointment, or the money to burn."

He waved that problem away. "I have a friend who'll take care of you. Know what sort of thing you want?"

"Yeah."

He looked at her, eyebrows raised, but she didn't elaborate. *I can explain it to an artist. Not to you.*

"Okay. I'll fix something up. Getting inked is… I don't know, it helps when you're hurting."

I'm not hurting, she wanted to say, but it would be a lie. She *wanted* to lie, as she'd lied that time when she'd had a rank test go all wrong, a catastrophic pile-up of circumstances that led to failure. When they'd asked her if she was okay, she'd smiled through gritted teeth and pretended it was nothing – and regretted forever after that she'd held everything inside a false front instead of admitting to her misery and anger. "I suppose we'll see about that," she said with a shrug, hoping he'd have the sense to let the subject go.

He did. "How's your head? You want an ice pack for it? Some ibuprofen?"

"Ice would be good." Fatigue washed over her, more pressing than aches and pains now that hunger wasn't clawing at her. "But I really just want to go to bed."

"I think we can manage both of those things."

Music woke her, heavy bass chords and Eamonn singing, *"Getting inked today, gonna be okay / Scratch of the needle, love that feeling / New tattoo today, gonna be okay / Scratch of the needle, addictive and healing..."* He sat beside her on the edge of the bed, fully dressed, with his hair still damp from the shower, playing his iconic blue Warwick Corvette bass – his favorite concert instrument, and Nell still couldn't quite believe she'd searched that information out on the internet one night. It was unmistakable, though; a shimmering metallic threadburst edged the bleached-ocean varnish of the custom-built bass.

"What are you singing?"

He grinned. "Just doodling around to wake you up."

"You made that up just now?"

"Sure. But you do need to get up. My tattoo artist doesn't usually work Tuesdays, but you've got a special appointment."

This is really happening? I'm getting a tattoo? Nell moved to sit up, then froze with a suppressed groan at the stiffness and pain in her back and neck. At least her head seemed to be all right – she prodded the area with careful fingertips, and although it was tender and bruised, she had only the mildest headache, barely even noticeable, and no signs of nausea or dizziness as she inched herself to a sitting position. "Do I have time for a shower?" she asked. Hot water would help with the muscle aches.

"Sure." He stood and held out a hand to pull her to her feet.

I don't need help. But as her back cramped again, she took his hand and let him ease her into a standing position. "Thanks."

"You know where the towels are. I'm going downstairs for a minute to put this baby away, then I'll be back up in case you need anything."

As soon as he'd gone, she dug into her gear bag for her street clothes, the ibuprofen in her first aid kit, and the spare underwear she kept in a pouch with her just-in-case tampons. Then she headed for the bathroom.

She lingered under the hot spray for a few minutes longer than usual, because it felt so good on her aching back and stiff neck, but she wasn't the sort of person to take long showers, preferring to be efficient and keep her water use to a minimum. And who could dawdle with a first tattoo appointment waiting?

He met her on the stairs; he was coming up to find her as she headed down. "You're all set? Let's go. We'll get something to eat on the way; I told her I'd bring breakfast."

"Her?"

"My tattoo artist, and now yours."

I'm not going to ask. I'm not. "Ex-girlfriend?"

Eamonn chuckled. "Ghostflower is more likely to hit on you than me, babe. I've known her since high school. She's a good friend and a fantastic artist."

"That *can't* be her real name."

"It's what she prefers."

"Did she do your angel?"

"Yeah. She's done all my ink. You can trust her."

Nell nodded. The artwork on his body was testimonial enough.

There was a bakery below the second-floor tattoo studio, the strong aroma of cinnamon rolls wafting from it immediately noticeable as Nell got out of Eamonn's truck. This was evidently the "breakfast" he'd meant, since he headed straight for the bakery door instead of the one with the sign that said *TATTOOS UPSTAIRS*.

She followed him in, just in time to hear him asking one of the bakery workers for a dozen cinnamon rolls. *How many does he think we can eat?* And she wasn't sure she could face a giant, sweet, sticky bun just then, anyway.

"Can I help you?" another of the bakery workers asked her.

"Maybe. I'm looking for something breakfast-y that isn't sweet."

"Sure. We've got some savory breakfast rolls just coming out of the oven now – they've got a caramelized onion and apple jam filling, with toasted pecans and vegan pepper jack cheese. Would that work for you?"

"That sounds amazing."

"You don't want a cinnamon roll?" Eamonn asked, coming over as the bakery worker vanished into the back of the shop.

"Honestly? Not really."

The bakery worker returned with a paper bag, and Nell fished a ten-dollar bill out of her pocket.

"Add it to my order," Eamonn said, gesturing for her to put her money away.

"No. You can't always be paying my way. I've got this." She turned back to the bakery worker, holding out the money. "And I'll have a large tea as well, please. In fact, I'll pay for his coffee too."

"Nell!" He looked as though he wanted to say *you can't* but realized that would be a mistake.

"It's okay," she said. "You can get Ghostflower whatever it is that she drinks. I know you're a rock god and all that, but sometimes I *need* to pay for my own food and get your coffee. It... keeps the balance."

He paid for the box of cinnamon rolls and a coffee for the tattoo artist. She thought he'd dropped the subject. But as they were fixing their drinks at the cream and sugar station, he said, "Nell, I want to take care of you. I'm in a position where it's nothing for me to get your food and drink. Why shouldn't I?"

She shook her head. "Rub it in, much?"

He snapped his head around to look at her, equal parts offended and rueful. "I didn't mean–"

"And that's *why* you have to let me pay my own way or treat you sometimes. Otherwise, I feel like a charity case, whether you mean it or not." And then, firmly changing the subject, "This bakery is great."

He nodded, accepting her point *and* the subject change. "The tea and coffee are pretty basic, but the baked goods are on point. Coming here is kind of a pre-tattoo ritual for me. Shall we head up?"

"I'm ready."

Going out the bakery door and in through the neighboring door took only a moment. The stairs, trim, and handrails looked original to the building – old hardwood, well-maintained and smooth with varnish – but had new-looking grip strips for safety. The walls were white, with a trail of black tattoo art leading up the stairs. There was a buzzer just inside the door with a sign that said, *Please ring if assistance is needed. Elevator access is available at the back of the building.*

Nell had expected a warren of dark hallways and cubicles, like a dark version of a doctor's office, but as they reached the top of the stairs, she found herself in a big open space instead. The front third of the room had varnished hardwood floors and sleek black couches. Big windows overlooking the street let in a flood of natural light. Portfolio books lay on a low coffee table, and an antique reception desk was positioned at one end, with a skinny teenager in baggy black clothing lounging on a chair behind it.

The rest of the space had black and white checkerboard tiles on the floor and was clearly the tattoo artists' workspace, with an assortment of padded chairs and tables to sit and lie on, a couple of wheeled workstations that looked almost medical, and several freestanding adjustable lamps. This part of the studio was cordoned off from the sitting area with a purple velvet rope that made Nell think of a nightclub entrance or red-carpet gala. A big man with bodybuilder-style muscles lay on one of the tables, and an artist in a Doctor Who t-shirt and cargo shorts looked up from his work on the man's chest.

"Hey, Easy," he said. "Ghost'll be back in a minute. Stell, this is Ghostflower's eleven o'clock. Good friends."

"Hiya," said the teenager behind the reception desk, holding out a clipboard. "Got your paperwork all up here."

Easy took the clipboard and handed it to Nell. "That's for her, not me. She's getting her first ink today. I'm just here to supply the cinnamon rolls." He opened the box and set it on a side table in the sitting area.

"You freaks better save at least one of those for me," said the artist with a grin.

"Don't worry, Justin, I brought a dozen this time," Easy told him.

A tall woman with rainbow hair and dragon tattoos wrapped around both arms strode into the workroom from a door at the back. "I smell cinnamon rolls, don't I?" She laughed, a deep, warm laugh. She crossed the workspace, stepped over the velvet rope, and drew Easy into an enthusiastic hug. "It's good to see you, man."

"Always feels like home, coming here," Easy said in return, so softly that Nell almost didn't catch it, though she was only a few feet away. Then he turned and waved her over. "Nell, this is Ghostflower."

Nell stepped up and shook Ghostflower's hand, feeling as though she were meeting a master at a national event, someone who might be judging her rank test or competition ring. "Nice to meet you." She just barely managed to avoid calling the tattoo artist *ma'am*.

"Honored to be the one doing your first ink," Ghostflower said. She had a firm handshake and genuine interest in her dark eyes. "Lemme just grab a cinnamon roll and we can talk about what you want, 'kay? You want one?"

"I got a savory roll instead," Nell explained, holding up her paper bag. "I know Eamonn loves his sweets in the morning, but some days I just can't."

That made Ghostflower laugh. "Sit and eat! I'll be right there."

Nell unwrapped her roll and bit into it. *So good!* The filling had just a tiny hint of sweetness from the apples and caramelized onions, mixed with the crunch of pecans and the creamy goodness of melted pepper jack.

Ghostflower sat down beside her with a sketch pad. "Now, tell me what sort of tattoo you're thinking of."

"On my left shoulder blade," Nell said. "I've thought about this for years. Do you know what I mean by lettering that's both strong and fluid?"

"Absolutely. And what are we spelling out?"

Nell shot a glance at Eamonn, who was at the window looking down into the street as he sipped his coffee. She held out a hand for Ghostflower's pencil and printed one word lightly at the top of the page. "It's the most important thing about me," she said. *Integrity.*

ETTING A TATTOO DIDN'T HURT, EXACTLY. IT WAS MORE of a scratchy, pinch-poke feeling. There were moments of *ouch* – when the tattoo machine's needles hit nerves in the skin, maybe, like tiny pressure points here and there – but mostly it was tolerable. She imagined the lettering taking shape on her shoulder blade. *Integrity.* Ghostflower had drawn the word in her sketchbook, in broad capital letters with swirling serifs, both strong and flowing, just as Nell had described. After they'd talked some more, the artist had added a sun rising behind and through the letters, because the sun rises every day, no matter what, and is always there above the clouds. Nell couldn't directly see the back of her own shoulder, but Ghostflower had made a stencil from the sketch and placed it according to Nell's request, then showed her in a pair of mirrors. *This is me. This is right.* With every prick of the tattoo machine, the beautiful artwork was becoming her own ink, part of her skin.

Losing the Wildforest job had taken nothing from her but temporary security. A rest from her sport as well as the workforce grind – a true vacation – was maybe something she'd needed for a while. As the scratching discomfort went on and on, Nell found a place inside herself where it didn't matter so much that she'd lost control of her life. *Maybe it's a sign. Time for the next step, whatever it is. It will be okay.*

And that felt good.

It came almost as a surprise when the needles stopped and the artist's gentle hands wiped the area with something cool. "All done,"

Ghostflower said. "Want to take a look before I put the Dermalize on?" Out came the mirrors again. The finished work was perfect, beautiful, even with the slightly angry skin around it.

Eamonn wandered over to take a look.

He stood just behind her, where she couldn't see him unless she twisted around, and neither the sore muscles in her lower back nor the brand-new tattoo on her shoulder blade wanted her to do that.

What did he think of it? Had he paid attention to the design before this? Nell couldn't be sure. It wasn't as though Ghostflower had shown him the sketchbook, or even drawn his attention to the transfer when she applied it.

This isn't about you, she wanted to tell him. But then again, maybe it was. She'd been imagining variations of this tattoo for several years, and yet she'd put off finding an artist and getting it done – too busy, no time to heal, maybe afraid to commit all the way to something so permanent. So now, because *he* suggested it and had a tattoo artist friend? Or now, because she deep down needed him to know how important integrity was to her, so much that she'd make it part of her skin to prove the point?

"Fuck me, Nell, that ink looks good on you," he said softly, and she wished she could see the expression on his face. "Gorgeous work as always, Ghostflower."

Ghostflower's warm chuckle sounded pleased. "You warm my heart, Peasy. Want anything yourself, while you're here? Just putting the Dermalize on, Nell, then you're done." Her capable hands touched the newly tattooed area with care, covering it with something that felt adhesive. Out of the corner of her eye, Nell could see that it was some kind of translucent film. *Peasy? Oh… Easy-peasy. Too funny.* Who would have thought the great and famous rock bassist would be nicknamed Peasy by his best friend?

"Yeah, maybe. Could you fit her name on me somewhere?"

What? "Eamonn, no!" Nell knew not to move while Ghostflower was sticking the protective wrap over her tattoo, but she twisted her head around as much as she could. "That's a little too flipping permanent, given how long we've known each other, don't you think?"

He chuckled and came around to where she could see him properly. "You're part of my story now, Nella-bella, no matter what happens going forward. I want you on my skin. I'm not expecting any promises of forever."

And that took the breath out of her. It was so much over the top, such a wild romantic gesture far too soon, and yet – *I'm not expecting any promises of forever.* Why did that sting a little, even as she swallowed a lump in her throat at the sweetness of him saying she was part of his story?

"You can get up now, Nell," Ghostflower said.

As Nell got to her feet, her lower back protesting movement more than the tattooed shoulder, Ghostflower was already peeling off her purple latex gloves and heading to the sink to wash up before putting on a new pair. Stell from the front desk hurried over to clean and reset the workstation, disinfecting the tattoo machine and sliding a fresh plastic sleeve over it, fitting on a disposable grip, setting out new needle cartridges in sealed blister packs.

"This isn't a good idea," Nell muttered.

Stell snickered, not looking up from the job at hand. "I've heard *that* before."

"Settle down, Stell," Ghostflower said mildly. She looked Eamonn over. "Shirt off. I'm thinking just under your collarbone, left side? Trust me to freehand it, or you want a stencil?"

He peeled off his shirt and tossed it to Nell, who caught it without thinking. It smelled like him – the body wash and deodorant he used, his skin, a faint tang of clean sweat. Ordinarily, if someone tossed a shirt at her, she'd toss it back or step aside and let it hit the floor, saying *I'm not your laundry maid*. But she was momentarily entranced by his spectacular bare torso, smooth muscles and ink and the light dusting of golden hair she found so beautiful, and then the moment to act had passed and she was left holding the shirt. She wasn't sure what she was supposed to do with it, but Stell noticed and said, "We got hooks on the wall for that."

Nell knew she'd missed something while she was hanging up the shirt, because she turned back to see a strange expression on Ghostflower's face as the artist shaved and disinfected the skin below Eamonn's left collarbone – affectionate, wistful, and maybe a little worried. They were talking in soft voices and it wasn't meant to be overheard, but Nell had sharp ears. "You falling in love, Peasy?"

Hearing the answer to that question, whatever it was, couldn't be good. "I'm going down to the bakery to get another tea," Nell said in a bright enthusiastic-instructor tone. *See? I'm leaving. Please have your awkward conversation while I'm not here.* "Does anyone want anything?"

There was no awkwardness later when they all went out for dinner. Ghostflower was kind and friendly, Justin turned out to have a wicked sense of humor, and even though Stell didn't talk much and was a good decade younger than the rest of them, the apprentice seemed glad to be included and smiled whenever Nell made eye contact. Eamonn sat close to Nell the whole time, often resting a hand on her thigh or wrapping an arm around her waist.

I could get used to this, she thought. His friends were good company. She could imagine her friend Amy fitting in with them too. It all seemed very comfortable and pleasant, and she kept waiting for the bubble to pop, the dream to end.

They stopped for ice cream cones to end the night, and walked back all together to where they'd parked, licking their ice cream in contented pleasure. "Want to try a taste of mine?" Eamonn offered, holding his cone out to Nell – he'd chosen cherry, creamy pink with bits of candied fruit and swirls of jam.

"Sure." She took a small lick, then held out her lemon ice cream to him, knowing that the tartness of it would make his mouth pucker after the sweet cherry. "Try mine."

She grinned at the expression on his face when he tasted it.

Ghostflower gave Nell a hug before leaving and Justin shook her hand. Stell waved goodbye from the back seat of Ghostflower's car, a little flutter of fingertips, and then it was just the two of them, standing in the street next to Eamonn's truck.

He opened the door for her, and because her back and neck still hurt and her head throbbed a bit and her freshly tattooed shoulder felt tender, she let him help her up into the seat.

"My place okay?" he asked, getting into the driver's seat.

"I should go home," Nell countered, though her heart wasn't in it.

He cocked an eyebrow at her. "Why?"

She didn't have an answer for that.

"Come on, lovely." His gaze turned sensual and his voice thickened, dropping into an undeniably sexy tone. "My bed is bigger than yours."

Why does he have to be so flipping irresistible? An answering tingle of desire flickered over her like lightning, just from the look in his eyes and the promise in his voice. "Don't know how much fun I'll be," she muttered, not wanting to admit to feeling pain, but not sure how much in the way of mattress gymnastics she could take.

He stifled a groan, but she still heard it. "You know I'm happy just to hold you," he said ruefully. He bit his lip, breathed out slowly. And that little demonstration of self-control set her fizzing like the fuse of a Roman candle – burning toward an explosion, no stopping what was started.

"I want more than that," she blurted out. "I'm just not sure how well I can ride you with my back messed up like this."

At that, he shot her a grin that was pure sinful heat. "All I needed to hear is that you want me." He put the car into gear. "Buckle up, babe. Let's get home."

In his sunshine-yellow bedroom, Eamonn helped Nell take off her t-shirt, easing it over the newly tattooed shoulder and lifting it straight up so she wouldn't have to bend or twist her back. Then he stripped down to his boxer briefs and flopped onto the bed, grinning at her, cupping his obvious erection through the cotton with one hand and patting the bed beside him with the other. "How d'you want to do this?"

"I..." She looked at the bed, and at him. "Being on top takes more hip action than I can manage tonight, and... lying down, I move around too much when I'm on my side, so I have to be pretty much flat on my back with something wedged under for support..." The obvious conclusion was inescapable and added an unaccustomed edge of vulnerability to her wanting him. She'd never accepted a passive position, always able to control their movement, always taking an active part in arriving at their mutual pleasure. Never pinned down.

It took him only a moment to reach the same conclusion. He gazed up at her, his expression taut, his eyes so dilated with desire that they appeared darker than their usual blue. "Are you going to let me climb on top of you tonight?"

She hadn't expected it to be that much of a turn-on for him. He liked a little bit of power exchange with his lovemaking – that had become clear enough, since telling him firmly what to do or what she needed could bring him to a point of helpless urgency – but she'd assumed he only went for the more submissive side of things. Apparently, though, it worked both ways for him, and the unexpected switch gave her a disturbing thrill of anticipation, an uncertain melting feeling that was unwelcome but not entirely unexpected. The idea of giving up control to him should not be so appealing. And yet, she was drawn to it, moth to flame.

With a small nod, she undressed down to her underpants and got onto the bed, carefully settling onto her back and adjusting the pillow under her head.

He stroked a hand down her belly to the waistband of her boyshorts and pinged it gently against her skin. "You said you needed something for support under your back. Take these off, and I'll get you a towel."

Ooh, he has an assertive mode! She hadn't seen that in him before – cocky and flirtatious, yes, but never with such a commanding tone. *Interesting... and reassuring.* She didn't always find it easy to let go of the instructor role and be fully a student, but that was necessary in order to train to a higher level, and there was a certain kind of peace in obeying commands. *Could it be the same with a lover I trust?* As he vanished into the bathroom for a moment, she gingerly inched the underwear down over her hips.

Eamonn returned at almost the same moment that Nell realized she was stuck. The sore muscles in her back protested any attempt to raise her legs, lift her hips, or curl to the side to get her underpants off. If she'd been standing, gravity would have done the job. As it was, she couldn't push the stretchy cotton past her fingertips' reach where it constrained her upper thighs. *Crap.*

He saw the problem immediately and tried not to laugh, but she could see it in his eyes. "Nobody's perfect all the time," she said. The grin he'd tried to suppress spread across his face like sun from behind clouds, and she contemplated wrenching herself up through the pain so she could flip him and pin him down.

"No," he agreed. "That's true. But you? You're pretty close, most of the time." He wedged the folded towel under her lower back, giving it some support, then ran a teasing hand over her upper thighs where her underwear had slid to a stop in its current partially lowered position. "And this? Sexy."

She tried to part her legs further and couldn't. Squirmed as his fingers brushed closer but still didn't touch. The muscles in her back protested, and she winced.

"No moving." He shook his head, teasing but also serious. "Neither of us is into pain, so you need to lie still, lovely. Let me do the work."

"All right," she gritted out, refusing to add *sir* although it was there in her mind.

He placed his free hand firmly on her abdomen to hold her steady, and then at last his fingers dipped down to stroke her where she needed it, slowly, far too slowly, but still blissful.

Her hips tilted a little to get more and his hand stilled, denying her.

"You're freaking killing me," she muttered.

He laughed, all too pleased with himself, cocking an eyebrow at her impatience. "Just relax. I'll get you there."

He continued his slow, tantalizing strokes – not fast enough or deep enough to satisfy her. The underwear binding her thighs prevented her from spreading them to get more of his touch. Her various aches receded in a haze of wanton urgency, and a wordless growl of frustration escaped her before he finally helped her kick her underwear away.

By the time he rolled the condom on and settled himself over her, she'd almost lost the capacity for coherent thought. His weight and strength on top of her invited an emotional surrender and relinquishing of power she wasn't sure she was ready to give.

"You're safe with me, Nella-bella," he reminded her, his voice low and thick with desire, then he chuckled affectionately. "And anyway, I'm pretty sure you could still kill me from there. But just... lie back and let me love you, okay?"

It was true. She could easily get a foot onto his hip, and from there... As he held himself above her, poised to enter but waiting for encouragement, she truly realized she'd never need to do it – unless someday he might be willing to play *that* game with her. She smiled and reached down between them to guide him in.

Without her usual focus on controlling and guiding the action, all Nell could do was lie back and *feel*. Somehow, Eamonn wasn't just thrusting into her body, but driving himself into her soul.

They slept in, and woke to sunshine trickling in around the edges of the curtains. A glorious day, clearly, and Nell could barely get out of bed.

"But you weren't this bad yesterday," Eamonn said, concern in his eyes.

"Second day," she grumbled. "It's always worse. Just need a hot shower."

He helped her to the bathroom and got into the shower with her, holding her against him under the hot spray so the water could flow over her back, angling her so that not too much of it would hit her left shoulder. She could feel his morning wood against her stomach but he didn't try to make anything of it, thankfully seeming to understand that she was too achy just then for any kind of fun, even though the skin-to-skin embrace felt good. "Are you sure you don't need to see a doctor?" he asked, wincing in sympathy when she shifted her weight and grimaced.

"It's only a pulled muscle. I'm fine. This is helping."

"I've got some Voltaren gel, if you want it after we're done here."

"That'd be great. Just a few minutes more like this..."

The steaming water streamed around them, beading on the Dermalize covering their new tattoos. Some pale pinkish-yellow fluid had collected underneath his, but she could still make out the letters of her name, permanently inked into his skin just under his collarbone. *Ridiculous man. Why?*

"Integrity, huh?" he said, nodding toward her left shoulder. "It means that much to you?"

She wondered how much fluid had gathered under the wrap covering it, how clearly the strong letters and graceful swirls could be seen. "It's... everything I am. Doing right, doing my best, trying my hardest even when no one will know. I–"

She could see the pulse beating in his throat, near a small tattooed star. "I admire that," he said, so softly that it was almost inaudible against the falling water.

After the shower, he was uncharacteristically quiet, getting dressed without any of his usual flirting and humor. Nell followed suit, putting on her sports bra and slightly damp underwear, feeling thankful that she'd thought to wash them out in the sink the night before. Damp was better than dirty or going bare.

Then, as he rubbed the aromatic pain-relief gel into her lower back, he said, "It matters to you, that I haven't told Blade how sorry I am." It was a statement, not a question, and he stood behind her so she couldn't see his face.

"You know I've accepted that it's none of my business," she reminded him.

"But would you... think better of me if I did?"

She whipped around to face him, annoyed that he was putting this burden onto her. *Why are we having this dead-end conversation again?* "It shouldn't matter what I think of you. Integrity is an inside-yourself thing. Yes, I think you'd be happier if you *tried* to resolve what happened, but for yourself and maybe for him, not for me."

His face looked bleak and hard. "Happier? You've got to be kidding me. Security'll throw me out on my ass before I can even say I'm sorry, and then what?" He sighed. "But I know what I have to do. At least I'll have tried. Will you come with me?"

"What?" *I can't have heard that correctly,* Nell thought.

"I can't do this alone. Will you – *please* – come with me?"

No! "Look, you can't do something like this because of what I said, or to make me 'think better of you.' It doesn't work like that." She wanted to roll her eyes, or stomp her feet in frustration, and most of all she wanted to make him *see* that you couldn't fake integrity to buy respect.

"I know!" he snapped back. They stared at each other. She could see his frustration simmering, mirroring her own. "T-shirts are in the top drawer there, if you want one. I'll be in the kitchen," he said, when the silence had stretched too far.

She took her time brushing her teeth. *Is this almost-arguing crap a thing that couples do?* She didn't generally care enough to let anyone get under her skin, or mind that they didn't understand something important to her. Still a bit on edge, she wasn't sure if she wanted to borrow one of his t-shirts, but eventually poked through his drawer and selected one with a Warwick logo.

As she descended the stairs, she smelled hot butter and something cake-like. When she got to the kitchen, she found a mug of tea steaming on the kitchen island breakfast bar for her and Eamonn methodically making pancakes with his back to the door.

She could tell by the tensing of his shoulders that he'd heard her come in, but he didn't turn or say anything.

"Thanks for the tea," she said, to break the silence.

"No trouble." He slid a pancake from pan to plate, added butter to the pan, poured more batter. Then, "I miss them. I want to try to fix things, but I'm a fucking coward, all right? I can't do it without you."

Well. Nell took a sip of tea, looking at his stiff back. "Right. So, you *are* being a coward, and the first step to fixing that is recognizing it and making the decision to do something about it."

He spun around, looking shocked that she'd just agreed with his self-assessment.

She grinned. "What? You thought I'd be nice and assure you that you're not a fraidy-cat at all? Me?" That drew a half-laugh from him. Then the sizzling sound and browning-butter smell from the frying pan behind him grew a bit stronger. "Don't let that pancake burn."

Just in time, he turned to flip it. "Thanks."

"I'm glad you've decided to try to fix things with your bandmates," she told him. "I know it takes courage. And... I *will* come with you. Not because you *need* me, not because you can't do it without me – you absolutely could – but because you *want* me with you. That means something to me."

"Nella-bella, I want you with me all the time." He lifted the last pancake out of the pan and added it to one of the plates, which he then brought over to set in front of her. "And especially for this. I'm so ashamed and afraid to face them, but you were right all along. I need to do it. Thank you." Having said that, he seemed to relax. "What d'you like on your pancakes? Ah, that is, I hope you like pancakes. I've got syrup, jam, whipped cream, cinnamon sugar..."

"You and your sweet stuff in the morning! Got any peanut butter? If not, I like them fine just plain."

He produced a jar of peanut butter from the cupboard, then grabbed his own plate of pancakes and loaded them up with syrup and whipped cream before sitting down at the island bar next to her. "I've got to tell you, though..." A note of doubt crept into his voice, and he forked up a big mouthful of pancake, effectively stopping what he was going to say.

Nell deliberately rolled her eyes at him. "What? You've already told me some pretty dark crap. Whatever it is now can't be worse, honestly."

He swallowed, cleared his throat. "I want you to come with me. More than anything. But we... have to do it my way."

"And what exactly is *your way*?"

"I've seen you being a ninja. You haven't seen me being a rock god yet."

"I absolutely have seen you *being Easy* – at the hospital, among other times. You're flirty and charming and you smile a lot. That's not so terrible."

"It's more than that. I can't roll up in an old t-shirt and a budget rental car – it's a first-class flights and limos kind of deal. I know to expect media attention and camera flashes, and you'll be with me, so..."

"Oh." Nell thought about that for a moment. How bad could it be? People took pictures of her competing at tournaments all the time. Then something else he'd said struck her. "You said flights. As in, taking an airplane? Just where *are* your bandmates right now?"

Eamonn shrugged and said, "Time Rock." It sounded as though he thought she'd know what that meant, but no, so she made an exaggerated inquiring face at him, and he threw his hands out in a *forgive me* gesture. "California."

"Right." She'd assumed they'd be here because he was, even though that made little sense once she thought about it.

"You don't *have* to come," he said, with hardly any hesitation in his voice, but she suspected he was regretting his words even as he spoke them.

"I promised," she told him. "Don't worry, I don't break my promises. I'll go with you." She could see the relief in his posture and his smile, and the way he dug into his pancakes with more appetite.

"Good." He spoke between bites, but not with his mouth full, which she appreciated. "I'll book our tickets." Bite of pancake, sip of coffee. "You'll probably want to go home for a bit to pack, and all that?"

Nell almost choked on a mouthful of tea. "Uh, when are we going?"

"Got to see when we can get a flight. Tomorrow, or maybe this evening."

Slow down! "Tomorrow is good," she said firmly.

❤

As soon as Eamonn had dropped Nell off at her place, once she was inside the front door of her building and out of his sight, she texted Amy: *I need to look like a rock star's girlfriend. By tomorrow. What do I do?*

Amy sent back a shocked-face emoji, almost immediately followed by the chimes of an incoming video chat request.

Nell let it chime away as she hustled the rest of the way up the stairs and down the hall to her apartment, then answered it with one hand as she unlocked the door and let herself in with the other.

"Nell! What's going on?" Amy asked as soon as they were connected. "Are you going to a costume party? Why not go as a rock star instead of just the girlfriend?"

"It's not a costume party. I've, uh, kind of been seeing someone."

Amy gasped. "Bestie, you're telling me that you've hooked up with a musician? *So* out of character – I'm impressed! So, are you going to a show or just a party? Who are you trying to impress? Bandmates? Manager? Or letting other women know he's taken?"

"The media, actually." Nell grinned at Amy's stunned expression. "I'm told it's very likely there will be pictures taken at the airport."

"Are you telling me I'd, like, recognize his name?"

"Well, his name is Eamonn, but... Easy Yarrow."

"No shit! *Easy*, as in the bass player who was kicked out of Smidge?!" Amy stared at Nell through the phone screen, her face a mix of envy and concern. "Nell, you know he's not exactly the good guy in any of the stories I've heard..."

Nell sighed. "He's told me what really happened. People make mistakes, right? It's what you do afterward that matters."

"Hmm." Amy didn't look or sound convinced. "Funny thing, a guy I know is touring with Smidge now. I could call him up, try to get the other side of the story for you."

"No! Promise me, Amy. Don't say anything to anyone. Eamonn's going there to apologize to them, to Smidge. Do *not* mess this up for him. But that's why I need help. I'm going with him, and I'm–"

Amy waved a shushing hand at the screen as she interrupted. "You're *you*, Nell. That's not a bad thing. Don't let anyone tell you to change."

"Thanks for the vote of confidence," Nell said, letting a bit of sarcasm bleed through in her voice. "The point is, I don't want to be mistaken for a bodyguard or PA or something."

"You do *walk* like a bodyguard." Amy giggled. "Oh, come on, bestie, don't be mad – you know you move like you're going to take people apart if they look at you wrong. But I see what you mean. And your work clothes make you look like a PA. Shit, I wish I were at home!" She tapped her fingernails against her phone screen, and the clicking sound echoed through the speaker. "Hold on, I think Johnny's performing in Seattle right now. I'll call you back."

"Who's Johnny?" Nell asked, but Amy had already ended the connection.

Practical action is best, she told herself. She took a load of pajamas and underwear down to the laundry room in the basement, then decided to look up Time Rock and find out what it was.

Ten minutes later, she was even more overwhelmed. It seemed that back in the 90s, some rock promoter had bought a vineyard overlooking Lake Hennessey in the Napa Valley and turned it into a concert venue. From what she could tell, a number of events were held there throughout the year, but the biggest of all was the Time Rock Music Festival, in which newer bands were paired up with bands whose first big hits had been recorded in past decades, each pairing sharing a stage as they alternated sets and then performed a few songs together. The official website showed glamorous pictures of beautiful people gathered around open-air bars and spectacular stages, lots of bare skin shining with sunscreen and sparkles, leather and metal accessories everywhere, rock t-shirts cut low and tied high on women or tight and de-sleeved on men. Grapevines and the blue twinkle of a lake view graced the soft-focus distance in every shot. *Crap.* She couldn't imagine fitting in with all that. *Give me a taekwondo tournament over this any day.* A trace of reluctance settled in her stomach. *But I promised.*

Her phone buzzed, alerting her to a new message from an unknown number: *Hi Nell, this is Johnny. Amy gave me your number. I can meet up with you this afternoon if you like, take you shopping?*

"Shopping?" Nell said out loud, momentarily taken aback. *Really kind of you,* she texted back, *but I think Amy maybe gave you the wrong idea. Wasn't planning on a shopping spree.*

I know you're on a budget, but she says you don't own any jeans, came his reply. *Trust me, I've been to Time Rock. You need a pair of jeans. Let's meet at the Westlake Center Starbucks and go from there.*

Faced with that, she agreed to meet him at three o'clock. Was there something wrong with preferring loose-fitting workout pants and stretchy, comfortable yoga pants? She asked how she would recognize him.

Pretty sure I'll be the only guy with pink hair, Johnny texted in reply.

♥

Nell made a point of arriving twenty minutes early, partly because she disliked even the risk of being late, and partly to counteract her reluctance – shopping in general used up time better spent doing other things, plus this particular trip involved buying an item of clothing she didn't want, with money she didn't have to spare, for an event that didn't appeal to her. She didn't love having strangers involved in her business, either, which Amy knew very well.

The tattoo wrap on her shoulder itched, and she wanted it off.

She sat by a window in the Starbucks, grimly sipping her tea, wondering whether Amy's friend Johnny was an on-time person or a late one. *Probably late.*

But he was five minutes early.

He *did* have pink hair – vivid neon pink hair, buzzed short around the back and sides, a couple of inches longer and expertly styled on top. Lean and toned in a way that made her think he might be an athlete, he walked into the coffeehouse like he owned it. *That's some confidence,* Nell thought with grudging respect. She stood up and raised a hand in a small wave so that he'd know she was the person he was looking for.

He returned her wave with a smile and pointed to the lineup, indicating that he'd order something and then join her.

In a relatively short time, he'd acquired some kind of iced coffee drink and was striding up to her table, his hand out for her to shake. "You must be Nell. I'm Johnny. Good to meet you." He sat down, took a sip of his drink, hauled his backpack onto his lap, and said, "While we're sitting here, let's talk about makeup. Get that out of the way."

What the ever-loving hell? "I really don't know what Amy told you, but–"

"You've met a musician dude and are going to Time Rock with him, and you don't want to be mistaken for a roadie or PA or something, so you need to look like a Girlfriend with a capital G."

"Sure, but I know how to put on eyeliner. And I'm not going to coat my face with all kinds of gunk."

Johnny laughed. "Amy told me you'd say that. You wear sunscreen, don't you? So all I want you to do is use this instead." He took a small makeup bag out of his backpack and extracted a pastel-green pump bottle. "Sunscreen moisturizer with skin brighteners – think of it like, oh, a super-subtle hint of shimmer, barely even noticeable. But it'll give you that music festival glow you want."

Shimmer. Ick. But Nell nodded her acceptance. *Barely even noticeable* didn't sound so bad. And she *had* asked for help, so it would be foolish to refuse it now. "Okay. What else do I need to do?"

He reached into the makeup bag again and brought out a fat jet-black eye pencil, a round eyeshadow container with glittery contents the color of an almond cookie, and a brush, all of which looked brand new, still sealed with plastic bands. "This is a super easy look you can't screw up. Smudgy black liner will give you a good rock festival vibe – just draw it on thick, top lid and bottom, and smudge it a little with your finger – it's supposed to be messy. Then you take your brush and do your whole upper lid with this shadow, and you're done. It's so sheer, you really can't go wrong. Add mascara if you like, but don't worry if that's not your jam. Either way, you won't look like an office girl."

"Thank you," she said, a bit nonplussed, and put the items into her purse. "How much do I owe you?"

He waved that away. "You don't owe me anything at all. Amy and I go back a long way. I owed *her* a favor and a bit of money. She told me taking care of you today would put us square."

Nell bit her lip. "I hate to be awkward, but I don't feel right taking the makeup as a gift. You don't even know me."

"I got it in a swag bag at an event and it doesn't fit my look, so it's yours. My time is well spent if anything I say or do helps you walk around Time Rock like you own it and have a blast with your man. Shall we go find you some jeans now?"

She blinked at him. "Your look?"

He batted his eyelashes at her and pouted, and for a moment became entirely feminine in body language and expression, then relaxed back into being Johnny. "When I'm in drag, you'd call me Ripped Creme."

No wonder she'd thought him both graceful and athletic. The name even sounded a bit familiar, though she couldn't be sure how or where she'd heard it. "No wonder you know so much about makeup, then."

"That, and I can sew almost anything, but even *I* have to shop for my jeans. So maybe you'll trust me to help you find something you'll like?" he asked, with an encouraging smile. "Let's take our drinks and walk. I've got a few different shops in mind, and don't worry, I won't forget you're on a tight budget."

Two hours, three stores, and what felt like four dozen pairs of jeans later, Nell was ready to give up. "Jeans just plain don't suit me," she said to Johnny, doing her best to keep the frustration out of her voice. "I feel bad for wasting your time."

He shook his head. "Helping someone find her inner queen is never a waste. I'm taking you to Bee Cute. It's a teeny bit pricier, but they can fit anyone. I get *my* girl jeans there, okay?"

She sighed but nodded. As they walked, she said, "I don't think it's the fit."

"No? Well, here we are."

Bee Cute had denim like Nell had never seen it. Laced up, cut away, bedazzled, acid washed, rainbow tie-dyed...

A motherly-looking older woman with waist-length hippie hair came out from behind the counter to greet Johnny. "Hey, hey, Rip! I can't wait 'til your season of *Drag Dolls* airs, so exciting. What can we find for you today?"

"Ruby! I'm not supposed to talk about it. Wait for July, darling." He let her hug him, then drew Nell forward. "I have a hard-to-fit friend here. She's going to Time Rock and needs some truly fuck-off jeans."

Nell cringed. She couldn't help it. "I really just need something normal that doesn't make me look too..." *Hard. Unfeminine. Too much muscle. Thighs like tree trunks. Chunky Booty.* Every disparaging comment she'd ever overheard came roaring back into her mind. In athletic pants or running shorts, she was an athlete, a competitor, but in jeans...

Johnny took a look at her face and said, "Shit, Nell, what is it?"

She shrugged. "I've worked hard for my body. I'm proud of it. But... it's an athlete's body, not a girly one. My butt and thighs are, uh, not small. And anything that fits me at the waist is wrong in the butt and too tight in the thighs. I look like a tank."

"I hate to break it to you," said the shopkeeper, "but his thighs are bigger than yours, and Ripped Creme can work stretch denim like nobody's business."

Johnny wasn't laughing. "I wish I'd come to meet you in drag today. I could do this so much better as Rip. Fuck." He rubbed the back of his neck. "Okay, look, you're trying to hide yourself in jeans, picking baggy boyfriend styles, but more fabric isn't better here. I want you to let Ruby find you something tight and sassy to show off what you've got. When AC/DC sang about American thighs, they weren't talking about toothpicks. Strong thighs are sexy, so make that work *for* you."

Nell raised her eyebrows, trying not to let too much of her disbelief show. "At this point, I'll try anything on."

Ruby bustled away, and Johnny said, "Your musician boyfriend – has he got a band shirt for you to wear, or..."

"Oh, I don't think – it would be awkward. He's, uh, estranged from his... I think you'd call them ex-bandmates at the moment. I don't want to say too much."

Johnny gave her a sharp look. "I only know of one band at Time Rock this year that recently dumped their *bassist* for being a nefarious prick. Please tell me that's not your man?"

Crap. "He does play bass, but–"

"Nell. We *are* talking about Easy and Smidge, aren't we?"

"If you have to know, we're going to Time Rock so he can apologize for what he did. People make mistakes."

Now it was Johnny's turn for raised eyebrows and polite disbelief. "You know he had a pretty bad reputation even before that incident, don't you?"

All she could think of was Eamonn saying *I'd only ever felt part of Smidge when we were all high* and *it felt less like being abandoned after a show if I was busy screwing my brains out.* "And wasn't all of Smidge rolling about in a confetti storm of drugs and groupies not so long ago? Don't half the rock stars out there end up partaking one way or another, at least for a while? As far as I can tell, he's mostly guilty of being a recreational drug user who *didn't* turn into an addicted moral message, as though it's somehow worse that he could walk away from it at will, while everyone forgives the sad rehab cases."

"Point taken. Guard your heart, is all I'm saying. Amy wouldn't want you to get hurt, and nor do I. Does she know who you're seeing?"

"Yes."

"Well, you're definitely playing in the big league. Let's find you some body armor." He gestured toward Ruby as she returned with an armful of denim in various shades.

Right away, Nell pointed to the bubblegum pink fabric sticking out of the pile. "No pink. That's a hard limit for me. And I'm not wearing anything that laces up the outside of the leg, either," she added, eyeing some lacing and grommets. Johnny and Ruby looked at each other and snickered.

Ruby looked Nell up and down, considering. "You don't look like a goth girl to me, so maybe not the all-black look in the summer heat, either." Nell wouldn't have minded black, but Ruby had already moved on. "Here's a cream pair, and we could try these mid-blue ones, and – oh, this acid wash would look fantastic on you!"

Acid wash should go back to the Eighties, Nell grumbled to herself, stifling resentment as she found herself bundled into a changing cubicle with the light blue jeans. But the denim was soft to the touch and stretched comfortably over her thighs. The back pockets were embroidered with a scattering of silver stars. *I could wear these.*

Ruby clapped when Nell came out of the changing room. "Looks like you've found your brand! And it's on a two-for-one promotion right now, so you should pick up a second pair. Let's see..." And Nell ended up walking out of Bee Cute with the acid wash jeans *and* a pair of pale grey capris in her shopping bag. Johnny had a bag too, although she wasn't sure what he'd bought.

"Happy with those?" he asked, as the two of them stepped out into the street. "Because they look more than fine. Your legs and ass are on fire, cutie."

Nell nodded. "These'll do." She almost tacked on a half-hearted *don't call me cutie,* but she recognized that it was a genuine compliment and couldn't bring herself to object.

"What about a rock shirt for your top half?"

"I'm good." Nell grinned. "I have a Dexter Gordon Club House Session t-shirt."

He laughed out loud at that. "Bringing jazz to a rock festival. I like it." He turned to look her in the eyes and said, "My buddy Rhys from back home is touring with Smidge right now. He'll be at Time Rock. He's a good guy – Amy knows him too – so if you have any problems, find him. I'm going to message him to watch out for you."

Eamonn isn't going to hurt me, she wanted to say, but she only smiled. "Thanks, Johnny."

At the bus stop, as her bus was pulling in, Johnny pushed his plastic shopping bag from Bee Cute into her hands. "Here. Gift. Bet you won't wear this, but... I dare you. Go knock Time Rock on its ass." And he was striding away down the crowded sidewalk before she could say or do anything in response, and the bus door was open, the driver waiting, so she didn't have a choice but to board it.

HAT NIGHT, NELL HAD TROUBLE SLEEPING. *THIS IS ridiculous,* she thought, cautiously rolling over and flipping her pillow for the hundredth time.

When Eamonn had called to say they had a flight booked for 11:45 AM the next day, he'd also asked if she wanted to go out for dinner and then stay the night with him. She'd said no.

The idea of spending so much time with someone, when she was used to her own place and space, had her a bit on edge. *I don't want to get dependent on his company.* But she had to admit that she'd be sleeping better with his big warm body next to hers. At least her back pain had subsided to mild discomfort, and the bruise on the side of her head only hurt when she touched it.

Eventually, sleep did come. She then slept through her alarm and had to rush her workout and shower – not an auspicious start to a travel day.

Her phone pinged. A message from Amy popped up – *No hair ties! Hair loose, use mousse. Wear the new jeans!*

Nell laughed ruefully and took off the yoga pants she'd planned to wear. *That woman knows me too well.* With a shrug, she finger-combed a handful of mousse through her still-damp hair. Instead of her usual sunscreen, she applied the sunscreen moisturizer Johnny had given her, and the barely-there shimmer just looked healthy and summery. *Fine.* A little bit of smudgy eye pencil, and she was done. *I'll do eyeshadow and mascara at Time Rock, but this is enough for now.*

She double-checked the contents of her backpack and purse. The Dexter Gordon t-shirt and grey denim capris were there, folded and ready, along with a sleep shirt and matching shorts, a tank top and a pair of athletic shorts, underwear and socks. *Deodorant,* she thought, and added it to the bag. With a shake of her head, she tucked her yoga pants in where she'd taken the acid wash jeans out, and added her bathing suit and a stretchy black velour going-out shirt, just in case. For the plane, she'd decided to wear a martial arts t-shirt – a way of saying *this is who I am* to the cameras and curiosity she'd been warned about. *Makeup bag, check. Tablet, earbuds, phone, check. Two books, just in case, check.*

That had to be everything. But then she bit her lip and looked at the Bee Cute shopping bag she'd thrown on top of her dresser. *I dare you,* Johnny had said.

She opened the bag.

Flashes of reflected light splashed everywhere as she extracted the gift and held it up. He'd given her a pair of blue denim cutoff shorts, the same brand as her new jeans – very short and bedazzled all over the pockets and side seams with what looked like hundreds of sparkling rhinestones. *No way. I refuse. And anyway, I didn't agree to any dare.* She stuffed the shorts back into the bag and threw it back onto her dresser.

She jammed her sandals into the top of the bag and set her black athletic shoes by the door, ready to put on. *Toothbrush,* she remembered, and grabbed it from the bathroom. *All set.* And she still had ten minutes until Eamonn had said to be ready.

Filling time was never a problem. She gave the cactus a bit of water, then tested out the stretch of her jeans with some kicks and a few segments of her form. *Not bad.* She laced on her shoes. When her phone buzzed to let her know that Eamonn had arrived, she picked up her backpack and purse and headed out the door.

Go knock Time Rock on its ass, Johnny had said.

Oh, ever-loving hell. Nell dashed back into her bedroom and grabbed the Bee Cute bag from her dresser. *I'm still not wearing them, but I'll take them with me for luck.*

♥

The limousine was enormous. Not a party bus, but the next thing to it, the kind that took ten or twelve people to proms and weddings.

Nell came to a dead stop on the front steps of her apartment building. Neighbors who'd never paid her the slightest bit of attention were staring – at the shining black vehicle, then at her, then at the doorway to the building as though maybe she'd just come out by random chance while the bride or prom queen was delayed.

The chauffeur got out and came around to open the door, and when Nell didn't immediately rush over and hop in, Eamonn unfolded himself from the limo's comfortable interior and got out. *No, not Eamonn. This is Easy.* The low profile was gone.

Biker boots, a black leather vest. His tight chocolate brown t-shirt had the sleeves rolled to show off his inked arms. Heavy silver rings gleamed on his fingers. He'd done something to his hair to enhance its natural blond waves into a sexy tousled bedhead style, and his weekend beard had been trimmed to a fine stubble. He looked expensive and dangerous.

He leaned against the side of the limo and grinned at her, arms crossed, pleased maybe that his giant form of transportation had brought her to a standstill. There was something challenging and unpredictable about him today, a wildfire energy she hadn't seen in him before. They stared at each other. Would he come to her or would she go to him? She had a bad feeling that if he made that move, it would involve a public kiss, and there was already more attention on them than she felt comfortable with.

Take command of the situation. She closed the distance between them with confident strides and rose up on her tiptoes to plant a quick kiss on his stubbled jaw. Before he could react, she tossed her backpack into the vehicle, said a quick "thank you" to the chauffeur, and got in.

"I can put your bag in the trunk, ma'am," the chauffeur said.

There's lots of room in here, Nell wanted to say, but both men seemed to expect that bags would go in the trunk as a matter of course, so she handed it out for the chauffeur to take.

Through the limo door, she could see that more people were starting to gather, many of them taking pictures as Easy smiled and waved. A couple of women scuttled up and begged to take a selfie with him, and she could hear him say loudly enough for the rest of the crowd to hear, "Just this one, since you lucky ladies asked first, then I've got to go catch a plane with my girlfriend."

In the next moment, he was climbing into the limo. There was a ridiculous amount of room, but he sat right beside her and put his arm around her shoulders, smiling out at the bystanders and waving once more as the chauffeur closed the door.

"What was that all about?" Nell asked, shrugging his arm away once there was no one to see.

He glanced at her in surprise but didn't seem to realize there was a problem. "Oh, well, I'm not hiding anymore. I wanted to be recognized, so I got recognized." The big car's motor thrummed into life and pulled out into traffic, heading for the airport.

"No, I mean that *performance.* Being a cocky ass. Waiting for me to come to you. Telling those women they were lucky. Not thanking the driver."

Eamonn laughed. "I'm a rock god, baby. I told you. It's a different world."

"No." She pushed herself away from him to sit on the opposite bank of seats. "That's crap. There *is* no world in which you're excused from thanking people and being respectful and kind. Don't fool yourself that it's okay. And don't think I can't hear the difference when you call me *baby* like *that,* either."

His brows lowered. He looked taken aback and pouty. "That's quite a lecture. Are you going to hit me now?"

She seethed. It would be so easy to kick him, right from where she sat. But she knew she never would – her self-control was far too deeply ingrained to be broken by petty temptation. "I only ever defend myself. Are you planning to give me cause?"

That jolted him. "No! Look, I'm sorry I called you *baby.*"

"Don't be obtuse. I'm used to your pet names by now. The problem is in the way you said it."

He ran a ringed hand through his hair, ruining his careful styling. "It's not enough that you've pushed me into trying to apologize to people I'd planned never to see again? You're going to tell me how to talk, now?"

Nell leveled her last-warning instructor stare at him. "You don't have to do anything you don't want to do, and you can talk however you like. But you'd better tell your driver to let me off anywhere that's convenient, because I really don't need to stick around and take this kind of crap."

"Very funny," he said, with a sour twist to his mouth.

"I'm not kidding. You said you wanted to fix things with your bandmates – was that the truth, or just some line you were feeding me? Because no one is pushing you anywhere. You can take that back or let me out of this car. Your choice." A sad lump of regret filled her throat as soon as she'd spoken the words. He was beautiful and funny and the best sex she'd ever had, and it would be hard to walk away from that. But she knew she'd stand by the choice she'd just given him. *I'm not here to carry the weight of your fear or regret. You're a grown man; own your crap.* And it bothered her how viscerally she hoped that he would.

The only sound was the smooth hum of the limousine's motor, punctuated by the occasional honk or heavy engine sound from the traffic outside.

"Fuck me," Eamonn grumbled at last. "I know you're not. I'm just nervous." And when she raised her eyebrows at him, he added, "Sorry."

The relief she felt was flat-out ridiculous. *I could have walked away,* she told herself. "Nerves are okay, but don't take them out on me."

For a moment, she saw a flicker of answering relief in his face – they'd dodged a rough landing there – and then it shifted into something a lot more playful and seductive. "Yes, ma'am," he said softly, with a sultry gaze, heavy-lidded. *I've been a bad boy,* he seemed to be saying. *Discipline me.*

She crossed her arms, tempted but unwilling to give in, even as she wondered how the shorter stubble on his jaw would feel against her skin. "No. You don't get to play games with this and make it about sex. Use some flipping self-control and turn your rock god persona into someone who's not an ass."

A hint of red washed up from his shirt collar and he looked away. "I just give people what they want."

He really believes that. And in that moment, she felt sad for him. "Your dirty-sweet smiles and flirty winks are what they want, Eamonn. Look at how Jessalyn and the nurses ate up your charm and went all googly because you brought flowers."

"Got to be nice to people in hospitals – they're usually having a tough enough time already." He shrugged.

"And you don't think you could make your driver's day a little bit better with a smile and some appreciation? How about actually talking to your bandmates, telling them how you feel, instead of just playing a part?"

"Ouch. Low blow," he said.

And it was; she knew that. *Crap.* "I'm not at my most confident right now either," she admitted. Saying those words horrified her a bit – she prided herself on always projecting confidence and keeping everything under control. But he'd admitted he was feeling nervous, and she'd paid him back by digging at the way he'd handled his bandmates. *An unacceptable slip of self-discipline.* "This is completely not my world, and I'm feeling a bit... on edge. I do think you should be yourself with your bandmates, as much as you can, but I could have put it in a kinder way."

He nodded his acceptance of that. "I guess I'm about to find out what being real with them feels like. And you're about to find out what being a rock star's girlfriend feels like."

"We can do it," she said, injecting as much brightness and confidence into her voice as she could to mask her dread, and turned to look out the window.

They were nearing the airport, heading toward the departures drop-off zone.

"Maybe this wasn't so smart," he muttered to himself.

"What?" She glanced over at him, only to see him shaking his head. "Come on, tell me."

"I didn't think this through. I haven't been to an airport without a bodyguard since Smidge first got big enough for us to be recognized."

That made Nell laugh, then she stifled it as she saw that he was genuinely concerned. "You're with *me*, Eamonn. I'm not going to let anything happen to you." As the car slowed to a stop, she laid a hand on his arm. "Stay here while I get a cart for our bags."

"The driver can do that," he said.

She gave him her instructor face. *We're doing this my way.* "I'm getting a cart and having a look around. I'll let the driver get the bags out of the trunk, though. Stay in the car 'til I tell you, okay?" Focusing on safety banished her uncertainty and put her back in control of the situation. Without waiting for his response, she opened the door and got out, surprising the chauffeur who had come around to open it. "Oh, hi there. I'm just going to grab a cart, if you'll get our bags from the trunk."

"Sure, ma'am." Nonplussed, but professional.

The airport was about as busy as she'd have expected for June, but most of the travelers seemed to be focused on their own needs and weren't paying much attention to others, although a few glanced over in passing at the giant limousine. *Good.* No one appeared to be loitering or triggered her sense of threat.

She watched as the driver loaded the cart with the contents of the trunk – her backpack, his expensive-looking black Rollaboard bag, and a guitar case. *We didn't need the cart.* She'd expected him to travel with more stuff, somehow.

Backing down from the plan she'd laid out wasn't going to happen, though. *Nope. We're taking the cart.*

With only carry-on items, they'd be able to bypass the checked-baggage counter and head straight for security. It felt strange to be traveling without her gear bag, which she always had to check because even training weapons weren't permitted in carry-on bags and most of her flying experience involved going to tournaments. "Thank you," she said to the driver. "You can let your other passenger out now." She stood back, watching. A test, of sorts.

He emerged from the limo in a smooth motion, looking practiced and confident, as though the whole world was his stage. It didn't matter that his audience was a handful of travelers who'd stopped to gawk at the size of the limo, not knowing who was in it. He doled out winks, waves, and nods of acknowledgment to anyone who made eye contact, all with that flirty, dirty grin of his – then he checked himself and turned to the chauffeur for a moment, saying, "Thanks very much, man. You want an autograph or selfie, now's the time to ask."

"We're not supposed to, sir," the uniformed man began, then paused and dug his phone out of a pocket, "but I'd love to get a picture to show my girl." So Easy leaned in for a photo moment before turning his attention to Nell.

"You're pushing the cart," she said. "I want both my hands free, just in case."

She positioned herself on his right, half a pace ahead of him – not enough to be obvious but enough to have a good view of anything approaching his left side – and stuck there through security and all the way to their gate. Nothing happened. Sure, a few people did double-takes as they passed, pointed their phone cameras in his direction or elbowed a companion with a *look over there* expression, but there was no threat. No one even approached.

Eamonn turned to her as they boarded the plane. "I guess I didn't need to worry about needing a bodyguard," he said with a shrug, and a hint of a blush colored his cheekbones. "Airports seemed to generate more of a fuss... before. Maybe I'm just washed up."

"Always better to be safe," Nell assured him. "And there were plenty of people eyeballing you and sneaking photos; you can still draw a crowd. They just had the good sense not to get too close to *me*." *You move like you're going to take people apart if they look at you wrong,* Amy had said, and Nell wasn't going to let that sting. *So what if I do?* She was here, wasn't she, boarding a first-class flight with an actual rock star?

"Excuse me, sir, you can't bring your instrument on board, you're going to have to – oh!" The flight attendant at the door of the plane blinked as she got a good look at Eamonn's face, then double-checked his boarding pass. "Er, Mr… Yarrow, that's one of your concert basses, I guess?" She looked flustered. Her nametag said *Pam*.

"Sure is. This one's my favorite, my blue Warwick. Not going in the cargo hold, sorry. They told me the crew would find somewhere safe for it."

Pam turned pink and nodded. "Of course. Our pleasure. I can put it in the coat closet for you, sir." She held out her hands to take the guitar case, which had clearly risen in status with her recognition of its owner.

He gave her a dazzling smile, Easy the rock god at his very best. "Thank you, darling. And you don't need to be formal – call me Easy."

With an impressed "Wow! Thank you!" Pam carried the precious instrument away, leaving Eamonn and Nell to find their seats; the first-class recliners seemed huge compared to the economy seating Nell was used to. *Maybe it's not so terrible to be taking a break from training for a few days.* For years, all her travel had been to tournaments and seminars, never a real vacation.

Pam came over to offer them pre-takeoff beverages, so Nell shortly found herself sipping a mimosa in comfort while the economy passengers boarded. "*Sláinte,*" Eamonn said and clinked his glass against hers. "Time to enjoy your vacation." He looked a little grim and downed his drink too fast. *Worrying about what's waiting for him at the end of the flight,* Nell thought, but didn't say anything. Apologizing for a wrong done to someone wasn't easy, and no words could lighten that load for him.

❤

When their flight landed in Sacramento, Pam came over to them while the plane was still taxiing; she offered snacks and more drinks to soften the inconvenience as she asked them to stay in their seats while the other passengers disembarked.

"Something wrong?" Eamonn asked.

The flight attendant gave them a big *everything's fine* smile. "Your security escort is on the way to the gate and should be ready for you in, like, two minutes. Do you have a car service booked, or is someone meeting you?"

Nell glanced over at Eamonn, who had a quizzical expression on his face, one eyebrow cocked. "Car service, but... I didn't arrange for any security escort," he said.

"There's a little media cluster gathered in arrivals and the airport has reason to believe they're waiting for you. So, a complimentary VIP escort is being arranged – I swear it will only be a couple of minutes."

"See?" Nell said once Pam had moved away. "You're still famous."

He gave her a look of pity for her ignorance and slumped against the back of his seat, resigned to waiting. "They're just looking for dirt. Guess I'm going to give it to them."

"Well, what are you supposed to do in this sort of situation?"

"Kin always said – he's this music-industry public relations guy we had around – he always said to just smile and wave and keep walking, keep moving, and if you have to give 'em unprepared sound bites, make it two words: great night, thank you, awesome crowd, love you, no comment. *You can't get into trouble with pairs of words,* he told us."

"Is that what you're going to do?" she asked.

Eamonn grinned, thoughtful and slightly mischievous. "I don't know."

♥

They disembarked from the courtesy cart at the escalator and rode down two stories to the ground-floor concourse, carrying their bags this time, with a uniformed security officer ahead of them and another behind. They could see that Pam's described "cluster" of people with cameras and microphones, gathered around the foot of the escalator, had attracted curious bystanders and grown into something of a crowd.

"Take my hand," Eamonn said into Nell's ear. "And don't let go 'til we get to the car."

She shook her head. "I need both hands free, just in case."

"We have two airport security people with us. Just trust me on this."

Recognizing that she wasn't an expert on the current situation, she conceded the point and reached out to grip his hand. *At least I'm on the right side.*

"Smile for the cameras," he reminded her, and they stepped off the escalator, into the crowd.

The security officers kept anyone from getting too near, but the core knot of media followed closely as they moved toward the exit to the car service pickup area, some holding out microphones, others holding up cameras. Their shouted questions seemed to jumble into each other, but Nell heard "confront" and "revenge" and "make trouble" – looking for dirt, indeed. Eamonn kept on smiling, walking in silence, until they reached the sliding glass doors beyond which a limousine waited for them.

There, he let go of Nell's hand and turned to face the crowd, gesturing for silence. The security officers looked surprised – everyone looked surprised – and a hush came over all of them, waiting for him to speak. "I'm here because I owe someone an apology," Eamonn said, his voice firm and clear. "I hope he accepts it." More quietly, he added, "Thank you very much," to the security officers, then wrapped an arm around Nell's waist and swept her through the doors, away from the rising clamor of requests for more detail, more comments, more. The security officers blocked anyone from following them through the doors, and they handed their bags to the chauffeur and got into the waiting limousine without incident.

"That was unexpected," Nell blurted out.

Eamonn nodded slowly. "I didn't exactly plan it. I just – hearing them shout about confrontation and revenge, they were so wrong, and..."

She reached out and laid a reassuring hand on his thigh. "It was good. Honest. Makes me proud of you."

He blinked away something that could have been a mote in his eye, or moisture. "Well, I don't know if we've got a chance of getting to Blade before some reporter does, but it's worth a shot. I'm going to ask the driver to find us a Starbucks drive-thru before we hit the freeway, though. Chai latte?"

"Please."

♥

Even with a stop for coffee, the drive into the Napa Valley didn't take much over an hour. Glorious blue sky stretched from horizon to horizon, only broken by a few tiny clouds like shreds of cotton candy, and the powerful black car ate up the miles as its occupants sipped from their to-go cups in air-conditioned comfort.

Eamonn wasn't saying much, mostly playing with his phone or looking out the window, a rather grim expression on his face. Nell could see he didn't want to be prodded or talked at.

Eventually, the limousine turned off the highway onto a side road, and shortly thereafter turned again down a long driveway, passing under an arch covered with climbing roses to approach a building with creamy stucco walls and terracotta roof tiles. A glossy wooden sign welcomed them to Rancho Rosal Inn.

"Are we staying here?" she asked.

"*They're* staying here. Smidge booked the whole place. There's a good chance I'll be thrown out on my ass, but I expect they'll be nice to you."

The driveway curved up to a u-shaped drop-off area in front of the hotel. Double French doors had *Reception* etched into frosted glass panes, and a hand-lettered sign taped to the glass read *sorry, no rooms available*. A few feet to the right, an archway with a wrought-iron gate gave a glimpse of a courtyard and pool. A fit man in a black Smidge crew t-shirt sat on a folding chair just inside the gate – he turned to look at the limousine pulling up but didn't leave his seat.

The vehicle stopped. The driver's door opened and closed; he'd be coming around to open the door for Eamonn and Nell at any moment. Behind the tinted windows, they looked at each other. He seemed anxious, doubtful.

"You've got this," she said, reaching out to give his thigh a reassuring stroke.

"Kiss me for luck," he rasped, his voice gone dry. So she leaned in and pressed her lips to his. He kissed her back with desperation, transmitting his tension, then it melted into something sweeter, better. He tasted of coffee.

They broke apart when the driver opened their door. Eamonn gestured for Nell to get out ahead of him. *Ladies first*, she could imagine him thinking. Or maybe he just wanted to delay the inevitable for a few more seconds.

The man at the gate didn't seem fazed when Nell emerged from the limo – perhaps it wasn't unusual for random females to turn up wherever the band was staying – but as soon as he recognized Eamonn behind her, he tensed and his face went professionally blank. "Easy. No one told me you were coming. They expecting you?"

"Hey, Ramón. No, I thought I'd surprise them if I could get here before the gossip reporters did." Eamonn strolled casually toward the gate, gripping Nell's hand with a firmness that told her his laid-back body language was faked.

Ramón looked wary. "Maybe you should have called first, find out if they want to see you. Not all surprises are good ones."

"I'm not here to cause trouble, man. Trust me. This is my girlfriend Nell; would I have brought her with me if I'd wanted to start something?"

"Girlfriend?" Ramón blinked. "That's... different." He looked at Nell with new interest and seemed to be softening. "You're not his usual kind of groupie, baby."

"Two points." Nell spoke calmly and firmly, the instructor explaining concepts to a student who'd misunderstood. She didn't want to antagonize the man, who might be their key to getting inside the hotel – the easy way, at least – but nor was she willing to let anyone talk to her in that insulting tone. "One, I'm not a groupie. I don't even listen to rock music much. And two, you do not have permission to call me *baby*. I answer to Nell, Miss Whelan, or ma'am."

There was a moment's pause, then Ramón burst out laughing. "I... can't... even..." he managed to gasp between chuckles. "You're just so... *unexpected.*"

"Better get used to it," Eamonn said with a grin.

"You two planning to be around here much?" Ramón asked, sounding more curious than antagonistic.

"Look, I'm here to apologize to Blade." Eamonn held out a hand in what was almost a pleading gesture. "My best chance to do that is if you'll let me in so I can find him and say it face to face. I have no idea what'll happen afterward."

"They've got a new bass player, you know." The slightly belligerent edge to Ramón's voice as he relayed this fact made Nell wonder whether Eamonn had been less than pleasant to him in the past.

"Hard to do without one," Eamonn shot back, his good intentions apparently souring.

Flipping hell. Nell gave his hand a squeeze, hoping he'd remember that their goal was to get inside, not win a pissing contest with a crew member guarding the gate. "So, Ramón? Can I ask you something?"

"Sure."

"Were you specifically told not to let Easy through the gate? I'd understand if you didn't want to disobey a direct order like that..."

Ramón shook his head. "I've been with this crew a good bit of time now. I get told if they're expecting someone they want to see. Otherwise, they trust me to use my judgment."

She gave him an encouraging smile. "So, what would it take to get us inside? I promise you, we're here to make things right, that's all."

"Well, I don't know. Your man's attitude with the crew doesn't make us want to do favors..." And under his breath he added, "Arrogant ass."

Nell had lots of experience with students who added things under their breath, thinking the instructor wouldn't hear or would somehow let it pass. "Oh? I should think arrogance is pretty common among rock stars. Doesn't it just go with the territory?"

Ramón squirmed a little. "Lots of the time, sure. Smidge, though – Angel always treats us right, one of the few true gentlemen of rock, so it sets our standards high. And Dice has the biggest heart in the world, he'd literally help us do our jobs if we let him. Blade can be prickly when he's in a mood, it's true, but he apologizes afterward like a man should, and he'll party with the crew like we're brothers."

"I guess they don't feel like they have to prove over and over they belong on the stage and not back with the groupies," Eamonn snapped, then reddened as both Nell and Ramón turned to stare at him. "I didn't mean–"

"Of course you belong on the fucking stage, man," Ramón said at once, cutting off whatever Eamonn would have said. "You may be an ass, but you're a gifted one." He sighed, an exaggerated concession, and got up to open the gate. "Oh, go on in. Maybe they'll be glad to see you."

"Thanks," Eamonn said. "I almost wish you'd said no, because facing Blade after all that is one of the toughest things I've ever had to do."

Ramón gave a dry chuckle and punched Eamonn on the arm in encouragement, perhaps a little harder than necessary, as he passed through the gate.

Right on the pressure point, Nell thought. And they were in.

No one noticed the two visitors at first.

The central courtyard was almost breathtakingly beautiful. Crystal clear water reflected the sky from a sunken central Art Deco swimming pool and matching hot tub tiled in shades of turquoise. Chairs grouped around patio tables invited guests to sit by the pool, and three men sat around one of them, poring over a stack of papers. Climbing roses rambled up the creamy plaster walls; stairs at either end of the courtyard led to the second-floor rooms, where a walkway with a wrought-iron railing wrapped around the courtyard, serving as both a balcony and an outdoor hallway. Here and there people came and went, carrying boxes or instruments or clothing – Rancho Rosal was a luxury boutique hotel, but the crew who'd taken it over were there to work, at least at this hour.

A man emerged from one of the ground-floor rooms with a mixing console in his arms and some cables draped around his shoulders. He almost walked right by Nell and Eamonn, then did a double take and paused. "Easy?"

"Hey, Trick. I'm just here to see the guys, nothing bad, only to talk. Point me in the right direction?"

The man gave Eamonn a doubtful look, but jerked his head toward the stairs, muttering, "Don't get me involved, dude. I didn't see you; I want nothing to do with this."

Nell and Eamonn headed up the stairs in silence. *Which room?* Some of the doors stood open; others were closed. The swimming pool glinted with sunlight in the courtyard below, and roses twined around the railing bobbled in the mild breeze, everything so peaceful and postcard perfect.

A door at the far end of the walkway opened and a woman came out – a young-looking beauty with a halo of vintage-movie-star curls and a silver ring in her lip, wearing a floaty grey dress that clung to her obviously pregnant belly. She didn't see them at first, but when she did, she froze, her eyes opening very wide. "Oh, good Lord," she gasped. Her voice wasn't loud, but the sound carried clearly. "You... you can't be here! Oh, this won't be good..." She turned back toward the room she'd come from, her hands raised as if to stop the inevitable from happening.

"Sweetheart, what–" a deep, raspy voice called from inside the room, then a lean man with spiky dark hair and multiple facial piercings stepped out into the corridor, saw them too, and fell silent.

Not good, Nell thought, recognizing the Smidge guitarist and the absolute burning rage rising in his face, just as Eamonn stepped past her.

He must have thought he'd have a chance to say a few words, to begin his apology, but Blade – it *was* Blade – lunged forward in fury and landed a hard punch that split Eamonn's lip and rocked him backward a few staggering steps. Then Blade closed the gap and delivered a few more punches, and Eamonn began almost automatically to defend himself and return blows, so that the pair of them were fighting in earnest, blood splattering messily from Eamonn's lip.

"Blade! Christopher, please stop!" the pregnant woman called out, wrapping her arms protectively around her belly. She clearly didn't know what to do and was afraid to approach the fight. "Angel! Dice! *Help!*"

Smidge's lead vocalist and drummer dashed out of their rooms, along with an electric-orange-haired woman whose spectacular breasts strained her crew t-shirt and the bib of her overall shorts, and two men who looked like security or bodyguards raced up the far-end stairs from the courtyard.

Well, Eamonn won't hit me. I can break this up, now that help is here to keep them apart. Nell eyed the fighters, watching for the right moment to slide herself between them. She used her right shoulder and hip to check Eamonn backward, creating space, then chambered her left knee up and planted a firm sidekick into Blade's abdomen with enough force to send him tumbling onto his backside. She kept her eyes on him just long enough to make sure that the blond vocalist and the pregnant woman were holding his arms and talking him down, then she turned and wrapped her arms around Eamonn to prevent him from doing anything foolish until he too had calmed himself.

Blood from Eamonn's lip and nose was smeared over his chin and down his shirt, and Nell realized with some annoyance that it had transferred to her shirt as well. "*That* went well," she said quietly, for his ears only, drawing a rueful laugh from him.

By this time, the security crew had reached them and were pacing warily around.

"I came to apologize," Eamonn said, talking over Nell's shoulder, his eyes fixed on Blade. The genuine ring of sincerity in his voice was unmistakable. "I'm sorry."

Nell relaxed her arms and turned a bit so she could see what was going on. Blade had gotten to his feet and was clearly still seething. The pregnant woman had her arms around him and was trying to lead him away, but he stood like a rock, his mouth open as though he wanted to say something but was too flooded with feelings to find words.

"Go with Crys, dude," the blond man said to him. "Let her calm you. We'll sort this out." Then he turned to Nell and Eamonn, wry humor in his face. "Maybe a surprise appearance wasn't the best choice, Easy? And who's this?" Behind him, the drummer – at least, Nell felt fairly sure that the tall man with the bandana and floppy brown hair was Smidge's drummer – gave a nod in their direction and then followed Blade and the pregnant woman into one of the rooms, pulling the door closed behind him. The orange-haired woman moved to stand with the security men, not intruding on the conversation but near enough to keep an eye on everything.

"Nell, meet Angel, Smidge's lead singer and front man. Angel, this is my girlfriend Nell." Eamonn's voice was thick, his nose clogged now, his lip swelling.

Angel held out a hand for her to shake, and when she took it, she found he had a firm, confident grip. *The handshake of a reliable person. Interesting, for a rock star.*

"You're going to want to get cleaned up," Angel said, eyeing the blood. "Room 20 at the end of this floor is empty; you two can have that one. Go settle in and have a wash, then we'll talk. Got bags?"

"Still in the car we came in out front, I should think," Nell said. "And his bass." It occurred to her, now, how unwise it had been to leave their things in the hired limousine – especially his instrument – but his mind had been on the apology he'd have to make, and her mind had been on him.

Angel nodded at one of the security men, who headed off down the stairs. "Aidan'll bring your stuff up. Just... do me a favor and stay in your room until I've talked to Blade, okay?"

"You've got it," Eamonn said.

At that, Angel cocked an interested eyebrow. "What happened to your *maybe I will and maybe I won't* line?"

Without thinking, Eamonn started to wipe his nose with the back of his hand, winced, and looked down at the bloody smear as though it were the most fascinating thing in the world. "A smart woman convinced me that it's time to drop the asshole rock star act, at least around you guys, so…"

That drew an incredulous grimace from Angel. "And what the fuck made you think *that* act would be a good idea in the first place?"

Eamonn shrugged. "Dunno. I just wanted to fit in, man. You all were so tight, younger than me and so mad about the label pushing you to drop your bassist, and I came in for that audition thinking I needed to be all cool to impress everyone. Tried to play Han Solo to your Skywalker, and it all went to shit."

"I like this version of you better," Angel said, shaking his head with reluctant humor. "Now go clean up. Room 20 – oh, key cards. Sally?" He looked around 'til his eyes found the orange-haired woman.

She pushed off the wall and came over to them, fishing in the bib pocket of her overalls as she walked. "Got them right here." She drew out a packet of key cards and thumbed through them until she found the ones she wanted. "A key card for you, and a key card for you…" She grinned and gave them a big Oprah gesture. "Everybody gets a key card. Nice to meet you, Nell. I'm Sally." She turned to Eamonn, then, shaking her head with an amused twist to her mouth. "Sorry, Easy – Harrison Ford did it better." Everybody laughed.

"I'll talk to Blade," Angel said, "see if I can get him to sit down with you." He turned to walk away, then looked back for a moment. "Is that lip going to want stitches?"

chapter

13.

"JUST ONE MORE," SAID THE MAN IN THE SKULL-PATTERNED bandana as he guided the needle in and out of Eamonn's lip. He tied a neat surgeon's knot and cut the suture. "All done."

"Thanks, Jed." Eamonn got up from the desk chair where he'd been sitting for the procedure.

Jed packed up his medical kit and straightened to his full height, stretching and rolling his shoulders as he peeled off his latex gloves. "Better to have the stitches and make sure your pretty smile isn't spoiled. I can't promise no scarring, but I've done my best to minimize it."

"I don't mind a man with scars," Nell said. She sat cross-legged on the king-sized bed, a position which had provided a good view of the stitching procedure.

Eamonn smirked at that, but Jed nodded. "Sure. It's less attractive if the vermillion border – the lip line – heals unevenly, though. A few stitches can make all the difference." He took an instant cold pack out of his kit and gave it a squeeze and shake to activate it before tossing it to Eamonn. "You'll want to ice that eye, Easy. You're going to have a spectacular shiner either way, but try to keep the swelling down as much as you can. Nice to meet you, Nell." And then he was gone, gently closing the door behind him.

Eamonn flopped onto the bed next to Nell with a groan, holding the cold pack against his left eye.

"You need to learn how to duck," she told him.

He gave her a rueful chuckle for that but shook his head. "Maybe he needed to hit me. I deserved it. So, I'm wearing my apology on my face for a few days."

"Nope. No way. You may deserve a lot of things, but *never* stay still and let someone hit you. Promise?" She put every bit of serious concern she had into her voice and expression, wanting him to see how important it was, but he had the cold pack obscuring his face so she couldn't look him in the eyes.

"I'm tough enough to handle it."

"That's not the point." Nell had seen plenty of black eyes and stitches, and gotten a few herself without complaining – it wasn't a question of toughness. "You take an accidental hit or you don't get out of the way fast enough, whatever. But the instinct to evade should be automatic."

"Right." He tossed the cold pack toward her and sat up. "Babe, I'm going to take a quick shower. I was sweating a little on the way in." With something that was sort of a shrug, he peeled himself the rest of the way off the bed and vanished into the bathroom.

She felt somehow rebuked. It had been hard for him to come here at all, and now she'd criticized him for not managing to dodge Blade's furious onslaught, when he'd had no training and everything had happened so fast. She crossed the room to the bathroom door, intending to knock and see if she could join him, but then she hesitated. *Wouldn't he have asked me, if he wanted company?* Inside the bathroom, the shower came on with a gush and then splashing sounds as Eamonn stepped under the spray – the water would be darkening the gold of his hair and running over the ink on his torso and arms.

Nell sighed and sat down on the floor to stretch out her back. Only minor twinges still reminded her that she'd pulled a muscle earlier in the week.

A knock on the door startled her. The security guy had already brought their bags and Jed had fixed up Eamonn's face. Could Blade be ready to talk so soon?

When she opened the door, the man waiting there pushed past her into the room like he had every right to do so. She felt a prickle of apprehension, but he wore a Smidge crew t-shirt, so she held out a hand to him, saying, "Hi, I'm Nell. Nice to meet you."

The man took her hand but didn't shake it. Instead, he held it in a rather too intimate grip, his thumb caressing her knuckles. "I'm Donnie," he said, "but you can call me Big D." He snickered at his own words, seeming pleased with himself. He was not a big man, being of average height and somewhat weedy in build, so the nickname – probably self-bestowed – was doubtless intended to imply intimate size. "I guess you're one of Easy's groupies? You've got sexy titties, baby, and he never minds sharing."

Nell tried to pull her hand away without making an issue of it, but Donnie tightened his hold slightly, just enough that her fingers wouldn't easily slide out. He seemed intent on raising her fingers toward his mouth, making her shudder at the thought of contact with his scraggly goatee and potentially germy lips. She jerked her hand downward in a sharp motion, breaking his grip, and took a step backward to put space between them. "Not a groupie, and even if I were, that wouldn't give you the right... What do you want?"

He laughed, but it sounded fake. "I thought I'd bring Easy a little welcome-back gift. Is he around?"

"In the shower."

Donnie extracted a small paper bag from his pocket. "Give him this, just tell him Big D says it's on the house." Then he looked at her and winked. "If you're with Easy, you must be a party girl, right? I can hook you up with whatever you need."

Flipping crap. Puzzle pieces started to fall into place. "You mean... you're his, uh, supplier?" She kept her expression neutral, showing none of the revulsion she felt. *Get the facts first. Let him incriminate himself.*

"That's right. I take care of people on this tour. Whatever you're into, I can get it for you."

Confirmed. This piece of walking excrement was the dealer hidden inside Smidge's crew, the monster who'd kept on supplying drugs right under Angel's... well, *nose* would be a bad pun, wouldn't it? "I thought this tour was supposed to be clean now. How have they not fired you?"

Donnie smirked. "Oh, I'm safe enough. I joined the crew after Blade's first rehab, see, and he'll never rat me out to daddy Angel in case the craving gets too bad and he wants me to hook him up again. And there are plenty of crew who want one thing or another, keeping me in business. We just don't, you know, tell the grownups. Now, can I fix you up with a little something? First one's always free for a new client."

"No drugs," she told him. "And Eamonn doesn't want your poison, either. You need to leave."

"Oh, but he does," Donnie said, inching closer to her with a cocky grin. "And what are you even here for, if you don't fuck or get high?"

He was into her personal space now. *Not okay.* "You need to leave now."

"Nah, I think I'm going to wait for Easy. Seems I can't trust you to give him his candy." He tucked the paper bag back into his jacket pocket with a nasty chuckle. "And now that I have both hands free, let's see if maybe you do fuck after all."

In a quiet but clear voice that any of her students would have recognized as meaning a line had been seriously crossed, she said, "You need to back the hell up and leave. Right now."

He didn't, of course.

And because he was right in front of her, reaching for her hips, it was the easiest thing in the world to shove her forearm across his throat and grip his shoulder for leverage as she rammed a knee between his legs. She'd caught his wrist with her free hand out of instinct, and as he crumpled, she flipped him over to land face down, pinning him with a knee in the small of his back and his arm twisted into a hammerlock. Adrenaline and satisfaction flowed through her.

"Ah... what's going on?" Eamonn's surprised voice broke into her awareness. She looked around to see him standing in the bathroom doorway, wearing nothing but a peach-colored towel wrapped around his hips.

She didn't even try to keep the disgust out of her voice. "This... person showed up with a *gift* for you, and since I refused his offer of *a little something* for myself, he seemed to think my only other purpose could be sexual. I warned him to leave. Twice. He didn't listen."

"Well, shit. Donnie, really?"

Donnie mumbled something but his face was against the carpet, so the words were muffled.

"Get up," Nell ordered, exerting a bit of pressure on the arm she still had in a hammerlock to let him know he didn't have a choice.

"How was I to know? You've always shared your groupies," Donnie grumbled, resentment plain on his face. Nell felt a surge of fury at that. Her hands tightened on his arm and it took significant willpower not to wrench it higher behind his back as retribution for the words, even though she wasn't sure where to pinpoint her anger. She glanced at Eamonn and knew she was letting accusation and doubt show on her face, but she didn't care.

For a brief moment, the bassist looked older than his years, his expression sad and tired as he said, "You've never understood. It was fun, sure, but I gave myself as a gift to them, not the other way around. And groupies aren't candy bars to be shared – they're people with free will – *they* can share their good times with anyone they want. Even you."

Nell felt her expression softening. Put that way, it didn't sound so gross, and the whole matter had to be complicated for him after growing up with a groupie mom. That would be something to sort through at another time, when they didn't have scum for company. "Moving on," she said, "Donnie apparently has something in his pocket for you. Do you want it?"

Unbelievably, Eamonn smiled at the question, standing there in nothing but a towel and his tattoos. "Honest answer, Nell? Of course I *want* it. But I'm going to say no anyway. I promised you I wouldn't touch the stuff as long as we're together, and I'm trying to do this integrity thing right." And there was absolutely no reason the word *integrity* on his lips should give her a stab of happiness somewhere near her heart, but it did.

Donnie spat on the carpet. "You're supposed to be fucking addicted, Ease."

Eamonn shrugged. "Wrong again. I guess I'm not wired for addiction; I've always been able to walk away from stuff that screws other people up. I *like* getting high, sure, but I don't *need* it." He looked at Nell, talking to her, not Donnie. "That's probably why I didn't take Blade's problem seriously until it was too late – I figured he could stop if he really wanted to, because I always could."

"You heard him." Nell hauled Donnie around to face the door and let him go, giving him a bit of a push on his way. "Time to leave. I suggest you vanish altogether, before I have to talk to Angel and maybe law enforcement. I don't want to see you again."

Instead of taking the hint, Donnie turned back, scowling. "I'm not scared of you, bitch."

Nell took a half-step forward and smiled as he shrank back a little. Big words from a pathetic excuse of a person. "Do I need to put you on the ground again?" she offered, almost hoping he'd give her a reason to do it.

"Nah, this tour has gotten boring anyway," Donnie mumbled. "Sad day when all the guys have turned into pussies, but whatever." This, he said in the kind of undertone that was meant to be overheard.

"Get out of here, Donnie. Don't come back," Eamonn told him.

Donnie was almost out the door when he turned back a final time. "I don't get it, man. You *lived* to party with the boys..." And then, faced with stony glares from both of them and not a fragment of forgiveness, he was gone.

Eamonn sighed, turning to Nell. "I guess that's what it looked like to everyone – and I thought I *did* live to party with them." He sat down on the edge of the bed and was silent for a moment, looking thoughtful, regretful. Much as she liked looking at him in just the towel, Nell decided it was time for him to either get dressed or get naked, and he didn't seem in the mood for making out. She grabbed a t-shirt and boxer briefs from his bag, meaning to toss them into his lap – or at his head if that would shake him out of his mood. The expression on his face stopped her, though, and then he kept talking. "I was trying to hold onto something I'd never really had. Like I was reaching for starlight, only to discover I was grasping at a reflection in a puddle in a gutter." He shook his head. "I should have been looking up. I should have – how didn't I see? I only needed to do better."

"That's a song, man," came a deep, raspy voice. Blade stood in the doorway, with Angel beside him. The pair of them looked like darkness and light, Blade in black jeans and a black sleeveless shirt, Angel in a tight white t-shirt and pale faded jeans. "You need to write that down."

"Oh, hey, guys," Eamonn said, standing up and looking down at the towel he still wore. "I, ah, need to get dressed…"

"No, really, Easy," Blade said. "Write those lyrics down before you forget. Please? I can *feel* the chords for them." He paused, with a hesitant look at the damage he'd done to Eamonn's face. "If you'd consider writing with us, that is."

Eamonn stared at them, sinking back down to sit on the bed with disbelief written in every line of his face and body, and it was Nell who found a hotel notepad and pen on the writing desk and brought it over to him. She saw how his hand shook as he wrote down the words, and realized he didn't answer Blade because he couldn't trust his voice not to wobble. "Believe in yourself," she said softly, for his ears only. "Funny that it's happening now, after everything, but let it happen."

"Equal split of the songwriting credits?" Angel offered, his tone warm and encouraging, when Eamonn held out the scribbled sheet of notepaper for him and Blade to take. "It's what we always do when we're writing together – better than arguing over who did how much or what's creation versus arrangement and production."

"I'm confused," Eamonn muttered. "I thought we were still at the apology part, and now we're *writing* together?"

Blade grimaced. "Fuck, I'm sorry I hit you, man. Still working on my temper."

"No – no, I deserved all of that–" Then Eamonn interrupted himself with a glance at Nell and a half-smile. "I mean, I need to learn to duck. But the apology, that's from me to you. I knew you were getting clean and I... it was selfish and wrong of me to ruin that for you. Been ashamed ever since. I'm sorry." He said this with such sincerity that Nell felt almost embarrassed to be standing there, witnessing what should perhaps have been a private moment between him and Blade. She looked over at Angel and their eyes met; he looked a bit uncomfortable too, but moving away could break the spell of the moment.

"It's okay, Easy. Bygones, and all that." Blade held out a hand and Eamonn took it. The handshake seemed suspended in time for an instant, everyone in the room holding their breath as the moment of forgiveness and healing took place.

"Maybe I needed that last blast and the fallout that came from it to really be sure my dance with heroin was over for good," Blade added, with a little shudder. "We'll never know. But – did you know Crys and I got engaged the next day?"

"You what?" Eamonn launched himself to his feet in surprise, then grabbed at the towel that threatened to slide off his hips. "Congratulations! I saw something about that, but figured it was just another bit of Kin's public engineering."

"We have a few things to tell you, I think," Angel said, with a dry laugh. "Including the part where we severed our ties with Kinney Wicks PR. Come along to my suite when you're dressed, Easy. It's number 27, near the other end of the walkway. Bring your bass; we'll jam a bit before dinner, maybe see what this turns into." He held up the paper with Eamonn's lyrics on it. Then he turned to Nell, giving her a kind smile and eye contact to assure her she wasn't an afterthought. She recognized the professional technique when she saw it; he must have been taught how to make people feel special at meet-and-greets and that sort of thing. "Nell, you're welcome to join us, or I can have Sally show you around the place and introduce you to some people."

Nell smiled. "If Sally isn't otherwise busy...?" *I'm not going to crash the writing session Eamonn's been dreaming about for years.*

"I'll send her to find you," Angel said. Blade nodded – agreement, farewell, or both – and they left, closing the door behind them.

"I can't believe it," Eamonn said. He dropped his towel, flashing her a glimpse of his perfect body, and skinned into the clothes she'd placed near him on the bed. "This isn't a dream, right?" He seemed so full of excitement and happiness, an eager smile ready to break out like sunshine at any moment as he took a glance in the desk mirror and finger-combed his hair into place. Then he grabbed his instrument case. "You're okay if I go do this, Nell?"

"I'm fine. Go!"

He planted a kiss on her lips, brief but sweet, and whisked out the door, humming to himself.

He doesn't need me anymore, she thought. But that was a good thing, wasn't it? She'd never wanted to be needed. She'd never wanted him to be tied to her. *I can just enjoy my vacation now, then I'll go back home and sort my real life out.*

♥

"Got a bathing suit?" Sally asked, leaning against the doorway.

"I do." *This time*, Nell added in her mind with an inward grin, remembering the hot tub at Champagne Cascades. Not that the suit looked much different from her underwear, to be honest – a practical, athletic two-piece that wouldn't come adrift if a person actually swam in it, almost solid black except for a tiny dash of scarlet trim. "But I've got a fresh tattoo on my shoulder, and I think swimming was on the list of things to avoid."

Sally nodded. "How fresh? Do you still have Saniderm or Dermalize or something covering it?"

"Two days ago, and yes."

"Right. So, you shouldn't, like, completely submerge it, but the plastic film will keep any splashes out if you want to come sit in the shallow end and cool off with us. That's all we're doing, anyway – Crys is too pregnant for anything active, and the heat's killing her, so we're doing a fair bit of hanging out in the pool."

Oh, the pregnant one who looks too young and sweet to be here. "That's Blade's girlfriend?"

"Yep, and you'll want to meet the rest of the Smidgettes too – we have more female crew than most tours, which might be because I've been involved in the hiring part." Sally laughed, a full-blown peal of someone enjoying life. "We have fun. Come on, put your suit on and let's head down."

❤

The pool was every bit as beautiful up close as it had been on first impressions, very clean and well-maintained. One end had wide, shallow steps leading down into the water – perfect for sitting to cool off and chat – and three women were already there, enjoying the pool, deep in conversation. Nell wondered what their jobs were; one wore an athletic bathing suit a lot like hers and had a boyish haircut and more piercings than Blade, another had artful pink and purple streaks in her hair and a tiny lime-green bikini, and the third, in a British flag bikini, looked more like a secretary or something from the neck up but had a massive tattoo across most of her back. They looked over as she and Sally approached, and Nell clearly heard, "Is that her?" carry across the water, though she wasn't sure which one had said it because they were all talking at once, and it was jumbled up with "Come on, Sal," and "Hey, there."

As they reached the edge of the pool, Sally said, "Everybody, this is Nell." Then she waved a hand toward the women in the pool, pointing them out in turn. "Kimmy, with the piercings, is our drum tech. Ruby is our monitor engineer. I did her hair – isn't it pretty? And Trish is the tour accountant."

"Come on in," said Trish, with a trace of an English accent in her voice. "The water's lovely." Nell stepped into the pool and sat down on one of the higher steps, keeping her freshly-inked shoulder well out of the water.

Sally wriggled out of her overall shorts and t-shirt, revealing a shimmering metallic Wonder Woman bikini that did an impressive job of lifting and supporting and enhancing her spectacular curves. A sparkling gem twinkled in her pierced belly button. "I love that this place has a pool!" She made her way to the deep end, where she dove in and swam the length of the pool to the shallow end to join the other women. *Smidgettes?*

"So, you're dating Easy?" Ruby asked, almost at once. "Actually *dating* him, not just casual fucking?"

"Ruby!" Trish exclaimed, with a *we don't ask that kind of question* look.

Nell shrugged. "I don't mind. We *are* exclusively dating each other, but it's just a fun time. I mean, I don't have any illusions. I don't expect it to last."

"Why not?" Crys asked, from the deck of the pool. Nell hadn't seen her approach. The others made space for her and she eased her way into a sitting position in the water, adjusting her maternity tankini – black with pink polka dots – over her belly.

Because nothing lasts, Nell thought. *Got to grab life while it's good.* A shiver ran over her spine and she pushed away the thought of things ending with Eamonn. It wasn't reasonable to feel tragic about the inevitable; he was there for a good time, nothing more, and so was she. "Our lives are too different," she said. "There's nothing practical keeping us together. Why would someone like him keep someone like me around?"

Sally laughed. "You'd make a fantastic bodyguard, for starters. I saw how you split up that fight. But I agree, not all relationships need to be one-way tickets to the wedding zone – ugh – no offense, Crys!"

"We wouldn't be in such a drama about it if this unexpected blessing hadn't come along." Crys gave her belly a pat and rub, as if cuddling or comforting the little one inside it. "I thought we'd have at least a year to plan and get used to each other, but now I'm trying to decide if I want my wedding pictures to have a baby bump or an infant in them, and I'm running out of time."

"You know I think before is best," Trish said. "You won't be much in the mood for a party once the baby comes."

"But who wants to look like a white whale getting married?" Ruby wrinkled her nose, then covered her mouth with a hand as she realized how that sounded. "You totally *don't* look like a whale, Crys, truly!"

"Didn't Erva say her sister got married after her baby was born and leaked milk through her gown?" Kimmy looked around. "Where is Erva, anyway?"

"Having a nap," said Sally. "She was on the bus that broke down yesterday; they were really late getting in. Erva's one of the lighting crew," she explained in an aside to Nell.

Crys sighed, swishing her hands back and forth in the water, watching the ripples. "Do you think I could find a dress that would even fit me like this?"

"Honestly, honey, you won't have to find a dress. Just decide what you want, and Blade'll fly in a designer to create something beautiful and unique for you," Sally assured her. "You know I've got connections, rising stars who'd drop anything to work on a wedding dress for the Smidge guitarist's bride-to-be. I can see you in something delicate and lacy – maybe Tasha Antrova?"

As the talk of designers and dresses swirled around her, Nell tuned out, thinking instead about Sally saying she'd make a fantastic bodyguard. *It's true; I would.* She'd enjoyed taking charge of Eamonn in the airport, scanning the space around them, prepared for anything. For a moment, she allowed herself to imagine what it would be like to travel with a rock band, wearing a t-shirt that said *SECURITY* instead of business casual blouses or taekwondo whites. She'd sleep on tour buses and in hotels with pools, travel the world, and no two days would ever be the same.

But then reality reasserted itself. *That's ridiculous.* She'd never cope with the lack of routine. She needed her tidy apartment with its cactus on the table and rank certificates on the wall. And what about her training? This was supposed to be her year, her serious run at getting her red letters. Taking a shot at the World Champion title would take a phenomenal effort, but she'd never been more fit and had already talked to Master Simran about the coaching and strategy she'd need for it, assuming she could get a good enough job to pay for the extra training and travel. There was definitely no room in that picture for rambling around with rock stars in an unpredictable way.

"How much longer do I have to keep this plastic covering on my tattoo?" she asked Trish quietly, figuring the accountant would know since she had such a huge back piece.

Trish peered at the wrapping on Nell's shoulder. "Nice lettering. Ghostflower's work?"

"You know her?"

"I know of her, enough to recognize her style, and I've met her a couple of times at after-parties and such. I like my traditional ink, but she does beautiful blackwork and watercolor work. Anyway, I had mine done before these waterproof wraps were a thing, but three to five days is what I've heard. You don't have too much seepage so you could probably take it off soon-ish."

"Mum wants me to make things legal at the courthouse and keep it quiet so she can tell her friends we got married before anything happened," Crys was saying to the others. "But I *do* want a wedding."

"Your mother's a trip," Sally replied, her voice kind, as she put a comforting hand on her friend's shoulder.

Kimmy leaned toward them, obviously horrified at the thought. "You deserve a proper romantic wedding, Crys," she said firmly. "Whenever it happens."

All this talk of weddings... Nell tried not to roll her eyes. She'd never been able to understand why people wanted such a show, such a circus of silly outfits and public promises. What was the point? Commitment was commitment, and you either had it or you didn't – to a person, to a job, to a goal. An exchange of rings and flowery words wouldn't hold someone who didn't want to be there.

The man Nell and Eamonn had met on the way in, the one who'd said he didn't want to get involved, came over to the side of the pool. "You want to get dressed for dinner, Ruby?" he asked. "It's almost six."

"Coming, sweet man," Ruby said, getting out of the water at once.

"Thanks, Trick," Kimmy added. "We were talking and lost track of time."

The others chimed in with their thanks too. They all stood, dripping, splashing, and helped Crys to her feet before leaving the pool to find their towels. "The dining room's in there," Sally told Nell, pointing to a pair of French doors, just as a man in a white dress shirt and tie – a waiter? – opened them from inside. "We eat at six, so hurry down as soon as you're dressed."

♥

Eamonn was back in their room when Nell got there. "Hey, lovely," he said when she walked in. His voice lilted with happiness, his face full of light and joy despite the stitches in his lip and the bruise developing in dramatic shades of purple and blue around his left eye. "How was the pool?"

"Nice, refreshing. How was...?" She wasn't sure quite what to call it. A writing session? A reunion? Bonding?

He grinned. "Amazing. They're so talented. We could have gone on and on. 'Reaching for Starlight' has so much potential, I can't even believe it. My words, Nell! And then I told them I'd started a little doodle about getting tattooed the other day, so we worked on that one a bit too. *Getting inked today, gonna be okay / Scratch of the needle, love that feeling...*" He sang under his breath, so pleased with the world. Again, she could feel him slipping away from her, back into the rock star life he'd come from.

She peeled off her wet bathing suit and dashed into the shower, rinsing off as quickly as she could. *Dinner's at six, and punctuality is an element of discipline.* If she focused on that, there'd be no time to think too much about the future.

But as she hurried out of the shower, drying herself as she went, she walked slap into him – or maybe he deliberately placed himself in her path and wrapped his arms around her when they collided. "I was having fun, but I missed you," he said into her ear.

Every particle of air in the room went dry and developed a static charge.

She felt acutely naked, wrapped only in an unsecured and slipping towel, pressed against the fully dressed length of him. She could feel the metal ridges of his rings against the bare skin of her back, the denim of his jeans rough against her thighs below the edge of the towel.

I have to get dressed, she tried to say, but it came out as, "Umm..." *He smells so good.* For a moment, she nuzzled against him, inhaling and reveling in the contact and contrasts as his hands caressed her back then slid down inside the towel to cup her buttocks and play at the top of the cleft there.

He bent his head to lick and nip at the tender skin of her neck, just below one ear. "Nell," he said on a breath that was almost a growl, "do you want me?"

"But... dinner..." she managed to choke out, though everything in her was crying *yes.*

"You don't think I can make you come in under five minutes?" he asked with a wanton chuckle, his voice thick with urgency, his breath warm on her ear. "Because I totally can. And we'll still get to dinner on time. You up for it?"

"Yes. Oh, yes!"

"Good." With a quick tug, he had the towel on the floor, and in the next moment her back was against the nearest wall and he was on his knees in front of her, gazing up at her like she was something glorious and delicious and perfect, the rising sun and doughnuts and a really awesome song all in one.

Without breaking eye contact, he raised one of her legs to hook over his shoulder, stroking her inner thigh with teasing fingers – it should have been awkward, too intimate, too much, but he'd already proved to her how good he was with his tongue, and all she could think of was the pleasure he would give her. Until now, she'd never fully understood the line in *Rocky Horror Picture Show* about shivering with anticipation.

"I was kind of afraid you wouldn't like the rocker side of me so much." He ran the knuckles of his other hand lightly over her most sensitive flesh, spreading the slippery wetness around, using his rings to make her gasp. "Doesn't seem to be a problem, does it? Fuck me, you're lovely." Then he took a firm grip of her hips and leaned in like he was eating an ice cream cone, licking and sucking until she moaned and squirmed and was utterly dependent on the wall to stay upright. And it wasn't five minutes, wasn't even two minutes before she came right to the edge of a whole galaxy of swirling bliss, teetering on the precipice, left frustrated and wanting as he pulled away. "Hold on," he murmured, "hold on," and she didn't know if he was talking to her or to himself as he surged to his feet, fumbling to open his pants with fingers made clumsy by urgency.

I'd help, but if I let go of this wall, my legs won't hold me. The thought fused in her brain and didn't translate to her mouth. "Eamonn, Eamonn," she heard herself saying.

Then his cock was jutting free of his pants and he was ripping open a condom packet, every passing second unbearable until he lifted her up and gasped, "Legs around my waist, Nella-bella. I want to do you against the wall until we both see stars." He pushed into her, filling her, big and hot and hard, as his mouth sought hers in a deep, wet kiss that demanded her total surrender. It barely took a couple of thrusts before the bliss she'd felt before swirled around her again, and this time it spiraled up to consume them both in an infinite ocean of starry darkness.

They slid down the wall together – had his knees buckled? – and ended up in a sated heap on the floor. "Wow," she sighed. "That was so amazing, I wanted it to go on forever..."

"I could get used to the idea of forever with you," he said against her skin, softly enough that she couldn't be sure of what she'd heard.

chapter

14

HOSE WORDS WERE STILL ECHOING IN NELL'S MIND AS she and Eamonn entered the dining room. *I could get used to the idea of forever with you.* Had he really said it? *No such thing as a forever partner,* she reminded herself, *but I'd sure like to keep him for a while.*

It was still a few minutes before six – as he'd promised, they'd made it on time – but the dining room was nearly full. The dozen round tables were elegantly set with crisp white linens and silver bowls of roses, contrasting sharply with the pierced and tattooed crew who filled the chairs, not fancy at all in their jeans and crew shirts, some with shaved heads and others with bandanas or ponytails. A gradual hush fell over the room as one after the other, they noticed Eamonn, until all eyes were on him as he made his way over to the table where the band sat, with two vacant chairs clearly saved for him and Nell. Acknowledging with an ironic grin that he was the cause of the silence, he waved a greeting to the crew before turning away to take his seat at the table. "Well, they've all realized I'm here, now," he said in an undertone to Nell as he pulled out the chair next to Sally and gestured for her to sit. He was about to lower himself into the remaining vacant seat when the dark-haired man on the other side of him stood and held out a hand to shake. He didn't have quite the same rock-and-roll air as the others – he looked almost preppy in a soft blue Henley and jeans that were neither ripped nor tight.

"Hi, I'm Rhys Davies. Stage name's Risk," said the man, with a tentative but friendly smile. *The replacement bassist. Amy's friend.*

242

For a split second, Nell could see Eamonn's reflexive desire to retreat into his usual armor and shield of being an ass, to refuse the offered hand and respond with something offensive or sardonic. But then he took a breath and reached out, shaking Rhys's hand firmly, if briefly. "Easy Yarrow," he said.

"I know." Then Rhys reddened. "I mean–"

"It's okay," Eamonn said. "This is my girlfriend Nell." So Rhys reached across and shook her hand too.

I think you know my friend Amy, Nell wanted to say, but it didn't seem to be the right moment with the entire room watching them. "Nice to meet you. Let's sit?" she suggested. They did, at which point the hum of conversation picked back up in the rest of the room. The show was over.

That explained the staring and silence, at any rate. It wasn't just that Easy was back; the crew had known his replacement was present and must have been waiting for a confrontation, some kind of dramatic scene. There'd been enough drama earlier that Nell felt glad neither man seemed inclined to give anyone more to gossip about.

"So, does the crew always eat with the band?" she asked Sally, mostly to make conversation and draw attention away from the two bassists sitting side by side.

Sally shook her head. "Depends where we are, but usually, no. Since we booked out the whole place, though, Rancho Rosal offered us a nice rate on meals for everyone. Saves us from having to bring in other food for the crew, keeps their kitchen staff and servers working, and it would be silly for a handful of people to sit in here eating with linens and silverware while everyone else was out in the courtyard with takeout boxes."

"Our crew gets taken care of, one way or another," Angel added from across the table. "Some of them tell stories about other tours where they were just handed their *per diem* money and had to fend for themselves at whatever truck stop or gas station they passed through, even getting left behind if they weren't back in time, but Phil – our road manager – always has a plan to make sure everyone eats properly and gets on the buses before they roll. And then Sally is basically everybody's big sister, and Jed was an ER nurse before he came to us so he's in charge of... well, you saw him fix Easy up."

"It's like a big road family," Dice put in. "Every family's got a few skeletons and hard-to-handle relatives, but we make it work."

Nell thought of Donnie. *That's some skeleton.* But families dealt with all kinds of things, didn't they? She could see why Eamonn had missed them.

The table fell silent again as one of the servers came around, placing a basket of breadsticks on the table and then cups of soup in front of everyone – some kind of spicy corn chowder.

Rhys was watching all of them with an amused look on his face. "Maybe we should just talk about the elephant in the room, huh? One band doesn't need two bassists."

"Later," Angel said, in a firm tone that didn't allow for argument. "We'll talk upstairs after this." It was very much a *not in front of the children* sort of thing, but Nell thought he was right – it wasn't a conversation to have with listening ears around, even their crew. If she had questions about staffing or who got what teaching hours at the dojang, she wouldn't ask about it in front of the students either, no matter how much she cared about them or wanted them to succeed.

Dinner after that was pleasant but not exactly comfortable. Crys kept looking anxiously from Rhys to Eamonn and sometimes over at Angel, and even with Blade's arm around her, she seemed tense. Sally made bright conversation about Time Rock and the band that was set to share the stage with Smidge – Gumdrop Conspiracy had been at their peak in the late '80s and early '90s. Their glory days were already fading before Nell had reached high school; Crys, who had to be almost a decade younger, looked blank at the mention of them although she nodded when Sally mentioned their big hits "Sugar All Around" and "Green-Eyed Annie," both of which had been extensively sampled and covered by newer bands. Dice drummed on the edge of the table and said he didn't think one joint rehearsal session would be enough.

Once everyone had cleared their plates of enough chicken mole and rice to be believably done eating, and crewmembers from the other tables had begun to get up and leave, Angel pushed his chair back. He got up and went over to the bar in one corner of the dining room, and came back with two bottles of Jameson Black Barrel. "I'm thinking we might need this," he said. A wry look between him and Blade acknowledged that they would once have used something much stronger to take the edge off difficult conversations. "So. Band meeting, my suite. Bring a glass if you want a drink."

♥

Angel's suite was furnished in much the same rustic-luxury style as the room Eamonn and Nell had been given, only larger, with a half-wall and two steps up separating the bedroom area from the lounge, which had a couch, loveseat, and armchair in mocha leather arranged around a coffee table.

"He said 'band meeting' – are you sure I should be here?" Nell asked Eamonn quietly, hesitating at the door.

With the hand that held a plate of chocolate caramel torte he'd taken from the dessert table on the way out of the dining room, Eamonn gestured for her to enter; in his other hand, he carried a couple of tumblers he'd acquired at the same time. "Band meeting just means inner circle. Look, Crys and Sally are here too."

Crys was settled in one corner of the big couch, sipping soda water with a slice of lemon, Blade beside her with a protective arm around her shoulders. Angel took up the couch's third seat, leaning forward as he poured whiskey into three glasses on the coffee table.

Sally perched on the arm of the couch next to Angel, waving Nell and Eamonn forward to take the loveseat. "Lots of room, make yourselves comfortable and let's fill your glasses."

Eamonn clunked the two tumblers he carried onto the table. "While we're waiting for the others," he said, "I should warn you, the tour's going to be short a driver when it's time to hit the road."

Angel poured a generous slug into each one. "How's that? Also, cheers." He picked up his glass and held it aloft.

"*Sláinte*. Well, let's put it this way – Smidge had a dealer in the crew. He's gone now."

"I thought we got rid of Roach a long time ago," Angel said slowly.

"We did," Sally confirmed. "But I suspected there might be another. It was one of the drivers?"

The two of them turned to look at Blade, who couldn't hide a flush of embarrassment rising up his neck. He took a too-big sip of his whiskey and grimaced at the burn of it, or maybe at what he had to say. "Donnie had a lot of dirt on me," he muttered. "After Seattle, I told him to stay away from me if he wanted to keep his job with the tour, didn't want to push him further than that."

"Or maybe part of you wanted him to stick around in case you changed your mind, dumbass?" Angel asked, his words harsh but his expression kind. "You know it doesn't help to keep temptation within reach."

"Maybe at first, I don't know," Blade said, shame evident on his face. "I'm such a fuck-up."

Crys gave his thigh a sympathetic squeeze, then took his hand and laid it on her belly. "No, love! You're stronger than anyone I know, and you've got us to live for now," she reminded him.

"I've been clean since San Diego, I swear, but... I've thought about it. I knew Donnie was around, knew he'd get me some if I asked."

"I know it's hard, man," Angel said. "But you didn't give in, and you won't." Beside him, Sally nodded her agreement. The three of them were looking at Blade with so much love and affection and concern that witnessing it made Nell feel mildly uncomfortable.

I have no business being here for this. But she couldn't very well get up and leave. Turning away to give them at least a modicum of privacy, she caught the look on Eamonn's face and almost gasped at the complex mix of surprise and guilt and envy there. *Flipping hell. There's an inner circle within the inner circle, and he's just been admitted to it.*

Everyone's eyes were drawn to the door as footsteps echoed outside along the walkway. Dice came in, tossing a coffee mug from hand to hand like a juggling ball as he walked. He caught the mug and turned it right side up as he reached the coffee table, and held out a hand for Angel to pass the whiskey bottle.

Rhys followed. He too had a mug in his hands, but his was full of coffee. "I hope we didn't keep you waiting," he said. "We stopped by the coffee station."

"I can see that." Sally looked pointedly at the mug Dice was pouring whiskey into.

"I know, I know," Dice said, "but the mugs were right there while Risk was getting his coffee, so I wasn't going to go looking for a glass." He dragged the desk chair over and turned it around to sit astride it, waved for Rhys to take the armchair.

"Sally, would you like to sit here?" Rhys asked.

"Nah, I'm good like this," Sally replied, patting the arm of the couch where she was perched.

So Rhys sat. "You guys–" he began, looking earnest, but Eamonn cut him off.

"I didn't come back to take your job or make things awkward. I wasn't even thinking about that. I just needed to see Blade and apologize for what went down last year."

"But you *are* staying," Angel put in, somewhere between a statement and a question.

"I never expected..." Eamonn shook his head in disbelief. "But I don't want to take someone else's dream job away to get mine back. I could... I could play keyboards, or..."

And Rhys laughed. Kindly, gently, and with no malice; still, he was definitely laughing. "When I was in school, I *would* have called it my dream job. Maybe even up until now, part of me thought it was. The thing is – I'm an actor, really, more than I'm a musician. So I'm ready to bow out gracefully here. It's not a problem."

That stunned everyone into silence.

"I mean it," Rhys said. "Don't get me wrong, it's been a blast. I've loved playing bass with Smidge, I truly have. But I survived by *acting* you, Easy. Must have watched hundreds of videos to learn your body language and playing style, and I was *being you* on stage the whole time. It's not something I can keep up forever. My agent's getting calls for me – this higher profile thing is kind of working in my favor – and the band needs the real you, not me faking it. I'm definitely keeping the name Risk Davies as an actor, though."

A welcome sense of relief came over the room as it sank in that the difficult conversation they'd been steeling themselves for wouldn't be necessary.

"I get that," Blade said at last. "It's probably like the way I feel when we have to pretend stuff for a photo shoot or music video. I can do it, but fuck, it's way too much effort to keep up for long."

"That's just you. I *liked* being a mechanic for the 'Empty Girl' video," Dice pointed out with a grin.

Angel gave the younger drummer an affectionate look. "I doubt you'd enjoy actually fixing airplanes for a living."

"It'd be all right if I had Kimmy to help me. She can fix anything."

The others laughed, poured more drinks, and the conversation broke into multiple threads – Blade grumbling about the outfits they'd worn for the "Empty Girl" video, Crys asking about Rhys's future and the calls his agent had been getting, Angel teasing Dice about hero-worshiping his drum tech. "Did you meet Kimmy earlier?" Eamonn asked Nell. "Very short hair, lots of piercings. She's a good drummer in her own right, could probably cover for Dice if he were out sick, and she really can fix anything."

"Can I ask how you're going to handle the... transition?" Rhys's question brought everyone's attention back to the business at hand. "If at all possible, I'd like to go out without burning bridges or looking bad, you know? Reputation is gold for me right now. Does your label handle something like this?"

Angel sighed. "The *gentlemen* at Arleigh Hayward keep offering us new public relations people, but anyone they send or endorse will just be another spy for them." His emphasis on *gentlemen* suggested the label's bosses were anything but that. "We need to figure this out on our own."

"Let's see..." Sally called up the schedule on her phone. "There's that party tonight, the radio show tomorrow morning, then your rehearsal slot with Gumdrop Conspiracy in the afternoon. Saturday, we've got sound check and the show, and then Sunday there's a VIP brunch followed by a photo-and-autograph session. I know Kin would have set up a press conference, but I don't see when, and I don't know who or how."

"So, let's do it on stage," Eamonn said. "It's a platform, we'll be in control, so we just... do it. Rhys can go out and play the first couple of songs, then – let's say I could pull together a piano part for 'Star Shot Down' – we could play one all together before I get up and take over the bass. I'm kind of enjoying the idea of playing keys with a hoodie on and my head down so people are trying to figure out who I am, then coming up to the front and pushing my hood back..."

"I like it," said Angel. "You'll need to stay out of sight until Saturday for this to be effective, though. Are you good with that?" He seemed satisfied with Eamonn's nod.

Blade raised a ringed eyebrow. "You play concert-quality keyboards?" Curiosity was evident in his tone, rather than doubt.

"Piano was my first love," Eamonn assured him. "We just need to find me an instrument."

♥

The band, with Rhys, set off to some pre-festival industry party with their security people. The rest of the crew, given a night off-duty, had already vanished into their rooms or headed out to a bar in downtown Napa where apparently road crew from other bands were meeting up.

The courtyard was quiet in the deepening dusk, only broken by insect noises and the occasional gentle slap of water against the side of the swimming pool. "You want to watch a movie?" Eamonn asked Nell.

"What kind of movie?"

"Let's just see what our choices are."

"All right. As long as it's not some cringy so-called comedy. I don't find sex jokes and people embarrassing themselves funny."

That made him grin. "Fair. I like science fiction and action and adventure, nothing too gory, but I'll watch whatever you pick."

For no reason that made any sense to her, hearing him name her favorite genres annoyed her. "You weren't supposed to be so perfect," she blurted out. She hadn't meant to say it out loud, but there was something about Eamonn Yarrow that made her filters and defenses fail at the worst moments.

"Perfect, am I?" His voice was light and teasing, but the fractional hesitation before he spoke and the absurd lurch of hope in his eyes said otherwise.

Don't look at me like that, you ridiculous man. And the worst part was that she liked the way he was looking at her. "I just... approve of your taste in movies?" Then, more briskly, she added, "Honestly, a cup of tea to go with the movie would be even more perfect, but I didn't see a kettle or anything in our room."

"Well, then," he said, with a slightly lopsided smile, "there's that coffee station in the reception area – it probably has tea too."

There were, in fact, insulated carafes at the coffee station alongside the mugs, and a decent selection of tea bags, so Nell was able to make a pot of decaf cinnamon vanilla tea to take back to their room. Eamonn took a mug of coffee, shrugging when she asked him if it wouldn't keep him awake. "I'll be sleepy by the time I'm ready to sleep," he said.

A small mountain of pillows filled the head of their bed, more than anyone would need for sleeping but very nice to lean against while watching the television on the opposite wall. Rancho Rosal offered several streaming services in addition to cable channels, so their choice was almost unlimited – they ended up watching *Apollo 13*, which both remembered seeing at some point in their teens but hadn't watched again since then.

Just as the ending credits came up, Eamonn's phone pinged. He reached to grab it from the nightstand and his face took on a look of dismay as he read the message.

"What is it?" Nell asked.

For answer, he held out his phone. Angel's text message said: *Check the news. Major car crash, media saying members of Gumdrop Conspiracy may be involved.* Scrolling through the newsfeed on his phone with one hand, he switched the television to the local cable news station with the other.

It was the lead story. A reporter on the scene stood in front of what had evidently been a multi-car disaster. At the center of the blocked-off intersection, the crumpled remains of a black sports car were wrapped around the nose of a three-ton truck, with other cars in various states of peripheral damage nearby. A uniformed figure closed the rear doors on one of the ambulances and it raced away, sirens wailing; a firetruck and two police cars were also on the scene, their lights pulsing in the background as the reporter spoke into a microphone. "At this point, two individuals have been removed from the black Lamborghini and taken to Emergency in the ambulance you just saw leaving. One appeared to be receiving oxygen and it looked to us as if the paramedics were taking spinal precautions, but the other's face was covered." She paused for a moment, looking suitably somber. "We have not been able to confirm their identities, but the car is licensed to Orion Giery, front man of Gumdrop Conspiracy. Was he in the car? We know the band members are here in Napa to perform at Time Rock on the weekend. Other minor injuries are being treated at the scene. I'm Ashley Mint, and I'll keep you updated as we uncover further information." The news moved on to local politics and Eamonn switched it off.

"Well, shit," he said, then, "I'm not being heartless – it's a hell of a tragedy – but also we were supposed to perform with them on Saturday. Now what?"

"Do – did you know them?" Nell asked.

"Not really. Mom does, I think, or at least did at one time. They were huge when I was a little kid, then kind of fizzled out. Still touring and doing festivals and stuff but... they let the party life get to them. No-shows, temper tantrums, arrests, going on stage too wasted to perform competently – all that shit. Bet you a doughnut it'll come out that Giery was driving drunk or high or both when..." He shuddered, and she wondered if he was thinking of near misses he'd had. "A band's got to grow out of that stuff to survive. I've been given something here, a second chance, a gift... I want us to be looked up to when we're older, the way the Bad Luck Opals are, not just aging party boys like Gumdrop Conspiracy."

His determination was a beautiful thing, and yet... *His 'us' is the band,* Nell told herself. *That's where he sees his whole future.* And she couldn't fault him for following his restored dream, just as she'd never give up on her plan to attain mastership and someday own a martial arts school. "You should call your mother," she suggested, as gently as she could. "If she did know these guys, maybe you ought to break the news to her before she sees it online or something."

"Good thought," he said. "Yeah." He looked at his phone but didn't dial.

"Bad news calls are hard to make, I know. You want me to take a walk, give you some space?"

He looked over at her, snuggled up all cozy in the bed. "No, lovely. You look so nice and comfortable. Stay here and keep the bed warm. I'll get some fresh air while I call Mom." He leaned over and kissed her temple. "Be back soon."

She was half asleep by the time he came back in, only vaguely aware of him lifting the covers and sliding into the bed beside her.

♥

By morning, it was confirmed that Orion Giery had died, and Gumdrop Conspiracy drummer Timothy Redwell was in critical condition with spinal trauma and a collapsed lung. "Looks like I owe you a doughnut," Nell said to Eamonn over breakfast in the dining room, as the entertainment news industry exploded with reports that Giery and Redwell had been mixing alcohol, cocaine, and ecstasy before getting into the car.

"Shit, no," Eamonn said. "I wasn't serious about betting on that, though I wish I'd been wrong."

"He's always saying 'I bet you' this and that," said Sally, who was sitting with them. "If you don't shake on it, you don't have to pay." Erva, a tough-looking woman with tightly braided hair and arm muscles that rivaled Nell's, nodded her agreement.

"It's just an expression. Anyway, I don't bet on sure things, and Giery hasn't – *hadn't* been sober in two decades." He grimaced at the shift to past tense, pushed his chair back and stood up. "I'm going to get some more coffee. Anyone want anything?"

The doors to the dining room banged open and Blade stormed in, snarling curses. Angel and Dice followed close behind him, more in control but equally incensed. "Oh, they're not happy," Sally commented. "Okay, Jed's talking to Blade. Erv, you wanna go wake Crys up? She's the best at settling him down. I've got Angel." She looked around for support, then her gaze settled on Eamonn. "You're not the ass I thought you were. Think you could take Dice? Just, you know, get him a coffee, see if he wants to eat something." She turned to Nell. "You might have figured out that Blade is our rage-y one. Angel's pretty calm but he feels things deeply when they affect the band, you know? Dice... I don't know, he's the band's easygoing little brother, but he still might be upset if the radio interview went really sour – oh, and there's Risk–" Sally added as the actor slipped into the dining room, looking concerned.

"We have a mutual friend," Nell said. "I'll go talk to him."

She grabbed her mug from the table and crossed the room to where Rhys stood. He seemed to be observing the crew's response to the angry band members, perhaps absorbing and storing expressions and reactions for his future use as an actor. As he saw her approach, he gave her a tired smile. "It's been an interesting morning."

"No doubt," she agreed. "I was just going to get more tea. Join me?"

"Sure. I've been hoping for a chance to talk to you – we have a friend in common, I think?"

Nell rolled her eyes. "Amy. She called you, didn't she? Or... Johnny did? For some ridiculous reason, no one thinks I can take care of myself when it comes to men."

Rhys shrugged. "Both called, separately. They *did* ask me to look out for you if you showed up here. This rock star world can be a hard place, and your friends don't want you getting hurt."

They got their tea and coffee, and Rhys loaded a plate with scrambled eggs and waffles. "Should we go sit with Easy and Dice?" Nell asked, seeing that the two were sitting at an empty table together.

Rhys gave her a thoughtful look. "You know, let's just sit over here for a bit. We can join them later."

He wants to talk. "Okay. You might as well unload whatever's on your mind." She sat down at the unoccupied table nearest them. *Letting him get the words out now is probably easier in the long run than trying to avoid the conversation.*

He seemed a bit uncomfortable as he sat down next to her. Cleared his throat. "I wouldn't even say anything if Amy hadn't asked me about Easy and to watch out for you. But Amy's my friend and she cares about you, so – here we are."

"And I'm an adult woman with a relatively lethal physical skill set and no romantic illusions. What's the concern?"

Rhys inched his chair away from her a little, maybe even unconsciously, and raised his hands in an *I didn't mean to offend you* gesture. "You know Easy parties pretty hard, right?"

Seriously? "I've heard about the drugs and the groupies, but the worst he's done around me is have a few drinks, and never to the point where it goes from fun to gross. So..."

"All I really have is gossip," Rhys said. "It's a whole other story, but I met the other guys right around the time Easy got kicked out, so I don't know him first-hand. Maybe he's changed from what he was, or the stories I've heard were exaggerated. I just hate to see anyone get their heart broken."

"Someone acknowledging that I actually have a heart – that's a novelty," Nell said, with a bit more bitterness bleeding into her words than she'd intended. "Pretty sure it's shatterproof, though."

The actor gave her a long look, cynical but kind. "Shatterproof heart, huh? Well, if you're just here for a good time and some mattress fun..."

His words hit a conversational lull in the dining room and carried.

Eamonn turned, plainly having heard. His eyes met hers.

Flipping hell. Nell scrambled for something to say that would defuse the moment, some way to deflect Rhys's comment, and came up blank. It couldn't be done. She'd never meant for there to be more than sex between her and Eamonn, but somehow, that wall had fallen – brushing him off as nothing but mattress fun would be cruel, and worse, it would be a lie. *Time to live your values, Miss Whelan,* she told herself. *Integrity's worth nothing if you bail out when it gets hard.* "He's more than that," she said, her voice firm and clear. "So much more." *When feelings get involved, they leave a mess. But there it is.* She stood up and walked out of the dining room, abandoning her tea, because she couldn't deal for another moment with what she'd just admitted to herself in front of everyone. Feeling rattled, she compounded her embarrassment by bowing at the door as though she were leaving a dojang, not a dining room. *Oh, craptastic.* She fled.

Eamonn caught up to Nell in the courtyard. "You forgot your tea," he said, holding the mug out – still hot and three-quarters full. She could see a grin twitching at the corners of his mouth.

"I abandoned my tea," she clarified, but took it from him anyway. "Thank you."

"So... you've caught feelings for me after all, Nella-bella?" His eyes were bright with intensity, blue as the sky and the pool.

She grimaced, feeling the heat of a blush wash over her. "I wasn't planning on it, but yeah."

"Is that so awful?" He held out his arms, cautiously, ready to hold her if she wanted to be held but letting her make that choice.

"No! I just – feelings are messy. I don't see how we fit into each other's life. I don't want to get hurt. And yet..." She took a big sip of her tea, clinging to the mug with both hands, fighting an urge to throw herself into his embrace and use ridiculous words like *mine* and *always*. "I've only known you a couple of weeks, but I don't want it to end."

"It didn't take weeks for me, or days, or even hours. I could swear I was struck by lightning the first moment I saw you in the Frog and Ball, sipping your Frosty Peach and reading your book. I felt like I'd been given the biggest gift in the world when you walked into the photocopier room at Wildforest. I won't hurt your heart, lovely. We'll find a way to make it work."

"Yeah, that's just chemistry."

"Hey, if you can call it something more, so can I." He gazed down at her with his eyes full of... something that was too much to put a name to at that moment. "Maybe it's too soon to say I'm falling–"

"Please don't. I like you more than I thought possible – more than I like most people, honestly. Let me get used to that idea for a while before you push it further, okay?"

"So... you're not telling me never?"

"Go slow for me," she said softly.

He bit his lip, nodded. "I can do that. And you? Believe in me. Believe my feelings for you are real and my intentions are good." For a moment, there was something raw and almost pure in his face. Then, almost as if he knew it was bordering on too much for her, he arched one eyebrow and a flirty, dirty smile spread across his face. "Also, you can acknowledge that I'm the best lover you'll have in this lifetime, gorgeous."

After one split second of astonishment, she collapsed into laughter, to the point that he reached out to steady her tea mug before she spilled it. "Oh, you–"

"It wasn't *that* funny," he said after a minute, as she was still gasping with small snorts of disproportionate humor.

"No," she said, wiping her eyes and straightening herself out, "I'm laughing because it's too damn true." And because laughing was close kin to crying, and his sense of humor clicked with something inside her and made her want to believe, and fall with him, and have it all. "I—"

Then Angel came crashing out of the dining room into the courtyard, on his phone, saying, "I'm sorry, what was that? I think I didn't hear you clearly. You want us to perform with a local Gumdrop Conspiracy *tribute* band tomorrow? ... Yes, I do have some concerns. ... I'm wondering about their experience and professionalism, whether they've played a festival before, whether one rehearsal is enough for them to sync with us. ... Well, it's not what we signed on for, and I'm not seeing the benefit to us in risking–"

Nell swallowed the words she wasn't sure she wanted to say anyway, as Eamonn turned toward Angel with a silent *what's going on* gesture.

Angel waved at them to wait while he wrapped up his phone call. "Look, we'll be happy to cover a Gumdrop Conspiracy song as a memorial for Giery during our set, and express our concern and best wishes for Redwell, but– ... That's right, we're completely willing to go do our set solo if necessary. ... Yes, I'd appreciate that. Looking at other options would be great. Thanks, let me know." He ended the call and sighed.

"Gumdrop Conspiracy tribute band?" Eamonn asked.

"That was the organizer's thought – it's fantastic exposure for the band, I'm guessing the festival gets to pay them next to nothing, and we get stuck on stage with an unknown quantity who may or may not even know our songs. Well, they're 'looking at other options' now, so we'll see. And coming right after this morning's disaster of a radio show..."

"Do you want to tell us what happened with that?" Nell asked, when Angel trailed off into grim recollection, staring into the depths of the swimming pool as though he'd like to drown someone in it.

"All the interviewer wanted to talk about was drugs. He started out with Giery's car crash and death and how drugs and partying were involved, and kept going at us about our history, needling Blade especially with hurtful questions, wanting to know if he was afraid of ending up like that. Blade lost it when the dude implied that Crys was getting cold feet about marrying him because of his past heroin use and asked if he was ashamed of his unborn child growing up knowing his father was an addict. It was pretty much chaos after that. None of the questions at any point were about music or performing."

"Well, shit," Eamonn said, though he didn't seem surprised. "It's not uncommon," he explained in an undertone to Nell. "Unfortunately, 'poke at Blade until he loses his shit' is a popular game in some corners of the media." His phone buzzed, and he glanced down at it, then looked puzzled. "Huh. Mom just texted 'Cavalry is coming.' Weird."

Angel shrugged, with a *no clue* look on his face.

Eamonn typed something, then his phone buzzed again. "She says, 'Stay where you are.' No explanation. I hate it when she's cryptic." But he smiled affectionately all the same as he put the phone back in his pocket. "I guess I'll have to wait and see."

"Well, we're not going anywhere this afternoon unless Time Rock gets us a new match in time to use our rehearsal slot," Angel said. "No sense in dragging our asses over there if it's just us. Maybe Mama Mandy is planning a visit."

As they stood there, a coffee mug rocketed into the swimming pool and Blade stomped by them, glowering, his combat boots scraping on the tiles of the pool deck. Jed followed, saying, "Hey, man. Breathe, okay? They've said much worse before."

The sound of a door opening on the upper level caught Nell's attention. Crys shuffled out to the stairs and made her way down, barefoot and clearly fresh out of bed in a matching sleep set and robe printed with candy hearts, with a concerned Erva hovering behind her. *Pregnancy looks flipping uncomfortable and exhausting,* Nell thought, watching the younger woman struggle down the steps at a painfully slow top speed to get to her fiancé.

The two met as Crys reached the bottom of the stairs, and the tough, angry guitarist melted into his woman's embrace, the fury bleeding out of him. They could barely make out his words, muffled against her, but it sounded like, "Know it's not true, but I don't like them talking about you that way."

"Let's just get married," Crys suggested softly. Her words were only meant for Blade, but she spoke clearly enough that the sound carried. "I don't need a fancy dress or a big event; I don't need anything but you. Let's just do it here, this weekend. Surely we can find a priest – or a judge or something?"

"I thought she wanted a wedding," Nell said, but neither Eamonn nor Angel had been part of that conversation.

Angel shrugged, though an affectionate smile showed how much he cared for his friends. "They'll figure it out, now that he's calmed down. At least it was only a coffee cup in the pool – back before he met her, there would have been a big mess."

"Learning self-control is a process," Nell agreed.

Eamonn looked thoughtful. "You said she wanted a wedding." He took a deep breath and strode over to Blade and Crys. "You know, Blade, if a lady wants a proper wedding, she should have one."

Blade shot a hard glance at him, then turned his attention back to Crys, his expression softening. "Fuck. Yeah. You want a white dress and flowers and cake, sweetheart?"

Crys's eyes met Nell's, torn between two wishes – the young woman obviously loved Blade and was more than willing to get married without any of the usual attendant fuss, but there was a little gleam of longing in her face for something more memorable than just signing legal papers in front of a judge. And it didn't seem fair to have to give that up, if one wanted it. "These things are not mutually exclusive," Nell said firmly, and everyone turned to look at her. "Think about it. Shouldn't be that hard to scare up a cake and a bouquet, even at short notice. And even a dress."

"Really?" Crys asked, her whole expression lighting up. "I absolutely want to get married this weekend – now that we've decided, I want it more than anything – but it *would* be nice to feel like a bride."

"Anything you want," Blade said.

It struck Nell that she'd pretty much just volunteered herself as wedding coordinator. *Flipping hell. I don't even like weddings. But...* "Okay. Crys, let's talk to Sally and we'll take it from there."

Crys hugged her.

Angel's phone rang.

The sound of a vehicle reached them from out front, followed by voices.

And then the gate opened and Amanda Joy Yarrow entered the courtyard in a blaze of magenta feathers, followed by a group of instantly recognizable older men.

The Bad Luck Opals.

A BIZARRE FLUTTER OF PANIC AND EXCITEMENT WASHED over Nell. She hadn't cared in the slightest about meeting Smidge – they were famous, sure, and she'd heard their music on occasion, but she wasn't a *fan* in whatever way those things were measured. She'd listen to Kamasi Washington or Cécile McLorin Salvant ahead of a rock band any day. But the Bad Luck Opals were something else, shooting her straight back to her teenage years, with posters on her walls and in her locker like every other girl. Mad Gilbert may have been her first love, but she'd had intense enough crushes on the Opals too.

It was almost unfair how much the same they looked, though silver threads streaked their hair and character lines creased their smiles and the corners of their eyes. Joel Bonamour had cut his hair short since those days, but the guitarist still had a flirty, soulful look and eyes that could melt hearts and panties. Drummer Rudy Matchett's hair was more Morgan Freeman than Jimi Hendrix now, bassist Troy Turgen tipped a fedora over what was probably a receding hairline or bald spot, and keyboardist Carl Arascain's once-fiery red mop had faded to thinning strawberry. Front man Keith Zamarron still rocked a full mane of long dark hair, as he always had, and his face still looked full of wicked fun as he grinned around at their surprise. *There's something familiar about him,* Nell thought, *but she couldn't place it. Maybe it's just memory. I stared at their posters enough, back then.*

"Yes," Angel was saying into his phone. "They're here now. They just arrived at our hotel. ... No, totally unexpected, we didn't arrange it. ... Huge honor indeed, I'm aware they've never been willing to play Time Rock, and I – ... Of course we know some of their songs, not an issue at all. We'll be ready for tomorrow. ... Thanks."

Eamonn showed no restraint at all in racing over to his mom and wrapping her in a hug before shaking hands with the Opals, who greeted him with kindness, saying things like "Nice to see you again, buddy," and "Well, you've grown up some since we last had you backstage."

Zamarron clapped a friendly hand on his shoulder and said, "Been following your career, Easy. Was a little worried last year, but it looks like things are good, yeah? You know you can call any time if you need anything – you don't need to wait for Mandy to ask us."

Angel joined them, letting Eamonn make the introductions, shaking hands and saying what an honor it was to meet them. Blade drifted over to join them, still holding Crys's hand, looking awed in the presence of rock royalty. "It's so cool to have a discography that spans over three decades," he muttered.

"You guys'll get there," Zamarron said kindly.

"I understand from the festival organizers that you've stepped in to fill the gap left by Gumdrop Conspiracy's tragedy," Angel said. "That's incredibly kind, especially when you've never been willing to play Time Rock before."

Zamarron shrugged. "Time Rock doesn't give guarantees about a match-up. Not all younger bands are... professional."

Matchett chuckled. "What Zam means is he's always been afraid we'd get paired with some hopeless, unrehearsed, drug-addled mess. Our time is too valuable to come out here for that."

"It's a good thing you lot aren't on that road anymore," Bonamour added. It wasn't clear whether he meant their own band history or having to perform with the rolling disaster that Gumdrop Conspiracy had become.

"Anyway, I'm told there's a rehearsal space booked for us at the venue this afternoon," Zamarron said. "D'you know anything about the security situation and crowds before we head up there?"

Angel shook his head. "Not sure, to be honest. This is our first run at Time Rock too. But we could just jam here instead – got the whole place to ourselves. Would that suit better?"

The Opals nodded, looking at each other to group-confirm the plan.

"I like it. I'll have someone bring our instruments over." Then Zamarron cocked an eyebrow and grinned. "Now, any chance us weary travelers could get some coffee while we wait for those instruments to arrive?"

He looks so familiar, Nell thought again – and it clicked. He was dark where Eamonn was fair, but the eyebrows were identical. *Flipping hell.*

Fortunately, Eamonn had already moved to lead the way to the coffee station in the reception area, and Zamarron's arm was around his shoulder, the other men following. But Nell's eyes met Mandy's, and the older woman froze for a fraction of a moment before slowly approaching. *She must know. And she saw that I... saw it. But Eamonn?*

"So nice to see you again, honey," Mandy said, and quite unexpectedly wrapped Nell in a hug.

After everyone had been supplied with their beverage of choice and the Bad Luck Opals' instruments had arrived, the two bands sequestered themselves in a conference room next to the dining room to figure out their set lists and practice together.

Mandy Yarrow unwound her giant feather boa to expose a sequined vest and tailored white satin capris. "Is there somewhere I can put this? Feathers are fun for making an entrance, but a bit inconvenient after that."

"Come up and put it in our room," Nell offered. So Mandy followed her up the stairs and into room 20 to deposit her armful of magenta feathers on top of the dresser.

"You saw it," Mandy said, after a bit of awkward silence.

"I saw what?" Nell asked, curious to see if Mandy would spell things out.

"The resemblance – the eyebrows, mostly, but there are other things. Earlobes, jawline. Gossips have always looked at blond and blue-eyed rockers to guess about Easy's father, but he got his coloring from me."

"Eamonn doesn't know?"

"Oh, honey, even Zam and I don't know for sure, never wanted to poke around with DNA tests and such. It's better left alone."

Nell felt cold. "Why?" she asked.

Mandy shrugged. "I chose to keep my baby, and he's mine. End of story."

"Okay, that's fair. But... you can see it, I saw it. With them performing together this weekend, someone else is going to notice, and then what?" *If it explodes all over the tabloids, will he be happy to finally know? Will he be hurt or angry that no one told him before?*

"I'll talk to Zam, I guess," Mandy said, closing her eyes as though the thought was painful. But why would it be, if she was close enough to her old lover to call him to the rescue? Presumably, she was staying at his hotel, maybe even in his room. And the Opals' front man had looked like he'd be proud to claim a closer association with Eamonn.

"Why would that be so bad?" Nell asked. "You get along with him, don't you?"

"I love him, honey, always have. But we don't do commitment, just good times."

And that, somehow, made Nell feel sad. *Nothing fully works without commitment.* It was what broke boards, won sparring matches, achieved goals. *So, love without commitment is... what?* She took a deep breath, seeing two diverging paths ahead of her clearly. *I don't want to end up like that.* "It's never too late. But you do what you want."

Mandy grimaced, her mouth so like her son's. "I guess I'll have to talk to both of them. Not this weekend, but soon."

Nell nodded. "Now, do you want to go down and listen to the rehearsal session, or – I'm assuming you're familiar with the number of women crew here. Would you rather have a visit with them?"

"The Smidgettes are great fun, but I'll always choose my boys and their music, every chance." Mandy put her sunglasses back on and headed for the door. "I can find my way down, honey. Join me there if you like, or I'll see you at dinner."

When Mandy was gone, Nell slumped onto the bed, her hands trembling with adrenaline. *I can't do this.* Eamonn belonged here – his *us* was his band, and now it seemed he was about to be crowned heir to rock royalty. Maybe that conversation wouldn't happen for a week or two, if the tabloids and gossip websites didn't explode with the resemblance overnight, but one way or another, it would come out, and the world's eyes would be on him. She saw no place for herself in that. *I can't be a glamorous groupie, or a blushing bride.* Without consciously making a decision, she found herself on her feet, rapidly stowing her things into her backpack. *Better to just be gone.*

She took a last glance around the room, feeling sick. Took her key card out of her pocket and laid it on the dresser. *Should I leave a note? Or just… text him later?*

Going home was sensible. She'd find a job and carry on with her training. Maybe if she got her red letters, she'd call him. As an employed person and World Champion, she'd have something to offer a rock god. She smiled to herself as the thought crossed her mind of him coming around to see her when he happened to be home in Seattle, taking her to the Frog and Ball for a drink or meeting her at the Coffee Witch. *Yeah, no.* He was far too wrapped up in making music and at last belonging with his band. And with the Opals as their mentors, there was no limit to their future.

Love without commitment is a hollow, shallow thing – but to give my heart to someone whose commitment lies elsewhere? Never. So it's time to go.

She picked up her bag and turned to leave, and there was Eamonn in the doorway, swinging in around the doorframe, saying, "Have you noticed my pedal tuner anywhere in here? It's a black box about five inches long with a silver knob and an LED screen. I know I brought it, and it's not in my..." Then his voice trailed off into a frozen silence.

"No," she said in a wobbly voice that didn't sound like hers. "I don't know."

"Nell. Please tell me I'm not seeing what I think I'm seeing." He gestured at the backpack on her shoulder, then around at the room devoid of her things, with an awful, slapped, sickened expression on his face.

Crap. He looked stunned, broken. *It wasn't meant to be like this. He was supposed to be busy, happy. I was just going to slip away.* "You don't need me anymore," Nell blurted out.

"What? Of course I fucking do." He stood looking at his hands, as though he didn't know what to do with them. His voice sounded raw like he might be holding back actual tears.

"You have your band again," she tried to explain, "and now that your father is–" Their eyes met. "Oh, ever-loving hell, I didn't mean to say–"

He sounded suddenly very tired as he said, "I do own a mirror or two, babe. I can recognize my own face when I see it, just as well as you can. It's not like I'm going to be surprised if they ever decide to tell me."

"But will you be all right when it happens? Because with the two of you on the same stage, I think more people are going to see the resemblance. It's going to come out sooner rather than later."

"You say that like you're still planning to leave," he said, his voice cracking.

She looked away from him, couldn't bear to see his eyes. "I don't belong here. I can't just give up everything I've worked for to tag along with a rock band like a groupie, getting free room and board in exchange for sex."

"Fuck me." The agony in his voice forced her to look at him; he sank to his knees in front of her. "Don't leave me, lovely. We'll give you a job – you can work security, get paid – you don't have to share a room with me if you don't want to. Or live at my house in Seattle, and I'll come home between concerts, whenever I can. Anything."

Nell dropped her backpack; it thumped onto the hardwood at her feet. "You don't have to kneel for me," she said slowly, and the hope brightening up his eyes was almost worse than anything else, because she wanted that hope, needed it, and felt an answering flare of possibility rising in her to meet it.

"I'd do a lot more than kneel to keep you," he told her. "I swear I don't expect you to be a groupie or a bride – just be my ninja woman, my gorgeous independent woman with heavenly tits and a razor-sharp mind, and we'll figure the rest out as it comes."

"I don't know." She struggled to find words around the ache in her heart. "How can it work between us, when we both have higher commitments to other priorities?"

He shook his head, still on his knees, looking up at her. "You're wrong, Nell. Those aren't *higher commitments*, they're part of who we are. We can be all in as partners without having to sacrifice what we breathe for, what we do best. I want you at my concerts; I want to be at your tournaments."

That sounded sweet. *Tempting.* But was it too good to be true? When the needs of his band inevitably conflicted with the demands of her sport, what would they choose? "Get up, already," she told him. "I won't leave right this minute, at least."

"That's something," he muttered, getting to his feet with a sigh. "Could you consider talking to me if there's a problem, instead of just disappearing?"

"I thought you wouldn't miss me, now that you're happy with your band again."

He gave a short bark of incredulous laughter. "Well, I would. It would fucking break my heart to find you gone, okay?"

It was breaking mine to leave, she thought, grateful for the reprieve, no matter how temporary it might be. "I promise I won't disappear."

"Good." He grabbed her hand and pressed a fervent kiss to the back of it. "I'll do my best to show you we can make this work." Then his phone pinged, and he gave her a hesitant grin. "They're waiting for me. Think you could help me find that pedal tuner, then come down and listen to us jam? If you'd like to, that is."

♥

That night, Keith Zamarron took a party of thirteen out for dinner at an excellent steakhouse in St. Helena – ten musicians, plus Mandy, Crys, and Nell. "Call me Zam," he said. "Most everyone does."

"Thirteen is *not* bad luck," Nell had overheard Sally telling Angel, right before they left. "I refuse to come with you just to make up a number. Anyway, I'm not dressed for it, plus Erva and I have plans."

Sally's company would have been nice, but Nell understood.

She felt a bit underdressed at the fine restaurant in her grey denim capris and black velour top, but most of the men were in jeans, Mandy still wore her sequins and feathers, and Crys looked like a little girl at a birthday party in a ruffled lilac maternity smock that really didn't help her appear old enough to be there. At least they were eating in a private wine-cellar dining room that would keep cameras and prying eyes and ears out.

Nell was seated between Eamonn and Joel Bonamour, which was still a bit difficult to get her mind around. "I saved up for a whole year so I could go see you on the *Dark Jewelry* tour," she said, and then felt ridiculous for saying something he must have heard so many times. "Absolutely worth it," she added, taking a gulp of her gin and tonic.

"I enjoyed that tour," the older guitarist told her. "Some of my best memories are from that year. But every tour has its own highs and lows. I'm guessing you weren't even born when we released *Pseudochromatic Effect,* and now here we are."

"*Elder Dragons* is the best work we've done yet, though," his drummer said from across the table. "And that's as it should be. Our best work should always lie ahead."

"Matchett's right," said Zam. "Every band should strive for better each time."

"That's our hope for our next album," Angel said. "We've started working on some new stuff, but we signed a wretched contract with Arleigh Hayward back when we were newbies lured with champagne and girls, and we just can't see a way out of it."

"I'll talk to our guys at Valancy," Zam offered. "They're old-school, mostly-legal gangsters, but their loyalty and support for us are through the roof. Maybe they can help you."

Angel nodded thoughtfully as waiters circulated with bottles of Chateau Montelena Chardonnay and Mayacamas Cabernet Sauvignon.

The food was overwhelming perfection. Baskets of fresh sourdough bread sat on the table, with oil and balsamic vinegar for dipping. To begin, everyone was served a choice of crispy spring rolls or delicate *pâté en croûte* with apricot relish, followed by heirloom tomato salad or avocado gazpacho. Mandy and most of the men opted for grilled filet mignon with horseradish cream, but Crys and Zam chose the Pacific halibut, and Nell decided to try the seared maitake mushrooms on a bed of zucchini risotto. All of these were accompanied by crisp green beans with toasted almonds and truffle frites with parmesan aioli.

Sitting across the table from Nell and a couple of seats down, Crys sipped her cranberry and soda and picked at her fish. When Blade offered her a bite of his steak, she shook her head and rubbed her belly. *Just how pregnant is she?* Nell wondered. *Could she be going into labor?*

Later, as everyone dipped their dessert spoons into delicate vacherins, peach and champagne sorbets layered between rounds of crunchy meringue, Crys wasn't at the table. Nell ate a few bites, then got up, leaning down to murmur next to Eamonn's ear that she'd be right back.

♥

Nell found Crys in the bathroom – at least, there was muffled sobbing coming from the only occupied toilet stall. *Oh, crap. Tears.* Sometimes students in the children's class cried; it was best to be practical with them. "Uh, hey, Crys? The fact that you're crying tells me something's wrong. Can we troubleshoot?"

The wet sniffles stopped, followed by a nose-blowing sound, and then the younger woman emerged from the stall, red-eyed but in control of herself. "Could we just... pretend this moment never happened?" Crys asked, her voice a bit shaky.

Nell put a cautious hand on her shoulder, thinking that some comfort was in order but not knowing her well enough to offer a hug. "Is the baby okay?"

Crys looked down at her belly with a watery smile, her eyes shining with love. "Thank God, yes! Lots of kicking tonight."

"Well, that's good. Are you feeling sick? In pain?"

That prompted a small snort of amusement. "Only the usual for thirty-six weeks pregnant. We're both healthy and it's almost over, so I shouldn't complain."

Nell could respect that. From training in a male-dominated, relatively stoic sport, she knew all about putting a good face on discomfort and pain – she might joke or grumble, but never whine or cry. So, if Crys faced things that way too, why the tears? "You want to talk about whatever's wrong, then?"

This got a moment of hesitation, then Crys's eyes welled up again and she pressed her lips together to hold back more tears.

"It's okay. Breathe. Baby's fine, you're fine, Blade is fine."

Crys nodded.

"Better. Good. Now, tell me what's bugging you, hmm?"

The words tumbled out of Crys then, a bit jumbled and sob-interrupted, but Nell could follow the gist of it well enough. "I'm sorry – it's just hormones – I'm not normally like this but the last couple of months I've been all over the place. I love Blade so much, I just want to be married... so people like that awful radio show can't talk, but... Mummy will think I gave in to what she wanted... and I'm tired all the time and I feel like a whale and everything hurts..."

"Okay, right. So, hormones. Let's just accept that you wouldn't be crying if you weren't flooded with a preggo-chemical cocktail."

Crys gave a weak chuckle at that. "Truer than you could imagine."

"I'm not sure I ever want to experience that," Nell said with a shudder. "But look, if you *don't* want to rush into a wedding this weekend, I'll back you up, talk to people for you. No one should push you into–"

"No! I don't want to wait," Crys said, her words tumbling out in a rush. "Blade is the other half of my soul, and... I guess I could be married in a potato sack if I had to. It's just that... right before we left for dinner, I overheard Sally telling Erva she doesn't have time to find or make a wedding dress this weekend. It shouldn't matter – it *doesn't* matter – but..." The younger woman swallowed against another upswelling of emotion, then very quietly said, "It was just the last straw, you know? I guess a part of me *did* want to feel pretty on my wedding day! I can let that go – I *can* – but it broke me a little, and I have to put myself back together and pretend I don't mind." She looked down at herself, fingering the ruffles on her lilac smock. "I just expanded again, it seems, and this is the only pretty dress I have that fits, so I guess I'll be wearing it again on Sunday."

Nell felt a surge of grim sympathy. She'd never wanted a wedding dress, but she knew how right her uniform felt at a tournament: crisp, gleaming white, tied with a black belt that bore her name in gold letters. Sometimes being dressed for an occasion did matter. And there was something admirable about the fact that Crys loved her man enough to let go of a vision she'd wanted and dreamed about, or at least accept that it was turning out differently from what she'd planned. *Isn't there a way she can have it all? Shouldn't there be?* And a little stray thought inside her asked, *Am I wondering that for her, or myself?* Could it be possible to let go of her structured life and throw herself all in with Eamonn, on the road and at his house in Seattle, and still train and take her shot at the championships? *Everyone has their own version of happily ever after.* If she could find a way for Crys to have her dream wedding... "Look, I'm going to text a guy I know. If anyone can magic up an emergency wedding dress, he can do it."

"Really?" Crys looked so hopeful and appreciative that Nell worried she might not be able to deliver.

I haven't done anything yet, she thought, but got her phone out and texted Johnny: *I know this is random and we barely know each other, but can I ask a giant favor?*

Almost immediately, he texted back: *You can ask, sure. Can't promise I'll do it 'til I know what you want. Is everything okay, though?*

Better than okay, she replied. *But here's the thing – Smidge's guitarist Blade is engaged, his fiancée Crys is almost nine months pregnant, and they've decided to get married here at Time Rock. Which means she needs a maternity wedding dress for Sunday evening. Any chance you'd want to get involved?*

He replied with a heart emoji, then added, *You're not messing with me?*

I know it's probably not enough time, she typed. *But you said you sew your own costumes, this poor kid wants to get married before she pops, and I don't know who else to ask.*

Johnny sent her an emoji of a laughing face. *You haven't watched Drag Dolls, have you? It's more than enough time. You're literally offering me the chance to make a wedding dress for what could be the bride of the fucking year, and she's my buddy Rhys's friend on top of that – of course I'm interested. Is she there with you? Can we voice chat, or better yet, video?*

Nell showed Crys the message. "Are you okay with me putting Johnny on video so we can talk?"

Crys blinked. "How do *you* know Johnny? I've only met him once – it was at a Smidge concert, the same night I met Blade. *He* can make a wedding dress for me?"

"Let's talk to him," Nell said, and connected the call.

"Well, look at you, mama-to-be!" Johnny said, as soon as he saw Crys. "Congratulations!"

"Hi, Johnny! Thanks!" she replied, then, "Can you *really* make me a wedding dress in time for Sunday?"

"Of course I can. But we need to talk about budget." Johnny gave them a rueful grimace through the screen. "I wish I could wave the money side of it away for you, lovey, but I've got to be practical."

"Absolutely!" Crys pursed her lips, thinking. "Blade told me to spend however much I wanted on a dress, and I can't haggle with one of Rhys's best friends, so... just tell me whatever you think is right."

"Well, it's going to take probably twelve work hours for me – that'll add up to about nine hundred – and then depending on the style of dress and the kind of fabric, we're looking at a couple hundred there if you want nice stuff, plus any lace or beading or sequins... Oh, and I'm going to need to buy a duplicate of your current most comfortable bra if I can find it here, 'cause I can build a bodice around it and know that it'll support everything in a good way. How about twelve hundred?"

Crys agreed, without hesitation but with a touch of concern. "That's an awfully good deal. I've been looking at a *lot* of wedding dresses lately, and they're mostly more than that, even with a wait time of several months for delivery. Are you sure it's enough?"

He assured her it was, and launched into a series of questions about what sort of dress she imagined for herself, sleeves or no sleeves, lace or no lace, hotfix Swarovski crystals, and a discussion of silk chiffon.

It's practically a crime to spend that kind of money on a dress for a single day's use, Nell thought. *I could never do it.* But people often balked at the cost of martial arts training too, she reminded herself, and Johnny should be paid for his professional skill. *The money will at least do some good, going to him.*

Nell wondered if Eamonn was the sort of man who wanted a wedding, or if being legally wed would matter to him. *I hope not.* All this fuss struck her as a burden and a jinx – and maybe there *could* be such a thing as a forever partner, but did it have to be at that price?

"I'll need a bunch of other measurements too," Johnny was saying. "That'll get me started, and then I'm going to need to get down there to fit it to you and make some adjustments."

Crys nodded happily. "Yes! We'll arrange plane tickets for you. Bring Tab, if he wants to come – you might as well have a vacation, and Napa's beautiful. I know Rhys will be glad to see you, and so will I."

At that, Nell felt a tiny bit of unexpected envy. Maybe there *was* something to be said for gathering friends together to celebrate happiness. Or maybe it was just that she'd had a taste of that happiness herself and wanted more – so badly, she hardly dared let herself think about it.

♥

As Nell and Eamonn got back to their room, sated with fine dining and enough alcohol to take the edge off inhibitions, she stopped just outside their door. "All right," she said.

"What?" he asked, as he swiped his keycard to open the door.

"You can lift me over the flipping threshold for once, if you want. Just this once."

He grinned. "Really?"

When she nodded, he swept her up into his arms and carried her into the room, kicking the door shut behind him as he headed for the bed.

She'd only wanted to prove that she could trust him to lift her – without worrying about whether he thought she was heavy, without trying to control the situation and gain the upper hand – but as she relaxed into the strength of his lift and let her head rest on his shoulder, she was struck by the sweetness in his eyes and the happiness and affection that hovered in the upturned corners of his mouth. *He's happy. We're happy?* The thought was both comforting and frightening. *Wishes coming true...*

As he laid her on the bed and settled beside her, he asked, "Nella-bella, about your training – how much, how often do you really need to be at your dojang in Seattle?"

Given the loving way he'd been looking at her, that wasn't the question she'd expected to hear, but she knew the answer, having thought about it many times over the past few days. "At this level, I should be able to manage my own training a lot of the time, and Master Simran can fix me up to be a guest at other dojangs in our organization, wherever I am. I'd want to get home for a session with him now and then, and I have to do as many tournaments as possible if I'm going to make a serious run for World Champion this year – but again, we have those all over the continent, so..."

Eamonn seemed satisfied by this. "Whatever I need to do to make that happen for you so we can stay together, I'll do it. Plane tickets, whatever."

She'd fended him off from saying he was falling in love earlier, so he didn't say it now, but she could see it in his face. *Falling for you. Forever partner.* Against all odds, she felt it too, wanted to hear it, wanted to say it, but the words wouldn't come. *Too soon. I can't.* So she sat up and said instead, "If you can flip me over, you can be on top tonight."

He laughed. "Go easy on me?"

Later, as she drifted into sleep, wrapped in Eamonn's arms, Nell felt surprisingly content. *Cuddling. Who would have thought I'd enjoy it?*

♥

The next day dawned with bustle and perfection – bustle, because it was a show day and everyone had work to do; perfection, because the sky was a clear and glorious blue and Smidge would be performing with the Bad Luck Opals in just a few hours.

At breakfast, Sally handed Nell a Smidge security t-shirt and crew lanyard. "Here you go."

Nell blinked. "Oh? But I'm not–"

"You are. We added you as security personnel this morning, subject to your agreement, of course. It clears you to go anywhere with Easy, we're short one bodyguard because we only ever had four and the guys are five with both Easy and Rhys, and you can protect him like no one else."

This was true. He'd be safest with her, and yet... "I'm his girlfriend. I don't want to pretend to be an employee."

Sally looked slightly embarrassed. "I understand that. But you know, if you're going to be with him long-term, you'll be with *us.* You'll need a job; security is your natural fit, am I right? So, start as you mean to go on – crew shirt, sexy legs, and girlfriend hair. The world will just need to understand that Easy's woman is also his bodyguard. You've got some cute shorts or a skirt or something, right? If not, one of us will find you something. I'll do your hair, but I have to squeeze it in between all the million other things on deck, so be ready when I shout for you."

I will need a job. That truth was undeniable. *Oh, what the ever-loving hell, why not?* "Okay. Incidentally, we've got Crys's wedding dress issue under control now. Not sure if you follow drag queens much, but Johnny performs as Ripped Creme and – okay, I don't know a lot about this, but there's a competition show called *Drag Dolls*–"

"Honey, it's my favorite show!" Sally lit up. "I've seen Ripped Creme in the trailers for the upcoming season, which is pretty much a guarantee of talent. The competitors design and make the most gorgeous outfits for themselves and then walk a runway in them and do wild stuff to prove the construction is solid and won't fall apart. Those queens can sew the ass off your average wedding dress designer, and fast! Genius idea."

"Thanks. I helped Crys book plane tickets for Johnny and his partner Tab, arriving this evening. I just need to know if there's a room for them here or if we have to find them somewhere to stay."

That drew a chuckle from Sally. "A rock tour can always make space for extra bodies to crash. Since Donnie took off, Quingshan's had their room to himself, so I'll get him to move in with Phil – as road manager, *he* doesn't generally have to share, but he won't mind for a couple of nights – and that'll open up a room."

"Thanks. I'll let Johnny know," Nell said. "Anything else I can do to help?"

"Rancho Rosal can provide a cake and champagne, and I've got the marriage license sorted, so that just leaves flowers... Could you call around, see if you can find a florist who'll do it? Concert days are just too busy for me to have an extra minute."

"Sure."

Sally shot Nell a look of sincere appreciation. "Man, Blade's going to owe both of us for making this happen. Got to run, I'll text you when I'm ready to do your hair."

Back in her room, Nell put on the security shirt, then extracted the Bee Cute shorts from their bag and stepped into them. Chose running shoes in case she actually needed to take protective action. Nodded to herself. The combination said *more than* – more than just a fighter, more than just a girlfriend. The shorts were a bit much, but maybe over-the-top was necessary for a rock festival, and she could live with a disco ball butt for one afternoon.

Angel and Blade and Dice and Rhys were whisked away to sound check by a limousine. Nell, with artfully tousled loose hair and what felt like a face full of glitter – Sally had added some kind of sparkly gel to her eyelids and cheekbones – was sent to wait in the passenger seat of an unmarked cargo van, where she waited for her man. He needed to be at sound check, but without anyone catching on, so they were planning to slip him in. Someone named Phil waited in the driver's seat.

Then the cargo door opened at the back and Easy got in and sat down among the equipment. He was definitely Easy in that moment – something beyond the Eamonn Yarrow she knew – in full rock-star mode, kitted out with rings and gelled-up hair and a little bit of eyeliner for the stage, his black eye muted with concealer. "Let's go. I want to see what kind of piano they've got for me, and I'm hoping to have time to play a little so I can get used to it."

Easy stood with Nell and Sally and Crys, just out of sight backstage as Angel walked out to greet the crowd, followed by Blade, Dice, and Rhys. "It feels funny watching from back here," he said in Nell's ear. "I should be out there."

"It's only two songs," she reminded him. The piano waited for him, and "Star Shot Down" was the third song on their set list. Gary, the bass tech, stood by with his blue Warwick Corvette, ready to bring it out for him to play "My Tainted Baby" after that.

Angel thanked the audience for coming to see them and acknowledged the tragedy that had befallen Gumdrop Conspiracy, but promised they were in for a huge treat. Word had already spread about the Bad Luck Opals' arrival, and connections had been made, so a thunderous cheer rippled over the crowd. The first song raced by, and the second.

Then it was time. Easy slipped on the extra-large black hoodie Sally held ready for him, big enough to drape forward and hide his face. "Go," she said.

He turned to give Nell a quick kiss. "I love you," she blurted out, without quite meaning to.

"Fuck me." The dazzling delight on his face was a gift.

"Go!" said Sally again. "That shit can wait."

Easy strode out onto the stage, head down to keep his face hidden, but joy vibrating in every line of him – a man who could make magic, walk on water, touch the sky.

And the familiar opening notes of "Star Shot Down" sounded new and extraordinary with a keyboard in the mix.

The transition happened every bit as smoothly as they'd hoped. On the last verse, Easy raised his head and shook his hood back, and a spotlight came up to highlight his instantly recognizable face and blond hair. A collective gasp and then screams and shouts reacted to the revelation. And when the song came to an end, Easy got up and approached Rhys. The two bassists shook hands, making it clear to everyone that there were no plots or hard feelings going on.

Angel came over and handed his microphone to Rhys, who said, "It has been an honor and a privilege to play with Smidge, it really has. But my first love is acting and I've got a big chance I have to take, so I'm handing the role of bass player back to the man it belongs to, and I'm hoping you'll all come see me on the big screen sometime not too far in the future."

"Thanks for everything, Risk," Angel said. "And welcome back to Smidge, Easy!" Gary ran out to hand Easy his blue bass and plug him in.

The rest of the set was electric, beautiful, charged with an extra energy that had even the crew listening afresh and opening their eyes in wonder at what they'd been missing, or maybe something they'd never heard before, because Easy was on fire with something that had never lit him up before.

When the Bad Luck Opals emerged onto the stage for their set, shaking hands and high-fiving Smidge as they transitioned off for a break, the crowd burst into an extra-loud roar of applause and approval. And in all that thunder, Easy forged his way off the stage ahead of the others, straight to Nell, where he swept her into his arms and kissed her.

It was glory unlike anything she'd felt before, an electric storm. "Did you mean it?" he gasped, coming up for air.

I love you. She'd said it. She meant it. "Yeah. I kind of realized it last night. Needed to find the right moment to say it. I don't want to live my life without commitment, even if it feels safer that way, so... I'm letting myself love you. I'm all in."

He looked dazed at that, kissed her again, her neck, her hair. "Nella-bella, my lovely ninja woman, you have no idea. I've given a lot of love away in my life and never had it returned until now. I love you with every bit of my being, and I'm shaking at the thought that you could feel even a little bit of the same for me."

It was overwhelming, and at the same time so lovely to be cared for with such passion, not just of the body but of the heart. She wanted to feel it with all of her, more than kissing, but the stage manager smacked Easy on the arm and said, "You're back on in five minutes," so she had to make do with five more minutes of making out, right down until he had to run back onstage and Sally took her aside to fix her face and hair.

♥

At five in the afternoon on a beautiful June Sunday in wine country, Christopher Blakehart and Crystal Murphy were married in the rose garden at Rancho Rosal Inn.

The bride wore a delicate gown of tapioca silk chiffon that enhanced and framed her baby bump – *it's romantic,* Johnny had said, *we're not trying to hide it* – with a handful of tiny palest-pink rosebuds pinned into her halo of curls.

The Bad Luck Opals were present for the ceremony, accompanied by notable groupie Amanda Joy Yarrow. Rising drag star Ripped Creme, who'd designed the bride's dress, was there with partner Tab Galloway. Neither the bride's parents nor the groom's parents attended, but Angel's parents had flown in for the occasion, considering Blade to be almost a son to them as well, and Dice's father, an Episcopal priest, performed the ceremony. The Opals' keyboardist, Carl Arascain, provided the music, including a rock-edged mashup of "Ode to Joy" and Blade's theme from "Love Bound" as the happy couple signed the requisite papers after saying their vows, with Angel and Sally as witnesses and honor attendants.

"Arascain's doing a nice job of the music. I could see recording a version of this, maybe as a collab with the Opals," Eamonn said quietly to Nell. "But... you'd probably want jazz at *your* wedding." It wasn't quite a statement, nor a question.

She swallowed an odd lump in her throat. "I don't know that I want a wedding," she told him. "I hope my commitment to you is enough. If I'm letting myself do this, I mean it for life, you know – all in. The question is, do *you* need that signed in law and sealed in front of people?"

"You're enough for me, Nella-bella, just as you are," he assured her, taking her hand and giving it a squeeze.

She hesitated before bringing up the other thing, but had to say it. "I, uh, also don't know how I feel about having children. I've always assumed I wouldn't."

He gave her a slightly wry grin. "I'm not asking for promises on that, either." And she sighed in relief. "Would you wear a ring, if I got you one?" he asked.

"Maybe a silicone one," she said. "Something I can wear while training. Not right away. But, you know, Christmas or something."

"All right, then," he said.

"You were just... negotiating the right to a future proposal, weren't you?" she asked, with a surprised chuckle.

"You know, I kind of was," he said. "A *spend your life with me* proposal, that's all. No weddings required."

She smiled. "Maybe in time, I'll let you do the romantic thing. We'll see."

the end

want more

in your life?

ROCK ICON READY

Kimmy & Dice's story

IS COMING

Acknowledgments

THIS BOOK WAS A CHALLENGE TO WRITE, AND TOOK MORE than twice as long as I'd expected. Thank you to everyone who waited patiently for it – I hope the wait was worth it.

Rock God in Exile is so much a product of my experiences in martial arts. To be clear, I'm nowhere near Nell's skill level; I began as a white belt at 37 years old, and have often wondered or imagined what I'd be capable of now if I'd started as a child. But seven and a half years later, I'm preparing to test for my second-degree black belt in ATA taekwondo. That test will take place two days before this book is published.

This book would not exist without all those experiences, and particularly the encouragement and support of my instructor and friend Tiffany John, who not only answered (and demonstrated practical answers to) uncountable questions about self-defense, martial arts, and high-level competitions, but also helped me persevere when *Rock God in Exile* got hard to write, talked me through problems when I got stuck, and sat with me in library and coffee shop writing sessions to get the last bit done.

My teenage daughter, with whom I got into taekwondo in the first place, has listened to and encouraged me through the writing process. I'm profoundly lucky to have her and her little brother as my children, and to have a husband who always encourages me in my sport and my writing.

Jamie Stroud, drummer for Six Foot Cherry, talked to me about the role of the bass in a band, which was extremely helpful.

My brother Peter answered medical questions for me.

Heather helped me name Rancho Rosal Inn.

When I got my first tattoo in preparation for writing the tattoo studio scene in chapters 10 & 11, tattoo artist Justin Albrice answered my questions and let me take photos of his equipment setup. Taylor Beadell kindly read the relevant pages to confirm I'd got the mechanics of it right.

The vegan breakfast roll with caramelized onion and apple jam filling that Nell eats before her tattoo was inspired by a recipe from The Vegan Caveman (@vegancaveman on Instagram).

I deeply appreciate the sensitivity reader feedback I got on Johnny's scenes from Cameron Mackenzie, also known as The Queen of East Van, Isolde N. Barron.

Thank you also to Jennifer at Romance Rehab for the professional beta reader feedback, and especially for the missing scene that I hadn't realized the book needed until she pointed it out. Emily Bell and Sonja Feichtinger were kind enough to beta read for me as well, and both brought up really important points that I'm glad I was able to address.

Andy and Deseré helped me talk out plot issues when I got stuck.

Jenna gave me a great critique of the opening chapters.

My editor, Tanya Oemig, managed to fit me into her full schedule earlier than I had any right to expect, and did her usual fabulous job of catching my missteps and giving the manuscript a professional polish.

All of this expertise has come together to make the book better than it might otherwise have been. Of course, any errors are my own.

Appreciation is also due to our cover model, Ryler Stevens, who did a fantastic job of being Easy for the camera. And as always, I am in awe of Tiffany's photography skills.

Finally, thank you to my Sweethearts – my street team and book chat group – who have done so much to support and encourage me during the process of this book. This group has grown a bit over the past couple of years, and I appreciate every one of you.

As I've said before, publishing isn't a solo act. I couldn't do this without you all.

About the Author

Kella Campbell can usually be found in Vancouver, Canada.

She writes mostly romance, because love and relationships are what she finds most interesting about life and in fiction.

She likes tea and chocolate and happily-ever-after endings.

kellacampbell.com

9 780099 215258